NEW TOEIC
START
新制多益
給新手的聽力閱讀解題攻略

作者 • Mu Ryong Kim / The Mozilge Language Research Institute
譯者 • 江奇忠 / 彭尊聖　　審訂者 • Helen Yeh

MP3

目 錄

Parts 5 & 6
句子填空和段落填空

Part 7
閱讀單篇文章／多篇文章

1 各類型試題說明

2 各類型文章說明

中譯解析

坊間針對新制多益而出版的參考書很多，但在這麼多的書籍中，幾乎沒有以首度接觸多益的應試者為對象而撰寫的參考書。此外，也幾乎沒有教材是設計給讀者藉由新多益來培養商業溝通活用能力。許多參考書都將焦點放在機械式地反覆背誦新多益模擬試題。但這種方式對已具備一定英文程度的考生來說，雖能幫助應考，但對於提升溝通能力卻十分有限，因此本書除了有幫助讀者在考試上取得佳績短期目標，更有培養商業溝通實戰能力的長遠目標。

我們通常把學習英語想成是一段不斷背誦陌生單字和複雜文法的過程，這個想法也讓一般人相信這是考多益時得高分的唯一方法。這種錯誤的想法，透過英文教育只會使英語學習過程失了方向。有效的英語學習是讓自己具備「理解並再運用的能力」，若要具備此能力，要接觸道地的英語溝通方式，觀察英語母語人士是如何自然地彼此交流，熟悉英語母語人的思考方式，並加以吸收內化。

本多益入門書的目標有兩個：

第一，累積新多益考試得高分必備的基礎實力。對此，本書活用許多出現在日常生活中的素材作為考題，讓讀者能無負擔地熟悉新制試題。也針對備考，收錄適當分量的商業對話和文章。另外，更調整文章難易度和選項結構，讓初試者能輕鬆上手。透過這些，除了能培養基本實力，也能在準備新多益考試的過程中給予很大的幫助。

第二，培養能在新多益考試中得高分且能活用的溝通能力。我們熟悉的機械式英語學習方式，不僅無聊且無效。將這種英語學習方式，說是「理解再重組」的過程，實在有些難為情。正確的英語學習，應該要培養理解能力，而不是為了應付考試而不斷背誦。因此本書盡量用較簡易的例句來說明，讓英語學習真正變成培養理解能力的過程。

本書有許多文法說明，為了讓讀者在打基礎的階段中，熟悉英語的思考方式。但是學習文法，並不只是背誦陌生用語和複雜規則，有效的文法學習過程，是了解英語母語人士是用何種方式將世界和經驗再重組出來的。這個再重組過程是以兩個要素組成，那就是詞序，以及單字和含意的關聯，所以這兩者也是本書的主要目標。

衷心祝福準備考新制多益考試的考生們，實現自己寶貴的夢想，不斷進步，學習有成！

為了讓讀者建立讀書計劃並每天規律地練習，本書均衡地設計了各章節的份量。
各單元均分成四個階段，讓讀者能每天輕鬆練習。

單元結構

Ⓐ 輕鬆上手

為了有助於理解多益各個 Part 的試題類型，本書提供將**難度及長度大幅縮減**的範
例試題，讓讀者有效掌握基本概念。

Ⓑ 基本題型

為了**實際演練並確認理解前一階段提過的概念**，提供兩到三組的試題讓讀者做答。

Ⓒ 題型練習

經過「輕鬆上手」和「基本題型」後，讀者可以自己試著作答沒有說明和翻譯的
範例試題，之後參考下一頁的 Script ／答案／解析。

Ⓓ 應用練習

透過作答符合本章學習概念的**多益模擬試題**以結束學習，得出最終的成績。
可以依頁數標示，翻頁本書後面的解答頁，確認正確答案，參閱中譯並閱讀解析。

各 Part 測驗

○ QUICK TEST

每結束三到六個章節後，會出現 QUICK TEST，將這段時間學習過的內容，快速
且確實地做個整理。若有不足的部分，再回到該章節，從基本類型開始複習研讀。
做錯的試題，下次再錯的可能性很高，所以一定要將基本類型了解透徹，清楚知
道做錯的原因。

○ PRACTICE TEST

每結束一個 PART，可以營造類似真實應考的情境來做與正式多益擬真的模擬題。
利用這個機會了解知道自己哪裡考得好，哪裡考得不好後，再複習一下基本題型
和應用練習。

多益介紹

○ **何謂多益？**

TOEIC 代表 Test of English for International Communication（國際溝通英語測驗）。多益測驗乃針對英語非母語人士所設計之英語能力測驗，測驗分數反映受測者在國際職場環境中與他人以英語溝通的熟稔程度。參加本測驗毋需具備專業的知識或字彙，因為測驗內容以日常使用之英語為主。多益測驗是以職場為基準點的英語能力測驗中，世界最頂級的考試。2012 年在全球有超過七百萬人報考多益測驗，並在 150 個國家中有超過 14,000 家的企業、學校或政府機構使用多益測驗，同時在全球超過 165 個國家施測，是最被廣泛接受且最方便報考的英語測驗之一。

○ **新制多益的結構**

結構	Part	各 Part 內容		題數	時間	分數
聽力測驗 Listening Comprehension	1	照片描述		6		
	2	應答問題		25	100	45 分	495 分
	3	簡短對話		39			
	4	獨白		30			
閱讀測驗 Reading Comprehension	5	句子填空（文法／字彙）		30			
	6	段落填空		16	100	75 分	495 分
	7	閱讀	單篇文章理解	29			
			多篇文章理解	25			
Total		7 Parts		200 題	120 分	990 分

○ **報名方式**

共有網路報名、通訊報名、臨櫃報名 和 APP 報名四種。
詳情請參考多益網站（http://www.toeic.com.tw）。

○ **考場用品**

有效身分證件、2B 鉛筆及橡皮擦。

○ **考試時間**

TOEIC 測驗時間約 150 分鐘，測驗中無休息時間。
（基本資料填寫約 20–30 分鐘、聽力測驗約 45 分鐘、閱讀測驗是 75 分鐘。）

Notes

PART

1

照片描述

題型 **01** | 人物照片

 輕鬆上手

多益 Part 1 的題型是看著某張照片，聽四個描述該照片的選項，並在這四個選項中選出最符合照片的描述。本書只有在 Practice Test 時才會用四個選項練習，之前都用三個選項練習。

和其他 Part 不同，Part 1 的線索是照片。也就是說，不會事先在文字或聲音中給出線索，因此要做一邊看著照片，一邊思索關鍵字彙的練習。因為每道試題不會超過六句，所以是屬於心理負擔較小的試題類型。

例題 🎧 001

Script

(A) The man is opening the window.   (A) 這位男子正在打開窗戶。

(B) The man is making a call.   (B) 這位男子正在打電話。

(C) The man is using a computer.   (C) 這位男子正在使用電腦。

解析 因為立刻可以看出男子正在使用電腦，所以答案是選項 (C)。

在人物照片的類型中，要注意照片中人物的主要動作是什麼。上個例題中，男子的主要動作就是使用電腦。

另外，因為 Part 1 的句子都較簡短，所以心理負擔會比較小。但是一定要先一邊看著照片，一邊思索關鍵字彙，之後再仔細聽錄音並選出正確的選項。

Ⓑ 基本題型

❶ 一人照片　🎧 002

Select the one statement that best describes what you see in the picture.

Script

(A) The boy is swimming in the river.
(B) The boy is driving a car.
(C) The boy is riding a bicycle.

(A) 這個男孩正在河裡游泳。
(B) 這個男孩正在開車。
(C) 這個男孩正在騎腳踏車。

解析 一看照片，立刻會注意到，有個小孩正在騎腳踏車，所以答案是選項（C）。

單字 drive 駕駛 ｜ ride a bicycle 騎腳踏車

Select the one statement that best describes what you see in the picture.

Script

(A) They are washing the dishes.
(B) They are shaking hands.
(C) They are watching TV.

(A) 他們正在洗碗盤。
(B) 他們正在握手。
(C) 他們正在看電視。

解析 一看照片，立刻會注意到有兩名男子正在握手，答案是選項（B）。你會發現選項都是英文短句，而且多半是在描繪日常生活中會接觸到的情境，所以要事先熟悉這些常用用語。

單字 wash the dishes 洗碗盤 ｜ shake hands 握手

C 題型練習　🎧 004

Select the one statement that best describes what you see in the picture.

1.

(A)　　　(B)　　　(C)

2.

(A)　　　(B)　　　(C)

答案和解析

1. Answer (A)

Script
(A) She is painting a picture.
(B) She is reading a book.
(C) She is playing with a dog.

解析 一看照片，立刻會注意到有個小女孩正在畫圖。所以答案是選項(A)。

翻譯 (A) 她正在畫圖。
(B) 她正在讀書。
(C) 她在跟一隻狗玩。

單字 **draw** 畫圖

2. Answer (B)

Script
(A) The man is breaking something.
(B) The man is eating something.
(C) The man is writing something.

解析 照片裡有個看起來像醫生的男子正在寫字，所以答案是選項(C)。

翻譯 (A) 這名男子正在破壞某樣東西。
(B) 這名男子正在吃東西。
(C) 這名男子正在寫東西。

單字 **break** 破壞

D 應用練習　　　▶ 解析 P. 454　　🎧 005

Select the one statement that best describes what you see in the picture.

1.

(A)　　(B)　　(C)

2.

(A)　　(B)　　(C)

題型 02 以室內為背景的照片

Ⓐ 輕鬆上手

在 Part 1 中會出現以室內為背景的照片,也會出現以室外為背景的照片。在這些照片中,有時會出現人物,有時則不會出現。

室內背景照片因為是在室內,所以一定會出現地板、牆壁、窗戶這類的常見的空間素材。仔細看看這些素材有什麼特徵,對解題會很有幫助。

照片試題算是比較單純的試題類型,時常會拿日常用語來出題,所以要熟背基本的用語當作準備。

例題 🎧 006

Script

(A) A man is writing something on the blackboard.

(B) Some children are playing in the room.

(C) There are a lot of desks in the classroom.

(A) 一名男子正在黑板上寫字。

(B) 有些孩子正在房間裡玩耍。

(C) 教室裡有很多書桌。

解析 這是一張空教室裡有很多課桌椅的照片。所以答案是選項(C)。

單字 blackboard 黑板

照片裡一個人也沒有，但卻有選項說有一名男子、有些孩子，甚至還出現完全無關的說明，這些都是常見的錯誤答案陷阱。

 **基本題型**

❶ 室內背景＋人物 🎧 007

Select the one statement that best describes what you see in the picture.

Script

(A) A man is sleeping on the sofa.

(B) A man is giving a speech.

(C) There are few people in the room.

(A) 一名男子正在沙發上睡覺。

(B) 一名男子正在演講。

(C) 會場中的人很少。

解析 一看照片，就注意到一名男子正站在觀眾前演講，所以答案是選項（B）。

單字 speech 演講

❷ 室內背景　　　　　　　　　　　　　　　　🎧 008

Select the one statement that best describes what you see in the picture.

Script

(A) A woman is sitting on the bed.　　　(A) 一名女子正坐在床上。
(B) There are a lot of pictures on the wall.　(B) 牆上掛著很多張照片。
(C) There is a lamp near the bed.　　　(C) 床邊有一盞檯燈。

解析 一看照片就看到一張床，床旁邊有檯燈，所以答案是選項(C)。

單字 picture 照片 | lamp 檯燈 | near 靠近

C 題型練習 🎧 009

Select the one statement that best describes what you see in the picture.

1.

(A)　　(B)　　(C)

2.

(A)　　(B)　　(C)

1. Answer (A)

Script

(A) They are cooking some food.
(B) The woman is wearing glasses.
(C) There are three people in the kitchen.

解析 這是一張以兩個正在做料理的人為主題的照片,所以答案是選項(A)。

翻譯 (A) 她們正在烹煮食物。
(B) 這名女子戴著眼鏡。
(C) 廚房裡有三個人。

單字 cook 烹煮 | glasses 眼鏡

2. Answer (A)

Script

(A) The man is wearing headphones.
(B) There are a lot of people in the room.
(C) The man is leaving the room.

解析 因為男子正戴著耳機,所以答案是選項(A)。

翻譯 (A) 這名男子戴著耳機。
(B) 房間裡有很多人。
(C) 這名男子正要離開房間。

單字 headphone 耳機

D 應用練習　　　　　▶ 解析 P. 454　　　🎧 010

Select the one statement that best describes what you see in the picture.

1.

(A)　　　(B)　　　(C)

2.

(A)　　　(B)　　　(C)

題型 **03** 以室外為背景的照片

A 輕鬆上手

和以室內為背景的照片一樣,在以室外為背景的照片中,有時會出現人,有時不會。
人出現的時候,要確認人做了什麼動作、穿著怎樣的服裝這類的細節。相反的,沒
有人出現的時候,要確認有沒有樹木、橋、山等常在室外看見的素材。

準備多益聽力測驗時,要練習一邊聽英文句子,一邊聯想句子出現的使用情境。
Part 1 只需確認事實關係即可,但從 Part 2 開始,就要一邊聽問句、對話、獨白,
一邊思考在怎樣的情境下要用什麼用語,才能有效提升聽力實力。

例題 🎧 011

Script

(A) There are a lot of birds in the sky.
(B) A horse is running.
(C) There are a lot of trees.

(A) 天空有很多鳥。
(B) 有一隻馬在跑。
(C) 那裡有許多樹。

解析 一看照片就看到樹林裡有很多樹,所以答案是選項(C)。

B 基本題型

❶ 室外背景

🎧 012

Select the one statement that best describes what you see in the picture.

Script

(A) People are boarding the bus.
(B) There are a lot of cars on the road.
(C) Cows are crossing the street.

(A) 乘客正在上公車。
(B) 路上有很多汽車。
(C) 牛隻正在通過街道。

解析 一看照片就看到馬路上有很多汽車，所以答案是選項(B)。

單字 **board** 搭乘 │ **cross** 穿越

❷ 室外背景＋人物

Select the one statement that best describes what you see in the picture.

Script

(A) They are swimming in the sea.

(B) They are fighting.

(C) They are on the beach.

(A) 他們在海中游泳。

(B) 他們在打架。

(C) 他們在沙灘上。

解析 一看照片就看到有四個人在海邊，所以答案是選項(C)。

單字 **fight** 打架 | **beach** 海灘

C 題型練習

Select the one statement that best describes what you see in the picture.

1.

(A)　　(B)　　(C)

2.

(A)　　(B)　　(C)

答案和解析

1. Answer (A)

Script

(A) There is a large ship in the sea.
(B) There is an airplane over the ship.
(C) Birds are flying over the ship.

解析 一看照片，就看到大海中有一艘船，所以答案是選項(A)。

翻譯 (A) 海中有一艘大船。
(B) 船的上空有一架飛機。
(C) 鳥兒飛越船的上空。

單字 sea 海 | airplane 飛機

2. Answer (C)

Script

(A) People are fishing in the lake.
(B) Children are swimming in the lake.
(C) A woman is sitting near the lake.

解析 女子正坐在湖邊，所以答案是選項(C)。

翻譯 (A) 人們在湖中釣魚。
(B) 孩童們在湖中游泳。
(C) 女子正坐在湖邊。

單字 fish 釣魚

D 應用練習 ▶ 解析 P. 455 🎧 015

Select the one statement that best describes what you see in the picture.

1.

(A)　　　(B)　　　(C)

2.

(A)　　　(B)　　　(C)

Quick Test for **Part 1** 🎧016　▶ 解析 P. 455

Select the one statement that best describes what you see in the picture.

1.

2.

3.

4.

Practice Test

🎧 017   ▶ 解析 P. 456

LISTENING TEST

In the Listening Test, you will be asked to demonstrate how well you understand spoken English. The entire test will last approximately 45 minutes. There are four parts, and directions are given for each part. You must mark your answers on the separate answer sheet. Do not write your answers in the test book.

Part 1

Directions: For each question in this part, you will hear four statements about a picture in your test book. When you hear the statements, you must select the one statement that best describes what you see in the picture. Then find the number of the question on your answer sheet and mark your answer. The statements will not be printed in your test book and will be spoken only one time.

Sample Answer

Example

Ⓐ Ⓑ Ⓒ ⬤

Statement (B), "They're looking at the document" is the best description of the picture, so you should select answer (B) and mark it on your answer sheet.

1.

2.

3.

4.

5.

6.

Notes

PART

2

應答問題

題型 01 Do/Does 疑問句

 輕鬆上手

多益聽力測驗的 Part 2 和其他單元不同。其他單元可以事先看照片或試題題目，再聽音檔選出答案，但是，Part 2 完全沒有任何內容可看。因此，要培養單聽音檔就理解訊息並找出答案的能力。

在 Part 2 中，每題的第一個句子大致可分成一般疑問句、疑問詞疑問句和非疑問句（平述句和祈使句）三種。

解 Part 2 試題的核心技巧，就是要「聽清楚句子的第一個字」。有無聽清楚第一個字對於句子的理解程度會有很大的差異，一起來看看下列兩個句子：

Where shall we meet?	我們要在哪裡見面？
When shall we meet?	我們要在何時見面？

☞ 兩個句子的差異只有 Where 和 When，但是這兩個問句一個問地點，一個問時間，非常不同。由此可知，聽清楚第一個字非常重要。

在一般疑問句中，我們首先來探討 do/does/did 疑問句。句子的動詞是一般動詞時，要用助動詞 do、does、did 來幫忙形成問句或否定句。現在式用 do、does，過去式用 did，主詞是第三人稱單數時用 does。

◉ 現在式用 do	Do you like strawberries? 你喜歡草莓嗎？
◉ 現在式 + 主詞是第三人稱單數用 does	Does he like strawberries? 他喜歡草莓嗎？
◉ 過去式用 did	Did they like strawberries? 他們那時喜歡草莓嗎？

這樣的 do/does/did 疑問句，用 yes 或 no 來回答即可，也可以在 yes 或 no 之後加上原因。

Ⓐ Do you like strawberries? 你喜歡草莓嗎？

Ⓑ **Yes**, they taste good. 喜歡，草莓很可口。

Ⓑ 基本題型

❶ Do 疑問句 　　　　　　　　　　　　　　　🎧 018

Select the best response to the question or statement and mark the letter (A), (B), or (C) on your answer sheet.

(A) 　　　 (B) 　　　 (C)

Script

Ⓠ Do you live here?

(A) I don't want to leave now.

(B) Thank you.

(C) No, I don't.

Ⓠ 你住在這裡嗎？

(A) 我現在不想離開。

(B) 謝謝你。

(C) 不是，我不住在這裡。

解析 問句詢問目前是否住在這裡，所以答案是選項（C）。要注意選項（A）leave 和題目 live 的發音差異，leave 比 live 發音要更重一點。

❷ Does 疑問句　　　🎧019

Select the best response to the question or statement and mark the letter (A), (B), or (C) on your answer sheet.

(A)　　　(B)　　　(C)

Script

Q Does she have a house?

(A) She lives by herself.
(B) She has an apartment.
(C) She doesn't like horses.

Q 她有房子嗎？

(A) 她自己一個人住。
(B) 她有一間公寓。
(C) 她不喜歡馬。

解析 看到選項中都沒有 yes 或 no。所以可以知道問句所問的訊息就是答案，因此，回答說「她有公寓」的選項（B）是答案。

❸ Did 疑問句　　　🎧020

Select the best response to the question or statement and mark the letter (A), (B), or (C) on your answer sheet.

(A)　　　(B)　　　(C)

Script

Q Did you enjoy the movie?

(A) It was exciting.
(B) They don't like watching movies.
(C) You're very kind.

Q 你喜歡這部電影嗎？

(A) 很精彩。
(B) 他們不喜歡看電影。
(C) 你真客氣。

解析 本題的選項中都沒有 yes 或 no。答案是選項（A），因為字面上說「電影很精彩」，其實就是很享受電影的意思。就像這題一樣，理解話語真實的含意，比單純地按字面將英語翻譯成中文更重要。

單字 movie 電影　|　exciting 刺激的　|　watch 觀看

C 題型練習 🎧021

Select the best response to the question or statement and mark the letter (A), (B), or (C) on your answer sheet.

1. Mark your answer on your answer sheet.

2. Mark your answer on your answer sheet.

3. Mark your answer on your answer sheet.

Answer Sheet

1.	(A)	(B)	(C)
2.	(A)	(B)	(C)
3.	(A)	(B)	(C)

1. Answer (C)

Script | 翻譯

1. Do they speak Korean?	他們說韓語嗎？
(A) I met them yesterday.	(A) 我昨天和他們見面。
(B) When can you come?	(B) 你何時可以來？
(C) Just a little.	(C) 只會說一點。

解析 本題的選項中都沒有 yes 或 no。問句的意圖是想知道他們會不會說韓語，選項（C）回答「會說一點」，所以是答案。要注意，像選項（C）這樣的不完整句也可能會是答案。

2. Answer (A)

Script | 翻譯

Does he read novels?	他讀小說嗎？
(A) He hates reading books.	(A) 他很討厭讀書。
(B) He's bought a new house.	(B) 他買了一棟新房子。
(C) I find the novel interesting.	(C) 我覺得這本小說很有趣。

解析 問題詢問他是否讀小說，選項（A）回答「他討厭讀書」，所以可以推測他也一定討厭讀小說，答案是選項（A）。選項（B）和問句完全無關；選項（C）的內容並不能回答問句的問題，所以是錯誤答案。

單字 novel 小說 ｜ hate 討厭；憎恨

3. Answer (B)

Script | 翻譯

Did you go there by yourself?	你獨自一人去那裡嗎？
(A) I didn't buy anything.	(A) 我什麼都沒買。
(B) I went there with Peter.	(B) 我和彼德一起去的。
(C) Here you are.	(C) 給你。

解析 問題詢問是否一人單獨去那裡，選項（B）回答「跟彼德一起去的」，是正確答案。選項（A）和（C）與問句完全無關。

D 應用練習　　　　　　　▶ 解析 P. 458　　　🎧 022

Select the best response to the question or statement and mark the letter (A), (B), or (C) on your answer sheet.

1. Mark your answer on your answer sheet.

2. Mark your answer on your answer sheet.

3. Mark your answer on your answer sheet.

4. Mark your answer on your answer sheet.

Answer Sheet

1.	(A)	(B)	(C)
2.	(A)	(B)	(C)
3.	(A)	(B)	(C)
4.	(A)	(B)	(C)

題型 **02** Be 動詞疑問句

Ⓐ 輕鬆上手

be 動詞疑問句以 is、are、was、were 來起始句子,也就是把句中 be 動詞拿到句首成為疑問句。

be 動詞疑問句是單純地詢問「是什麼」或「是怎樣」。

◉ 詢問「是怎樣」　　Are you happy? 你快樂嗎?

◉ 詢問「是什麼」　　Are you a student? 你是學生嗎?

be 動詞和 there 搭配使用,表「有」的意思。

◉ 詢問「有什麼」　　Is there a coffee shop near here? 這附近有咖啡店嗎?

　　　　　　　　　　Are there any animals there? 那裡有動物嗎?

be 動詞疑問句中的 be 動詞,也可以和現在分詞或過去分詞搭配使用,表進行式或被動語態。

◉ be 動詞和現在分詞搭配使用,表進行式。

Are you trying to lose weight?
你在嘗試減重嗎?

◉ be 動詞和過去分詞搭配使用,表被動語態或狀態。

Was the party cancelled?
派對取消了嗎?

單字 lose weight 減肥 │ cancel 取消

由於 be 動詞疑問句的用法很多，所以回答時並不一定要用 yes 或 no，只要說出符合詢問意圖的字詞，也可以是答案。

請看例句。

Ⓐ Are **you happy?** 你快樂嗎？

Ⓑ **I'm depressed.** 我很沮喪。

☞ 雖然不是用 yes 或 no 來回答，但因為回答說「感覺很沮喪」，也就是 no 的意思，所以這樣回答也可以。

Ⓑ 基本題型

❶ 簡單式

🎧 023

Select the best response to the question or statement and mark the letter (A), (B), or (C) on your answer sheet.

(A)　　　(B)　　　(C)

Script

Q Are you a college professor?

 (A) I don't like that professor.

 (B) I teach high school.

 (C) I graduated from college in 1997.

Q 你是大學教授嗎？

 (A) 我不喜歡那位教授。

 (B) 我在高中教書。

 (C) 我在 1997 年時大學畢業。

解析 問題詢問對方是否為大學教授，選項（B）回答「在高中教書」，表示回話者不是大學教授，所以答案是選項（B）。選項（A）所提到的教授，與問句中的教授沒有關係，因此是錯誤答案。選項（C）說的是畢業年度，也跟是否為大學教授無關，也是錯誤答案。

單字 professor 教授 ｜ graduate 畢業

❷ 和 there 搭配使用的型態

Select the best response to the question or statement and mark the letter (A), (B), or (C) on your answer sheet.

(A)　　　(B)　　　(C)

Script

Q Are there any subway stations near your house?

(A) Public transportation is convenient.

(B) I left my house at nine.

(C) There are two subway stations nearby.

Q 你家附近有地鐵站嗎？

(A) 大眾運輸工具很方便。

(B) 我在九點出門。

(C) 附近有兩個地鐵站。

解析 本題選項也都沒有用 yes 或 no 來回答。選項（C）回答「有兩個地鐵站」，所以選項（C）是答案。選項（A）和（B）完全答非所問，都是錯誤答案。

單字 subway station 地鐵站 | public transportation 公共運輸工具 | convenient 方便的

❸ 被動語態和現在進行式

025

Select the best response to the question or statement and mark the letter (A), (B), or (C) on your answer sheet.

(A)　　　(B)　　　(C)

Script

Q Was his lecture called off?

(A) Can you call me at seven?

(B) I don't know.

(C) I think he's a good professor.

Q 他的講課取消了嗎？

(A) 你可以在七點時打電話給我嗎？

(B) 我不知道。

(C) 我認為他是位好教授。

解析 本題是 be 動詞和過去分詞搭配。動詞片語 call off 是「取消」的意思。答案是選項（B）。選項（A）和（C）不是正確答案，因為它們並沒有針對問句所詢問的內容作回答。

單字 lecture 演講 | call off 取消

C 題型練習

Select the best response to the question or statement and mark the letter (A), (B), or (C) on your answer sheet.

1. Mark your answer on your answer sheet.

2. Mark your answer on your answer sheet.

3. Mark your answer on your answer sheet.

Answer Sheet

1.	(A)	(B)	(C)
2.	(A)	(B)	(C)
3.	(A)	(B)	(C)

答案和解析

1. Answer (B)

Script

	翻譯
Are you disappointed with your score?	你對自己的分數感到失望嗎？
(A) Nobody wants to talk to me.	(A) 沒有人想和我說話。
(B) At least I did my best.	(B) 至少我盡力了。
(C) I won't let you down.	(C) 我不會讓你失望。

解析　詢問對成績是否感到失望，選項（A）是完全無關的回答；選項（C）是談論未來的事，所以也不能選。答案是選項（B），「至少我盡力了」這句話，有種自我安慰的意思。

單字　**disappointed** 失望的　┃　**at least** 至少

---

2. Answer (B)

Script

	翻譯
Is there a bank around here?	這附近有銀行嗎？
(A) I've never been to Bangkok.	(A) 我從沒去過曼谷。
(B) There's one on Fifth Street.	(B) 第五街有一家。
(C) You're welcome.	(C) 不客氣。

解析　要選擇符合問句所問的內容來當作答案，答案是選項（B）。選項（A）是完全無關的回答；選項（C）是當對方說 Thank you 時最常使用的回答句，所以不能選。

單字　**bank** 銀行

---

3. Answer (C)

Script

	翻譯
Are you looking for a new job?	你在找新工作嗎？
(A) Don't mention it.	(A) 小事一樁。
(B) I went to the post office yesterday.	(B) 我昨天去郵局。
(C) I'm happy with my current job.	(C) 我對現在的工作很滿意。

解析　這是稍微複雜一點的試題。選項（A）是當對方說 Thank you 時，最常用的回答。因為問句是用現在進行式，所以回答也要用現在式，因此選項（B）是錯誤答案。詢問「在找新工作嗎」，選項（C）回答「很滿意現在的工作」，意思就是並沒有在找新工作，所以選項（C）是答案。

單字　**look for** 尋找　┃　**mention** 提到　┃　**current** 目前的

D 應用練習

▶ 解析 P. 459

🎧 027

Select the best response to the question or statement and mark the letter (A), (B), or (C) on your answer sheet.

1. Mark your answer on your answer sheet.

2. Mark your answer on your answer sheet.

3. Mark your answer on your answer sheet.

4. Mark your answer on your answer sheet.

Answer Sheet		
1. (A)	(B)	(C)
2. (A)	(B)	(C)
3. (A)	(B)	(C)
4. (A)	(B)	(C)

題型 03 Have/Has 疑問句

Ⓐ 輕鬆上手

疑問句中，以 have、has、had 起始的疑問句，叫做**完成式疑問句**。現在完成式用 have 或 has，過去完成式用 had。

◉ 現在完成式疑問句中，主詞不是第三人稱單數時，用 have 做疑問句開頭。

Have you ever been to Canada?	你去過加拿大嗎？
Have they visited us before?	他們以前拜訪過我們嗎？

◉ 在現在完成式疑問句中，主詞是第三人稱單數時，要用 has 做疑問句開頭。

Has he ever been to Canada?	他去過加拿大嗎？
Has he visited us before?	他以前拜訪過我們嗎？

◉ 現在完成式疑問句並非一定要用現在完成式來回答，可以用符合疑問句內容的現在式或過去式來回答。

Ⓐ **Have** you ever been to Canada?	你去過加拿大嗎？
Ⓑ I went there last summer.	我去年夏天去過那裡。

☞ 因為去年夏天去過，所以肯定地回答「有去過」。

◉ 過去完成式疑問句，用 had 起始疑問句。此種問句在日常生活中較不常被使用，所以在多益考試中較不常出題。

Had they bought a new car?	他們曾買過新車嗎？

B 基本題型

❶ 現在完成式 Have 疑問句（1）

🎧 028

Select the best response to the question or statement and mark the letter (A), (B), or (C) on your answer sheet.

(A)　　(B)　　(C)

Script

Q Have you contacted the travel agency?

(A) I've traveled around the world.
(B) Call me anytime.
(C) I've been too busy.

Q 你和旅行社聯繫過了嗎？

(A) 我曾環遊世界。
(B) 隨時都可打電話給我。
(C) 我一直都太忙了。

解析 這個問題也可以不用 yes 或 no 來回答。詢問聯絡旅行社了嗎，選項（C）回答「太忙了」，意思就是沒有聯絡，所以是答案。選項（A）和（B）都和所問不符。

單字 contact 聯絡 ｜ travel agency 旅行社

❷ 現在完成式 Have 疑問句（2）

🎧 029

Select the best response to the question or statement and mark the letter (A), (B), or (C) on your answer sheet.

(A)　　(B)　　(C)

Script

Q Have they finished writing the report?

(A) I haven't met them before.
(B) They are asking for an extension.
(C) They attended the conference.

Q 他們的報告寫完了嗎？

(A) 我以前沒見過他們。
(B) 他們正要求延期。
(C) 他們參加了大會。

解析 選項（A）雖然用現在完成式來回答，但語意不合，不能選它做答案。詢問他們寫完報告了嗎，選項（A）卻回答說「從未見過他們」，牛頭不對馬嘴。選項（B）回答「他們要求延期」，意思是報告還沒寫完，所以選項（B）是答案。

單字 report 報告 ｜ extension 延期 ｜ attend 參加 ｜ conference 研討會

❸ 現在完成式 Has 疑問句　　　🎧 030

Select the best response to the question or statement and mark the letter (A), (B), or (C) on your answer sheet.

(A)　　　(B)　　　(C)

Script

Q Has she worked abroad?

(A) She lives with her parents.

(B) She's a good student.

(C) She worked in France last year.

Q 她在國外工作過嗎？

(A) 她和雙親住在一起。

(B) 她是好學生。

(C) 她去年在法國工作。

解析 詢問女子有沒有在國外工作的經驗，所以答案是選項（C）。
其他選項和問句完全無關。

單字 abroad 國外

Select the best response to the question or statement and mark the letter (A), (B), or (C) on your answer sheet.

1. Mark your answer on your answer sheet.

2. Mark your answer on your answer sheet.

3. Mark your answer on your answer sheet.

Answer Sheet		
1. (A)	(B)	(C)
2. (A)	(B)	(C)
3. (A)	(B)	(C)

答案和解析

1. Answer (C)

Script

Have you passed your driving test?

(A) Driving can make you feel tired.

(B) She drives to work every day.

(C) I'm looking for another driving instructor.

翻譯

你通過路考了嗎？

(A) 駕駛會讓你感到疲倦。

(B) 她每天開車去工作。

(C) 我在找另一位路考教練。

解析 這是較複雜的試題。選項（A）和通過考試完全無關，選項（B）提到她，但因為這是另外一個人，所以也是錯誤答案。選項（C）提到要另外找一位路考教練，因為如果通過考試的話就不需要找教練了，所以可以推測，回話者沒有通過考試，答案是選項（C）。

單字 **pass** 通過 ｜ **driving test** 路考 ｜ **instructor** 教練

---

2. Answer (B)

Script

Have they invited us to dinner?

(A) We usually have dinner at seven.

(B) I've heard nothing from them.

(C) We're having pasta for dinner.

翻譯

他們有邀請我們去吃晚餐嗎？

(A) 我們通常在七點吃晚餐。

(B) 我一直沒聽到他們的消息。

(C) 我們晚餐要吃義大利麵。

解析 詢問他們是否有邀請我們吃晚餐，選項（B）回答「沒聽到他們的消息」，間接表示他們沒有邀請，所以選項（B）是答案。選項（A）和（C）是和問句完全無關的內容。

單字 **invite** 邀請 ｜ **pasta** 義大利麵

---

3. Answer (C)

Script

Has she found a new boyfriend?

(A) I don't know why she broke up with Jack.

(B) I've known her since childhood.

(C) She doesn't tell me about her private life.

翻譯

她找到新男友了嗎？

(A) 我不知道她為何與傑克分手。

(B) 我從小就認識她了。

(C) 她不跟我談論她的私事。

解析 這是較複雜的試題。詢問「她找到新男友了嗎」，選項（C）回答「她不跟我談論她的私事」，也就是不知道的意思，所以選項（C）是答案。

單字 **break up with** 與……分手 ｜ **childhood** 童年 ｜ **private** 私人的

D 應用練習

▶解析 P. 460　🎧 032

Select the best response to the question or statement and mark the letter (A), (B), or (C) on your answer sheet.

1. Mark your answer on your answer sheet.

2. Mark your answer on your answer sheet.

3. Mark your answer on your answer sheet.

4. Mark your answer on your answer sheet.

Answer Sheet

1.	(A)	(B)	(C)
2.	(A)	(B)	(C)
3.	(A)	(B)	(C)
4.	(A)	(B)	(C)

題型 **04** 助動詞疑問句

 A 輕鬆上手

就像會使用 do 和 have 幫助一般動詞形成疑問句，動詞時常會和助動詞搭配使用。不過這些助動詞與 do 和 have 不同，它們會在動詞上再增加一層含意。舉例來說，一般動詞原形前若加上 can，就增加了「能……」的意思。

這類的助動詞有 can、could、may、might、will、would、shall、should、must。回答助動詞疑問句，並非一定要用 yes 或 no 起頭，也並非一定要用助動詞來回答。

A	**Can** you swim?	你會游泳嗎？
B	I'm a good swimmer.	我是個游泳好手。

☞ 並沒有使用 yes 或 no 來回答，也沒使用助動詞來回答，不過對問句所問內容提出了解答。

重要的助動詞有 can 和 should。

A	**Can** I ask you a question?	我可以問你一個問題嗎？
B	What do you want to know?	你想知道什麼事？

☞ 詢問對方能否問他一個問題，對方反問「想要知道什麼」。

A	**Should** we postpone the meeting?	我們該延後會議嗎？
B	We don't have any other choice.	我們別無選擇。

☞ 問對方要不要將會議延後，對方說「別無選擇」，表示不得不將會議延後。雖然沒有用 yes 或 no 來回答，但作出了有肯定含意的答覆。

Ⓑ 基本題型

❶ can/could　🎧 033

Select the best response to the question or statement and mark the letter (A), (B), or (C) on your answer sheet.

(A)　　(B)　　(C)

> Script
>
> Q Can I talk to you for a minute?
>
> (A) I haven't talked to them yet.
> (B) I'm too busy right now.
> (C) Why didn't you call me last night?

> Q 我可以和你談一下嗎？
>
> (A) 我還沒和他們談。
> (B) 我現在太忙了。
> (C) 你昨晚為何沒打電話給我？

解析 雖然是用助動詞 can 來當開頭發問，但選項中都沒有 can。詢問「能和你談一下嗎」，選項（B）回答「現在太忙了」，意思就是沒辦法說話，所以選項（B）是答案。選項（A）有 talk，但卻是和「他們」說話，所以是陷阱答案。選項（C）完全答非所問。

❷ shall/should　🎧 034

Select the best response to the question or statement and mark the letter (A), (B), or (C) on your answer sheet.

(A)　　(B)　　(C)

> Script
>
> Q Should we accept their offer?
>
> (A) We can offer you a good salary.
> (B) Don't interrupt me.
> (C) I don't think that's a good idea.

> Q 我們該接受他們的提案嗎？
>
> (A) 我們可以給你優渥的薪水。
> (B) 別打擾我。
> (C) 我認為那不是個好點子。

解析 雖然是用助動詞 should 來問，但選項中都沒有 should。詢問「要接受他們的提案嗎」，選項（C）回答「不認為那是個好點子」，意思就是不要接受他們的提案，所以選項（C）是答案。

單字 accept 接受 ｜ offer 提案 ｜ salary 薪水 ｜ interrupt 打擾

Select the best response to the question or statement and mark the letter (A), (B), or (C) on your answer sheet.

(A)　　　(B)　　　(C)

Script

Q Shall we go out tonight?
　(A) I've already watched the movie.
　(B) I feel too tired.
　(C) Don't worry about your children.

Q 我們今晚要出去玩嗎？
　(A) 我已經看過這部電影。
　(B) 我覺得很累。
　(C) 別擔心你的孩子。

解析　「Shall we . . . ?」是「我們要不要一起去……?」的意思，表詢問對方要不要一起去做什麼事。詢問「今天晚上要不要一起出去」，最合適的回答是選項（B），選項（B）回答「覺得太累了」，意思就是不想出去。

單字　worry about　擔心

Ⓒ 題型練習　　　🎧 036

Select the best response to the question or statement and mark the letter (A), (B), or (C) on your answer sheet.

1. Mark your answer on your answer sheet.

2. Mark your answer on your answer sheet.

3. Mark your answer on your answer sheet.

Answer Sheet

1.	(A)	(B)	(C)
2.	(A)	(B)	(C)
3.	(A)	(B)	(C)

1. Answer (B)

Script	翻譯
Can you give me an example?	你可以給我個例子嗎？
(A) Why are you always complaining?	(A) 你為何總是在抱怨？
(B) Let me give you a good example.	(B) 讓我給你一個好例子。
(C) When can you fax the contract to me?	(C) 你何時可以把合約傳真給我？

解析 詢問「可以給我個例子嗎」，對這請求最合適的回答是選項(B)。選項(A)和(C)完全和提問無關。

單字 example 例子 ｜ complain 抱怨 ｜ contract 合約

---

2. Answer (B)

Script	翻譯
I think it's too bright here.	我覺得這裡太亮了。
(A) Can you stay a little longer?	(A) 你可以待久一點嗎？
(B) Should we turn off the lights?	(B 我們該關燈嗎？
(C) I was really surprised.	(C) 我真的很意外。

解析 發話者覺得該空間太亮了，選項(B)詢問「我們要關燈嗎」，意思是建議關燈會比較好，選項(B)是答案。

單字 bright 明亮的 ｜ turn off 關閉

---

3. Answer (C)

Script	翻譯
May I take your order, please?	請問可以為您點餐嗎？
(A) We're processing your order.	(A) 我們正在處理您的訂單。
(B) This dish is too spicy.	(B) 這道菜太辣了。
(C) I'd like two cheeseburgers.	(C) 我要兩個起司漢堡。

解析 這是在餐廳時常會聽到的問句。答案是選項(C)。選項(A)是處理訂單的人會說的話，顧客不會這樣說。選項(B)也是，在還沒訂餐的狀況下，顧客不會說出這種話。

單字 order 訂單 ｜ process 處理 ｜ dish 餐點 ｜ spicy 辣的

D 應用練習

▶ 解析 P. 461　　🎧 037

Select the best response to the question or statement and mark the letter (A), (B), or (C) on your answer sheet.

1. Mark your answer on your answer sheet.

2. Mark your answer on your answer sheet.

3. Mark your answer on your answer sheet.

4. Mark your answer on your answer sheet.

Answer Sheet		
1. (A)	(B)	(C)
2. (A)	(B)	(C)
3. (A)	(B)	(C)
4. (A)	(B)	(C)

Quick Test for **Part 2**

 038　▶ 解析 P. 462

Select the best response to the question or statement and mark the letter
(A), (B), or (C) on your answer sheet.

1. Mark your answer on your answer sheet.

2. Mark your answer on your answer sheet.

3. Mark your answer on your answer sheet.

4. Mark your answer on your answer sheet.

5. Mark your answer on your answer sheet.

6. Mark your answer on your answer sheet.

7. Mark your answer on your answer sheet.

8. Mark your answer on your answer sheet.

Answer Sheet

1. (A)   (B)   (C)

2. (A)   (B)   (C)

3. (A)   (B)   (C)

4. (A)   (B)   (C)

5. (A)   (B)   (C)

6. (A)   (B)   (C)

7. (A)   (B)   (C)

8. (A)   (B)   (C)

題型 01　Who 疑問句

A 輕鬆上手

疑問句中，以 have、has、had 起始的疑問句，叫做完成式疑問句。現在完成式用 have 或 has，過去完成式用 had。

疑問詞疑問句就是以疑問詞 who、when、where、what、which、why 起始的問句。和前面的一般疑問句不同，疑問詞疑問句絕對不能用 yes 或 no 來回答。疑問詞疑問句是針對已知事實獲得更進一步的消息或資訊所使用的問句，因此不會用 yes 或 no 來回答。

一起來看例句 :

> Ⓐ **Who** attended the conference?　誰參加了大會？
>
> Ⓑ₁ Mary did. 瑪麗參加了。　(○)
>
> Ⓑ₂ Yes, she did. 沒錯，她參加了。(×)

☞ 第一個回答是最適合的回答。提問的人已經知道會有人參加會議，只是不清楚是誰會出席，所以只要提供這個訊息，就會是正確答案。
第二個回答並不合適，第一，問句中沒有要對方回答是或不是的內容；第二，yes 或 no 是詢問對事情完全不知情的人時才會使用的回答。

疑問詞中的 who，大致有兩種用法：

❶ 作疑問句的主詞，表示「某人如何……」的意思。

Ⓐ **Who** passed the test? 誰通過了考試？

Ⓑ Only Kevin did. 只有凱文通過。

❷ 當作疑問句的受詞，表示「如何……是誰」的意思。在寫作中要用 whom，但在口語中，比較常用 who。

Ⓐ **Who** should I contact? 我該聯絡誰？

Ⓑ Call Amy right away. 立即打電話給艾美。

Ⓑ 基本題型

❶ 當作主詞的 who（1） 🎧 039

Select the best response to the question or statement and mark the letter (A), (B), or (C) on your answer sheet.

(A)　　　(B)　　　(C)

Script

Ⓠ Who is your supervisor?

(A) Yes, I'm in charge.
(B) No, I didn't do that.
(C) I report to Mr. Baker.

Ⓠ 你的主管是誰？

(A) 沒錯，由我負責。
(B) 不，我沒有做那件事。
(C) 我的主管是貝克先生。

解析 這是用疑問詞 who 來起始的疑問句，所以絕對不能用 yes 或 no 來回答。正答是選項(C)。仔細想想這個回答，詢問你的主管是誰，回答「要對貝克先生報告」，意思就是貝克先生是他的長官。要像這樣選出符合提問內容的選項。

單字 **supervisor** 主管 ｜ **in charge** 負責 ｜ **report** 稟報

❷ 當作主詞的 who（2）

040

Select the best response to the question or statement and mark the letter (A), (B), or (C) on your answer sheet.

(A)　　(B)　　(C)

Script

Q Who was selected to handle the matter?

(A) No, I was against the plan.

(B) Mary, in the accounting department.

(C) I'll see you tomorrow.

Q 被選上處理這件事的人是誰？

(A) 不，我之前反對這個計劃。

(B) 是會計部門的瑪麗。

(C) 明天見。

解析 因為是疑問詞 who 起始的疑問句，所以選項（A）絕對不會是答案。因為是用過去式提問，選項（C）卻用未來式回答，所以是陷阱選項。答案是選項（B）。要記得，不用完整句回答也有可能是正確答案。

單字 **select** 選擇 ｜ **handle** 處理 ｜ **accounting** 會計

---

❸ 當作受詞的 who

040 041

Select the best response to the question or statement and mark the letter (A), (B), or (C) on your answer sheet.

(A)　　(B)　　(C)

Script

Q Who should I talk to about the project?

(A) When can you complete it?

(B) Yes, we were successful.

(C) Kevin is in charge of it.

Q 我該找誰談這個案子？

(A) 你何時可以完成？

(B) 是啊，我們很順利。

(C) 凱文負責這個案子。

解析 因為是疑問詞 who 起始的疑問句，所以選項（B）可以立刻刪除。答案是選項（C）。詢問要找誰談這個案子，選項（C）回答「凱文負責這個案子」，意思就是要和凱文談。

單字 **project** 案子 ｜ **complete** 完成

Select the best response to the question or statement and mark the letter (A), (B), or (C) on your answer sheet.

1. Mark your answer on your answer sheet.

2. Mark your answer on your answer sheet.

3. Mark your answer on your answer sheet.

Answer Sheet

1.	(A)	(B)	(C)
2.	(A)	(B)	(C)
3.	(A)	(B)	(C)

1. Answer (C)

Script | 翻譯

Who invited you? | 誰邀請你？

(A) Yes, she's an excellent speaker. | (A) 沒錯，她是位優秀的演講者。

(B) No problem. | (B) 沒問題。

(C) I was invited by the CEO. | (C) 我是被執行長邀請的。

解析 因為是以疑問詞 who 起始的疑問詞疑問句，所以選項（A）絕對不會是答案。選項（B）是當對方說 Thank you 時時常出現的回答。答案是選項（C），因為是用被動語態回答，所以可能會覺得不太順，不過因為符合提問內容，所以是答案。

單字 excellent 優秀的

---

2. Answer (A)

Script | 翻譯

Who is working on the budget report? | 誰在處理預算案？

(A) That hasn't been decided yet. | (A) 還沒決定由誰負責。

(B) No, we're trying to balance the budget. | (B) 不，我們正嘗試平衡預算。

(C) Paul told me something strange yesterday. | (C) 保羅昨天告訴我有件奇怪的事。

解析 因為是以疑問詞 who 起始的疑問詞疑問句，所以選項（B）絕對不會是答案。選項（C）雖然回答了人名，但不符合提問內容，所以答案是選項（A）。詢問誰在做預算報告，選項（A）回答「還沒決定」。

單字 budget 預算 ｜ balance the budget 平衡預算 ｜ strange 奇怪的

---

3. Answer (B)

Script | 翻譯

Who did you vote for? | 你投票給誰？

(A) Yes, we won the election. | (A) 對，我們贏得選舉。

(B) I don't want to tell you. | (B) 我不想告訴你。

(C) No, I saw her yesterday. | (C) 不，我昨天有看到她。

解析 這是以疑問詞 who 起始的疑問詞疑問句，所以選項（A）和（C）絕對不會是正答。詢問投票給誰，選項（B）回答「不想告訴你」。

單字 vote 投票 ｜ election 選舉

D 應用練習　　　　　　　▶ 解析 P. 465　　🎧 043

Select the best response to the question or statement and mark the letter (A), (B), or (C) on your answer sheet.

1. Mark your answer on your answer sheet.

2. Mark your answer on your answer sheet.

3. Mark your answer on your answer sheet.

4. Mark your answer on your answer sheet.

Answer Sheet		
1. (A)	(B)	(C)
2. (A)	(B)	(C)
3. (A)	(B)	(C)
4. (A)	(B)	(C)

題型 02 | When/Where 疑問句

A 輕鬆上手

疑問詞 when 是問「何時」，where 是問「何地」，所以以這兩個疑問詞起始的疑問句，絕對不能用 yes 或 no 來回答。

When 可以和過去式、現在式、未來式搭配使用。
Where 要依據後接動詞來表現時間。

下列是 when 和 where 使用過去式的例句。

Ⓐ **When** did you meet Peter?	你何時和彼得見面？
Ⓑ Yesterday.	昨天。

☞ 詢問時間，直接回答「昨天」即可。

Ⓐ **Where** did you meet Peter?	你在哪裡和彼得見面？
Ⓑ At the airport.	在機場。

☞ 詢問場所，直接回答「在某處」即可。

下列是 when 和 where 使用現在式的例句。

Ⓐ **When** do you have lunch?	你何時吃午餐？
Ⓑ Usually at noon.	通常在中午。

Ⓐ **Where** do you have lunch?	你在哪裡吃午餐？
Ⓑ Usually at a fast food restaurant.	通常在速食店。

下列是 when 和 where 使用未來式的例句。

Ⓐ	**When** will the event take place?	活動將在何時開始？
Ⓑ	Next Tuesday.	下週二。

Ⓐ	**Where** will the event take place?	活動將會在哪裡舉行？
Ⓑ	At the Roberts Hotel.	在羅伯茲旅館。

Ⓑ 基本題型

❶ 過去式　　　　　🎧 044

Select the best response to the question or statement and mark the letter (A), (B), or (C) on your answer sheet.

(A)　　　(B)　　　(C)

Script

Q When did you write your first novel?

(A) Yes, it was a best-seller.
(B) When I was 20.
(C) I found the novel really boring.

Q 你在何時寫第一本小說？

(A) 沒錯，那是本暢銷小說。
(B) 在我 20 歲時。
(C) 我認為這本小說很無趣。

解析 因為是以疑問詞 when 起始的疑問句，所以選項（A）絕對不會是答案。選項（C）提到對小說的感覺，所以也是陷阱選項。答案是選項（B）。要記住，像選項（B）這樣沒有用完整句來回答，也有可能會是答案。

單字 **boring** 無聊的

❷ 現在式

Select the best response to the question or statement and mark the letter (A), (B), or (C) on your answer sheet.

(A)　　　　(B)　　　(C)

Script

Q Where do you live?

 (A) No, I haven't met him before.
 (B) I must leave now.
 (C) I live in Toronto.

Q 你住在哪裡？

 (A) 沒有，我以前未曾見過他。
 (B) 我現在得離開。
 (C) 我住在多倫多。

解析 因為是以疑問詞 where 起始的疑問句，所以選項（A）絕對不會是答案。選項（B）並沒有提到現在住在哪裡，所以也是錯誤選項。答案是選項（C）。

❸ 未來式

Select the best response to the question or statement and mark the letter (A), (B), or (C) on your answer sheet.

(A)　　　　(B)　　　(C)

Script

Q When will the meeting be over?

 (A) No, I won't tell anyone about it.
 (B) Hopefully at 2:00 p.m.
 (C) Yes, we signed the agreement.

Q 會議何時會結束？

 (A) 不，我不會告訴任何人。
 (B) 希望在下午兩點結束。
 (C) 沒錯，我們簽了協議。

解析 因為是以疑問詞 when 起始的疑問句，所以選項（A）和（C）絕對不會是答案。答案是選項（B）。

單字 **sign** 簽署 ｜ **agreement** 協議

Select the best response to the question or statement and mark the letter (A), (B), or (C) on your answer sheet.

1. Mark your answer on your answer sheet.

2. Mark your answer on your answer sheet.

3. Mark your answer on your answer sheet.

Answer Sheet

1.	(A)	(B)	(C)
2.	(A)	(B)	(C)
3.	(A)	(B)	(C)

答案和解析

1. Answer (B)

Script	翻譯

Where did they go for lunch? | 他們去哪裡吃午餐？
(A) No, I haven't had lunch yet. | (A) 不，我還沒吃午餐。
(B) To a Japanese restaurant. | (B) 在一家日本餐廳。
(C) Yes, it was delicious. | (C) 沒錯，餐點很可口。

解析 因為是以疑問詞 where 起始的疑問句，所以絕對不能用 yes 或 no 來回答。答案是選項(B)。不用完整句來回答也可以。

單字 delicious 可口的

---

2. Answer (C)

Script	翻譯

When do you plan on getting married? | 你何時打算要結婚？
(A) No, he's still single. | (A) 不，他還是單身。
(B) I didn't go to her wedding. | (B) 我沒有參加她的婚禮。
(C) That's too personal a question. | (C) 那問題太私人了。

解析 是以疑問詞 when 起始的疑問詞疑問句，所以選項(A)是錯的。選項(B)不符提問內容，所以答案是選項(C)。詢問對方何時結婚，選項(C)回答「那個問題太私人了」，意思就是不方便回答。

單字 get married 結婚

---

3. Answer (C)

Script	翻譯

When will you finish writing the article? | 你何時會寫完這篇文章？
(A) It was written by a famous professor. | (A) 是由知名教授所寫的。
(B) Yes, it contains some errors. | (B) 是啊，文章有一些錯誤。
(C) Hopefully by midnight. | (C) 希望在午夜前寫完。

解析 是以疑問詞 when 起始的疑問句，所以選項(B)絕對不會是答案。詢問何時結束，選項(C)回答「希望在午夜前」，所以選項(C)是答案。

單字 article 文章 | contain 包含 | error 錯誤 | midnight 午夜

D 應用練習　　　　　　　▶ 解析 P. 466　　　🎧 048

Select the best response to the question or statement and mark the letter (A), (B), or (C) on your answer sheet.

1. Mark your answer on your answer sheet.

2. Mark your answer on your answer sheet.

3. Mark your answer on your answer sheet.

4. Mark your answer on your answer sheet.

Answer Sheet

1. (A)	(B)	(C)
2. (A)	(B)	(C)
3. (A)	(B)	(C)
4. (A)	(B)	(C)

題型 **03** | How 疑問句

Ⓐ 輕鬆上手

疑問詞 how 是「如何」的意思,所以用 how 起始的疑問句,絕對不能用 yes 或 no 來回答。

how 除了當「如何」之意使用外,也有當其他含意使用的時候。

◉ 詢問交通方式

How do you go to work every day?　你每天如何去上班?

◉ 詢問心情狀態

How was your weekend?　你的週末過得如何?

◉ 詢問喜好

How do you like the new office?　你覺得新辦公室怎麼樣?

how 若放在形容詞或副詞前,則是「多少」的意思。

問數量 **How <u>many</u>** newspapers do you read every day?　你每天讀幾份報紙?
問價格 **How <u>much</u>** is that sweater?　那件毛衣多少錢?
問頻率 **How <u>often</u>** do you play tennis?　你多久打一次網球?
問時間 **How <u>long</u>** are you going to stay in Canada?　你要在加拿大待多久?

如上所示,how 的用法很多,要記住 how 要和不同單字搭配所產生的不同含意。

B 基本題型

❶ 簡單式
🎧 049

Select the best response to the question or statement and mark the letter (A), (B), or (C) on your answer sheet.

(A)　　(B)　　(C)

Script

Q How do I print this document?

(A) Your order is out of stock.

(B) No, I didn't use the printer yesterday.

(C) Sally can show you how to do it.

Q 我要如何列印這份文件？

(A) 你訂購的商品沒貨了。

(B) 不，我昨天並沒有使用印表機。

(C) 莎莉會教你怎麼印。

解析 疑問詞 how 是「如何」的意思，詢問要用什麼方法做某事。因為是疑問詞疑問句，所以選項（B）絕對不會是答案。因為並不是詢問訂購商品的狀況，所以選項（A）是錯的。回答「莎莉會教你怎麼印」的選項（C）是答案。

單字 document 文件 ｜ out of stock 沒貨

❷「方法」以外的意思

Select the best response to the question or statement and mark the letter (A), (B), or (C) on your answer sheet.

(A)　　　(B)　　　(C)

Script

Q How do you like your new neighbor?

(A) Yes, we've been working together for five years.
(B) I find him very friendly.
(C) You look young for your age.

Q 你覺得新鄰居怎麼樣？

(A) 沒錯，我們已共事五年。

(B) 我覺得他很友善。

(C) 你看起來比實際年紀年輕。

解析 因為是疑問詞 how 起始的疑問句，所以選項（A）絕對不會是答案。選項（C）不符提問內容。答案是選項（B），選項中的 find 是「經驗、體驗之後而得知」之意。

單字 neighbor 鄰居 ｜ friendly 友善的

---

❸ how ＋形容詞／副詞

050051

Select the best response to the question or statement and mark the letter (A), (B), or (C) on your answer sheet.

(A)　　　(B)　　　(C)

Script

Q How often do you visit the library?

(A) Almost every day.
(B) Yes, I've been there before.
(C) They're building a new library.

Q 你多久去一次圖書館？

(A) 幾乎每天去。
(B) 是啊，我以前去過。
(C) 他們正在建一棟新的圖書館。

解析 疑問詞 how 搭配副詞 often，表示詢問頻率。因為是疑問詞疑問句，所以選項（B）絕對不會是答案。選項（C）不符提問內容，所以答案是選項（A）。

Select the best response to the question or statement and mark the letter (A), (B), or (C) on your answer sheet.

1. Mark your answer on your answer sheet.

2. Mark your answer on your answer sheet.

3. Mark your answer on your answer sheet.

Answer Sheet

1.	(A)	(B)	(C)
2.	(A)	(B)	(C)
3.	(A)	(B)	(C)

1. Answer (B)

Script	翻譯
How can we protect our data?	我們要如何保護資料？
(A) No, I didn't bring it up at the meeting.	(A) 不，我並沒有在會議中提起這件事。
(B) We should install reliable security software on our computers.	(B) 我們應該在電腦中安裝可靠的防護軟體。
(C) Yes, my company is prospering.	(B) 沒錯，我的公司正在蓬勃發展。

解析 是疑問詞 how 起始的疑問句，所以選項（A）和（C）絕對不會是答案。選項（B）提到了保護資料的方法，所以選項（B）是答案。

單字 bring up 提出 ｜ install 安裝 ｜ reliable 可靠的 ｜ security 防護 ｜ prosper 蓬勃發展

---

2. Answer (C)

Script	翻譯
How did your presentation go yesterday?	你昨天的報告進行得如何？
(A) Yes, it was recommended by experts.	(A) 沒錯，那專家所推薦。
(B) He didn't go anywhere.	(B) 他什麼地方都沒去。
(C) It went smoothly.	(C) 進行得很順利。

解析 疑問詞 how 不是詢問方法，而是表示其他意思。因為是疑問詞疑問句，所以選項（A）不會是答案。因為問句並沒有提到「他」，所以選項（B）是錯的。答案是選項（C）。

單字 presentation 報告 ｜ recommend 推薦 ｜ expert 專家 ｜ smoothly 順利地

---

3. Answer (B)

Script	翻譯
How many items are on the agenda?	議程上有多少討論要項？
(A) No, we don't have much time left.	(A) 不，我們剩下的時間不多。
(B) We have a lot of things to discuss today.	(B) 我們今天有很多事項要討論。
(C) The book is out of print.	(C) 這本書已絕版。

解析 因為是疑問詞疑問句，所以選項（A）不會是答案。因為問句並沒有提到「這本書」，所以選項（C）是錯的。雖然選項（B）沒有提到具體數字，不過只要能回答問題也可以是答案。

單字 agenda 議程 ｜ discuss 討論 ｜ out of print 絕版

Select the best response to the question or statement and mark the letter (A), (B), or (C) on your answer sheet.

1. Mark your answer on your answer sheet.

2. Mark your answer on your answer sheet.

3. Mark your answer on your answer sheet.

4. Mark your answer on your answer sheet.

Answer Sheet		
1. (A)	(B)	(C)
2. (A)	(B)	(C)
3. (A)	(B)	(C)
4. (A)	(B)	(C)

題型 04 What/Which 疑問句

A 輕鬆上手

疑問詞 what 是「什麼」的意思，which 是「哪一個」的意思。一般都單獨當疑問代名詞使用，但也可放在名詞前，表限定的含意。無論任何情況，當它們成為疑問詞疑問句時，絕對不能用 yes 或 no 來回答。

◉ what 和 which **當代名詞使用：**

What is the best way to learn a foreign language?
什麼是學習外語的最佳方式？

What are you doing now?
你現在在做什麼？

What do you want from me?
你要我做什麼？

Which do you like better, apples or strawberries?
你比較喜歡哪種，蘋果或草莓？

Which is the capital of Canada? Toronto or Ottawa?
加拿大的首都是哪個？是多倫多或渥太華？

Which is more effective in increasing our sales?
哪個是增加我們銷售更有效的方式？

◉ what 和 which 當限定詞使用：

What subject in school is your favorite？ 你在學校最喜歡的科目是什麼？

What color is the new dress? 新衣服的顏色是什麼？

What kind of job are you looking for? 你想找什麼樣的工作？

Which movie is more interesting? 哪一部電影更有意思？

Which car would you like to drive? 你想開哪部車？

Which university are you going to this year? 你今年想讀哪一所大學？

Ⓑ 基本題型

❶ what 當代名詞使用 🎧054

Select the best response to the question or statement and mark the letter (A), (B), or (C) on your answer sheet.

(A)　　　(B)　　　(C)

Script

Q What do you do for work?

(A) Yes, you did a good job.

(B) I'm a graphic designer.

(C) I'm shocked at what happened to you.

Q 你從事什麼工作？

(A) 沒錯，你做得很好。

(B) 我是平面設計師。

(C) 我對你的遭遇感到很震驚。

解析 本問句是在詢問職業。因為是疑問詞疑問句，所以選項（A）絕對不會是答案。選項（C）不符所問的內容。答案是選項（B）。

單字 shock 震驚

❷ which 當代名詞使用

Select the best response to the question or statement and mark the letter (A), (B), or (C) on your answer sheet.

(A)　　　(B)　　　(C)

> **Script**
>
> **Q** Which is more fun to visit for tourists? Seoul or Tokyo?
>
> (A) No, Seoul is better than Tokyo.
> (B) I've never been to Asia.
> (C) I think they are equally fun.
>
> **Q** 造訪哪個都市對遊客而言比較好玩？首爾或東京？
>
> (A) 不，首爾比東京更適合。
> (B) 我從未去過亞洲。
> (C) 我認為兩者都一樣好玩。

解析 因為是以 which 起始的疑問詞疑問句，所以選項（A）絕對不會是答案。選項（B）並沒有說出哪個都市比較好，所以也不會是答案。答案選項（C）回答「兩個都市都一樣好」，這樣回答也可以。

單字 tourist 遊客 ｜ equally 一樣地

❸ what/which 當限定詞使用

055 056

Select the best response to the question or statement and mark the letter (A), (B), or (C) on your answer sheet.

(A)　　　(B)　　　(C)

> **Script**
>
> **Q** Which department do you want to work for?
>
> (A) No, I didn't accept their offer.
> (B) That's a brilliant idea.
> (C) The human resources department.
>
> **Q** 你想到哪一個部門工作？
>
> (A) 不，我沒接受他們的提案。
> (B) 那是個很棒的點子。
> (C) 人力資源部門。

解析 是以 which 起始的疑問詞疑問句，所以選項（A）絕對不會是答案。選項（B）並沒有回答問題想在哪個部門工作，所以是錯誤答案。答案是選項（C），直接說出部門。

單字 department 部門 ｜ accept 接受 ｜ offer 提案 ｜ brilliant 很棒的

C 題型練習　　　🎧 057

Select the best response to the question or statement and mark the letter (A), (B), or (C) on your answer sheet.

1. Mark your answer on your answer sheet.

2. Mark your answer on your answer sheet.

3. Mark your answer on your answer sheet.

Answer Sheet		
1. (A)	(B)	(C)
2. (A)	(B)	(C)
3. (A)	(B)	(C)

1. Answer (B)

Script

What should we do to attract more customers?

(A) No, the customer didn't complain.

(B) We need to invest more money in marketing.

(C) They are very attractive jobs.

翻譯

我們該做什麼才能吸引更多顧客?

(A) 不,顧客並沒有抱怨。

(B) 我們必須在行銷上投注更多資金。

(C) 它們是很吸引人的工作。

解析 這是用疑問詞 what 起始的疑問句,所以選項(A)絕對不會是答案。問要做什麼來吸引客人, 選項(C)回答「它們是很吸引人的工作」,跟問句完全無關。所以答案是選項(B)。

單字 attract 吸引 │ customer 顧客 │ complain 抱怨 │ attractive 吸引人的

2. Answer (C)

Script

Which will improve our productivity, flextime or higher salaries?

(A) Yes, our productivity has increased.

(B) No, I don't want high salaries.

(C) Flextime seems to be a better option.

翻譯

哪個可以改善我們的生產力,彈性工時或更高的薪資?

(A) 沒錯,我們的生產力增加了。

(B) 不,我不要高薪資。

(C) 彈性工時似乎是較佳的選項。

解析 這是意思較複雜的問句,不過因為是用 which 起始的疑問詞疑問句,所以選項(A)和(B) 絕對不會是答案。所以答案是選項(C)。

單字 improve 改善 │ productivity 生產力 │ salary 薪資 │ option 選項

3. Answer (B)

Script

Which brand do you prefer, Samsung or Apple?

(A) No, my wife and I hate apples.

(B) Definitely Samsung.

(C) I've never been to the United States.

翻譯

你較喜歡哪一種品牌,三星或蘋果?

(A) 不要,我和老婆都討厭蘋果。

(B) 絕對是三星。

(C) 我從未去過美國。

解析 這是 which 當作限定詞使用的疑問詞疑問句,所以選項(A)絕對不會是答案。選項(C)不 符問句所問內容。所以答案是選項(B)。

單字 brand 品牌 │ hate 討厭 │ definitely 絕對

D 應用練習　　　　　　　▶ 解析 P. 468　　　🎧 058

Select the best response to the question or statement and mark the letter (A), (B), or (C) on your answer sheet.

1. Mark your answer on your answer sheet.

2. Mark your answer on your answer sheet.

3. Mark your answer on your answer sheet.

4. Mark your answer on your answer sheet.

Answer Sheet

1. (A)　　　　(B)　　　　(C)
2. (A)　　　　(B)　　　　(C)
3. (A)　　　　(B)　　　　(C)
4. (A)　　　　(B)　　　　(C)

題型 05 | Why 疑問句

A 輕鬆上手

疑問詞 why 是「為什麼」的意思。因為形成的問句是疑問詞疑問句,所以絕對不能用 yes 或 no 來回答。

以 why 起始的疑問句,大致可分作三種:詢問原因、詢問目的,也可以和其他字詞搭配來詢問「做……如何?」。

◉ 詢問原因

Why were you late for the meeting? 你為何這次會議遲到?

Why was your flight delayed? 你的航班為何會延誤?

Why are you crying? 你為什麼哭?

Why is Mary smiling? 瑪麗為何在笑?

◉ 詢問目的

Why did you go to New York? 你為何要去紐約?

Why do you ride the bicycle to work instead of driving?
你為何騎腳踏車上班而不開車?

Why are you having a party? 你為何舉辦派對?

Why do you plan to study abroad? 你為何計劃到國外留學?

◉ 以「why don't you/we . . . ?」的方式起頭,詢問「你/我們去做……如何?」

Why don't you go swimming? 你為何不去游泳?

Why don't we take a break? 我們何不休息一下?

Why don't you email him about it? 你何不針對這件事寄電子郵件給他?

Why don't we visit Mary in the hospital? 我們何不去醫院探視瑪莉?

B 基本題型

❶ 原因
🎧 059

Select the best response to the question or statement and mark the letter (A), (B), or (C) on your answer sheet.

(A)　　　(B)　　　(C)

Q Why did you stop smoking?

 (A) No, I don't like spicy food.

 (B) Because it's not good for my health.

 (C) You used to smoke a lot.

 你為何戒菸?

 (A) 不,我不喜歡辣的食物。

 (B) 因為那對我健康有害。

 (C) 你以前的菸癮很重。

解析 這是用疑問詞 why 起始的疑問句,所以選項(A)絕對不會是答案。選項(C)不符問句內容。所以答案是選項(B)。比起清楚區分詢問原因還是詢問目的,選出符合問句的回答更重要。

單字 spicy 辣的 **│** used to 以前

❷ 目的

Select the best response to the question or statement and mark the letter (A), (B), or (C) on your answer sheet.

(A)　　　(B)　　　(C)

Script

Q Why are they developing a new product?

(A) Yes, I like that product.
(B) To remain competitive in the industry.
(C) We live in a developing country.

Q 他們為何要開發新產品？

(A) 沒錯，我喜歡那項產品。
(B) 要在業界保持競爭力。
(C) 我們生活在開發中國家。

解析 這是用疑問詞 why 起始的疑問句，所以選項 (A) 絕對不會是答案。選項 (C) 不符問句所問內容。所以答案是選項 (B)。

單字 develop 開發 │ competitive 具競爭力的 │
developing country 開發中國家

❸ 提議

Select the best response to the question or statement and mark the letter (A), (B), or (C) on your answer sheet.

(A)　　　(B)　　　(C)

Script

Q Why don't you just relax and enjoy yourself?

(A) Please make yourself at home.
(B) You don't have to feel nervous.
(C) I have a deadline to meet.

Q 你何不讓自己好好放鬆一下？

(A) 請別客氣。
(B) 你不用感到緊張。
(C) 我有截止期限要趕。

解析 這是較複雜的問句，勸對方何不放鬆自在一點，所以答案是選項 (C)，說明了不能接受建議的原因。選項 (A) 和 (B) 不符問句內容。

單字 relax 放鬆 │ make yourself at home 別拘謹 │ nervous 緊張 │
deadline 期限

C 題型練習

Select the best response to the question or statement and mark the letter (A), (B), or (C) on your answer sheet.

1. Mark your answer on your answer sheet.

2. Mark your answer on your answer sheet.

3. Mark your answer on your answer sheet.

Answer Sheet

1. (A)   (B)   (C)

2. (A)   (B)   (C)

3. (A)   (B)   (C)

答案和解析

1. Answer (C)

Why did you leave your last job?	你為何離開上一份工作？
(A) Yes, I was a dedicated employee.	(A) 是的，我是位全心奉獻的員工。
(B) Explain to me how it works.	(B) 向我解釋它的功用。
(C) Because I wanted a new challenge.	(C) 因為我想要新的挑戰。

解析 用 why 起始的疑問詞疑問句，所以選項(A)絕對不會是答案。選項(B)是和問句所問內容無關的錯誤答案。所以答案是選項(C)。

單字 dedicated 盡心盡力的 | employee 員工 | challenge 挑戰

---

2. Answer (B)

Why do you have two jobs?	你為何做兩份工作？
(A) No, we don't live in a spacious apartment.	(A) 不，我們住的公寓並不寬敞。
(B) To support my sick wife.	(B) 因為我老婆生病了。
(C) I used to live in France.	(C) 我過去住在法國。

解析 用 why 起始的疑問詞疑問句，所以選項(A)是錯誤答案。選項(C)和問句所問內容完全無關。所以答案是選項(B)。

單字 spacious 寬敞的

---

3. Answer (B)

Why don't you buy her flowers?	你何不買花給她？
(A) Yes, we had a great time in Spain.	(A) 沒錯，我們在西班牙玩得很愉快。
(B) Actually, she doesn't like them.	(B) 事實上，她並不喜歡那些花。
(C) No, she's not a rich woman.	(C) 不，她並不是位有錢的女人。

解析 這是較複雜的問句。問句建議對方買花送給她，選項(B)說出了不接受該建議的原因，所以是答案。選項(A)和(C)不符問句所問內容。

單字 actually 事實上

Select the best response to the question or statement and mark the letter (A), (B), or (C) on your answer sheet.

1. Mark your answer on your answer sheet.

2. Mark your answer on your answer sheet.

3. Mark your answer on your answer sheet.

4. Mark your answer on your answer sheet.

Answer Sheet

1.	(A)	(B)	(C)
2.	(A)	(B)	(C)
3.	(A)	(B)	(C)
4.	(A)	(B)	(C)

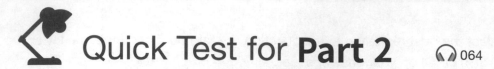 Quick Test for **Part 2**　　064　▶ 解析 P. 470

Select the best response to the question or statement and mark the letter (A), (B), or (C) on your answer sheet.

1. Mark your answer on your answer sheet.

2. Mark your answer on your answer sheet.

3. Mark your answer on your answer sheet.

4. Mark your answer on your answer sheet.

5. Mark your answer on your answer sheet.

6. Mark your answer on your answer sheet.

7. Mark your answer on your answer sheet.

8. Mark your answer on your answer sheet.

Answer Sheet

1. (A)　　　　　(B)　　　　　(C)

2. (A)　　　　　(B)　　　　　(C)

3. (A)　　　　　(B)　　　　　(C)

4. (A)　　　　　(B)　　　　　(C)

5. (A)　　　　　(B)　　　　　(C)

6. (A)　　　　　(B)　　　　　(C)

7. (A)　　　　　(B)　　　　　(C)

8. (A)　　　　　(B)　　　　　(C)

Practice Test

065 ▶ 解析 P. 472

Part 2

Directions: You will hear a question or statement and three responses spoken in English. They will not be printed in your test book and will be spoken only one time. Select the best response to the question or statement, and mark the letter (A), (B), or (C) on your answer sheet.

1. Mark your answer on your answer sheet.

2. Mark your answer on your answer sheet.

3. Mark your answer on your answer sheet.

4. Mark your answer on your answer sheet.

5. Mark your answer on your answer sheet.

6. Mark your answer on your answer sheet.

7. Mark your answer on your answer sheet.

8. Mark your answer on your answer sheet.

9. Mark your answer on your answer sheet.

10. Mark your answer on your answer sheet.

11. Mark your answer on your answer sheet.

12. Mark your answer on your answer sheet.

13. Mark your answer on your answer sheet.

14. Mark your answer on your answer sheet.

15. Mark your answer on your answer sheet.

16. Mark your answer on your answer sheet.

Practice Test

Answer Sheet

1.	(A)	(B)	(C)
2.	(A)	(B)	(C)
3.	(A)	(B)	(C)
4.	(A)	(B)	(C)
5.	(A)	(B)	(C)
6.	(A)	(B)	(C)
7.	(A)	(B)	(C)
8.	(A)	(B)	(C)
9.	(A)	(B)	(C)
10.	(A)	(B)	(C)
11.	(A)	(B)	(C)
12.	(A)	(B)	(C)
13.	(A)	(B)	(C)
14.	(A)	(B)	(C)
15.	(A)	(B)	(C)
16.	(A)	(B)	(C)

 Notes

PART

3

簡短對話

題型 **01**　掌握主題

A 輕鬆上手

Part 3 的解題順序分為三個階段：

| 階段一 | 推測對話內容 | ⇒ | 階段二 | 聽對話 | ⇒ | 階段三 | 找出正確答案 |

推測對話內容就是先看選項，然後推測對話的內容。不過，由於可能時間不夠而無法讀過所有的選項，所以閱讀的時候要把焦點放在名詞和動詞上，這是重要的訣竅。

例題 🎧 066

Q What are the speakers mainly talking about?	Q 對話者主要在談論什麼？
(A) The place for a local event (B) The time to meet with a client	(A) 當地活動的地點。 (B) 和客戶見面的時間。

Script

Ⓜ Do you know where the charity event will be held?	男 你知道慈善活動將在哪裡舉行嗎？
Ⓦ You mean the event for poor children in the city?	女 你是說為本市貧窮孩童所舉辦的活動？
Ⓜ Yes. One of my clients wants to go to the event.	男 沒錯。我的一位客戶想要參加這項活動。
Ⓦ Oh really? The charity event will be held in the Jackson Community Center.	女 喔，真的嗎？慈善活動的地點在傑克森社區中心。

解析 從上面這段對話內容可以知道，正確答案是選項（A）。對話中出現的 where the charity event will be held，在試題中被改寫成了 The place for a local event。

在聽對話內容的時候，將聽到的內容和選項做比對是很重要的。一般來說，選項都會將對話中出現的用語加以改寫（paraphrasing），所以在最後找出正確答案的階段，要一邊注意改寫用語一面找答案。

ⓑ 基本題型

❶ 主題在對話的前半部　　　🎧 067

Question 1 refers to the following conversation.

Q What is the main topic of the conversation?	**Q** 這段對話的主題是什麼？
(A) A job interview	(A) 工作面試。
(B) The woman's plans for this summer.	(B) 女子的夏季計劃。

Script

Ⓜ What are you up to these days?	男 你最近在忙什麼？
Ⓦ I've been busy preparing for my trip to Europe.	女 我一直忙著準備我的歐洲之行。
Ⓜ Right. You told me you're going there this summer.	男 對耶，你說過這個夏天要去那裡玩。
Ⓦ Yes, I'm quite excited.	女 是啊，我很興奮。

解析 對話的主題在對話前半部出現。男子問女子最近在做什麼，女子對此做出回答，這回答接著變成了這段對話的中心。所以正答是選項（B）。選項（A）完全沒有出現在對話中。

單字 up to 做什麼事 ｜ prepare 準備 ｜ excited 興奮的

Question 2 refers to the following conversation.

Q What are the speakers mainly talking about?

(A) A novel that the man needs to find

(B) The man's marketing research paper

Q 對話者主要在談論什麼？

(A) 男子想找的一本小說。

(B) 男子的行銷研究報告。

Script

W May I help you, sir?

M Yes. I'm looking for a novel called *Great Expectations*.

W It's right here. Would you like to check out this book?

M No. I just need to take a picture of the cover for my marketing research paper.

女 有什麼可以效勞嗎，先生？

男 是的，我要找一本叫《孤星血淚》的小說。

女 就在這裡。你想借這本書嗎？

男 不是，我只要拍一張封面的照片用在我的行銷研究報告裡。

解析 對話中提到了《孤星血淚》這本書，選項（B）雖然在男子的話中有提到，但並不是對話的主要內容。所以答案是選項（A）。

單字 **check out** 借出 | **marketing** 行銷 | **research** 研究

Directions: You will hear some conversations between two or more people. You will be asked to answer a question about what the speakers say in each conversation. Select the best response to each question and mark the letter (A) or (B) on your answer sheet.

1. What are the speakers mainly talking about?

   (A) Why the woman doesn't like wearing sweaters.
   (B) What to buy for their mother.

2. What is the main topic of the conversation?

   (A) Which city the woman will go to for her student exchange program.
   (B) Why the man applied for a student exchange program in July.

Answer Sheet	
1. (A)	(B)
2. (A)	(B)

答案和解析

1. Answer (B)　　　　**2.** Answer (A)

Script

1.

Ⓦ Jack, let's order a Christmas gift for Mom.

Ⓜ Sure. Have you thought about what to get?

Ⓦ I'm thinking of buying a sweater for her.

Ⓜ Don't you think she has too many sweaters?

2.

Ⓜ Mary, I heard you applied for a student exchange program.

Ⓦ Yes, I'll be leaving in July.

Ⓜ Great. Didn't you say you wanted to go to London?

Ⓦ I did, but it seems the school in Boston is just as good.

Script

> 女 傑克，我們來替母親訂聖誕禮物吧。
> 男 好啊，你有想過要買什麼嗎？
> 女 我考慮為她買一件毛衣。
> 男 你不覺得她的毛衣已經太多了嗎？

Script

> 男 瑪麗，我聽說你申請了交換生計畫。
> 女 沒錯，我會在七月出發。
> 男 太棒了。你不是說想去倫敦？
> 女 我是說過，但是看來波士頓的學校和那邊一樣好。

解析 女子提到，要訂購聖誕禮物給母親，接著對話就以此為中心展開，答案是選項（B）。選項（A）完全沒有出現在對話中，所以是錯誤答案。

翻譯 對話者主要在談論什麼？
(A) 女子不喜歡毛衣的原因。
(B) 要為他們的母親買什麼。

單字 **order** 訂購 ｜ **gift** 禮物 ｜ **wear** 穿戴

解析 這是較複雜的試題。一開始男子提到女子申請了交換學生的計劃，不過對話接著轉為女子想透過交換學生計劃去哪個城市，答案是選項（A）。選項（B）和對話內容相反，所以是誤答。

翻譯 對話主題為何？
(A) 女子要去哪個城市當交換學生。
(B) 男子為何申請在七月的交換學生計劃。

單字 **apply** 申請 ｜ **exchange** 交換

D 應用練習　　　　　　　　　　▶ 解析 P. 476　　　🎧 070

> Directions: You will hear some conversations between two or more people. You will be asked to answer a question about what the speakers say in each conversation. Select the best response to each question and mark the letter (A) or (B) on your answer sheet.

1. What is the main topic of the conversation?

   (A) The effects of smoking on public health
   (B) Reserving a table at a restaurant

2. What are the speakers mainly talking about?

   (A) Why the man couldn't sing in the contest.
   (B) How confidence leads to success.

Answer Sheet

1. (A)　　　　　(B)
2. (A)　　　　　(B)

題型 **02** 　掌握目的

Ⓐ 輕鬆上手

掌握目的的試題，和掌握主題的試題一樣，都要充分理解整篇對話的內容，就能較輕鬆地解題。

例題 🎧 071

Q What is the purpose of the man's call?

(A) To ask the woman to help him improve his French

(B) To ask the woman to visit France in the summer

Q 這名男子來電的目的是什麼？

(A) 請女子幫他增進法語能力。

(B) 邀請女子夏天去法國玩。

Script

Ⓜ I am having difficulty learning French.

Ⓦ Are you taking classes?

Ⓜ I am taking an online course because I don't have much time. But I do review what I've learned.

Ⓦ You should also preview what you'll learn.

男 我在學習法語時碰到困難。

女 你有上課嗎？

男 我有上線上課程，因為我沒有太多時間。但我上完課後都有複習。

女 你應該也要做課前預習。

解析 是不是電話對話並不重要。男子目前在學習法語上遇到了困難，所以問女子怎麼做才能提升法語的能力。答案是選項（A）。

單字 **improve** 增進 ｜ **review** 複習 ｜ **preview** 預習

Ⓑ 基本題型

❶ 掌握目的 (1)　🎧 072

Question 1 refers to the following conversation.

Q Why is the woman talking to the man?	**Q** 女子為何和這名男子對話？
(A) To impress the man with her knowledge	(A) 向男子展現她知識淵博。
(B) To look for jeans that will suit her	(B) 要找適合她的牛仔褲。

Script

W Excuse me. Do you have these jeans in a size three?	**女** 請問，這一款牛仔褲有三號尺寸的嗎？
M If you can't find them on the shelf, they may be out of stock.	**男** 如果架上沒有，可能就沒貨了。
W Can you look in the stockroom?	**女** 你可以到倉庫看一下嗎？
M All right. Well, we have sizes two and four.	**男** 好。我們還有二號和四號尺寸的。

解析 對話的內容是女子正在找適合她身材尺寸的牛仔褲，所以答案是選項（B）。

單字 impress 給……好印象 | knowledge 知識 | shelf 架子 | out of stock 沒貨 | stockroom 倉庫

❷ 掌握目的 (2)

Question 2 refers to the following conversation.

Q Why is the man talking to the woman?　　**Q** 男子為何和女子談話？

(A) To advise her to refill the tank of her car

(B) To advise her not to waste money

(A) 建議女子為她的車子加油。

(B) 建議女子不要浪費錢。

Script

M Look! You are almost out of gas!

W Oh, I'm low on gas? Then I should refill the tank as soon as possible.

M Well, there's a gas station right there. Let's go.

W But the price there looks ridiculously high. Can you look for another gas station?

男 你看！你的油快沒了！

女 喔，我的油快沒了？那我該盡快加油。

男 加油站就在那裡，我們過去吧。

女 但它的價格看起來貴得離譜。你可以再找別的加油站嗎？

解析 男子跟女子說話的原因是提醒女子車快沒油了，叫她快去加油，所以答案是選項（A）。選項（B）在對話的內容中完全沒有提到。

單字 low on 即將耗盡 | gas station 加油站 | ridiculously 不可思議地

Directions: You will hear some conversations between two or more people. You will be asked to answer a question about what the speakers say in each conversation. Select the best response to each question and mark the letter (A) or (B) on your answer sheet.

1. Why is the woman talking to the man?

(A) To encourage the man to go on a picnic
(B) To identify the people in the man's picture

2. Why is the man talking to the woman?

(A) To ask the woman to tell him about what she is reading
(B) To ask the woman to spend quality time with her children

Answer Sheet

1. (A)   (B)

2. (A)   (B)

答案和解析

1. Answer (B)

Script

1.

W Daniel, is this your picture?

M Yes, it was taken when I went on a picnic at a park near my house.

W I see. Who is this man on your left?

M He is my cousin, Leo. He is five years older than us.

Script

女 丹尼爾，這是你的照片嗎？

男 是的，這是我在家附近公園野餐時拍的照片。

女 原來如此。你左邊的男子是誰？

男 他是我的堂哥，李奧，他比我們大五歲。

解析 女子一邊看著男子的照片一邊問照片裡的人是誰，答案是選項（B）。選項（A）並沒有出現在女子的對話中。

翻譯 女子為何和男子談話？
(A) 鼓勵男子去野餐。
(B) 指認男子照片中的人。

單字 encourage 鼓勵 ｜ identify 指認

2. Answer (A)

Script

2.

M What are you reading, Alice?

W I'm reading an article about spending quality time with children.

M What does it say?

W It says you should spend some time each day playing with your children.

Script

男 愛麗絲，你在讀什麼？

女 我讀的這篇文章是關於如何與小孩共度有品質的時光。

男 內容說了什麼？

女 它說你每天應該花點時間陪孩子玩耍。

解析 男子問女子正在讀什麼，答案是選項（A）。選項（B）並不是男子說的內容，所以不是答案。

翻譯 男子為何和女子談話？
(A) 要女子告訴他正在讀什麼。
(B) 要女子和孩子有高品質的相處時間。

單字 article 文章 ｜
quality time 高品質時間

Directions: You will hear some conversations between two or more people. You will be asked to answer a question about what the speakers say in each conversation. Select the best response to each question and mark the letter (A) or (B) on your answer sheet.

1. Why is the woman talking to the man?

　(A) To find out more information about the man's bank
　(B) To ask the man to cash her check

2. Why is the man talking to the woman?

　(A) To promise to help her move into a new place
　(B) To ask her to go with him to a party

Answer Sheet

1. (A) 　　　　　(B)
2. (A) 　　　　　(B)

題型 **03** 掌握細節資訊 (1)

A 輕鬆上手

應試者遇上與細節資訊相關的試題時，必須清楚理解對話中的具體內容，包括特定地點或問題所在等各式各樣的內容。因為細節資訊相關試題的比重很高，所以將用兩個單元來學習這個主題。

在準備作答此類試題時，「推測內容」的技巧非常重要。一邊看印在試卷上的問題和選項，一邊推測對話的內容，對理解對話內容會很有幫助。

例題 🎧 076

> **Q** Why was the man surprised yesterday?
>
> (A) He did not practice common sense.
> (B) A bicycle nearly hit him.

> **Q** 為何男子昨天感到意外？
>
> (A) 他沒有用常識。
> (B) 有一輛腳踏車差點撞到他。

Script

> **M** I was almost hit by a bicycle yesterday.
> **W** That's terrible. Were you OK?
> **M** Yes. It was an unpleasant surprise, but I wasn't hurt.
> **W** A lot of cyclists don't practice common sense these days.

> **男** 我昨天差點被一輛腳踏車撞到。
> **女** 太糟了。你當時還好嗎？
> **男** 還好。那是場讓人很不愉快的意外，但我並沒受傷。
> **女** 最近有很多沒帶腦的自行車騎士。

解析 細節資訊試題和理解整篇內容的試題不同。要培養確認「事實」和「具體訊息」的習慣。從對話內容可以知道，正答是選項 (B)。選項 (A) 説的是對自行車騎士的不滿。

單字 practice 實行 ｜ common sense 常識 ｜ nearly 差點 ｜ terrible 糟糕的 ｜ unpleasant 不愉快的

Ⓑ 基本題型

❶ 找出細節資訊（1）　　🎧077

Question 1 refers to the following conversation.

Q Why does the woman want to be a lawyer?

(A) To become famous around the world
(B) To help women exercise their rights

Q 女子為何想當律師？

(A) 想要在全世界博得名氣。
(B) 幫助女性行使權利。

Script

W I need to study harder to get the job I want.

M What do you want to be? An English teacher?

W No. I want to be a lawyer. I want to help protect the rights of women.

M I'm sure you'll achieve your goal.

女 我要更努力念書以得到我想要的工作。

男 你想做什麼工作？英文老師嗎？

女 不是，我想成為律師。我想幫助保衛女性的權利。

男 我相信你會達成目標。

解析 女子要成為律師的原因是她想要捍衛女性的權利，所以答案是選項（B），對話中完全沒有提到選項（A）。

單字 exercise 行使 ｜ right 權利 ｜ protect 保護 ｜ achieve 達到

Question 2 refers to the following conversation.

Q What problem does the woman have?

  (A) She needs to find a person to perform in a play.

  (B) She does not like spending time with her coworkers.

Q 女子有什麼問題？

  (A) 她要找一個人幫她演戲。

  (B) 她不喜歡花時間和同事相處。

Script

W Our club is planning to put on a play for the festival.

M I heard about that. How's it going?

W It's going well, except for the fact that we don't have a narrator yet.

M Can't you find someone to do the job?

女 我們社團打算為了節慶表演一齣戲劇。

男 我聽說了，情況如何？

女 進行得還不錯，只是我們還沒找到人來擔任旁白。

男 你找不到人來擔任這項工作嗎？

解析 女子的舞台劇還缺一位旁白，所以答案是選項 (A)。選項 (B) 並沒有出現在對話中。

單字 perform 表演 ｜ coworker 同事 ｜ put on 演出 ｜ narrator 旁白

Directions: You will hear some conversations between two or more people. You will be asked to answer a question about what the speakers say in each conversation. Select the best response to each question and mark the letter (A) or (B) on your answer sheet.

1. Which is true about the man?

   (A) He can reduce his spending by $130 this month.
   (B) He will buy the computer parts later than planned.

2. Which is true about the woman?

   (A) She will learn Spanish this summer.
   (B) She is not likely to learn Chinese.

Answer Sheet

1. (A)　　　　(B)
2. (A)　　　　(B)

答案和解析

1. Answer　(B)　　　　　　**2.** Answer　(B)

Script

1.

Ⓜ Let's see how much of our pocket money we can use.

Ⓦ I usually spend $80 on clothing, but I don't need to buy clothes this month.

Ⓜ I was planning to spend $50 on some computer parts. But I can buy them later.

Ⓦ All right. Then we can reduce our spending by $130 this month.

Script

男 來看看我們有多少零用錢可用。

女 我通常會花 80 元買衣服，但我這個月不須買衣服。

男 我打算花 50 元買一些電腦零件，但我可以稍後再買。

女 很好，那我們本月可以減少 130 元的花費。

解析　本題詢問細節資訊。答案是和對話內容一致的選項（B）。選項（A）是女子和男子節省金額的總和，所以不是答案。

翻譯　關於男子的說明何者為真？
(A) 他在本月可以減少 130 元的花費。
(B) 他會比預期稍晚買電腦零件。

單字　**pocket money** 零用錢 |
part 零件 | **reduce** 減少

Script

2.

Ⓜ Why don't you take Chinese?

Ⓦ I have heard that it's too much work to learn Chinese characters.

Ⓜ Then, do you want to learn Spanish?

Ⓦ It is a language that I want to learn some day. But I don't want to learn it this summer.

Script

男 你何不學中文？

女 我聽說學中文字很困難。

男 那麼你想學西班牙文嗎？

女 那是我以後要學的語言，但我不想在今年夏天學。

解析　本題答案與對話內容相符，所以答案是選項（B）。女子想學西班牙文，但不想在今年夏天學，所以選項（A）是錯誤答案。

翻譯　關於女子的說明何者為真？
(A) 她在今年夏天會學西班牙文。
(B) 她不太可能會學中文。

單字　**learn** 學習 | **language** 語言

Ⓓ 應用練習 ▶ 解析 P. 478 🎧 080

Directions: You will hear some conversations between two or more people. You will be asked to answer a question about what the speakers say in each conversation. Select the best response to each question and mark the letter (A) or (B) on your answer sheet.

---

1. Which is true about the woman?

(A) She has been living in Florida for the past three years.

(B) Her driver's license will not expire in the next three months.

2. Which is true about the man?

(A) He has been working out for the past six years.

(B) He does not feel that he should restrict his diet.

Answer Sheet

1.	(A)	(B)
2.	(A)	(B)

題型 **04** 掌握細節資訊 (2)

Ⓐ 輕鬆上手

在 Part 3 中，沒有什麼比推測對話內容的能力更加重要。只有具備這種能力，才能在聽到的訊息中，找出和答案有關聯的訊息。毫無心理準備地聽，和推測內容之後再來聽有很大的差異，因此要養成這樣的習慣，那就是無論何時都要一邊推測內容的展開方式，一邊聆聽對話。

例題 🎧 081

Q Which is true about the woman?

(A) She believes that governments should make efforts to protect the elephants.

(B) She has been making efforts to protect Africa's elephants from hunters.

Q 關於女子的說明何者為真？

(A) 她認為政府應該努力保護大象。

(B) 她一直努力保護非洲大象不受獵人殺害。

Script

Ⓦ Have you heard that Africa's elephants are endangered?

Ⓜ Yes. The reason is that people kill the elephants to get ivory.

Ⓦ That's right. And the governments are responsible for the problem, too.

Ⓜ Do you think they haven't done enough to protect the elephants?

女 你聽過非洲大象瀕臨絕種嗎？

男 聽過，人類為了象牙而獵殺大象。

女 沒錯，而政府也要為這個問題負責。

男 你認為他們並沒有採取足夠的措施保護大象嗎？

解析 這是問細節資訊的試題。可以知道女子認為保護大象是政府的責任，所以答案是選項 (A)。選項 (B) 的內容完全沒有出現在對話中，所以是錯的。

單字 effort 努力 ｜ protect 保護 ｜ endangered 瀕臨絕種的 ｜ ivory 象牙 ｜ government 政府 ｜ responsible 負責的

Ⓑ 基本題型

❶ 找出細節資訊（1）

🎧 082

Question 1 refers to the following conversation.

Ⓠ Which is true about the woman?

(A) She does not have difficulty understanding Mr. Green's online course.

(B) She will go to graduate school to become a professor.

Ⓠ 關於女子的說明何者為真？

(A) 她對於理解格林先生的線上課程沒有困難。

(B) 她會到研究所就讀以成為教授。

Script

Ⓜ Becky, I heard you're taking Mr. Green's class.

Ⓦ Yes, I enrolled in his online course. I download his lessons every Wednesday.

Ⓜ How do you like it? I find it difficult to understand the content.

Ⓦ I don't have that problem, but the course is not the right level for me.

男 貝姬，我聽說你在上格林先生的線上課程。

女 是的，我報名他的線上課程。我每週三都會下載他的課程。

男 你覺得如何？我覺得內容很難懂。

女 我沒有那個問題，但那課程不適合我的程度。

解析 這是細節資訊試題。女子不覺得格林先生的線上教學課程很難，所以答案是選項（A）。選項（B）完全無法從對話中得知。

單字 **content** 內容 ｜ **graduate school** 研究所 ｜ **enroll** 註冊；報名

Question 2 refers to the following conversation.

Q Which is true about the man?	**Q** 關於男子的說明何者為真？
(A) He doesn't want to share his mother's recipe with anyone.	(A) 他不想把母親的食譜分享給任何人。
(B) His mother taught him how to make egg rolls.	(B) 他的母親教他如何做蛋捲。

Script

W Thank you for the wonderful dinner.	**女** 感謝你準備這頓豐盛的晚餐。
M I hope you enjoyed the food.	**男** 我希望你喜歡這些料理。
W I sure did. The egg rolls were fantastic.	**女** 我很喜歡，蛋捲很美味。
M I'm glad you enjoyed them. I used my mother's secret recipe.	**男** 很高興你覺得好吃，我用了母親的祕方。

解析 對話內容沒有提到選項（A），所以不是正確答案。答案是能從對話的內容中清楚得知的選項（B）。

單字 fantastic 很棒的 ｜ recipe 食譜

Directions: You will hear some conversations between two or more people. You will be asked to answer a question about what the speakers say in each conversation. Select the best response to each question and mark the letter (A) or (B) on your answer sheet.

1. Which is true about the woman?

(A) Thomas Hardy is her favorite novelist.
(B) She has recently bought a biography of Thomas Hardy.

2. Which is true about the woman?

(A) She wants others to respect her.
(B) She is trying to lose weight.

Answer Sheet

1. (A)   (B)

2. (A)   (B)

答案和解析

1. Answer (B) 　　**2. Answer** (A)

Script

1.

Ⓜ My favorite novelist is Thomas Hardy. I want to learn more about him.

Ⓦ I have a new biography of him. It was recently released. Would you like to borrow it?

Ⓜ Sure. Can I read it after you're done with it?

Ⓦ You can read it first. I've got plenty to read for now.

2.

Ⓦ I don't understand people who judge others by their appearance.

Ⓜ Why do you say that?

Ⓦ People give me terrible nicknames just because I am a little bit overweight. It's really annoying.

Ⓜ I'm sorry to hear that. You look fine to me.

Script

男 我最喜歡的小說家是湯瑪斯・哈迪，我想多了解他。

女 我有一本他的新傳記，最近才出版，你想借嗎？

男 當然，你可以在讀完後借我看嗎？

女 你可以先讀，我現在有很多其他書要看。

Script

女 我不了解以貌取人的人。

男 為何那麼說？

女 別人因為我有點胖就給我取很難聽的綽號，真的很煩。

男 很遺憾聽你這麼說，我覺得你看起來很順眼。

解析 選項（A）說的是男子不是女子，哈迪是男子最喜歡的小說家。所以答案是選項（B）。

翻譯 關於女子的說明何者為真？
(A) 湯瑪斯・哈迪是她最喜歡的小說家。
(B) 她最近買了湯瑪斯・哈迪的傳記。

單字 biography 傳記 | release 出版

解析 從對話的內容可以知道，答案是選項（A）。選項（B）並不是對話的內容，所以是錯誤答案。

翻譯 關於女子的說明何者為真？
(A) 她要別人尊重她。
(B) 她嘗試減重。

單字 judge 評斷 | appearance 外貌 | lose weight 減重

Directions: You will hear some conversations between two or more people. You will be asked to answer a question about what the speakers say in each conversation. Select the best response to each question and mark the letter (A) or (B) on your answer sheet.

1. Which is true about the woman?

   (A) She doesn't want her friends to remember her birthday.
   (B) She may feel lonely.

2. Which is true about the man?

   (A) He is looking for a new house.
   (B) He can't afford to buy a new house.

Answer Sheet

1.　(A)　　　　　(B)
2.　(A)　　　　　(B)

題型 **05** 掌握意圖

Ⓐ 輕鬆上手

掌握意圖的試題是新題型，此外，此處還增加了結合圖表的題型。這種題型要將**對話或獨白的內容**和行程表這類的**圖表資訊**做連結，以找出問題的答案。若要了解圖表資訊類型，可以藉由做 Practice Test，以更加清楚其出題方式。

掌握意圖的試題，要理解對話當事人說話的意圖為何。我們說每一句話時，都具有某種意圖，可能是要傳達訊息，也可能是要尋求對方同意。這些意圖可以透過上下文推敲出來。

例題 🎧 086

Q What does the woman mean when she says, "Well, I feel a little tired"?

(A) She wants to go to sleep.

(B) She does not want to go bowling.

Q 當女子說：「我覺得有點累。」是什麼意思？

(A) 她想去睡覺。

(B) 她不想去打保齡球。

Script

Ⓜ What do you want to do today?

Ⓦ I don't know. Do you have any suggestions?

Ⓜ How about going bowling?

Ⓦ Well, I feel a little tired.

男 你今天想做什麼？

女 我不知道。你有什麼提議嗎？

男 去打保齡球如何？

女 嗯，我覺得有點累。

解析 若要掌握意圖，就要看看前後的脈絡。男子建議去打保齡球，女子說她有點累，意思就是她不想去打保齡球，所以答案是選項（B）。

單字 suggestion 建議

Ⓑ 基本題型

❶ 掌握意圖（1）　🎧 087

Question 1 refers to the following conversation.

Ⓠ What does the woman mean when she says, "That sounds nice, but you're not a good cook"?

　(A) She believes that the man needs to take cooking classes.

　(B) She does not want him to cook for his mother.

Ⓠ 當女子說：「那聽起來很棒，但你不善於烹飪。」是什麼意思？

　(A) 她認為這名男子需要上烹飪課。

　(B) 她不要他為母親做菜。

Script

Ⓦ Why don't you think about something nice that you can do for Mom?

Ⓜ Maybe I can cook for her.

Ⓦ That sounds nice, but you're not a good cook.

Ⓜ I'll do something simple, but tasty.

女 你要不要想想可以為媽做點什麼不錯的事？

男 或許我可以為她做菜。

女 那聽起來很棒，但你不善於烹飪。

男 我會做些簡單但好吃的菜。

解析　對話的主題是希望男子能替他母親做些小事。了解這個對話脈絡，就知道答案是選項（B）。如果對話的主題是男子想成為廚師，也許選項（A）會是答案。若能充分理解對話的狀況，就能很順利地解掌握對話者的意圖。

單字　tasty 美味的

Question 2 refers to the following conversation.

> **Q** What does the woman mean when she says, "Didn't you check the weather forecast"?
>
> (A) She wants to be a weather girl.
> (B) The man could have predicted the weather.

> **Q** 當女子說：「你們沒看氣象報告嗎？」是什麼意思？
>
> (A) 她想要成為氣象播報員。
> (B) 男子原本可以預知天氣狀況。

Script

> **M** Last fall, I went hiking on a mountain with my brother.
>
> **W** That sounds exciting. Did you have fun?
>
> **M** No, we didn't. When we got to the top, the weather suddenly turned pretty bad.
>
> **W** Didn't you check the weather forecast?

> **男** 去年秋天我和我哥去爬山。
>
> **女** 聽起來很刺激，你們玩得愉快嗎？
>
> **男** 不，不愉快。我們攻頂後，天氣突然變得很糟。
>
> **女** 你們沒看氣象報告嗎？

解析 若能理解對話的狀況，就能很順利地解題。對話者在談男子登山時遇到糟糕的天氣狀況，所以答案是選項（B）。選項（A）並沒出現在對話中。

單字 weather forecast 氣象預報 ｜ weather girl 女氣象播報員 ｜ predict 預測

Directions: You will hear some conversations between two or more people. You will be asked to answer a question about what the speakers say in each conversation. Select the best response to each question and mark the letter (A) or (B) on your answer sheet.

1. What does the man mean when he says, "Please check if you have everything"?

(A) Someone might have stolen something from the woman.
(B) He is going to buy some presents for the woman.

2. What does the man mean when he says, "It might help"?

(A) There is no way to help the woman fall asleep.
(B) Doing some exercise will help the woman fall asleep.

Answer Sheet

1. (A)   (B)
2. (A)   (B)

1. Answer (A)　　**2.** Answer (B)

Script

1.

Ⓜ Julie, did you know your bag was open?

Ⓦ What? Oh, it is.

Ⓜ Please check if you have everything. Someone once opened my backpack and took my wallet without my noticing.

Ⓦ That's terrible.

2.

Ⓜ What's the matter? You look really tired.

Ⓦ I didn't sleep well last night. These days it's difficult for me to fall asleep.

Ⓜ Why don't you do some exercise? It might help.

Ⓦ Well, I think I just need to go to bed early.

Script

男 茉莉，你知道你的包包是開著的嗎？

女 什麼？喔，真的耶。

男 請檢查物品是否都還在。有人以前曾趁我不注意時開我背包偷走我的皮夾。

女 太糟糕了。

Script

男 怎麼了？你看起來很累。

女 我昨晚睡不著。近來我很難入眠。

男 你為何不做些運動？那可能有幫助。

女 我想我只需要提早上床。

解析 女子不知道自己的包包被打開了，男子提醒她並要她檢查一下，所以答案是選項（A）。選項（B）完全沒有出現在對話中。

解析 女子說她近來難以入睡，男子建議運動當作解決方法，所以答案是選項（B）。如果選項（A）是答案，男子就不會提出建議。

翻譯 當男子說「請檢查物品是否都還在。」是什麼意思？

(A) 有人可能偷了這名女子的東西。

(B) 他要為這名女子買一些禮物。

翻譯 當男子說「那可能會有幫助。」那是什麼意思？

(A) 沒有辦法可讓這名女子入眠。

(B) 從事一些運動可以幫助這名女子入眠。

單字 **check** 檢查 ｜ **wallet** 皮夾 ｜ **steal** 偷走

單字 **matter** 事情 ｜ **fall asleep** 入眠

D 應用練習   ▶ 解析 P. 480   ∩ 090

Directions: You will hear some conversations between two or more people. You will be asked to answer a question about what the speakers say in each conversation. Select the best response to each question and mark the letter (A) or (B) on your answer sheet.

1. What does the man mean when he says, "Is there any way you can fix it"?

(A) He is usually good at fixing things.

(B) He does not want to exchange his coat for a new one.

2. What does the man mean when he says, "Would that work for you"?

(A) He wants to check if the computer is working now.

(B) He wants to check if 3:00 would be fine with the woman.

Answer Sheet

1.   (A)   (B)

2.   (A)   (B)

Quick Test for **Part 3** 091　▶ 解析 P. 481

Select the best response to the question or statement and mark the letter (A), (B), or (C) on your answer sheet.

Questions 1–3 refer to the following conversation.

1. What is the purpose of the man's phone call?
   (A) To find out if he can fly to California at seven
   (B) To book a table at a restaurant

2. Which is true about the man?
   (A) He has never been to California.
   (B) He is likely to visit the facility at seven.

3. Will the man visit the facility by himself?
   (A) He will be accompanied by two people.
   (B) He does not know whether other people will join him.

Questions 4–6 refer to the following conversation.

4. What is the main topic of the conversation?
   (A) That the danger of global warming has been exaggerated
   (B) The many different ways to preserve the environment

5. What does the woman mean when she says, "I couldn't agree more"?
   (A) She believes that recycling is a good idea.
   (B) She does not believe that recycling is good for the environment.

6. Which is true about the man?
   (A) He is likely to make efforts to protect the environment.
   (B) He wants to be an internationally recognized scientist.

Answer Sheet

1. (A)   (B)
2. (A)   (B)
3. (A)   (B)
4. (A)   (B)
5. (A)   (B)
6. (A)   (B)

Practice Test

🎧 092　　▶ 解析 P. 483

Part 3
Directions: You will hear some conversations between two or more people. You will be asked to answer three questions about what the speakers say in each conversation. Select the best response to each question and mark the letter (A), (B), (C), or (D) on your answer sheet. The conversations will not be printed in your test book and will be spoken only one time.

Questions 1–3 refer to the following conversation.

1. What are the speakers mainly discussing?

    (A) Why the woman missed the man's concert
    (B) When they can meet to discuss the upcoming concert
    (C) The man's sister's hospitalization
    (D) The man's disappointing performance

2. Why couldn't the man attend the woman's event?

    (A) He went to a foreign country that day.
    (B) He didn't believe that her music was worth listening to.
    (C) He was having a meeting with an important client.
    (D) One of his family members was involved in an accident.

3. What does the woman mean when she says, "You should have come"?
    (A) She believes that the man was too careless.
    (B) She wanted to go to a foreign country with the man.
    (C) She's sorry that the man didn't attend her event.
    (D) She doesn't like the man's sister.

Answer Sheet

1. (A) (B) (C) (D)　　2. (A) (B) (C) (D)　　3. (A) (B) (C) (D)

Questions 4–6 refer to the following conversation.

Item	Bag
Color	
Size	
Owner's Name	
Phone Number	
Address	

4. Why is the woman talking to the man?

(A) She believes that the man is hiding something.

(B) She wants to date the man.

(C) She believes that the man is very kind.

(D) She wants to find her missing bag.

5. Look at the graphic. Which piece of information about the bag does the man not have?

(A) The color of the bag

(B) The size of the bag

(C) The owner's phone number

(D) The owner's address

6. What does the man mean when he says "Of course"?

(A) He is not sure if he can find her bag.

(B) He does not care about the woman.

(C) It is his duty to call the woman if he finds her bag.

(D) He thinks that the woman is too difficult to please.

Answer Sheet

4. (A) (B) (C) (D)   5. (A) (B) (C) (D)   6. (A) (B) (C) (D)

Questions 7–9 refer to the following conversation.

7. What are the speakers mainly talking about?

   (A) Whether Australia is better than Canada
   (B) Where they will go for winter vacation
   (C) When they will travel around the world
   (D) The reason why they hate cold weather

8. Which is true about the woman?

   (A) She has been living in Switzerland for three years.
   (B) She has been to Australia.
   (C) She is likely to go to Australia this winter.
   (D) She enjoys skiing.

9. Which is true about the man?

   (A) He has visited Canada many times.
   (B) Switzerland is his favorite country.
   (C) He prefers hot weather to cold weather.
   (D) He is likely to spend some time in a foreign country this winter.

Answer Sheet

7. (A) (B) (C) (D)   8. (A) (B) (C) (D)   9. (A) (B) (C) (D)

PART

4

獨白

題型 **01** 掌握主題

Ⓐ 輕鬆上手

準備 Part 4 的基本戰略和 Part 3 一樣，但和 Part 3 聽對話後回答問題不同，Part 4 是聽獨白然後回答問題。

而且比起 Part 3 口語式對話以短句為重心，Part 4 的句子變長了許多，而且探討的內容也較困難。最後要注意的是，因為進入 Part 4 之前，已經做了很多試題，所以會有注意力下降的問題。

要克服這些狀況，可以積極地推測即將聽到的獨白內容。和 Part 3 一樣，推測內容和不推測內容在分數會造成很大的差異。另外，平常可以多聽 CNN 這樣的英語節目，邊聽邊理解內容，這樣的練習會對應考很有幫助。

例題　🎧 093

> **Q** What is the main topic of the talk?
>
> (A) The reason why few tourists visit Shadow Castle
>
> (B) The structures of Shadow Castle

> **Q** 這段獨白的主題是什麼？
>
> (A) 暗影城堡的遊客稀少的原因。
>
> (B) 暗影城堡的結構。

Script

Welcome to the tour of Shadow Castle. Its name comes from its position on the rocky hill above town. When you enter the gate, you'll see a small hut on your right. That's where the gatekeeper stayed. The watchman, who stayed in the right tower, directed the gatekeeper to open or close the door. Now, walk past the front yard and you will see the royal house on the left.

歡迎蒞臨暗影城堡。城堡名字的由來是因為它俯瞰城鎮，聳立在多岩的山丘上。當你進入大門後，你會看到右邊有一間簡陋小屋，那是看門人的待命處。右邊高塔的守望人會指揮看門人打開或關閉大門。現在，走過前院，然後你就會看到左側的皇宮。

解析 這是參加導覽時會聽到的內容。雖然細節資訊很多，但整體看來，都是在解說暗影城堡的結構設施，所以答案是選項（B）。選項（A）並沒有出現在獨白中。

 基本題型

❶ 找出主題（1）   🎧094

Question 1 refers to the following talk.

What is the main topic of the talk?	這段獨白的主題是什麼？
(A) The many different ways to cook beans	(A) 各種料理豆子的方法。
(B) The reason why so many people enjoy eating beans	(B) 很多人喜歡吃豆子的原因。

Script

Do you enjoy eating beans? They are very healthy. Beans can be prepared in many different ways. You can boil or roast them. Beans can also be transformed into various foods, such as tofu. They can be used in dressings and sauces like Teriyaki sauce. Why don't you prepare dinner with some beans tonight?

你喜歡吃豆子嗎？豆子很健康。豆子的料理方式有很多種，你可以水煮或烘烤。豆類還可以做成不同類型的食物，像是豆腐。豆類也可以製作成像照燒醬這樣的佐料或醬汁。今天晚餐就來一點些豆子吃吧？

解析 主題出現在整篇獨白中，在介紹各種豆子料理的方法，所以答案是選項（A）。選項（B）的內容沒有出現在獨白中。

單字 **various** 不同類型的 ｜ **transform** 轉化

Question 2 refers to the following talk.

What is the main topic of the talk?

(A) The joy of giving presents to others

(B) Cultural differences in giving presents

這段獨白的主題是什麼？

(A) 送禮物給別人的喜悅。

(B) 送禮物的文化差異。

Script

Whether a present is small or big, it makes both the giver and the receiver happy. However, if you give something to someone from a different country, you should consider their culture. For instance, you should not give food or drinks to a Saudi Arabian host. It suggests they do not feed you well while you're there. You might be in trouble to give a knife as a present in Japan. It means that you want to cut off the relationship.

不論禮物輕重，都讓送禮和收禮雙方感到開心。然而，如果你要送禮給來自不同國家的友人。就應該考慮他們的文化。例如，你不該送食物或飲料給阿烏地阿拉伯主人。那表示在你做客時，他們沒有讓你吃飽。在日本送人刀子可能會為你帶來麻煩，那表示你想要切斷雙方的關係。

解析　這段獨白是在講不同文化送禮習慣的差異，所以答案是選項(B)。選項(A)在獨白一開始的地方有提到，但並不是整篇獨白探討的內容。

單字　consider 考慮 | culture 文化 | host 主人 | relationship 關係

C 題型練習   🎧 096

Question 1 refers to the following talk.

What is the main topic of the talk?

(A) The reason why hospitalization is not always a good idea
(B) How to treat someone who has been burned

Question 2 refers to the following talk.

What is the main topic of the talk?

(A) The tradition of Christmas crackers
(B) How to celebrate Christmas in Europe

Answer Sheet

1. (A)   (B)
2. (A)   (B)

1. Answer (B)　　　　**2.** Answer (A)

Script

1.

Here are some tips when someone gets burned. If it is a very bad burn, take the person to the hospital immediately. If it's not serious, cool the burned part with cold water. Then cover it with a clean cloth to protect it from the air. Be careful not to put oil on the burn because oil can make it worse.

2.

Crackers are a type of biscuit, usually salted. However, Christmas crackers are not some kind of food. They are a part of Christmas celebrations. A cracker is typically pulled by two people at the start of the Christmas meal. When it splits, it makes a loud noise. Inside are colored paper hats and tiny gifts. The paper hats look like crowns. People wear them while having their Christmas meal.

Script

以下是有人燒燙傷時的一些處理訣竅。如果燒燙傷很嚴重，立刻將患者送醫。如果燒燙傷不嚴重，用冷水冷卻燒燙傷處，然後用乾淨的布覆蓋以隔絕空氣。小心不要在燒燙傷處上油，因為油會讓燒燙傷處惡化。

Script

蘇打餅乾是一種餅乾，通常會加鹽。然而，聖誕拉炮不是某種食物，而是慶祝聖誕節的一部分。拉炮一般由兩個人在耶誕大餐開始前拉開，拉開後會有一聲巨響，裡面有五顏六色的紙帽和小禮物。紙帽看起來像皇冠，大家在享用耶誕大餐時會戴著紙帽。

解析 整篇獨白都在說明該如何處理燒燙傷患者，所以答案是選項（B）。選項（A），雖然有提到要送醫院，但這並不是整篇獨白的主題。

翻譯 這段獨白的主題是什麼？
(A) 住院治療不一定是好點子的原因。
(B) 如何治療燒燙傷的人。

單字 **burn** 燒傷 | **cloth** 布 | **protect** 保護 | **hospitalization** 住院

解析 這篇獨白是介紹聖誕節慶祝用品聖誕節拉炮，所以答案是選項（A）。獨白中完全沒提到歐洲，所以選項（B）是錯的。

翻譯 這段獨白的主題是什麼？
(A) 聖誕拉炮的傳統。
(B) 在歐洲如何慶祝聖誕節。

單字 **celebration** 慶祝 | **split** 分開 | **tiny** 小的

D 應用練習   ▶ 解析 P. 487   🎧 097

Directions: You will hear some talks given by a single speaker. You will be asked to answer a question about what the speaker says in each talk. Select the best response to each question and mark the letter (A) or (B) on your answer sheet.

Question 1 refers to the following talk.

What is the main topic of the talk?

(A) Why Hawaii is popular among tourists
(B) The ethnic makeup of Hawaii

Question 2 refers to the following talk.

What is the main topic of the talk?

(A) How to report phishing emails to managers
(B) How to deal with phishing emails

Answer Sheet

1. (A)   (B)
2. (A)   (B)

題型 02 | 掌握目的

A 輕鬆上手

掌握目的和掌握主題的試題一樣，都必須充分理解整篇訊息才能正確解題，此種試題的解題基本戰略是理解說話人所處的狀況。在 Part 4 中，會詢問電話留言、演說、會議議程的變更和升等公告等的獨白目的。

例題 🎧 098

Q Why is the speaker calling?

  (A) To tell the listener that she needs to find another professor

  (B) To schedule a meeting with the listener

Q 發話者為何打電話？

  (A) 告訴受話者她必須找另一位教授。

  (B) 和受話者安排會面時間。

Script

Hello, this is Professor Britney Wood at Carlston University. I heard you wanted to schedule a meeting with me on Wednesday the 20th. However, I'd be out of town from the 12th to the 26th. I'll be back to work on the last day of February. If you are available that day, I'll be happy to see you and discuss the project. Please get back to me when you can. Thank you.

您好，我是卡爾斯頓大學的布雷特尼・伍德教授。我聽說您要安排在 20 日週三和我見面。不過，我會在 12 日到 26 日之間出城，我將會在二月最後一天回來。如果您那天有空，我會很樂意和您見面討論計畫案。請撥冗回電，謝謝。

解析 受話者本來希望和發話者（也就是教授）在二月 20 號開會，但是教授二月最後一天才會回來，所以教授希望將開會時間改在二月最後一天，答案是選項 (B)。

Ⓑ 基本題型

❶ 找出目的 (1)

🎧 099

Question 1 refers to the following speech.

What is the purpose of the speech?	這段演講的目的是什麼？
(A) To claim that the speaker does not deserve the award	(A) 主張演講人沒有資格獲得獎項。
(B) To recognize the merits of other workers	(B) 認可其他員工的優點。

Script

I feel honored to receive the Employee of the Year Award. Although I have sold more than 500 cars this year, I do know that other employees have been much more professional than I am. Most of them really care about their customers. Some of them have helped me in a lot of ways. Therefore, I would like to say that all these wonderful employees are truly the "Employees of the Year."	獲得年度員工獎讓我感到很光榮。雖然我今年賣了 500 多輛車，但我清楚知道其他同事比我更專業。他們大多數人都很在乎客戶。有些同事都曾經在許多方面幫助我。因此，我想說所有這些很棒的員工都是真正的「年度員工」。

解析 這是掌握目的的試題，必須要理解整篇訊息。在演講中提到領到這個獎感覺非常光榮，接著又提到其他員工的優點，所以答案是選項 (B)。像選項 (A) 這樣跳躍式的思考並不能成為答案。

單字 **honored** 光榮的 | **award** 獎 | **professional** 專業的 | **deserve** 值得 | **recognize** 認可 | **merit** 優點

Question 2 refers to the following talk.

What is the purpose of the talk?

(A) To explain an effective way to motivate employees

(B) To ask that employers provide good working environments for workers

這段獨白的目的是什麼？

(A) 解釋激勵員工的有效方式。

(B) 要求僱主為員工提供良好的工作環境。

Script

As an employer, you may know that you need to motivate your employees. If they are not motivated, your company is likely to fail. Then, what is the best way to motivate your workers? Higher salaries? Better working environments? Well, experts say that the best way to motivate employees is to make them feel appreciated. There are many ways in which you can show your appreciation of the efforts of your workers.

作為僱主，你可能知道你必須激勵員工。如果員工沒有獲得激勵，你的公司可能會倒閉。那麼，激勵員工的最佳方式是什麼？高薪？更好的工作環境？專家說激勵員工的最佳方式就是讓他們覺得獲得賞識。有很多方式可以讓你對員工的努力表達感激之心。

解析 獨白的主要目的是要說明如何利用有效的方法激勵員工，所以答案是選項(A)。發話者根本沒有要求選項(B)，所以是錯的。

單字 **motivate** 激勵 | **expert** 專家 | **appreciate** 賞識 | **effective** 有效的

Directions: You will hear some talks given by a single speaker. You will be asked to answer a question about what the speaker says in each talk. Select the best response to each question and mark the letter (A) or (B) on your answer sheet.

Question 1 refers to the following speech.

What is the purpose of the speech?

(A) To say that majoring in history can help your career
(B) To say that majoring in history was the speaker's biggest mistake

Question 2 refers to the following telephone message.

Why is the speaker calling?

(A) To praise the listener for his sense of humor
(B) To schedule an interview with the listener

Answer Sheet

1. (A)   (B)
2. (A)   (B)

1. Answer (A)　　　**2.** Answer (B)

Script

1.

As you may know, I majored in history at this university. When I graduated, I didn't expect that I would be employed by a major company. I thought such companies would hire only those who majored in engineering or the sciences. At the same time, I didn't believe that my major would help me in any practical way. But all these thoughts turned out to be wrong. My experiences have taught me that history majors can have a bright future.

2.

Hello. This is Mary Cooper, at TSC Newspaper. I am calling because I'd like to interview you. You may know that I specialize in the field of business administration. I have interviewed hundreds of CEOs, but I have recently found out that you are a unique CEO in lots of ways. Could you tell me when you're available? I'm sure an interview with you will help our readers realize their strengths.

Script

你們可能知道我在這間大學主修歷史。當我畢業時,我沒有預期會被大公司僱用。我原先以為這樣的公司只會僱用主修工程或科學的學生。同時,我不相信我主修的科目會為我帶來任何實質幫助。然而所有這些想法最終證明是錯的。我的經驗讓我了解主修歷史也會有光明的未來。

Script

您好,我是 TSC 報社的瑪莉・庫伯。我來電的目的是想要訪問您。您可能知道我的專業領域是商業管理,我曾經訪問過數百名執行長,然而我最近發現您在許多方面都和其他執行長與眾不同。可以告訴我您何時有空嗎?我相信與您訪談可以讓我們的讀者了解自身的優勢。

解析　這是歷史主修者的演講。內容提到,歷史學位對他的職場生涯是有幫助的,所以答案是選項(A)。選項(B)和演講內容不符,是錯誤答案。

翻譯　這段演講的目的是什麼?
(A) 說明主修歷史對你的職涯有助益。
(B) 說明主修歷史是演講者的最大錯誤。

單字　**major in** 主修 ｜ **employ** 僱用 ｜ **practical** 實際上的

解析　聽到整個電話留言後,可以知道這是一通為敲定專訪時間而打的電話,所以答案是選項(B)。選項(A)和電話內容完全無關,是在製造錯誤選項時,常用的方法之一。

翻譯　發話者為何致電?
(A) 讚美受話者的幽默感。
(B) 和受話者約時間訪問。

單字　**specialize** 專長 ｜ **business administration** 商業管理 ｜ **strength** 優勢

Ⓓ 應用練習 ▶ 解析 P. 488 🎧 102

▶ 解析 P. 488

Directions: You will hear some talks given by a single speaker. You will be asked to answer a question about what the speaker says in each talk. Select the best response to each question and mark the letter (A) or (B) on your answer sheet.

Question 1 refers to the following speech.

What is the purpose of the speech?

(A) To claim that shy people can succeed
(B) To thank Ms. Smith for encouraging the speaker

Question 2 refers to the following telephone message.

Why is the speaker calling?

(A) To inform the listener that he will make efforts to address a problem
(B) To suggest that the listener write an agreement with the speaker

Answer Sheet

1. (A)   (B)

2. (A)   (B)

題型 **03**　掌握細節資訊 (1)

Ⓐ 輕鬆上手

Part 4 的細節資訊試題和 Part 3 一樣，必須清楚了解具體的方式或地點等的資訊。不過，Part 4 的細節資訊試題比 Part 3 更難，因為內容更長。所以在聽獨白前，一定要事先看一下試卷上的問題和選項，這樣就比較知道接下來要注意聽哪些細節。

一段獨白的展開方式，一般來說是依照以下的順序進行：
1) 陳述主題或介紹獨白者
2) 提到關心的事項或問題點 3) 說出關心事項或問題點的解決方案

由此可知，細節資訊一般來說都會出現在獨白的中段或後段，解題時要集中注意力聽這兩個地方。因為細節資訊類型試題的出題比重很高，所以本單元很重要，必須仔細閱讀。

例題 🎧 103

Ⓠ What does the speaker want the listener to do?

(A) To explain why the listener has not signed a contract

(B) To visit her office and sign the document

Ⓠ 發話者要受話者做什麼？

(A) 解釋為何受話者還未簽合約。

(B) 前往她的辦公室並簽署一份文件。

Script

Hello. This is Erica Brown, from the Human Resources Department. I am calling because I have recently found out that you haven't signed your employment contract with us. I'm not sure how this could have happened. In any case, you'll need to sign the contract in order to receive the many benefits that our company provides. Please visit my office as soon as possible.

你好，我是人力資源部門的艾芮卡・布朗。我來電是因為我最近發現你還未簽本公司的勞動合約。我完全不清楚怎麼會發生這種情況。無論如何，你必須簽訂這份合約，才能享受我們公司提供的許多福利。請盡快找時間來我的辦公室。

解析 這是細節資訊試題。電話留言提到受話者沒有簽勞動合約，接著又提到一定要簽，所以答案是選項（B）。選項（A）並沒有在電話留言中提到。

單字 contract 合約 | document 文件 | employment 僱用 | benefit 福利 | provide 提供

B 基本題型

❶ 找出細節資訊（1） 🎧 104

Question 1 refers to the following talk.

Why have the employees complained?

(A) Because they must acquire another language

(B) Because they are required to visit foreign countries

員工為何抱怨？

(A) 因為他們必須獲得另一種語言能力。

(B) 因為他們被要求到國外出訪。

Script

Some employees have recently complained that they don't understand why they are required to learn a foreign language. I must mention that I really relate to them. I know that learning a foreign language is hard work. I also know that we are a company that requires every employee to work really hard. It's no wonder these employees find it demanding to learn a foreign language in addition to doing their jobs.

一些員工最近抱怨他們不懂為何有必要學習外語。我必須說我非常理解他們的想法。我知道學習外語並不容易，我也知道我們公司要求每一位員工都很勤奮工作。難怪這些員工覺得還要學外語是增加他們的工作負擔，令人感到吃力的事。

解析 獨白裡有許多資訊，但最重要的是表達員工不滿的事情，就是他們必須學外語，所以答案是選項（A）。選項（B）沒有在獨白中提到，所以不是答案。

單字 complain 抱怨 | require 要求 | relate to 同理 | demanding 吃力的

Question 2 refers to the following telephone message.

When the listener visits Friendly Computers, who will he talk to? (A) Ms. Smith (B) Mr. Cooper	聽話人到訪友善電腦公司時，會和誰商談？ (A) 史密斯小姐。 (B) 庫柏先生。

Script

Hello. This is Paul Cooper, at Friendly Computers. I am calling because we have fixed your notebook computer. At present, it is working perfectly, so you can pick it up anytime you want. Unfortunately, I won't be available for the next few days, but I've asked Amy Smith to take care of your computer. If you have any questions, feel free to call her at 888-9376. Thank you.	你好，我是友善電腦公司的保羅·庫柏。我來電告知我們已經修好了您的筆記型電腦。目前，它的功能完全正常，所以您可以隨時來領取。不巧的是，未來幾天我都不在。所以，我已經請艾美·史密斯處理您電腦的事。如果您有任何問題，隨時打電話到 888-9376 給她。謝謝您。

解析 這是細節資訊試題。因為發話者庫柏先生會有幾天不在，所以他拜託史密斯小姐處理他的工作，因此答案是選項 (A)。

單字 **fix** 修理 ｜ **perfectly** 完美地 ｜ **available** 有空

Directions: You will hear some talks given by a single speaker. You will be asked to answer a question about what the speaker says in each talk. Select the best response to each question and mark the letter (A) or (B) on your answer sheet.

Question 1 refers to the following talk.

What will Ms. Brown talk about?

(A) What she has learned from failure
(B) How she has made her business succeed

Question 2 refers to the following telephone message.

Why would the listener contact Ms. Smith?

(A) To sell his used car
(B) To buy a new car

Answer Sheet

1. (A)   (B)
2. (A)   (B)

1. Answer (B)　　　　**2.** Answer (B)

Script

1.

Welcome to our first International Conference on Small Business Owners. Running a small business has never been easy. But if you learn from successful business owners, your business will succeed. Our keynote speaker is Mary Brown. She started a small business in 2012, and now her business serves the needs of customers from all over the world. She'll share her secrets with you.

2.

Hello. This is Amy Baker, at Friendly Cars. Our records show that you bought a car from us in 2002. So much time has passed since then. Did you know you can sell your used car to us? If you want to do so, contact Jack Black. Or you might want to purchase a new car. If so, contact Alice Smith. Remember that we are here to serve your needs. You can always count on us!

Script

歡迎參加第一屆小型企業主國際大會。經營小型企業一直都不是件容易的事。然而如果您向成功的企業主學習，您的企業就會成功。我們的主講人是瑪莉·布朗，她在 2012 年創立了小型企業，現在她企業所服務的客戶遍及全世界。她會和你們分享她的秘訣。

Script

你好，我是友善汽車公司的艾美·貝克。我們的紀錄顯示您在 2002 年向我們買了一輛車，時至今日已經過了很長的一段時間了。您知道您可以把二手車賣給我們嗎？如果您想賣，可以聯絡傑克·布雷克。或者您也可能想買一輛新車。若是如此，可以連絡艾莉斯·史密斯。請記住我們隨時都可以為您服務。我們是您可以永遠信賴的對象。

解析 這是細節資訊試題。想一想最後兩句的內容，就知道答案是選項（B）了。內容並沒有提到布朗小姐曾經失敗，所以選項（A）是錯誤答案。

翻譯 布朗小姐會講什麼？
(A) 她從失敗中學到的事。
(B) 她如何讓自己的事業成功。

單字 conference 研討會｜
keynote speaker 主講人｜
failure 失敗

解析 這是細節資訊試題。可以知道史密斯小姐是負責銷售新車的人員，所以答案是選項（B）。

翻譯 聽者為何將連絡史密斯小姐？
(A) 因為他想賣他的二手車。
(B) 因為他想買新車。

單字 record 紀錄｜used car 二手車｜
count on 信賴

PART
4
❶ 各類型試題說明

題型
03
掌握細節資訊
（1）

Directions: You will hear some talks given by a single speaker. You will be asked to answer a question about what the speaker says in each talk. Select the best response to each question and mark the letter (A) or (B) on your answer sheet.

Question 1 refers to the following talk.

Who will talk about how the company promotes employees?

(A) Ms. Smith
(B) Mr. Brown

Question 2 refers to the following telephone message.

Why did Ms. Johnson leave a phone number?

(A) Because she was having a problem with her landlord
(B) Because she wants the listener to call Mr. Smith

Answer Sheet

1. (A) (B)
2. (A) (B)

題型 **04** 掌握細節資訊（2）

A 輕鬆上手

多益聽力測驗將日常生活中的素材或商業活動加以活用編寫成試題，所以比起其他語言測驗難度較低，這是它的優點。但缺點是，在短時間內要探討眾多內容會令人稍微感覺負擔。

另外，英語發音除了美式、英式口音外，還要熟悉澳洲口音，這也會令人感到有壓力。由於這些困難無法在一夕之間解決，必須透過平日孜孜不倦地學習，才能逐漸克服。只要願意花時間來準備考試，分數必會有所進步。

例題 🎧 108

Q Why does the workshop provide free interpretation service?

(A) To help participants communicate with international writers

(B) To show that the workshop has been financially supported by Korean writers

Q 為何工作坊提供免費的口譯服務？

(A) 幫助與會者和國際作家溝通。

(B) 表示工作坊有受到韓國作家的資助。

Script

Welcome to our 10th International Writers' Workshop! Our workshop allows you to learn from the best writers from all over the world. For your convenience, we provide free interpretation service. So, don't worry about the language barrier. This year, a large number of Korean writers will take part in our workshop. They will share their unique perspectives with you.

歡迎光臨我們的第十屆國際作家工作坊！我們的工作坊可以讓您向全世界最優秀的作家學習。為了方便各位，我們提供免費的口譯服務，因此，別擔心語言障礙。今年為數眾多的韓國作家將參加我們的工作坊，他們將與你們分享獨特的觀點。

解析 這是細節資訊試題。從獨白中可以知道為了方便與會者能互相溝通、消除語言的隔閡，因此提供了免費的翻譯服務，答案是選項（A）。

 interpretation 口譯 | participant 與會者 | communicate with 溝通 |
international 國際的 | financially 財務上地 | convenience 方便 |
take part in 參加 | share 分享 | unique 特別的

B 基本題型

❶ 找出細節資訊（1）

🎧 109

Question 1 refers to the following talk.

Which department will employ social media experts?	哪一個部門會僱用社群媒體專家？
(A) The Human Resources Department	(A) 人力資源部門。
(B) The Marketing Department	(B) 行銷部門。

Script

Our board of directors has recently decided to use social media to promote our products. Unfortunately, we have not fully recognized the power of social media. As a result, our sales have been decreasing in many parts of the world. The board has allowed the Human Resources Department to hire 15 social media experts. At the same time, the Marketing Department will come up with ways to use social media.

本公司董事會最近決定要使用社群媒體推廣產品。遺憾的是，我們仍未透徹意識到社群媒體的力量。於是，我們的銷售量在世界各個地區不斷減少。董事會已經讓人力資源部門僱用 15 位社群媒體專家。同時，行銷部門也將提出使用社群媒體的方式。

解析 這是細節資訊試題。因為提到董事會准許人力資源部門僱用專家，所以答案是選項（A）。一般來說，僱用人員的工作都是由人力資源部負責的。

單字 board of directors 董事會 | promote 推廣 | recognize 意識

Question 2 refers to the following talk.

What does the President want staff members to do?	總裁要員工做什麼？
(A) To treat her daughter as if she were a coworker	(A) 將她女兒當作公司同事一般對待
(B) To treat her daughter as if she were Vice-President	(B) 將她女兒當副總裁般對待

Script

Susan's Hotel welcomes it's new staff members. One of the new staff member Susan Baker, is actually the hotel's President's only child. As you may know, the President doesn't want any staff members to treat Ms. Baker differently. She wants her daughter to learn how to serve the needs of other staff members. Only then can she learn how to serve our customers.

蘇珊旅館歡迎新進員工。其中一位進員工是蘇珊‧貝克，實際上是總裁的獨生女。你可能知道總裁不希望任何員工給予貝克小姐差別待遇。她希望她的女兒學習如何滿足其他員工的需要。只有那樣她才會學到如何服務我們的客戶。

解析 這是細節資訊試題。從內容可以判斷答案是選項（A）。因為提到不要有特別待遇，所以選項（B）不會是答案。

單字 **staff member** 員工 ｜ **president** 總裁 ｜ **coworker** 同事 ｜ **vice-president** 副總裁

> **Directions:** You will hear some talks given by a single speaker. You will be asked to answer a question about what the speaker says in each talk. Select the best response to each question and mark the letter (A) or (B) on your answer sheet.

Question 1 refers to the following telephone message.

When does Ms. Smith want to see the listener?

(A) At 5:00 p.m. on Wednesday
(B) At 2:00 p.m. on Friday

Question 2 refers to the following announcement.

What do you need to have in order to access certain areas?

(A) Your international driver's license
(B) Prior permission

Answer Sheet		
1. (A)	(B)	
2. (A)	(B)	

答案和解析

1. Answer (B)　　　　**2.** Answer (B)

Script

1.

Hello. This is Erica Johnson, from Carlston University. We are impressed by your qualifications. President Nicole Smith is especially interested in interviewing you in person. Since she'll be leaving for Paris next week, she wants to see you on Friday. What time would be convenient for you? The best time for Nicole would be 2:00 p.m., but she could see you another time as well. Please call me at 777-2255.

2.

Sometimes, we take safety for granted. But recent events in many parts of the world tell us that safety is a serious issue. Therefore, we require that you wear your identification card at all times. In addition, certain areas cannot be accessed without prior permission. Permission will be granted on a case-by-case basis. These measures are expected to help us stay safe.

Script

您好，我是卡爾斯頓大學的艾芮卡‧強尼。我們對您的資歷感到印象深刻。妮可‧史密斯校長尤其有興趣想親自面試您。由於她將在下週去巴黎，她想在週五和您見面。您在什麼時間比較方便？最適合妮可的時間是下午兩點，不過其他時間也可以。請打777-2255和我聯絡。

Script

有時我們將安全視為理所當然。然而最近發生在世上各地的事件顯示，安全是一個嚴重的問題。所以，我們要求你要隨時戴著證件。另外，某些區域要事先許可才得以進入。許可的申請將視個案而定。這些措施預計可以維護我們的安全。

解析 這是細節資訊試題。在電話留言中提到，星期五下午兩點，所以答案是選項（B）。

翻譯 史密斯女士何時要與聽者見面？
(A) 週三下午五點。
(B) 週五下午兩點。

單字 qualification 資歷 ｜ president 校長

解析 這是細節資訊試題。文章提到要進入某些特定區域，要經過事先許可，所以答案是選項（B）。

翻譯 你需要什麼物件才能進入某些區域？
(A) 你的國際駕照。
(B) 事先許可。

單字 take for granted 視為理所當然 ｜ identification 身分證明 ｜ access 進入 ｜ prior 事先 ｜ grant 給予

Directions: You will hear some talks given by a single speaker. You will be asked to answer a question about what the speaker says in each talk. Select the best response to each question and mark the letter (A) or (B) on your answer sheet.

Question 1 refers to the following telephone message.

How long has the bear been at the zoo?

(A) For almost five years
(B) For almost three years

Question 2 refers to the following local news.

What musical instrument does Mr. Johnson play?

(A) The flute
(B) The piano

Answer Sheet

1. (A)　　　　(B)
2. (A)　　　　(B)

題型 **05**   掌握意圖

A 輕鬆上手

Part 4 和 Part 3 一樣有掌握意圖的新題型以及圖表資訊題型，要將獨白內容和圖表訊息對照，之後可以在 Practice Test 中多做練習。

在 Part 4 掌握意圖的試題中，會詢問下列三種狀況：
1) 對話者為何這樣說
2) 話中含有什麼意圖
3) 話中隱藏什麼含意

所以整體來說，Part 4 的難度比 Part 3 還高。這樣的難度需要多做練習，要多聽長度稍長的獨白，邊聽邊理解，並思考不同情況下會出現何種意圖，以及因應該狀況會說出的話語。

例題 🎧 113

Q What does the speaker mean when he says, "I have never met your father"?

(A) He has spoken to the listener's father through the phone.

(B) He didn't have a close relationship with the listener's father.

Q 發話者說：「我從未見過你父親。」是什麼意思？

(A) 他曾透過電話與受話者的父親對話。

(B) 他和聽者的父親並不熟。

Script

Hello. This is Martin Green, from the Human Resources Department. You have been a valued employee of our company. That's why all of us at Green Company are sad for your loss. Losing a family member is one of the most difficult things in our lives. I have never met your father, but I'm sure that he was a wonderful person. If you need anything during these difficult times, don't hesitate to ask.

你好，我是人力資源部門的馬丁・格林。你在我們公司一向是位重要的員工，因此格林公司全體員工都為你的失去感到悲傷。失去親人是人生中最難熬的打擊，我仍未親自見過你的父親，但我相信他是一位很棒的人。如果你在這段難熬的日子裡需要任何協助，請務必告訴我。

解析 這獨白後半提到，沒有親自見過面所以不熟，不過可以確定他是位了不起的人。答案是選項（B）。

單字 relationship 關係 | valued 重要的 | hesitate 猶豫

B 基本題型

❶ 掌握意圖（1）　　　　🎧 114

Question 1 refers to the following talk.

What does the speaker mean when she says, "Their complaints are understandable"?	發話者說：「他們的不滿是可以理解的。」是什麼意思？
(A) She agrees with the employees.	(A) 她同意員工的看法。
(B) It is no wonder they complain about the company's decision.	(B) 他們對公司的決策不滿並不令人意外。

Script

Some employees have recently complained that they don't understand the company's decision to merge with Sally Construction Company. Their complaints are understandable. Merging with another company is a huge task, and some employees may feel threatened in lots of ways. But I want to say that there is nothing to worry about. We will continue to grow, and we won't lay off any employees.	有些員工近來抱怨他們不能理解公司與沙力建築公司合併的決策。他們的不滿是可以理解的。和另一個公司合併是項艱鉅的任務，而一些員工可能在許多方面都覺得受到威脅。但是我想告訴大家完全不用擔心。我們將持續成長，也不會解聘任何員工。

解析 女子說這句話的意圖是選項（B）。女子說員工們的抱怨是可以理解的，表示這的確是令人不滿的狀況。

單字 merge 合併 | threaten 威脅 | lay off 裁員

Question 2 refers to the following talk.

What does the speaker mean when he says, "You may think that's ridiculous"?	說話人說：「你可能認為那很荒謬。」是什麼意思？
(A) People may think selling smiles doesn't make any sense.	(A) 人們可能認為販賣微笑沒有任何意義。
(B) People don't want the speaker to sell smiles.	(B) 人們不希望發話者販賣微笑。

Script

As some of you may know, I have sold many different things over the past thirty years. I have received awards for selling large numbers of products. A lot of people want me to share my secret with them. Well, my secret is as simple as a smile. What I mean is that I have been selling "smiles" for the past thirty years. You may think that's ridiculous, but I'm not kidding. Sell smiles, and your products will sell like hot cakes.

你們有些人可能知道，過去 30 年我已經賣出了很多不同商品。我曾因販賣出許多產品而獲獎無數。許多人要我和他們分享我的秘訣，我的秘訣就像微笑那麼簡單。我的意思是說過去 30 年我一直都在販賣「微笑」。你可能認為那很荒謬。

但我可不是在開玩笑，販賣微笑會讓您的商品變成搶手貨。

解析 發話者的意思是選項（A）。發話者說你可能認為那很荒謬，但那真的是讓銷售變好的秘訣。

單字 ridiculous 荒謬的 ｜ award 獎項 ｜ secret 秘訣 ｜ hot cakes 搶手貨

C 題型練習

Question 1 refers to the following telephone message.

What does the speaker mean when she says, "Of course, you may not like our job"?

(A) The listener may want the speaker to alter the pants again.
(B) The listener may want the speaker to close her business.

Question 2 refers to the following local news.

What does the speaker mean when he says, "One of our reporters will interview this amazing student tomorrow"?

(A) Listeners don't want to know more about Alice Lynch.
(B) Listeners are encouraged to learn more about Alice Lynch tomorrow.

Answer Sheet

1. (A)   (B)
2. (A)   (B)

1. Answer (A)　　**2.** Answer (B)

Script

1.

Hello. This is Mary Smith, at Mary's Clothing. I am calling because we have just finished altering the pants you bought from us last Monday. I hope you'll like what we did for you. Of course, you may not like our job. In that case, you can contact me at 762-8982. Or you can talk to John Miller at 762-8983. I hope to see you soon. Thank you.

2.

Alice Lynch was born in Los Angeles. She moved to New York at the age of 15. In high school, she was often teased because of her accent. Since she was a sensitive student, she realized that differences could often lead to discrimination. As a result, she started a Website to say that it is wrong to discriminate against anyone because of their differences. One of our reporters will interview this amazing student tomorrow.

Script

您好，我是瑪莉服飾公司的瑪莉・史密斯。我來電是因為您上週一在我們店裡購買的褲子已經修改好了，我希望您會喜歡修改後的成品。當然，您也有可能不滿意我們的修改，在這種情況下，您可以打 762-8982 和我聯繫。或者您也可以打 762-8983 和約翰・米勒商談。我希望可以很快可以和您見面。謝謝您。

Script

艾麗絲・林區生於洛杉磯，她在 15 歲時搬到紐約。高中時，她因為口音常受到嘲弄。由於她生性敏感，她理解差異往往可能導致歧視。於是，她架設了一個網站，倡導歧視和自己不一樣的人是不對的事。我們的記者明天將會訪問這位優秀的學生。

解析 女子說這句話的意圖是選項（A）。發話者說也許您也有可能不滿意我們的修改，意思就是您可能會要求再修改。

翻譯 發話者說：「當然，您也有可能不滿意我們的修改。」是什麼意思？

(A) 聽者可能想要發話者再次修改褲子。

(B) 聽者可能想要發話者收掉她的企業。

單字 alter 修改 | pants 褲子

解析 發話者的意思是選項（B）。發話者說，明天會專訪這位學生，意思就是，希望大家繼續收聽。

翻譯 發話者說：「我們的記者明天將會訪問這位優秀的學生。」是什麼意思？

(A) 聽者不想再多了解愛麗絲・林區。

(B) 聽者被鼓勵明天更進一步地了解愛麗絲・林區。

單字 tease 嘲弄 | discrimination 歧視 | encourage 鼓勵

D 應用練習

▶ 解析 P. 491　　🎧 117

> **Directions:** You will hear some talks given by a single speaker. You will be asked to answer a question about what the speaker says in each talk. Select the best response to each question and mark the letter (A) or (B) on your answer sheet.

Question 1 refers to the following telephone message.

What does the speaker mean when he says, "I know that you need your car to get around"?

(A) He thinks that the listener should think about buying a new car.
(B) He thinks that the listener will use his car often.

Question 2 refers to the following talk.

What does the speaker mean when she says, "This is unacceptable"?

(A) The company does not pay attention to contact information.
(B) The company must have an employee contact information.

Answer Sheet	
1. (A)	(B)
2. (A)	(B)

Quick Test for **Part 4** 118 　▶ 解析 P. 481

Select the best response to the question or statement and mark the letter (A), (B), or (C) on your answer sheet.

Questions 1–3 refer to the following telephone message.

1. Why is the speaker calling?

   (A) To inform the listener that Professor Bauer has left the university

   (B) To inform the listener that he has failed a course

2. Which is true about the listener?

   (A) He is a student at Carlston University.

   (B) He was hospitalized last Thursday.

3. What does the speaker mean when she says, "I do know that your health is the most important thing right now"?

   (A) She believes that the listener wants to be a medical doctor.

   (B) She believes that the listener is making efforts to get better.

Questions 4–6 refer to the following advertisement.

4. Who is the advertisement aimed at?

   (A) Diplomats

   (B) Business owners

5. Which is true about Mr. Smith?

   (A) He does not believe that international politics can affect business.

   (B) He has written several books.

6. When can listeners meet with Mr. Smith?

   (A) On Wednesday

   (B) On Friday

Answer Sheet

1. (A)   (B)

2. (A)   (B)

3. (A)   (B)

4. (A)   (B)

5. (A)   (B)

6. (A)   (B)

Practice Test

🎧 119　▶ 解析 P. 495

Part 4

Directions: You will hear some talks given by a single speaker. You will be asked to answer three questions about what the speaker says in each talk. Select the best response to each question and mark the letter (A), (B), (C), or (D) on your answer sheet. The talks will not be printed in your test book and will be spoken only one time.

Questions 1–3 refer to the following telephone message.

1. Why is the speaker calling?

   (A) To encourage the listener to be more creative

   (B) To ask the listener when he will move to the United States

   (C) To ask the listener to give a speech at a conference

   (D) To inform the listener that he has won an award

2. Which is true about the listener?

   (A) He will visit Toronto on May 15, 2017.

   (B) He is recognized for his creativity.

   (C) He used to be a wealthy man.

   (D) He teaches engineering at college.

3. What does the speaker mean when he says, "Did you know that your award is worth $5 million"?

   (A) The listener must be wise enough to handle a lot of money.

   (B) The listener must be disappointed to learn that he has lost a lot of money.

   (C) The listener may be surprised to learn that he will receive a lot of money.

   (D) The listener may want to invest his money in medicine.

Answer Sheet

1. (A) (B) (C) (D)　　2. (A) (B) (C) (D)　　3. (A) (B) (C) (D)

Questions 4–6 refer to the following talk.

Employee Name	Language(s) each employee is learning
Mary Smith	Spanish
Charlie Johnson	Japanese
Jack Bauer	German, Spanish, Korean
Alice Baker	French

4. Look at the graphic. Who follows the company's advice?

(A) Ms. Smith

(B) Mr. Johnson

(C) Mr. Bauer

(D) Ms. Baker.

5. Which is true about Griffith International?

(A) It requires its employees to learn at least two foreign languages.

(B) Its founder was an immigrant from South Korea.

(C) It believes that learning foreign languages is useless.

(D) It is a clothing company.

6. What can learning a foreign language help you develop, according to the talk?

(A) Knowledge

(B) Creativity

(C) Social skills

(D) Balance

Answer Sheet

4. (A) (B) (C) (D)   5. (A) (B) (C) (D)   6. (A) (B) (C) (D)

Questions 7–9 refer to the following speech.

7. What is the speech mainly about?

   (A) Why the publishing industry is struggling financially

   (B) Why the publishing industry is unpopular among college graduates

   (C) The importance of the publishing industry in our society

   (D) The importance of expanding your knowledge

8. What is true about the speaker?

   (A) She believes that the publishing industry is not useful anymore.

   (B) She is an internationally recognized novelist.

   (C) She runs several publishing companies.

   (D) She believes that the publishing industry is essential for the survival of society.

9. According to the speaker, why should we expand our knowledge?

   (A) Because we want to lead a healthy lifestyle.

   (B) Because we need to find innovative ways to solve social problems.

   (C) Because we want to earn a lot of money.

   (D) Because we need to live peacefully with foreign countries.

Answer Sheet

7. (A) (B) (C) (D)   8. (A) (B) (C) (D)   9. (A) (B) (C) (D)

PARTS

5 & 6

句子填空
和
段落填空

題型 **01** 主詞和動詞

A 輕鬆上手

1. 動詞

所有句子都可以理解成「A＋B」的結構
☞ A 是主詞、B 是動詞。因此，所有句子都可以看成是「主詞＋動詞」的結構。

The dog **barked**. 這隻狗叫了。
☞ The dog 是主詞，barked 是動詞。

不過在動詞的部分，除了有像 bark 這樣的表具體動作的一般動詞外，還有像 am、are、is 表「是」的 be 動詞，和像 look 這樣的表「像」的連綴動詞。

◉ 表「是」的 **be 動詞**	The dog **is** cute. 這隻狗很可愛。 ☞ The dog 是主詞，**is** 是 be 動詞。
◉ 表「像」的連綴動詞	The dog **looks** cute. 這隻狗看起來很可愛。 ☞ The dog 是主詞，**looks** 是動詞。

2. 主詞

主詞一般都是名詞或代名詞。所謂的名詞，是指稱人或事物的詞。所謂的代名詞，就是當名詞再次出現時，用來指稱該名詞的詞。

The dog looked tired. 這隻狗看起來很累。
☞ dog 是名詞。

The dog looked tired. **It** ran 10 kilometers. 這隻狗看起來很累。牠跑了 10 公里。
☞ dog 是名詞，這名詞再次出現時，就用代名詞 it 來代稱它。

主詞的位置可以放虛構主詞 it。當不定詞作主詞使用時，會用虛構主詞來代稱。

It is wise **to respect** everyone. 尊重每一個人是明智之舉。
☞「to respect everyone」是 to 不定詞當主詞使用，但因為太長，所以用虛構主詞 it 放在主詞的位置上。

代名詞有**主格**、**所有格**、**受格**三種。另外還有代表「自己」之意的反身代名詞。

She loves him. **She** loves his smile. 她愛他。她愛他的微笑。
☞ she（她）是主格，his（他的）是所有格，him（他）是受格。

能修飾名詞的是形容詞，修飾動詞的是副詞。

She likes **pretty** dolls **very much**. 她非常喜歡漂亮的玩具娃娃。
☞ pretty 是形容詞，very 和 much 是副詞

B 基本題型

❶ 放主詞位置的字彙

1. The _____ of the city was impressive. 城市的美景讓人印象深刻。

(A) beautiful　　(B) beauty　　(C) beautifully　　(D) beautify

解析 空格要放能當作主詞的名詞。選項（A）是形容詞，選項（B）是名詞，選項（C）是副詞，選項（D）是動詞，所以答案是選項（B）。

單字 impressive 令人印象深刻的 | beautifully 美麗地 | beautify 使美麗

2. _____ produced many cars. 他們生產了很多汽車。

(A) Them　　(B) Their　　(C) They　　(D) Themselves

解析 主詞的位置若要放代名詞，要放主格代名詞。選項（A）是受格，選項（B）是所有格，選項（C）是主格，選項（D）是反身代名詞，所以答案是選項（C）。

單字 produce 生產

3. _____ is important to work hard. 努力工作很重要。

(A) It　　(B) What　　(C) There　　(D) Why

解析 to work hard 是主詞，要用虛構主詞 it 來代替。所以答案是選項（A）。

❷ 放動詞位置的字彙

4. The company _____ computers. 這家公司生產電腦。

(A) produce　　(B) produces　　(C) producing　　(D) to produce

解析 主詞是第三人稱單數，動詞若是現在式，要在原形動詞後加 s 或 es。動詞的位置不能放 -ing 現在分詞形或不定詞。所以答案是選項 (B)。

單字 produce 生產

5. These companies _____ with the government. 這些公司與政府合作。

(A) cooperates　(B) cooperate　(C) cooperating　(D) to cooperate

解析 主詞是複數，動詞也要用複數形。選項 (A) 是動詞的單數形，選項 (B) 是動詞的複數形，選項 (C) 是動詞的現在分詞形，選項 (D) 是不定詞形，所以答案是選項 (B)。

單字 cooperate 合作　|　government 政府

❸ 祈使句

6. Please _____ in this form. 請填寫這張表格。

(A) fills　　(B) to fill　　(C) filling　　(D) fill

解析 祈使句通常會省略主詞 you，動詞要用原形動詞。選項 (A) 是動詞的第三人稱單數現在式，選項 (B) 是不定詞，選項 (C) 是動詞的現在分詞形，選項 (D) 是動詞原形，所以答案是選項 (D)。

單字 fill in 填寫　|　form 表格

C 題型練習

Select the best answer to complete the sentence.

1. The _____ of the movie was delayed.
   (A) productive   (B) production
   (C) produce   (D) productively

2. _____ wrote many interesting novels.
   (A) Her   (B) Herself
   (C) Her was   (D) She

3. _____ was an honor to meet the singer.
   (A) There   (B) What
   (C) It   (D) Why

4. The company _____ many kinds of buildings.
   (A) construct   (B) constructs
   (C) constructing   (D) to construct

5. These people _____ an important role in society.
   (A) plays   (B) playing
   (C) to play   (D) play

6. Please _____ us at 338-9276.
   (A) call   (B) calls
   (C) calling   (D) to call

答案和解析

1. (B)

解析 空格在「the . . . of」之中，所以只能放名詞。選項(A)是形容詞，選項(B)是名詞，選項(C)是動詞，選項(D)是副詞，答案是選項(B)。

翻譯 這部電影的製作延期了。

單字 production 製作 | delay 延期 | productive 有生產力的 | produce 製造 | productivity 生產力

2. (D)

解析 主詞是代名詞時，要用主格。選項(A)是所有格或受格，選項(B)是反身代名詞，選項(C)是「受詞＋be動詞」，選項(D)是主格，所以是答案。

翻譯 她寫了許多本很有意思的小說。

單字 interesting 有趣的 | novel 小說

3. (C)

解析 本句的 to meet the singer 是主詞，要用虛構主詞 it 來代替，所以答案是選項(C)。

翻譯 和這位歌手會面是一項殊榮。

單字 honor 殊榮 | singer 歌手

4. (B)

解析 The company 是第三人稱單數，因為句子是現在式，所以要在原形動詞後加 -s 或 -es，答案是選項(B)。

翻譯 這家公司建造很多類型的建築物。

單字 construct 建造 | kind 類型 | building 建築物

5. (D)

解析 These people 是複數主詞，動詞要用複數形。選項(A)是動詞的單數形，選項(B)是動詞的現在分詞形，選項(C)是不定詞，選項(D)是動詞的複數形，所以是答案。

翻譯 這些人在社會中扮演重要角色。

單字 play a role 扮演角色 | society 社會

6. (A)

解析 這是沒有主詞的祈使句，所以要用原形動詞。選項(A)是原形，選項(B)是現在式第三人稱單數，選項(C)是現在分詞，選項(D)是不定詞，所以答案是選項(A)。

翻譯 請打 338-9276 和我們聯繫。

單字 call 撥打電話

D 應用練習　　　▶ 解析 P. 499

Select the best answer to complete the sentence.

1. The _____ of the bridge began in 2012.
   (A) construct
   (B) construction
   (C) constructive
   (D) constructively

2. The _____ of the washing machine required little effort.
   (A) operate
   (B) operational
   (C) operationally
   (D) operation

3. Finally, _____ made a formal request.
   (A) him
   (B) his was
   (C) he
   (D) himself

4. Eventually, _____ decided to leave Seoul.
   (A) their
   (B) them
   (C) themselves
   (D) they

5. _____ was foolish to trust him.
   (A) Where
   (B) It
   (C) These
   (D) They

6. _____ was a pleasure to meet you yesterday.
   (A) When
   (B) Them
   (C) They
   (D) It

7. The CEO _____ care of many things.
   (A) take
   (B) takes
   (C) to take
   (D) taking

8. The dessert _____ good.
   (A) taste
   (B) tasting
   (C) to taste
   (D) tastes

9. These leaders _____ better treatment of workers.
   (A) demands
   (B) to demand
   (C) demand
   (D) demanding

10. Please _____ the document carefully.
    (A) to read
    (B) reads
    (C) reading
    (D) read

題型 **02**　受詞和補語

A 輕鬆上手

● 句子如果要表達兩個人或事物之間的關係，會稍微再複雜一點，
　時常以「A＋B＋C」也就是「主詞＋動詞＋受詞」的型態出現。

They built a tower. 他們建造了一座塔。
☞ They 是主詞，built 是動詞，a tower 是受詞。

● 受詞的位置可以放名詞或代名詞。放代名詞的話，一定要用**受格**。

Everyone wants happiness. 每個人都想過得快樂。
☞ 受詞的位置放了名詞 happiness。

Everyone loves her. 每個人都愛她。
☞ 受詞的位置放了代名詞的受格 her。

● 像 at 或 in 這樣放在名詞或代名詞前的詞，稱作介系詞。
　介系詞後一定要接名詞或代名詞的**受格**。

They live in a large city. 他們住在大城市。
☞ 介系詞 in 後的受詞位置，放了名詞 (a large) city。

The nurse looked at them. 這位護理師看著他們。
☞ 介系詞 at 後的受詞位置，放了代名詞的受格 them。

◉ 句型也可以是「主詞＋動詞＋補語」，這時的動詞是具「有……的感覺」之意的 be 動詞或連綴動詞，補語的位置要放名詞或形容詞。

The clerk is **smart**. 這位店員很聰明。

☞ The clerk 是主詞，is 是動詞，smart 是補語。

◉ 句型「主詞＋動詞＋受詞＋受詞補語」就更複雜了。這時的動詞是不完全及物動詞：find（得知）、let（使）、make（造成），受詞如果是不定詞的話，要用虛受詞 it 來代替。

We find **it** difficult <u>to please everyone</u>. 我們發覺要取悅所有人很困難。

☞ We 是主詞，find 是動詞，it 是虛受詞，difficult 是受詞補語，to please everyone 是真受詞。

單字 tower 塔 ｜ clerk 店員 ｜ smart 聰明 ｜ please 取悅

Ⓑ 基本題型

❶ 動詞的受詞

1. Julie wants a good _____ for her daughter. 茱莉希望女兒能接受良好教育。

(A) educate　(B) education　(C) educational　(D) educationally

解析 空格要放能當受詞的名詞。選項（A）是動詞，選項（B）是名詞，選項（C）是形容詞，選項（D）是副詞，所以答案是選項（B）。

單字 educate (v.) 教育 ｜ education (n.) 教育 ｜ educational 有教育性的 ｜ educationally 有教育性地

2. Everybody praised _____. 每個人都讚美他。

(A) he　(B) yourself　(C) him　(D) he was

解析 動詞的受詞是代名詞時，代名詞一定要用受格。選項（A）是主格，選項（B）是代名詞 you 的反身代名詞，選項（C）是受格，選項（D）是「主格＋be 動詞」，所以答案是選項（C）。

單字 praise 讚美

❷ 介系詞的受詞

3. The library was built in honor of ＿＿＿＿. 建造這座圖書館是為了紀念他們。

(A) they　　(B) their　　(C) themselves　　(D) them

解析 介系詞受詞的位置如果是代名詞的話，一定要用受格。選項（A）是主格，選項（B）是所有格，選項（C）是反身代名詞，選項（D）是受格，所以答案是選項（D）。

單字 in honor of 為了紀念

❸ 主詞補語

4. The product is ＿＿＿＿. 這項產品很有用。

(A) use　　　(B) usefulness　　　(C) usefully　　　(D) useful

解析 空格是補語的位置，要放名詞或形容詞，用來補充說明主詞。選項（A）當名詞是「使用」之意，選項（B）則是「使用性」的意思，所以都是錯的不用考慮。選項（C）是副詞，不能當作補語使用，所以答案是形容詞選項（D）。

單字 use 使用 ｜ usefulness 有用性 ｜ usefully 有用地 ｜ useful 有用的

5. Seoul is a famous ＿＿＿＿ with a long history. 首爾是歷史悠久的名城。

(A) rural　　　(B) city　　　(C) rurally　　　(D) urban

解析 空格是補語的位置要放名詞，選項（A）和選項（D）是形容詞，選項（C）是副詞，答案是選項（B）。

單字 famous 知名的 ｜ rural 鄉村的 ｜ rurally 鄉村地 ｜ urban 都市的

❹ 虛構受詞

6. We find ＿＿＿＿ important to do our best. 我們發覺得盡力而為很重要。

(A) it　　(B) what　　(C) when　　(D) there

解析 find 需要使用虛受詞 it 來構成複雜句，所以答案是選項（A）。本句中的 to do our best 是真受詞。

單字 do one's best 盡力而為

Select the best answer to complete the sentence.

1. The professor gave a _____ about quality control.
   (A) presentation   (B) presentable
   (C) presentably   (D) presentational

2. Her family greeted _____ warmly.
   (A) we   (B) our
   (C) ourselves   (D) us

3. The coach was proud of _____.
   (A) their   (B) them
   (C) they   (D) themselves

4. Those items are not _____ in South Korea.
   (A) avail   (B) available
   (C) availably   (D) availability

5. The smartphone is a great _____.
   (A) invent   (B) inventive
   (C) invention   (D) inventively

6. The climate makes _____ difficult to live there.
   (A) here   (B) which
   (C) it   (D) where

答案和解析

1. (A)

解析 空格要放能當作受詞的名詞。選項(A)是名詞,選項(B)是形容詞,選項(C)是副詞,選項(D)是形容詞,所以答案是選項(A)。

翻譯 這位教授針對品管提出簡報。

單字 professor 教授 |
quality control 品管 |
presentation 簡報 |
presentable 可呈現的 |
presentably 可呈現地 |
presentational 表演的

---

2. (D)

解析 代名詞當作動詞的受詞時,代名詞一定要用受格。選項(A)是主格,選項(B)是所有格,選項(C)是代名詞 we 的反身代名詞,選項(D)是受格,所以答案是選項(D)。

翻譯 她的家人熱誠地歡迎我們。

單字 greet 招呼 | warmly 熱誠地

---

3. (B)

解析 代名詞當作介系詞的受詞時,代名詞也一定要用受格。選項(A)是所有格,選項(B)是受格,選項(C)是主格,選項(D)是 they 的反身代名詞,所以答案是選項(B)。

翻譯 教練以他們為傲。

單字 coach 教練 | proud 驕傲的

---

4. (B)

解析 空格是主詞補語的位置,所以要放名詞或形容詞。但是「那些產品」本身不會是選項(A)的名詞意義「效用」或選項(D)的名詞「使用可能性」,所以只能放選項(B)的形容詞了。選項(A)是動詞或名詞,選項(C)是副詞,選項(D)是名詞。答案是選項(B)。

翻譯 那些東西在南韓買不到。

單字 item 物品 |
avail (n.) 有益於;(n.) 效期|
available 可得到的 |
availably 可得地 | availability 可得性

---

5. (C)

解析 空格是主詞補語的位置,所以要放名詞或形容詞。不過因為空格前有冠詞 a,所以一定要放名詞。選項(A)是動詞,選項(B)是形容詞,選項(C)是名詞,選項(D)是副詞,所以答案是選項(C)。

翻譯 智慧手機是很棒的發明。

單字 invent 發明 | inventive 發明的 |
invention 發明 |
inventively 有創造力地

---

6. (C)

解析 make 之後需要放虛受詞 it 來構成複雜句,所以答案是選項(C)。本句中的 to live there 是真受詞。

翻譯 氣候讓那邊的生活變得很困難。

單字 climate 氣候

▶ 解析 P. 500

D 應用練習

Select the best answer to complete the sentence.

1. The two companies signed an
    _____.
    (A) agreeable
    (B) agreeably
    (C) agreement
    (D) agree

2. The zoo had _____ in raising
    healthy animals.
    (A) success
    (B) successful
    (C) successfully
    (D) succeed

3. The CEO blamed _____ for
    the failure.
    (A) their
    (B) they
    (C) themselves
    (D) them

4. The committee was pleased
    with _____.
    (A) us
    (B) we
    (C) our
    (D) ourselves

5. Melanie hosted the event
    instead of _____.
    (A) he
    (B) him
    (C) himself
    (D) he was

6. The apartment belongs to a
    famous _____.
    (A) active
    (B) actively
    (C) act
    (D) actor

7. Chinese is a good _____ as a
    language to learn.
    (A) choose
    (B) chosen
    (C) to choose
    (D) choice

8. The results were very _____.
    (A) satisfy
    (B) satisfactory
    (C) satisfactorily
    (D) satisfaction

9. City life is generally _____.
    (A) comfort
    (B) comfortably
    (C) to comfort
    (D) comfortable

10. The lack of time made _____.
    difficult to complete the project.
    (A) what
    (B) it
    (C) there
    (D) which

題型 **03** 修飾詞

A 輕鬆上手

◉ 所謂的**修飾詞**，就是用來修飾、形容、說明其他詞類的詞。修飾詞可以用來修飾名詞、動詞或整個句子。

Mary is a **talented** artist. 瑪莉是很有才華的藝術家。
☞ 用形容詞 talented 來修飾名詞 artist。

The airplane landed **safely**. 飛機安全降落。
☞ 用副詞 safely 來修飾動詞 landed。

Fortunately, the company made big profits. 幸運地是，這家公司獲利豐厚。
☞ 用副詞 fortunately 來修飾全句。

◉ 形容詞、形容詞片語、不定詞，這些詞可以修飾**名詞**。

Julia is a **popular** singer. 茱莉亞是很受歡迎的歌手。
☞ 用形容詞 popular 來修飾名詞 singer。

The picture **on the wall** looks strange. 牆上的這張照片看起來很奇怪。
☞ 用形容詞片語 on the wall 來修飾名詞 picture。

There was no room **to show them to**. 沒有任何房間可以向他們展示。
☞ 用不定詞引導的 to show them to 來修飾名詞 room。

◉ 副詞、副詞片語，這些詞可以修飾**動詞**。

The children smiled **happily**. 這些孩子笑得很開心。
☞ 用副詞 happily 來修飾動詞 smiled。

The CEO listened to her story **with patience**. 執行長耐心地聽著她的故事。
☞ 用副詞片語 with patience 來修飾動詞 listened。

◉ 修飾整句的工作，通常都交由副詞來做。

Unfortunately, the fire claimed several lives. 遺憾的是，火災造成數人身亡。
☞ 用副詞 unfortunately 來修飾全句。

◉「介系詞＋介系詞的受詞」這型式的介系詞片語，可當作形容詞片語或
副詞片語使用。

There were lots of complaints about the product. 有許多人投訴這項商品。
☞ 介系詞片語 about the product 是用來修飾名詞 complaints 的形容詞片語。

The staff treated the customers with kindness. 員工用善意對待客戶。
☞ 介系詞片語 with kindness 是用來修飾動詞 treated 的副詞片語。

單字 **talented** 有才華的 | **land** 降落 | **profit** 利潤 | **popular** 受歡迎的 |
strange 奇怪的 | **patience** 耐心 | **complaint** 投訴

B 基本題型

❶ 修飾名詞的形容詞和形容詞片語

1. The _____ method will help the company a lot.
這種創新方式將會對這家公司大有助益。

(A) innovatively　(B) innovate　(C) innovativeness　(D) innovative

解析 修飾名詞的工作，通常都交給形容詞。選項（A）是副詞，選項（B）是動詞，
選項（C）是名詞，選項（D）是形容詞，所以是答案。

單字 **innovatively** 創新地 | **innovate** 創新 | **innovativeness** 創新力 |
innovative 創新的

2. The _____ of the bridge will be delayed. 這座橋的建造將會延期。

(A) construct　(B) construction　(C) constructive　(D) constructively

解析 接受形容詞片語 of the bridge 修飾的詞是名詞。選項（A）是動詞，選項（B）是
名詞，選項（C）是形容詞，選項（D）是副詞，所以答案是選項（B）。

單字 **delay** 延期 | **construct** 建造 | **construction** 建造工程 |
constructive 建設性的 | **constructively** 建設性地

❷ 修飾名詞的不定詞

3. Experts say that there is enough food _____ the world's population.
專家說有足夠食物養活全世界的人口。

(A) to feed　　(B) feeds　　(C) fed　　(D) feed

解析 在能修飾名詞的形容詞片語中，也有不定詞。選項 (C) 的過去分詞通常要和介系詞 by 搭配才能修飾名詞，所以答案是選項 (A)。選項 (D) 的原形動詞不能修飾名詞。

單字 expert 專家 ｜ feed 餵養 ｜ population 人口

❸ 修飾動詞的副詞和副詞片語

4. The plan was carried out _____. 這項計劃被小心執行。

(A) care　　(B) careful　　(C) carefully　　(D) carefulness

解析 本句的動詞部分是 was carried out，能修飾這部分的詞是副詞。選項 (A) 是名詞或動詞，選項 (B) 是形容詞，選項 (C) 是副詞，選項 (D) 是名詞，所以答案是選項 (C)。

單字 carry out 執行 ｜ care 細心 ｜ carefully 小心地 ｜ carefulness 小心

5. The cake was _____ with a knife. 這塊蛋糕被用刀切開了。

(A) cutter　　(B) cut　　(C) cuts　　(D) cutters

解析 空格是接受副詞片語 with a knife 修飾的動詞。本句中的動詞要用 was cut 的被動形式，所以答案是選項 (B)。選項 (A) 是名詞，選項 (B) 是動詞的過去分詞，選項 (C) 是動詞的第三人稱單數現在式或名詞，選項 (D) 是名詞。

單字 cutter 刀具 ｜ cut 切

C 題型練習

Select the best answer to complete the sentence.

1. Many _____ ways were suggested by the panel.
   (A) difference   (B) differently
   (C) different   (D) differ

2. The _____ of the product was unexpected.
   (A) successful   (B) succeed
   (C) successive   (D) success

3. This is a useful method _____ customers.
   (A) attract   (B) attracts
   (C) to attract   (D) attracted

4. The machine was working _____.
   (A) proper   (B) property
   (C) properties   (D) properly

5. They _____ to each other in French.
   (A) talkative   (B) talkativeness
   (C) talkatively   (D) talked

答案和解析

1. (C)

解析 能修飾名詞的詞是形容詞。選項(A)是名詞，選項(B)是副詞，選項(C)是形容詞，選項(D)是動詞，所以答案是選項(C)。

翻譯 專家小組建議了許多不同的方式。

單字 different 不同的 | suggest 建議 | panel 小組 | difference 不同 | differently 不同地 | differ 相異

2. (D)

解析 能被形容詞片語 of the product 修飾的詞是名詞。選項(A)是形容詞，選項(B)是動詞，選項(C)是形容詞，選項(D)是名詞，所以答案是選項(D)。

翻譯 這項產品的成功出乎意料之外。

單字 success 成功 | product 產品 | unexpected 出乎意料的 | successful 成功的 | succeed 成功 | successive 連續的

3. (C)

解析 不定詞能當作形容詞片語來修飾名詞。選項(A)是原形動詞，不能修飾名詞。答案是選項(C)。

翻譯 這是吸引客戶的有用方法。

單字 useful 有用的 | method 方法 | attract 吸引 | customer 顧客

4. (D)

解析 本句的動詞部分是 was working，要用副詞修飾，選項(A)是形容詞，選項(B)是名詞，選項(C)是名詞的複數形，選項(D)是副詞，所以是答案。

翻譯 這台機器運作正常。

單字 work 運作 | proper 適當的 | property 財產 | properly 適當地

5. (D)

解析 接受副詞片語 to each other 和 in French 修飾的詞是動詞。選項(A)是形容詞，選項(B)是名詞，選項(C)是副詞，選項(D)是動詞的過去式，所以答案是選項(D)。

翻譯 他們彼此用法文交談。

單字 each other 彼此 | talkative 健談的 | talkativeness 健談 | talkatively 健談地

D 應用練習　　　　　　　▶ 解析 P. 501

Select the best answer to complete the sentence.

1. A _____ environment is
   important to teenagers.
   (A) stably
   (B) stable
   (C) stability
   (D) stabilize

2. The _____ writer published
   several novels.
   (A) create
   (B) creation
   (C) creatively
   (D) creative

3. The _____ of the computer
   changed many things.
   (A) invent
   (B) inventive
   (C) invention
   (D) inventively

4. Her _____ with the client was
   professional.
   (A) relate
   (B) relatively
   (C) relations
   (D) relationship

5. The doctor thought of a new
   way _____ cancer.
   (A) detect
   (B) detected
   (C) detects
   (D) to detect

6. Follow the correct procedure _____
   the data.
   (A) modify
   (B) to modify
   (C) modifies
   (D) modified

7. The new product was selling _____.
   (A) quickness
   (B) quicken
   (C) quickly
   (D) quickening

8. These insects are _____ found in
   South Korea.
   (A) rare
   (B) rareness
   (C) rarity
   (D) rarely

9. Sam _____ well with other
   employees.
   (A) interaction
   (B) interactive
   (C) interacted
   (D) interactively

10. His proposal _____ to surprising
    results.
    (A) leading
    (B) to lead
    (C) lead
    (D) led

Quick Test for **Parts 5 & 6** ▶ 解析 P. 503

Choose the one word or phrase that best completes the sentence.

1. The _____ of the payment was surprising.
   (A) receipt
   (B) receivable
   (C) received
   (D) receive

2. Fortunately, _____ reached a compromise.
   (A) them
   (B) they
   (C) their
   (D) themselves

3. _____ is always a good idea to question everything.
   (A) Those
   (B) They
   (C) It
   (D) When

4. The inventor _____ something new on a regular basis.
   (A) creates
   (B) creating
   (C) to create
   (D) create

5. Please _____ these instructions carefully.
   (A) following
   (B) to follow
   (C) follows
   (D) follow

6. The committee made a _____ from several candidates.
   (A) selective
   (B) selection
   (C) selectively
   (D) select

7. We collected _____ about their needs.
   (A) inform
   (B) informative
   (C) informatively
   (D) information

8. The bodyguard stopped _____ from entering the office.
   (A) themselves
   (B) them
   (C) they
   (D) their

9. Our parents were ashamed of _____.
   (A) us
   (B) we
   (C) ourselves
   (D) our

10. The success of the project depends on _____.
    (A) their
    (B) themselves
    (C) them
    (D) they

11. Thomas Edison was an outstanding _____.
(A) invent
(B) inventor
(C) inventive
(D) inventively

12. Writing is a creative _____.
(A) process
(B) processed
(C) processor
(D) to process

13. These rooms are _____.
(A) spaciously
(B) spacious
(C) spaciousness
(D) space

14. Her predictions were _____.
(A) alarmingly
(B) alarmed
(C) to alarming
(D) alarming

15. His efforts made _____ possible to conserve a lot of energy.
(A) which
(B) there
(C) it
(D) what

16. Few people are leading a _____ lifestyle.
(A) health
(B) healthily
(C) healthiness
(D) healthy

Questions 17–20 refer to the following passage.

_____ is not always wise to trust experts. Experts are only _____, and they
17.   18.
make many mistakes. _____ Therefore, it is important to use common sense
                         19.
instead of _____ on experts.
              20.

17. (A) What
(B) There
(C) It
(D) Where

18. (A) humanness
(B) humanely
(C) humanity
(D) human

19. (A) For example, many experts help companies make wise decisions.
(B) For instance, few experts predicted the beginning of the global recession in 2008.
(C) In addition, many people are certain that they can depend on experts.
(D) In fact, experts can make correct predictions.

20. (A) depend
(B) depends
(C) to depend
(D) depending

題型 **01** 名詞的功能

A 輕鬆上手

◉ 用來指稱人或事物的詞是**名詞**,名詞可當作一個句子的主詞。

Creativity is important for every employee. 創意對所有員工來說很重要。
☞ 名詞 creativity 是本句的主詞。

Every **agent** should sign up before the end of this month.
每個代理商都應在本月底前註冊。
☞ 接受 every 修飾的名詞 agent,是本句的主詞。

◉ 名詞也可當作動詞或介系詞的受詞。

Erica used her **creativity** to design a new product.
艾芮卡運用她的創意設計了一項新產品。
☞ 名詞 creativity 是動詞 used 的受詞。

These days, many companies are interested in **creativity**.
近來許多公司對創意產生興趣。
☞ 名詞 creativity 是介系詞 in 的受詞。

His company had to deal with a very strange **customer**.
他的公司必須和一位很奇怪的客戶打交道。
☞ 名詞 customer 是動詞片語 deal with 中,介系詞 with 的受詞。

◉ 名詞也可以當作**主詞補語**或**受詞補語**。

What we need is **creativity**. 我們需要的是創意。
☞ 名詞 creativity 是補充說明主詞的主詞補語。

Many experts consider it **creativity**. 許多專家認為那是創意。
☞ 名詞 creativity 是補充說明受詞的受詞補語。

◉ 名詞也可像副詞那樣單獨使用。

This **evening**, we have to finish up the financial report for the meeting tomorrow.
今晚我們必須完成明天會議要用的財務報告。

☞ 名詞 evening 是表時間的副詞。

單字 creativity 創意 ｜ employee 員工 ｜ agent 代理商 ｜ sign up 註冊 ｜
be interested in 對……有興趣 ｜ deal with 打交道 ｜ customer 客戶 ｜
consider 認為 ｜ financial 財務的

B 基本題型

❶ 當主詞的名詞

1. The _____ of smartphones is striking. 智慧手機的受歡迎程度讓人驚訝。

(A) popular (B) popularly (C) popularity (D) popularize

解析 名詞能當句子的主詞。選項（A）是形容詞，選項（B）是副詞，選項（C）是
名詞，選項（D）是動詞，所以答案是選項（C）。

單字 popularity 受歡迎程度 ｜ striking 驚訝的 ｜ popularly 受歡迎地 ｜
popularize 使受歡迎

❷ 當動詞或介系詞受詞的名詞

2. High demand caused a(n) _____ in prices. 高需求造成價格上漲。

(A) to increase (B) increased (C) increasingly (D) increase

解析 名詞能當動詞的受詞。選項（A）是不定詞，選項（B）是動詞 increase 的過
去式或過去分詞，選項（C）是副詞，選項（D）是名詞或動詞，所以答案是
選項（D）。

單字 demand 需求 ｜ cause 造成 ｜ increase 增加 ｜ increasingly 增加地

3. Nothing could account for her strange _____.
沒有什麼可以解釋她奇怪的舉動。

(A) behavior　(B) behave　(C) behavioral　(D) behaviorally

解析 名詞能當介系詞的受詞。選項 (A) 是名詞,選項 (B) 是動詞,選項 (C) 是形容詞,選項 (D) 是副詞,所以答案是選項 (A)。

單字 account for 解釋 ｜ behavior (n.) 舉動 ｜ behave (v.) 舉動 ｜ behavioral 舉動的 ｜ behaviorally 舉動地

❸ 當主詞補語或受詞補語的名詞

4. What matters is _____. 保持真誠最重要。

(A) sincerely　(B) sincerity　(C) sincere　(D) being sincerely

解析 名詞也可當主詞補語。選項 (A) 是副詞,選項 (B) 是名詞,選項 (C) 是形容詞,選項 (D) 是「being ＋副詞」,答案是選項 (B)。

單字 matter 重要 ｜ sincerely 真誠地 ｜ sincerity 真誠 ｜ sincere 真誠的

5. Her talent made her a _____. 她的才華讓她成為名人。

(A) celebrate　(B) celebrated　(C) celebrity　(D) to celebrate

解析 名詞也可當受詞補語。雖然形容詞也可當受詞補語,但因為空格前有冠詞 a,所以一定要放名詞。選項 (A) 是動詞,選項 (B) 是形容詞,選項 (C) 是名詞,選項 (D) 是不定詞,所以答案是選項 (C)。

單字 celebrity 名人 ｜ celebrate 慶祝 ｜ celebrated 著名的

C 題型練習

Select the best answer to complete the sentence.

1. His _____ are easy to understand.

   (A) instruct   (B) instructions

   (C) instructive   (D) instructively

2. The city accepted our _____.

   (A) proposal   (B) propose

   (C) proposed   (D) to propose

3. Too many people rely on the Internet for _____.

   (A) inform   (B) informed

   (C) information   (D) informational

4. Becoming famous was not her original _____.

   (A) intend   (B) intentional

   (C) intentionally   (D) intention

5. Many customers consider it a useful _____.

   (A) produce   (B) productive

   (C) product   (D) productively

答案和解析

1. (B)

解析 名詞可當作主詞。選項(A)是動詞，選項(B)是名詞，選項(C)是形容詞，選項(D)是副詞，答案是選項(B)。

翻譯 他的指示很容易理解。

單字 instruct (v.) 指示 |
instruction (n.) 指示 |
instructive 增進知識的 |
instructively 增進知識地

---

2. (A)

解析 名詞可當動詞受詞。選項(A)是名詞，選項(B)是動詞，選項(C)是動詞 propose 的過去式或過去分詞，選項(D)是 to 不定詞，答案是選項(A)。

翻譯 這城市接受我們的提案。

單字 accept 接受 | proposal 提案 |
propose 提出

---

3. (C)

解析 名詞可當作介系詞受詞的。選項(A)是動詞，選項(B)是形容詞，選項(C)是名詞，選項(D)是形容詞，答案是選項(C)。

翻譯 太多人依賴網路獲取資訊。

單字 rely on 依賴 | information 資訊 |
inform 通知 |
informed 消息靈通的 |
informational 新聞的

4. (D)

解析 名詞可當作主詞補語。雖然形容詞也可以，但因為空格前有 her，所以空格一定要放名詞。選項(A)是動詞，選項(B)是形容詞，選項(C)是副詞，選項(D)是名詞，答案是選項(D)。

翻譯 成名並不是她的原意。

單字 famous 有名的 | original 原本的 |
intention 意圖 | intend 有意 |
intentional 有意圖的 |
intentionally 有意圖地

---

5. (C)

解析 名詞可當受詞補語。雖然形容詞也可以，但因為空格前有冠詞 a，所以空格一定要放名詞。選項(A)是動詞，選項(B)是形容詞，選項(C)是名詞，選項(D)是副詞，答案是選項(C)。

翻譯 許多客戶認為這項產品很有用。

單字 consider 認為 | useful 有用的 |
product 產品 | produce 生產 |
productive 有生產力的 |
productively 有生產力地

D 應用練習 ▶ 解析 P. 505

Select the best answer to complete the sentence.

1. Economic _____ in South Korea was remarkable.
   (A) expand
   (B) expansive
   (C) expansively
   (D) expansion

2. The _____ of the museum was funded by the city.
   (A) renovate
   (B) renovation
   (C) renovated
   (D) to renovate

3. The company got _____ to build a new factory.
   (A) permission
   (B) permissively
   (C) permissive
   (D) permitted

4. They delayed their _____ by one hour.
   (A) depart
   (B) in departing
   (C) departure
   (D) to depart

5. We can count on their good _____.
   (A) willing
   (B) willingly
   (C) to will
   (D) will

6. These students took to _____.
   (A) voluntary
   (B) volunteering
   (C) voluntarily
   (D) be volunteering

7. What was impressive was their _____.
   (A) perform
   (B) performed
   (C) performance
   (D) to perform

8. What we need to have is _____.
   (A) diligent
   (B) diligently
   (C) be diligent
   (D) diligence

9. His efforts made him a great _____.
   (A) communicate
   (B) communicator
   (C) communicative
   (D) communicatively

10. Many experts considered it a good _____.
    (A) invest
    (B) to invest
    (C) investment
    (D) invested

題型 02 名詞的種類

 A 輕鬆上手

◉ 名詞大致可分作可數名詞和不可數名詞兩類。可數名詞又分成單數形和複數形。

The task **was** easy to carry out. 這個任務很容易完成。
☞ 主詞 task 是可數名詞單數,所以動詞要用單數形的 was。

These tasks **require** great skills. 這些任務需要具備很好的技能。
☞ 主詞 tasks 是可數名詞複數,所以動詞要用複數形的 require。

◉ 不可數名詞和可數名詞不同,它只有一種型態。不可數名詞不能和表「一個」的 a 或 an 或任何表數量的數字搭配使用。另外,不可數名詞當主詞時,動詞要用單數。

The company got **some** advice from an expert.
這家公司從專家得到一些建議。
☞ advice 是不可數名詞,不能和 an 搭配,但可以和 some 搭配使用。

Her advice always **makes** me think again. 她的建議總會讓我再三考慮。
☞ 在中文的理解,advice 是可數名詞,但在英文中它是不可數的。因為本句用 advice 當主詞,所以動詞要用單數 makes。

◉ 修飾名詞的詞類一般都是形容詞。不過名詞也可以修飾其他詞類。

You can submit the **application** form online. 你可以在線上繳交申請表。
☞ application 是名詞,form 也是名詞,application form 是複合名詞,這種詞類在多益中常常出現。

單字 task 任務 │ carry out 實現 │ advice 建議 │ expert 專家 │ submit 繳交 │ application form 申請表 │ online 線上

Ⓑ 基本題型

❶ 可數名詞

1. The _____ was done by a mechanic. 這項作業由一位技工完成。

(A) a job   (B) jobs   (C) these jobs   (D) job

解析 這個句子中,可數名詞 job 在主詞位置,因為動詞是 was,所以選項(B)和(C)不會是答案。The 後面不能接 a,所以選項(A)是錯誤答案。答案是選項(D)。要記得,可數名詞的單數形前面一定要有 a 或 the 這樣的冠詞。

單字 mechanic 技工

2. Many people are applying for such _____. 許多人正在應徵這樣的工作。

(A) job   (B) a jobs   (C) jobs   (D) the jobs

解析 job 是可數名詞,不能像選項(B)和(D)那樣使用。另外,如果像選項(A)那樣是單數形,它前面就一定要有 a 或 the,不過句子中並沒有 a 或 the,所以選項(A)也是錯誤答案,答案是選項(C)。可數名詞複數形,不能和 a 搭配使用,也不一定要和 the 搭配使用。

❷ 不可數名詞

3. They need more _____ for their new project.
他們需要為新案子尋找更多資訊。

(A) informations (B) an information (C) information (D) the informations

解析 用中文來理解，感覺 information 是可數名詞，但在英文中它是不可數名詞。所以不能像選項（B）那樣和 an 搭配使用，也不能使用選項（A）和（D）的複數形。答案是選項（C）。

單字 information 資訊 ┃ project 案子

4. This information _____ correct. 這項資訊正確無誤。

(A) are   (B) is   (C) being   (D) to be

解析 不可數名詞當主詞時，動詞一定要用單數，所以答案是選項（B）。選項（C）和（D）還要和其他動詞搭配，意思才完整。

單字 correct 正確的

❸ 複合名詞

5. The _____ rate was five percent per year. 利率是每年5%。

(A) to interest   (B) to interested   (C) interestingly   (D) interest

解析 名詞 interest 加上名詞 rate，是「利率」的意思。所以答案是選項（D）。因為大部分的副詞不能直接修飾名詞，所以選項（C）不會是答案。

單字 interest rate 利率 ┃ per year 每年

C 題型練習

Select the best answer to complete the sentence.

1. The _____ was placed by a regular customer.
    (A) those orders　(B) an order
    (C) order　　　　(D) orders

2. These _____ should be processed right away.
    (A) order　　　　(B) orders
    (C) an order　　　(D) the orders

3. We have some bad _____ for them.
    (A) a news　　　　(B) the news
    (C) these news　　(D) news

4. The latest news on the company _____ shocking.
    (A) are　　　　　(B) to be
    (C) being　　　　(D) is

5. They asked us how much the _____ fee was.
    (A) enter　　　　(B) entrance
    (C) to enter　　　(D) to entered

答案和解析

1. (C)

解析 這是用可數名詞 order 當主詞的句子，因為動詞是 was，所以選項(A)和(D)複數不會是答案。因為 the 之後不能接 these 或 those，所以選項(A)是錯的。the 之後也不能接 a 或 an，所以選項(B)也是錯的。答案是選項(C)。

翻譯 這張訂單是一位熟客下的。

單字 place an order 下訂單 | regular customer 熟客

2. (B)

解析 order 是可數名詞。因為 these 後要接複數名詞，所以選項(A)是錯的。these 也不能後接 an，所以選項(C)也不對。另外，these 後也不能有 the，所以選項(D)不用考慮。答案是選項(B)。

翻譯 這些訂單要立刻處理。

單字 order 訂單 | process 處理 | right away 立刻

3. (D)

解析 名詞 news 是不可數名詞，所以選項(A)和(C)都是錯的。因為空格前有 some，所以選項(B)也不對，答案是選項(D)。

翻譯 我們有一些壞消息要告訴他們。

單字 news 消息

4. (D)

解析 不可數名詞 news 是主詞，所以動詞要用單數，答案是選項(D)。選項(B)和(C)要搭配其他動詞才完整。

翻譯 這家公司最新的消息讓人震驚。

單字 latest 最新的 | shocking 震驚的

5. (B)

解析 名詞 entrance 加上名詞 fee，是「入場費」的意思，所以答案是選項(B)。動詞原形不能修飾名詞，所以選項(A)是錯的。

翻譯 他們問我們入場費是多少。

單字 entrance fee 入場費

Select the best answer to complete the sentence.

1. The _____ was issued by the government.
   (A) announcement
   (B) an announcement
   (C) announcements
   (D) these announcements

2. The _____ was written by a famous professor.
   (A) those reports
   (B) report
   (C) a report
   (D) reports

3. Those _____ were welcomed by the city council.
   (A) announcements
   (B) an announcement
   (C) the announcements
   (D) announcement

4. Those _____ were submitted by the special committee.
   (A) report
   (B) reports
   (C) a report
   (D) the reports

5. Few people in the city have _____ to clean air.
   (A) an access
   (B) accesses
   (C) access
   (D) the accesses

6. The factory does not have much _____.
   (A) an equipment
   (B) equipment
   (C) equipments
   (D) the equipments

7. Access to the information _____ denied.
   (A) were
   (B) being
   (C) was
   (D) to be

8. All equipment _____ working properly.
   (A) to be
   (B) are
   (C) being
   (D) is

9. The _____ manager was very competent.
   (A) to produce
   (B) production
   (C) productively
   (D) produce

10. The product failed to meet _____ standards.
    (A) safely
    (B) to safe
    (C) safety
    (D) in safety

題型 03　人稱代名詞

Ⓐ 輕鬆上手

◉ 提過的人事物再次出現時，要用**代名詞**來代稱。代名詞分作主格代名詞、受格代名詞、所有格形容詞。

1. 主格代名詞

在句中當作主詞的代名詞要用主格代名詞。

He is willing to take that risk. 他願意冒那個險。
☞ 代名詞是本句的主詞。

主格代名詞還有：I（我）、you（你／你們）、she（她）、it（它）、we（我們）、they（他們）等。

2. 受格代名詞

They criticized **us** for our strategy. 他們批評我們的策略。
☞ 代名詞 us 是動詞 criticized 的受詞。

介系詞的受詞是代名詞時，一定要用受格。

They are fond of **us**. 他們喜歡我們。
☞ 代名詞 us 是介系詞 of 的受詞。

受格代名詞還有：me（我）、you（你／你們）、her（她）、him（他）、it（它）、them（他們）等。

3. 所有格形容詞

I started **my** own business in 2012. 我在 2012 年創立自己的事業。
☞ 所有格形容詞 my 修飾名詞 business。

◉ 所有格形容詞還有：your（你的）、her（她的）、his（他的）、its（它的）、our（我們的）、their（他們的）等。

4. 所有格代名詞，表「誰的東西」＝「所有格形容詞＋名詞」。

Your apartment is small, while mine is large. 你的公寓很小，而我的公寓很大。
☞ 所有格代名詞 mine 表「我的某物」（＝我的公寓）的意思。

◉ 所有格代名詞有：yours（你的某物、你們的某物）、hers（她的某物）、his（他的某物）、ours（我們的某物）、theirs（他們的某物）等。

單字 **be willing to** 願意 ｜ **risk** 冒險 ｜ **criticize** 批評 ｜ **strategy** 策略 ｜ **be fond of** 喜歡 ｜ **own** 自己的

B 基本題型

❶ 主格代名詞

1. ＿＿＿＿ discussed the matter with us. 他們和我們討論這件事。

(A) Their　　(B) Them　　(C) With them　　(D) They

解析 空格是主詞的位置，所以要放主格代名詞。選項（A）是所有格，選項（B）是受格，選項（C）是「介系詞＋受格」，選項（D）是主格，所以答案是選項（D）。

單字 **discuss** 討論 ｜ **matter** 事情

❷ 受格代名詞

2. She guided ＿＿＿＿ along the bridge. 她沿著這座橋引導我們。

(A) we　　(B) us　　(C) our　　(D) to we

解析 因為空格位在及物動詞 guided 之後，所以要放受格代名詞。選項（A）是主格，選項（B）是受格，選項（C）是所有格，選項（D）是「介系詞＋主格」，所以答案是選項（B）。

單字 **guide** 引導 ｜ **along** 沿著

3. She designed the building for _____. 她為他們設計這棟建築物。

(A) their   (B) to their   (C) them   (D) they

解析 因為空格位在介系詞 for 之後,所以要放受格代名詞。選項(A)是所有格,選項(B)是「介系詞+所有格」,選項(C)是受格,選項(D)是主格。選項(A)之後還要再接名詞才合乎正確的文法,所以答案是選項(C)。

單字 design 設計

❸ 所有格形容詞

4. _____ success story inspired many young Americans.

他的成功故事鼓舞了許多美國年輕人。

(A) She   (B) Her   (C) Hers   (D) To she

解析 空格後的名詞 success story 是本句的主詞,所以空格要放修飾名詞的所有格形容詞。選項(A)是主格,選項(B)是所有格或受格,選項(C)是所有格代名詞,選項(D)是「介系詞+主格」。選項(D)文法不對,答案是選項(B)。

單字 success story 成功故事 | inspire 鼓舞

❹ 所有格代名詞

5. His talent is not as great as _____. 他的才華沒有你那麼優秀。

(A) yours   (B) to you   (C) your   (D) you

解析 這個句子將「他的才能」和「你的才能」做比較,所以答案是選項(A),是「你的……」之意,放進本句中就是「你的才能」了。

單字 talent 才華

C 題型練習

Select the best answer to complete the sentence.

1. _____ was having a business meeting with the staff.
   (A) Me   (B) My
   (C) I   (D) To me

2. We accept _____ as you really are.
   (A) your   (B) with you
   (C) yourself   (D) you

3. We competed with _____ in the Asian market.
   (A) they   (B) them
   (C) themselves   (D) their

4. _____ business trip was extended by a few days.
   (A) Him   (B) Himself
   (C) His   (D) He

5. Their food tastes good, but _____ tastes much better.
   (A) our   (B) us
   (C) we   (D) ours

答案和解析

1. (C)

解析 因為空格後是動詞 was，所以空格要放能當主詞的代名詞。選項(A)是受格，選項(B)是所有格，選項(C)是主格，選項(D)是「介系詞＋受格」，所以答案是選項(C)。

翻譯 我那時正在和員工進行商務會議。

單字 business meeting 商務會議 | staff 員工

2. (D)

解析 空格位在及物動詞 accept 之後，所以空格要放受格代名詞。選項(A)是所有格，選項(B)是「介系詞＋受格」，選項(C)是反身代名詞，選項(D)是受格或主格，所以答案是選項(D)。

翻譯 我們接受真實的你。

單字 accept 接受

3. (B)

解析 空格位在介系詞 with 之後，所以要放受格代名詞。選項(A)是主格，選項(B)是受格，選項(C)是反身代名詞，選項(D)是所有格，所以答案是選項(B)。

翻譯 我們和他們在亞洲市場競爭。

單字 compete 競爭 | market 市場

4. (C)

解析 本句的主詞是名詞 trip，所以空格要放修飾名詞的所有格形容詞。選項(A)是受格，選項(B)是反身代名詞，選項(C)是所有格或所有格代名詞，選項(D)是主格，所以答案是選項(C)。

翻譯 他的出差延長了幾天。

單字 business trip 出差 | extend 延長

5. (D)

解析 本句將「他們的食物」和「我們的食物」做比較，所以答案是選項(D)。

翻譯 他們的食物很美味，但我們的食物更好吃。

單字 taste 品嚐起來

D 應用練習　　　　　▶ 解析 P. 508

Select the best answer to complete the sentence.

1. _____ are developing a new medicine.
   (A) Our
   (B) Us
   (C) To us
   (D) We

2. _____ held strong opinions on government regulations.
   (A) Her
   (B) She
   (C) Herself
   (D) To her

3. He praised _____ for her bright ideas.
   (A) her
   (B) she
   (C) herself
   (D) to her

4. We approached _____ with a kind offer.
   (A) they
   (B) their
   (C) them
   (D) themselves

5. I depended on _____ to lead the discussion.
   (A) himself
   (B) him
   (C) with he
   (D) he

6. The employee complained to _____ about her working conditions.
   (A) we
   (B) our
   (C) with ours
   (D) us

7. We were impressed by _____ excellent service.
   (A) they
   (B) their
   (C) themselves
   (D) them

8. We are proud of the quality of _____ products.
   (A) we
   (B) us
   (C) ourselves
   (D) our

9. His paintings are not as famous as _____.
   (A) hers
   (B) she
   (C) herself
   (D) her

10. Our procedures are not as simple as _____.
    (A) they
    (B) their
    (C) themselves
    (D) theirs

題型 **04** 反身代名詞

Ⓐ 輕鬆上手

● 反身代名詞是「……自己」之意的代名詞。當主詞自己承受動作本身，或想要強調主詞時，就會使用反身代名詞。

Kevin injured **himself** while driving his car. 凱文開車的時候傷了自己。
☞ 本句是 Kevin 讓他自己受傷，所以要用反身代名詞 himself。

You must believe in **yourself** to succeed. 你必須相信自己可以成功。
☞ 本句是你應該相信你自己，所以要用反身代名詞 yourself。

● 反身代名詞有：himself（他自己）、myself（我自己）、yourself（你自己）、herself（她自己）、itself（它自己）、ourselves（我們自己）、yourselves（你們自己）、themselves（他們自己）等。

● 強調主詞的反身代名詞用法，稱作**反身代名詞的強調用法**。強調用法也可用在受詞。

The CEO answered the phone **herself**. 執行長親自接聽電話。
☞ 為了強調本句的主詞「執行長」而用 herself。強調用法的反身代名詞，要緊接在主詞之後，或整句最後。

Alice lived **by herself** in a small town. 艾利斯在一個小鎮獨居。
☞ 「by ＋反身代名詞」，是「獨自、獨力」的意思。

Skiing **in itself** is not that dangerous. 滑雪本身沒那麼危險。
☞ 「in itself」是「它本身」的意思。

單字 injure oneself 讓某人受傷

B 基本題型

❶ 反身代名詞的一般用法

1. Mary considers _____ a good worker. 瑪莉認為自己是個好員工。

(A) she　　(B) to her　　(C) for her　　(D) herself

解析 因為 considers 是及物動詞，所以空格要放受格代名詞。不過，因為句意中主詞 Mary 認為她自己是位好員工，所以要用反身代名詞，選項(D)是答案。

單字 consider 認為

2. We were pleased with _____. 我們對自己很滿意。

(A) we　　(B) ourselves　　(C) our　　(D) for we

解析 因為空格前有介系詞 with，所以空格要放代名詞的受格。不過，因為句意是我們自己對自己滿意，所以答案是反身代名詞選項(B)。

單字 pleased 滿意的

❷ 反身代名詞的強調用法

3. The mayor _____ prepared the food for us. 市長親自為我們準備食物。

(A) him　　(B) his　　(C) he　　(D) himself

解析 首先，沒有空格本句仍是完整句。主詞是 mayor，動詞是 prepared，選項中能放進空格的只有反身代名詞，所以答案是反身代名詞選項（D）。

單字 mayor 市長

❸ 反身代名詞的活用片語

4. John assembled the bookcase by _____. 約翰自己組裝書櫃。

    (A) he   (B) himself   (C) for him   (D) for he

解析 因為空格前有介系詞 by，所以空格要放代名詞的受格。by himself 是「獨自、親自」的意思，所以答案是選項（B）。

單字 assemble 組裝 ｜ bookcase 書櫃

5. Obesity in _____ is a risk factor for heart disease.
肥胖本身是心臟疾病的風險因素。

    (A) its   (B) for its   (C) to it   (D) itself

解析 因為空格前有介系詞 in，所以空格要放代名詞的受格。不過，in itself 是「它本身」的意思，所以答案是選項（D）。

單字 obesity 肥胖 ｜ risk 風險 ｜ factor 因素 ｜ disease 疾病

Select the best answer to complete the sentence.

1. We saw _____ in the mirror.

   (A) we   (B) our

   (C) ourselves   (D) for we

2. The hotel is proud of _____ for its unique location.

   (A) its   (B) to its

   (C) for it   (D) itself

3. The singer _____ organized the event for children in need.

   (A) herself   (B) she

   (C) her   (D) to she

4. The artist enjoys spending time by _____.

   (A) she   (B) for she

   (C) herself   (D) to she

5. An investment in _____ does not guarantee profits.

   (A) its   (B) itself

   (C) for its   (D) to its

答案和解析

1. (C)

解析 saw 是及物動詞，要後接受格代名詞。不過因為句子中要表達主詞看見自己，所以選項(C)是答案。

翻譯 我們在鏡中看見自己。

---

2. (D)

解析 因為空格前有介系詞 of，所以空格要放代名詞的受格。因為句意是旅館以自己為傲，所以答案是選項(D)。

翻譯 這家旅館對自己獨特的地點感到自豪。

單字 proud 驕傲 ｜ unique 獨特的 ｜ location 地點

---

3. (A)

解析 本句即使沒有空格仍是完整句，所以要放強調用法的反身代名詞，答案是選項(A)。

翻譯 這位歌手親自為需要幫助的孩童籌劃活動。

單字 organize 籌劃 ｜ event 活動

4. (C)

解析 因為空格前有介系詞 by，所以空格要放代名詞的受格。by herself 是「她自己」的意思，答案是選項(C)。

翻譯 這位藝術家很享受獨處的時間。

單字 artist 藝術家 ｜ spend 花(時間)

---

5. (B)

解析 因為空格前有介系詞 in，所以空格要放代名詞的受格。in itself 是「它本身」的意思，答案是選項(B)。

翻譯 投資本身並不保證帶來利潤。

單字 investment 投資 ｜ guarantee 保證 ｜ profit 利潤

D 應用練習　　　▶ 解析 P. 509

Select the best answer to complete the sentence.

1. The company prepared _____ for the merger.
   (A) itself
   (B) to its
   (C) for its
   (D) its

2. They had to protect _____ against discrimination.
   (A) they
   (B) themselves
   (C) for their
   (D) their

3. He was disappointed with _____ for failing his supervisor.
   (A) he
   (B) to his
   (C) himself
   (D) for he

4. I was ashamed of _____ for letting them down.
   (A) I
   (B) my
   (C) myself
   (D) to my

5. The doctor _____ greeted the new patient.
   (A) he
   (B) his
   (C) him
   (D) himself

6. The manager _____ attended the conference.
   (A) she
   (B) her
   (C) herself
   (D) hers

7. Unfortunately, the mechanic could not fix the car by _____.
   (A) he
   (B) himself
   (C) to him
   (D) for his

8. The director spent the holiday by _____.
   (A) she
   (B) to her
   (C) for hers
   (D) herself

9. Smoking in _____ is harmful to your health.
   (A) its
   (B) itself
   (C) for it
   (D) to its

10. Fishing in _____ does not harm the environment.
    (A) itself
    (B) to it
    (C) its
    (D) for its

題型 05 指示代名詞

A 輕鬆上手

◉ 所謂的**指示代名詞**，就是指出某人事物時使用的詞，也就是 this（這個）、these（這些）、that（那個）、those（那些）等。

指示代名詞中的 that 是「那個」的意思，those 是「那些」的意思，可以代替前面出現過的「the ＋名詞」，名詞單數時用 that，名詞複數時用 those。

The population of South Korea is larger than **that** of Canada.
南韓的人口數比加拿大更多。

☞ the population 是「the ＋名詞」，可以用 that 代替。
　因為 population 是單數，所以不能用 those，要用 that。

The best smartphones are **those** from South Korea. 最棒的智慧手機來自南韓。

☞ the smartphones 是「the ＋名詞」，可以用 those 代替。
　因為 smartphones 是複數，所以不能用 that，要用 those。

Those who are interested in swimming can enjoy themselves here.
對游泳有興趣的人可在這裡盡情享樂。

☞ 「those who . . .」的意思是「那些……的人」，因為 those 是複數，所以動詞也要用複數形。

◉ 「anyone who . . .」的意思是「任何……的人」，沒有關係代名詞 who 的話，anyone 可以接現在／過去分詞來修飾。現在／過去分詞也可以在 those 沒有接關係代名詞 who 時修飾 those。

Anyone who has artistic skills can apply to our school.
只要有藝術才能的人都可以申請我們的學校。

☞ 「anyone who . . .」是「任何……的人」的意思，沒有 who 的話，anyone 可以接動詞 -ing 或 -ed 來修飾。

Those who want to discuss the matter should submit a report.
想要討論這個議題的人應該繳交報告。

☞ 「those who . . .」是「那些……的人」的意思。

單字 population 人口 ｜ artistic 具藝術感的 ｜ skill 才能 ｜ discuss 討論 ｜
matter 議題 ｜ submit 繳交

B 基本題型

❶ 指示代名詞 that/those

1. The economy of the United States is similar in size to _____ of Europe.
美國的經濟規模和歐洲的類似。

(A) one (B) that (C) it (D) those

解析 the economy 是「the ＋名詞」，可以用 that 代替它並後接其他字詞。所以答案是選項（B）。因為 economy 是單數形，所以選項（D）those 不是答案。

單字 economy 經濟 ｜ similar 類似的

2. Our products are more expensive than _____ of our competitors.
我們的產品比競爭對手的還貴。

(A) those (B) they (C) ones (D) that

解析 our products 可以用 those 代替，並後接其他字詞。所以答案是選項（A）。因為 products 是複數形，所以選項（D）that 不會是答案。

單字 product 產品 ｜ expensive 貴 ｜ competitor 競爭對手

❷ those who

3. _____ who could not go to the concert were disappointed.
不能參加音樂會的人都很失望。

(A) That　　(B) These　　(C) Those　　(D) This

解析 因為能表現「那些……的人」的字是 those who，所以答案是選項（C）。
本句的動詞是 were，是複數動詞，所以要用複數的 those。

單字 disappointed 失望的

❸ anyone (who) / those (who)

4. _____ interested in learning English should read this book.
對學習英文有興趣的人都該閱讀這本書。

(A) That　　(B) It　　(C) This　　(D) Anyone

解析 本句本來是「anyone who is interested . . .」，這時動詞 -ing 或 -ed 前的「關係代名詞＋be 動詞」可以刪除。所以答案是選項(D)。

單字 interested 人有興趣的

5. _____ staying in our hotel can access the Internet free of charge.
我們旅館的房客都可以免費使用網路。

(A) That　　(B) No　　(C) Those　　(D) Who

解析 本句本來是「Those who stay . . .」，這時刪除 who 的話，要把動詞 stay 改成 staying。或者可以理解成，本句本來是「Those who are staying . . .」，刪除了「關係代名詞＋be 動詞」。所以答案是選項（C）。

單字 access 使用　|　free of charge 免費

C 題型練習

Select the best answer to complete the sentence.

1. The climate of Hawaii is much milder than _____ of Scotland.
   (A) one   (B) ones
   (C) that   (D) those

2. The opinions in this book are _____ of the authors.
   (A) that   (B) those
   (C) one   (D) ones

3. _____ who are developing the new software are highly creative.
   (A) Those   (B) One
   (C) These   (D) That

4. _____ who has a good imagination can write a good novel.
   (A) Those   (B) Anyone
   (C) That   (D) This

5. _____ who want to buy furniture online should visit this website.
   (A) Anyone   (B) That
   (C) It   (D) Those

答案和解析

1. (C)

解析 the climate 是「the ＋名詞」，可以用 that 代替它並後接其他字詞。所以答案是選項（C）。因為 climate 是單數，所以選項（D）those 不會是答案。

翻譯 夏威夷的氣候比蘇格蘭的溫和得多。

單字 climate 氣候 ｜ mild 溫和的

---

2. (B)

解析 the opinions 可以用 those 代替，並後接其他字詞。所以答案是選項（B）。因為 opinions 是複數，所以選項（A）that 不是答案。

翻譯 這本書的主張都是作者的意見。

單字 opinion 主張 ｜ author 作者

---

3. (A)

解析 有「那些……的人」之意的字是 those who，所以答案是選項（A）。本句的動詞是 are，是複數動詞，所以要用複數的 those。

翻譯 開發新軟體的人都非常有創意。

單字 develop 開發 ｜ highly 非常地 ｜ creative 有創意的

4. (B)

解析 「anyone who . . .」是「任何……的人」之意，答案是選項（B）。若用選項（A）Those，who 後的動詞要改成 have，因為 those 是複數。

翻譯 想像力不錯的人可以寫出傑出的小說。

單字 imagination 想像力 ｜ novel 小說

---

5. (D)

解析 「those who . . .」是「那些……的人們」之意，答案是選項（D）。若用選項（A），who 後的動詞要改成 wants，因為 anyone 是單數。

翻譯 想上網購買家具的人可以瀏覽這個網站。

單字 furniture 家具 ｜ online 網路的 ｜ website 網站

Select the best answer to complete the sentence.

1. Our strategy is quite different from _____ of our main competitor.
   (A) those
   (B) this
   (C) ones
   (D) that

2. My first impression of the city was similar to _____ of my best friend.
   (A) one
   (B) that
   (C) these
   (D) those

3. Some say that the palaces in France are larger than _____ in South Korea.
   (A) those
   (B) one
   (C) that
   (D) this

4. Our decisions are much better than _____ of our chief competitor.
   (A) that
   (B) it
   (C) those
   (D) they

5. There are _____ who make an effort to improve our community.
   (A) anyone
   (B) this
   (C) one
   (D) those

6. _____ who wish to attend the conference should contact Ms. Lee.
   (A) Anyone
   (B) Those
   (C) One
   (D) This

7. _____ involved in the accident can help from the hospital.
   (A) It
   (B) Who
   (C) No
   (D) Anyone

8. _____ who wants to sell products should learn how to communicate well.
   (A) Those
   (B) Anyone
   (C) This
   (D) Ones

9. _____ interested in marketing can take these courses.
   (A) That
   (B) No
   (C) Those
   (D) It

10. _____ trying to lose weight should work out regularly.
    (A) Those
    (B) That
    (C) This
    (D) Who

題型 06　其他代名詞

Ⓐ 輕鬆上手

● 有一些代名詞的用法較複雜，一定要正確熟記。

If you don't have a smartphone, you should buy one.
如果你沒有智慧手機，就應該買一支。
☞ 代名詞 one 可以代替可數名詞的單數形，
　　本句的 one 是用來代替 a smartphone。

Some workers are more motivated than others. 有些勞工比其他勞工更積極主
動。☞ 代名詞 others 是「其他人」的意思。

Some of her ideas are remarkable. 她有些想法很棒。
☞ 代名詞 some 表「全部中的一部分」。

There was no one left on the bus. 車上沒有人了。
☞ 和當作代名詞用的 none 不同，no 不能當作代名詞使用。
　　像本句這樣，no 可當作限定範圍的限定詞使用。

Both of the new factories are located in rural areas.
新成立的兩間工廠都座落在鄉村。
☞ 代名詞 both，是指稱兩個人事物的代名詞。

All of the products have been discarded and there are none left.
所有產品都遭丟棄，無一留存。
☞ none 是指稱「no ＋全部數量的名詞」的代名詞，表示量的時候用單數，
　　表示數的時候用複數。

單字 motivate 積極 ｜ remarkable 很棒的 ｜ factory 工廠 ｜ locate 座落 ｜
rural 鄉村的 ｜ product 產品 ｜ discard 丟棄

Ⓑ 基本題型

❶ one, others

1. A more expensive shirt is not always better than a cheaper _____.

一件昂貴的襯衫不會總比便宜的襯衫好。

(A) it   (B) that   (C) one   (D) ones

解析 代名詞 one 可以代替可數名詞的單數形。本句中，one 可以代替 shirt，所以答案是選項（C）。

單字 shirt 襯衫

2. Some companies are better than _____ in satisfying consumers.

有些公司比其他公司更能滿足消費者。

(A) their   (B) others   (C) which   (D) other

解析 代名詞 others 表「其他所有的」。本句中，others 的意思是「其他所有的公司」，答案是選項（B）。

選項（D）other 單獨存在時不能當作代名詞使用。

單字 company 公司 | satisfy 使滿意 | consumer 消費者

❷ some, no

3. _____ of their statements don't make any sense.
他們的一些聲明說不通。

(A) Any   (B) It   (C) Some   (D) One

解析 代名詞 some 表「全部中的一部分」。答案是選項（C）。因為本句的動詞部分以 don't 開始，所以選項（D）不會是答案。選項（A）any，要放在 not 之後。

單字 statement 聲明 ｜ make sense 說得通

4. Unfortunately, _____ employee in this department is creative enough for the task. 遺憾的是，這部門的員工都不夠有創造力以進行這項任務。

(A) no   (B) none   (C) an   (D) another

解析 因為本句的主詞是 employee，所以空格要放可以修飾 employee 的詞。答案是選項（A）。no 作為限定詞，可以放在可數名詞或不可數名詞前。

單字 employee 員工 ｜ department 部門 ｜ creative 有創造力的

❸ both

5. A good company cares about _____ quality and quantity.
優良的公司會質量兼顧。

(A) neither   (B) either   (C) nor   (D) both

解析 在多益中常出現的重要片語有 both A and B，是「A 和 B 兩者都」的意思。答案是選項（D）。

單字 care 在乎 ｜ quality 品質 ｜ quantity 數量

Select the best answer to complete the sentence.

1. The best products are the _____ that exceed your expectations.
   (A) one   (B) ones
   (C) that   (D) those

2. One guest was eating a slice of cake, while _____ were drinking wine.
   (A) the others   (B) other
   (C) the   (D) another

3. Sadly, there weren't _____ employees who tried to save the company.
   (A) none   (B) any
   (C) no   (D) every

4. Her company has three branches, while his company has _____.
   (A) no   (B) an
   (C) none   (D) the

5. There were two candidates, but the college didn't admit _____ of them.
   (A) neither   (B) either
   (C) none   (D) every

1. (B)

解析 空格要放能代替可數名詞複數形 products 的詞。所以答案是選項 （B）。選項（A）可以代替單數形。 另外，the 之後不能緊接 that、 those。

翻譯 最好的產品是超越你期望的產品。

單字 exceed 超越 ｜ expectation 期望

2. (A)

解析 因為空格後緊接 were，所以空格 要放表複數的代名詞。答案是選項 （A）。 選項（B）的 other，不能單獨當作 代名詞使用。

翻譯 一位客人在吃蛋糕，而其他客人在 喝酒。

單字 guest 客人 ｜ while 當

3. (B)

解析 空格要放搭配否定句的代名詞。答 案是選項（B）。 選項（A）的 none，在英文中 not 和 none 不能同時出現在一個句子中， 所以是錯誤的。 選項（C）和（D）不能當代名詞使用。

翻譯 遺憾地是，沒有任何員工嘗試解救 這家公司。

單字 sadly 遺憾地 ｜ save 解救

4. (C)

解析 因為空格前有及物動詞 has，所以 空格要放當作受詞的名詞或代名詞。 在選項中，能當作代名詞的只有選項 （C）none，所以是答案。

翻譯 她的公司有三個分支機構，而他的公 司完全沒有。

單字 branch 分支

5. (B)

解析 either 的意思是「兩者中任何一者」， 與 not 連用則代表兩者皆否，所以答 案是選項（B）。因為有 didn't，所以 不能再接 neither 或 none。 選項（D）只能當作限定詞使用，所以 不能放在代名詞的位置。

翻譯 有兩位候選人，然而這所大學沒有接 受任何一位。

單字 candidate 候選人 ｜ admit 接受

D 應用練習　　　　　▶ 解析 P. 511

Select the best answer to complete the sentence.

1. At our theater, you can buy two tickets and get _____ free.
   (A) every
   (B) the
   (C) another
   (D) no

2. Of her two daughters, one is a doctor and _____ is a lawyer.
   (A) the other
   (B) others
   (C) the others
   (D) another

3. They have known _____ for 20 years.
   (A) their
   (B) each other
   (C) no
   (D) other

4. Family members should help _____.
   (A) other
   (B) every
   (C) the
   (D) one another

5. Can I keep _____ of these souvenirs?
   (A) no
   (B) an
   (C) any
   (D) other

6. The staff didn't carry out _____ of those tasks.
   (A) none
   (B) neither
   (C) nothing
   (D) any

7. _____ of our competitors is considering that option.
   (A) No
   (B) Other
   (C) None
   (D) They

8. _____ of the events was organized by the committee.
   (A) None
   (B) The
   (C) Others
   (D) Every

9. You can choose _____ tea or coffee.
   (A) both
   (B) neither
   (C) either
   (D) nor

10. _____ the doctor nor the patient was surprised by the test result.
    (A) Either
    (B) Both
    (C) Or
    (D) Neither

Quick Test for **Parts 5 & 6** ▶解析 P. 512

Choose the one word or phrase that best completes the sentence.

1. The _____ of a new department was suggested by the panel.
   (A) creative
   (B) create
   (C) creation
   (D) creatively

2. Our company developed a close _____ with the college.
   (A) relatively
   (B) relation
   (C) relate
   (D) relative

3. What really matters is _____.
   (A) honest
   (B) honestly
   (C) to honest
   (D) honesty

4. These _____ need special care.
   (A) machines
   (B) the machine
   (C) a machine
   (D) machine

5. They bought second-hand _____.
   (A) furnitures
   (B) a furniture
   (C) the furnitures
   (D) furniture

6. Mary didn't know that her _____ was lost.
   (A) baggages
   (B) baggage
   (C) a baggage
   (D) the baggages

7. _____ supported the new policy.
   (A) Them
   (B) Their
   (C) Themselves
   (D) They

8. Her mother raised _____ to be generous.
   (A) she
   (B) for she
   (C) her
   (D) to her

9. Melanie is one of _____ best students.
   (A) his
   (B) him
   (C) himself
   (D) he

10. She introduced _____ to them.
    (A) she
    (B) for her
    (C) for she
    (D) herself

11. Jack learned to be kind to _____.
    (A) he
    (B) himself
    (C) for his
    (D) for he

12. Happiness in _____ is good for your health.
    (A) its
    (B) to its
    (C) with its
    (D) itself

13. The consumer market of Japan is much larger than _____ of South Korea.
    (A) one
    (B) those
    (C) that
    (D) these

14. The traditions of the United States are similar to _____ of Britain.
    (A) that
    (B) one
    (C) ones
    (D) those

15. _____ wishing to succeed should be generous.
    (A) Other
    (B) Anyone
    (C) It
    (D) No

16. _____ of the suggestions is acceptable to the department.
    (A) Both
    (B) Others
    (C) The others
    (D) Either

Questions 17–20 refer to the following email.

Thank you for _____ email. Paying me at the end of the month _____ fine
            17.   18.
with _____. _____ I hope you have a wonderful time in the United States.
     19.   20.

17. (A) you
    (B) your
    (C) yourself
    (D) yours

18. (A) are
    (B) were
    (C) to be
    (D) is

19. (A) me
    (B) I
    (C) myself
    (D) my

20. (A) Where in France will you stay?
    (B) Your company must pay me right now.
    (C) Why did your company borrow money from the bank?
    (D) I will fax a copy of my bankbook to you on Tuesday.

題型**01** 單複數一致

A 輕鬆上手

◉ 單複數一致的原則：主詞是單數，動詞就用單數形；主詞是複數，
動詞用複數形。

A good work of art **inspires** people. 好的藝術作品激勵人心。

☞ 因為主詞是單數，所以動詞要用單數形 inspires。主詞是複數的話，
動詞就要用複數形 inspire。

Another suggestion was made by the professor.
另一項建議是由該教授提出的。

☞ 主詞 suggestion 接受 another 修飾。another、each、every 是搭配可
數名詞單數形的限定詞。因為主詞是單數，所以動詞要用單數形 was。
主詞是複數，動詞就要用複數形 were。

A number of workers were against the proposal. 有些工人反對這項提案。

☞ a number of 是「一些」的意思，因為是複數，所以動詞一定要用複數
形 were。

◉ 接受 few、a few、several 修飾的詞一定是複數，主詞是複數，動詞也要用
複數形。主詞若是「the number of ＋複數名詞」（……的數量），動詞則
要用單數形。

Both she and her husband have been to Toronto. 她和她丈夫都去過多倫多。

☞ 主詞是 both A and B，動詞要用複數形。

The picture on the wall describes a small village. 牆上的照片描繪一個小村莊。

☞ 本句的主詞是 the picture，on the wall 只是修飾主詞的地方副詞，所以動詞要用單數形 describes。

單字 inspire 激勵 ｜ suggestion 建議 ｜ professor 教授 ｜ against 反對 ｜ proposal 提案 ｜ describe 描繪 ｜ village 村莊

Ⓑ 基本題型

❶ 主詞為不可數名詞或單數名詞

1. Every child _____ protection. 每個孩子都值得受到保護。

(A) deserve　　(B) to deserve　　(C) deserving　　(D) deserves

Every child 是單數名詞，動詞要用單數形，所以答案是選項（D）。
選項（B）是不定詞，選項（C）是動名詞或現在分詞，兩種都不能當動詞使用。

單字 deserve 值得 ｜ protection 保護

2. Each candidate _____ to be interviewed by the CEO.
每一位候選人都需接受執行長的面試。

(A) need　　(B) needs　　(C) to needing　　(D) needing

解析 candidate 是可數名詞的單數形，所以要找符合它的動詞單數形，答案是選項（B）。選項（D）的 V-ing 不能當動詞用。

單字 candidate 候選人 ｜ interview 面試

❷ the number of 和 there is/are

3. The number of foreign workers _____ growing in South Korea.
南韓的外勞數量正在成長。

(A) are   (B) to be   (C) being   (D) is

解析 the number of 的意思是「……的數量」，片語中的主詞是 number，所以動詞要用單數形，答案是選項(D)。選項(B) 和(C) 不能當動詞使用。

單字 **foreign** 外國的 ┃ **grow** 成長

4. There _____ a laboratory between the two buildings.
這兩棟建築物之間有一間實驗室。

(A) are   (B) is   (C) being   (D) to be

解析 「There is/are . . .」是「有……」的意思，be 動詞後若接單數名詞，動詞就要用單數形；名詞是複數的話，動詞就要用複數形。因為 a laboratory 是單數，所以答案是選項(B)。

單字 **laboratory** 實驗室

❸ 介系詞片語

5. Those pictures on the wall _____ a small town.
在牆上的那些照片描繪一個小城鎮。

(A) describes   (B) describing   (C) describe   (D) to describe

解析 片語 on the wall 是用「介系詞＋名詞」所構成的，不能當主詞。本句的主詞 pictures 是複數，所以動詞也要用複數形，答案是選項(C)。

C 題型練習

Select the best answer to complete the sentence.

1. Seeking professional help _____ always a wise thing to do.
   (A) are   (B) being
   (C) to be   (D) is

2. Every employee _____ an asset to the company.
   (A) being   (B) to be
   (C) is   (D) are

3. Few cities _____ more attractive than New York.
   (A) are   (B) to be
   (C) being   (D) is

4. There _____ many restaurants that serve Korean food.
   (A) is   (B) are
   (C) being   (D) to be

5. Efforts to save the elephants in Africa _____ being made.
   (A) is   (B) to be
   (C) being   (D) are

答案和解析

1. (D)

解析 動詞 V-ing 形可以表「做……的這件事」的意思，稱之為動名詞。動名詞當作主詞時，被視為單數形。所以答案是選項(D)。

翻譯 尋求專業的幫助永遠都是明智之舉。

單字 seek 尋求 | professional 專業的

---

2. (C)

解析 every 是「每個」的意思，要和單數名詞搭配使用，因此動詞也要用單數形，答案是選項(C)。

翻譯 每一位員工都是公司的資產。

單字 employee 員工 | asset 資產

---

3. (A)

解析 因為 few 是「很少、幾乎沒有」的意思，所以很容易以為要和單數名詞搭配，但是，few 之後一定要接複數名詞，因此動詞也要用複數形，答案是選項(A)。

翻譯 很少城市比紐約更有吸引力。

單字 attractive 有吸引力的

4. (B)

解析 如果句形「There + be 動詞」後接名詞複數，be 動詞就要用複數形；後接名詞單數，be 動詞就要用單數形。因為 restaurants 是複數形，所以答案是選項(B)。

翻譯 有很多餐廳供應韓式料理。

單字 serve 供應 | Korean food 韓式料理

---

5. (D)

解析 在本句中 to save elephants 是修飾 efforts 的不定詞片語。因為主詞是 efforts，所以動詞要用複數形。答案是選項(D)。

翻譯 有心人士努力拯救非洲的大象。

單字 effort 努力 | save 拯救

D 應用練習　　　　▶ 解析 P. 514

Select the best answer to complete the sentence.

1. Many _____ worried about the safety of those campers.
   (A) was
   (B) were
   (C) being
   (D) to be

2. Few _____ aware of the danger of using social media.
   (A) to be
   (B) being
   (C) was
   (D) were

3. Half of the cakes _____ baked by Emily.
   (A) were
   (B) was
   (C) being
   (D) to be

4. Some of the equipment _____ developed by a Canadian company.
   (A) being
   (B) to be
   (C) were
   (D) was

5. A few buildings _____ left without water.
   (A) to be
   (B) being
   (C) was
   (D) were

6. Several passengers _____ taken to a local hospital.
   (A) was
   (B) were
   (C) to be
   (D) being

7. The woman who has lost her necklace _____ unhappy.
   (A) to look
   (B) looking
   (C) looks
   (D) look

8. The people who _____ against the plan felt uncomfortable.
   (A) being
   (B) to be
   (C) was
   (D) were

9. The lake surrounded by forest trees _____ beautiful.
   (A) looks
   (B) look
   (C) to look
   (D) looking

10. The interviewer who asked him a lot of questions _____ disappointed.
    (A) to be
    (B) being
    (C) were
    (D) was

題型 **02** 簡單式

Ⓐ 輕鬆上手

所謂的時態,就是將動詞原型依時間而做出變化。

英文時態有過去式、現在式和未來式:

過去式 在動詞原型後加 ed

現在式 在動詞原型後加 -(e)s

現在式 在動詞原型前加 will 或 be going to

Accounting generally **deals** with checking financial accounts.
會計一般是在處理檢查財務帳目。

☞ 動詞 deal 後加了 -s 表示主詞是第三人稱單數,時態是現在式。
現在式表示是一般、普遍存在的情形。

The CEO **delivered** a powerful speech **yesterday**.
執行長昨天發表了震撼人心的演講。

☞ 動詞 deliver 用了過去式 delivered。過去式時常會和 yesterday 這樣清楚表達
過去時態的用語搭配使用。

The marketing department **won** the award **in 2016**. 行銷部門在 2016 年獲獎。

☞ 動詞 win 用了過去式 won。本句也有清楚表達過去時間的時間用語 in 2016。
在過去式中,過去式動詞常會搭配表達過去時態的時間用語。

Tomorrow, there **will** be gentle winds in most parts of the country.
明天國內大部分區域都會吹著和風。

☞ 未來式,時常會在動詞的原型前,加 will 或 be going to。

The bus **arrives** at 10:00 tonight. 這輛巴士會在今晚十點抵達。

☞ 雖然動詞是現在式，但在意思上卻有表達未來的意思。大致來說，動詞若有「去、來、出發、到達」的含意，就會用現在式表未來。

The report **is scheduled** for publication **in April**. 這份報告預計在四月出版。

☞ 表未來時，會用 will/be going to 或現在式來表現。表「預計要……」之意的「be scheduled . . .」，也是其中之一。

單字 accounting 會計 ｜ generally 一般 ｜ financial 財務的 ｜ account 帳目 ｜ deliver a speech 發表演講 ｜ gentle 和緩的 ｜ country 國家 ｜ schedule 安排計劃 ｜ publication 出版

B 基本題型

❶ 現在式

1. The company usually _____ its employees to have paid vacations.
這家公司通常允許員工休年假。

  (A) allow   (B) will allowed   (C) allowing   (D) allows

解析 首先，選項（B）文法錯誤，因為 will 要後接原型動詞。選項（C）不能用來當作動詞使用。因為 company 是第三人稱單數，所以答案是選項（D）。

單字 allow 允許 ｜ employee 員工 ｜ paid vacation 有薪假

❷ 過去式

2. We _____ the package six days ago. 我們在六天前收到包裹。

   (A) receive   (B) received   (C) have received   (D) has received

解析 ago 時常要和過去式搭配使用。如果有 ago 的話，就不能使用像選項（C）和（D）那樣的現在完成式，所以答案是選項（B）。

單字 receive 收到 ｜ package 包裹

3. At one time, the building _____ the tallest structure in the world.
這棟大樓曾經是世界最高的建築物。

   (A) were   (B) being   (C) was   (D) will was

解析 表「曾經有一度」之意的 at one time，是要和過去式搭配的片語。一般動詞的過去式都只有一個，但 be 動詞卻有 was、were 兩個。答案是選項（C）。

單字 at one time 曾經 ｜ structure 建築物

❸ 未來式

4. The year 2020 _____ the 10th anniversary of the foundation.
2020 年將是這個基金會的十週年。

   (A) were   (B) will be   (C) have been   (D) are

解析 本句的主詞是 2020 年，年度被視為是單數，所以動詞要用 is；不過，因為主詞 2020 年是未來的時間，所以時態是未來式，未來式要在原型動詞前加 will 或 be going to，所以答案是選項（B）。

單字 anniversary 週年 ｜ foundation 基金會

5. Her new album _____ to be released next year.
她的新專輯將在明年發行。

   (A) were due   (B) has be   (C) will due   (D) is due

解析 「be due to . . .」也是表未來的片語，它是「預計要……」的意思。答案是選項（D）。

單字 be due to 將會 ｜ release 發行

C 題型練習

Select the best answer to complete the sentence.

1. Our regular business hours _____ Monday through Friday,
   11:00 a.m. to 8:00 p.m.
   (A) is   (B) are
   (C) to be   (D) being

2. The shipment _____ processed two weeks ago.
   (A) was   (B) were
   (C) have been   (D) has been

3. The North American market once _____ up half of their sales.
   (A) make   (B) made
   (C) making   (D) have made

4. The international conference _____ held next month.
   (A) were held   (B) will have
   (C) will be   (D) being

5. We _____ to acquire Japanese companies.
   (A) is looked   (B) were looked
   (C) was looking   (D) are looking

答案和解析

1. (B)

解析 現在式和現在進行式不同，現在式有經過一段較長的時間的含意。答案是選項 (B)。
選項 (C) 和 (D) 不能當動詞使用，所以不能放在本句的動詞位置。

翻譯 我們的正常營業時間是週一至週五，早上 11 點到晚上 8 點。

單字 regular 一般的 ｜ business hour 營業時間

---

2. (A)

解析 ago 是最常和過去式搭配使用的代表字彙，答案是選項 (A)。因為 shipment 是單數，所以要用 be 動詞的單數形 was。因為有 ago，所以不能用選項 (C) 和 (D) 的現在完成式，這點要注意。

翻譯 這批貨物已在兩週前處理完畢。

單字 shipment 貨物 ｜ process 處理

---

3. (B)

解析 因為 once 是「曾經」的意思，表「過去曾做發生某事」，所以要用過去式。答案是選項 (B)。

翻譯 北美市場曾占他們一半的銷售額。

單字 once 曾經 ｜ make up 構成 ｜ sales 銷售額

4. (C)

解析 表未來最常用的方法就是在動詞原型前加 will。因為會議是被舉行，所以要用被動語態 be held，所以答案是選項 (C)。

翻譯 國際大會將在下個月舉辦。

單字 conference 大會 ｜ hold 舉辦

---

5. (D)

解析 表未來的用語還有一種，就是 be looking to，是「正在尋找……的方法」。因為主詞是 we，所以答案是選項 (D)。

翻譯 我們正在尋求收購日本公司。

單字 be looking to 正在尋找 ｜ acquire 收購

D 應用練習 ▶ 解析 P. 516

Select the best answer to complete the sentence.

1. Each year, millions of Americans _____ to make a difference.
   (A) volunteer
   (B) to volunteer
   (C) volunteering
   (D) volunteers

2. Mary _____ to work every day.
   (A) commute
   (B) has commuted
   (C) having commuted
   (D) commutes

3. Sales _____ up by 15 percent last year.
   (A) have gone
   (B) has gone
   (C) went
   (D) will go

4. Clara _____ transferred to the Chicago office last month.
   (A) were
   (B) will
   (C) being
   (D) was

5. Farming _____ once a growing industry in South Korea.
   (A) will
   (B) was
   (C) were
   (D) have been

6. At one time, we _____ merging with the insurance company.
   (A) considering
   (B) will considering
   (C) considered
   (D) will considered

7. We _____ develop new strategies.
   (A) was gone to
   (B) was going to
   (C) is gone to
   (D) are going to

8. It _____ be difficult to control the situation.
   (A) is going to
   (B) were going to
   (C) are gone to
   (D) was gone to

9. When you _____ in Tokyo, call Mr. Park immediately.
   (A) will arrive
   (B) arriving
   (C) arrive
   (D) to arrive

10. We will cancel the event if it _____.
    (A) will rain
    (B) to rain
    (C) rain
    (D) rains

題型 **03** 完成式和進行式

A 輕鬆上手

◉ 一般提到一個動作，就會想到該動作的開始、進行和結束。在英文中，進行和結束，分別由進行式和完成式來表現。

時態	時間	句構
現在進行式	此時正在發生的事	be 動詞現在式 + V-ing
過去進行式	過去某個時間正在進行的事	be 動詞過去式 + V-ing
現在完成式	連接過去和現在	have/has + 動詞的過去分詞
過去完成式	1. 連接過去到過去的時間 2. 比過去更早之前發生的事	had + 動詞的過去分詞

We **are holding** a discussion about the future of our company.
我們正在討論公司的未來。

☞ be 動詞的現在式 are，加上動詞的 -ing 型 holding，形成現在進行式。

Julie **was writing** a news article when the phone **rang**.
電話響時茉莉亞正在寫一篇新聞報導。

☞ be 動詞的過去式 was，加上動詞的 -ing 型 writing，形成過去進行式。本例句非常重要，因為過去正在進行的事被其他事情打斷時，原來進行的事要用**過去進行式**，打斷的事要用**過去式**。

◉ 不是所有的動詞都能成為進行式。在英文中，不能改變的事，就不能使用進行式。

We **know** that hard work pays off. 我們知道努力會有回報。

☞「知道」某個事實後，「知道」這個狀態就不能改變了，所以 know 不能用進行式，所以像 We are knowing 這樣的寫法是錯誤的。

◉ 現在完成式被認為是連接過去和現在，所以不能和表過去的字詞搭配使用。

This is the best movie that we **have ever seen**. 這是我們看過的最棒的電影。

☞「have seen」是 have 加上動詞 see 的過去分詞 seen。這是現在完成式，表從過去到現在看過的電影中最棒的一部。

By the time she was 25, Erica **had read** a hundred books.
在她 25 歲時，艾瑞卡已經閱讀了 100 本書。

☞「had read」是 had 加上動詞 read 的過去分詞 read。這是過去完成式，表示艾瑞卡到 25 歲時，已經讀了 100 本書。

單字 discussion 討論 | future 未來 | article 文章 | pay off 回報

B 基本題型

❶ 現在進行式和過去進行式

1. The company _____ for a talented graphic designer.
公司正在找一位有才華的平面設計師。

(A) are looking　(B) is looking　(C) were looked　(D) was looked

解析 這是在徵才廣告中常看到的句子。由於是正在發生的事，所以答案是選項(B)。因為主詞是第三人稱單數，所以選項(A)不是答案。因為是公司主動進行動作，所以被動式的選項(C)和(D)是錯的。

單字 talented 有才華的

2. All the guests _____ a good time yesterday. 昨天所有賓客都玩得很愉快。

(A) was having　(B) has had　(C) will had　(D) were having

解析 yesterday 是過去的時間，表過去那段時間正在發生的事，所以答案是選項(D)。因為主詞是複數，所以選項(A)不是答案。選項(C)文法錯誤。

單字 guest 賓客

❷ 不能使用進行式的動詞

3. Programmers _____ how the computer works. 程式設計師了解電腦如何運作。

(A) is understanding   (B) understand

(C) are understood   (D) are understanding

解析 understand 是英文中不能使用進行式的動詞，所以答案是選項（B）。因為不能使用進行式，所以選項（A）和（D）不用考慮。程式設計師不是被了解，所以選項（C）也是誤答。

單字 programmer 程式設計師 ｜ work 運作

❸ 現在完成式和過去完成式

4. The economists have recently _____ their predictions for 2020.
經濟學家最近對 2020 年發布了預測。

(A) release   (B) released   (C) releasing   (D) releases

解析 連接過去和現在要用現在完成式，所以答案是選項（B）。若要形成現在完成式，have 之後不能接選項（A）動詞原型、選項（C）動詞 -ing 型、選項（D）第三人稱單數現在式。

單字 economist 經濟學家 ｜ release 發布 ｜ prediction 預測

5. Nobody knew that the meeting _____ cancelled. 沒人知道會議已被取消。

(A) have been   (B) having been   (C) had been   (D) has being

解析 會議取消是比大家知道更早的事，所以要用過去完成式，答案是選項（C）。選項（D）文法錯誤。

單字 meeting 會議 ｜ cancel 取消

C 題型練習

Select the best answer to complete the sentence.

1. At the moment, we _____ on developing a new menu.
   (A) was focused
   (B) were to focusing
   (C) are focusing
   (D) focusing

2. This time next week, we _____ to New York.
   (A) are flew
   (B) will be flying
   (C) are been flying
   (D) was flying

3. Business owners generally _____ new regulations.
   (A) hate
   (B) are hating
   (C) was hating
   (D) were hating

4. The shipment _____ yet.
   (A) haven't arrived
   (B) isn't arrived
   (C) aren't arrived
   (D) hasn't arrived

5. Next month, the professor _____ science for 15 years.
   (A) have taught
   (B) will have taught
   (C) will taught
   (D) had taught

答案和解析

1. (C)

解析 因為是現在正在發生的事，所以要用現在進行式。答案是選項(C)。
因為主詞是 we，所以不能接像選項（A）那樣用 be 動詞單數。

翻譯 目前我們專注於開發新菜單。

單字 at the moment 目前 ｜ focus on 專注於 ｜ develop 開發

---

2. (B)

解析 表未來某個時間正在發生的事，要用「will be ＋ V-ing」。這叫做未來進行式，答案是選項(B)。

翻譯 下週此時，我們會飛去紐約。

單字 fly 飛

---

3. (A)

解析 本題在形容一般的現象，所以答案是選項(A)。

翻譯 企業主一般來說都討厭新規定。

單字 owner 擁有者 ｜ generally 一般來說 ｜ regulation 規定

4. (D)

解析 yet 時常出現在現在完成式的句子中。因為過去配送的東西到現在還沒收到，所以答案是選項(D)。
因為 arrive 是不及物動詞，所以不能用選項（B）和（C）的被動語態。

翻譯 貨物還未送達。

單字 shipment 貨物 ｜ arrive 抵達

---

5. (B)

解析 句意連接現在和未來的時間，所以要用未來完成式「will ＋ have ＋ V-ed」，答案是選項(B)。

翻譯 下個月，該教授將已教了 15 年的科學。

單字 professor 教授

D 應用練習　　　▶ 解析 P. 517

Select the best answer to complete the sentence.

1. According to experts, the economy _____ better.
   (A) is getting
   (B) are gotten
   (C) will gotten
   (D) getting

2. The public library _____ to a new location in May.
   (A) are moved
   (B) moving
   (C) to move
   (D) is moving

3. Michael didn't attend the ceremony because he _____ with a client.
   (A) were met
   (B) would met
   (C) was meeting
   (D) is meeting

4. All of us _____ overtime next month.
   (A) will be working
   (B) would worked
   (C) has worked
   (D) works

5. The area _____ of high mountains.
   (A) consist
   (B) is consisting
   (C) consists
   (D) was consisting

6. This pamphlet _____ information about all annual events.
   (A) contain
   (B) containing
   (C) were containing
   (D) contains

7. They have already _____ writing the marketing report.
   (A) finish
   (B) finished
   (C) finishing
   (D) to finishing

8. Our company _____ in business for almost 10 years.
   (A) have being
   (B) was having
   (C) has been
   (D) has being

9. By the time we came home, Jack had already _____ for the airport.
   (A) leaving
   (B) leaves
   (C) left
   (D) be left

10. By the end of the week, we _____ over 500 copies.
    (A) has sold
    (B) are been selling
    (C) would sell
    (D) will have sold

題型 **04** 主動和被動語態

Ⓐ 輕鬆上手

◉ **主動語態**：動作是由主詞執行

◉ **被動語態**（be 動詞＋ p.p.）：動作是被主詞所承受，做動作的人事物可以放在介系詞 by 之後。當時態改變，只要改變 be 動詞即可。

The museum **was designed by** an American architect.
這間博物館由一位美國建築師所設計。
☞ 博物館是被設計的對象，所以要用被動語態「be 動詞＋ p.p.」。

The new system **is being developed** by a Korean scientist.
新系統正由一位韓國科學家開發。
☞ 系統正在被開發，所以要用進行式被動語態「be 動詞＋ being ＋ p.p.」。

◉ 在完成式被動語態「have 動詞＋ been ＋ p.p.」中，have 動詞配合句子的時態做改變就可以了。

The area **had been studied** by the professor. 這個區域已經被這位教授所研究。
☞ 地區已經被教授研究，所以要用完成式被動語態「have 動詞＋ been ＋ p.p.」。

◉ 句型「**be 動詞＋ p.p. ＋ to 不定詞**」也很常見，to 不定詞常用來做受詞補語。

They **were advised to** leave the building. 他們被建議離開這棟建築物。
☞ 他們是被建議的對象，所以要用被動語態。

● 不是所有的動詞都能使用被動語態。首先，不及物動詞因為沒有承受動作的對象，原則上都不能使用被動語態。另外，及物動詞中也有不能使用被動語態的動詞。

That jacket doesn't suit Kevin. 那件夾克不適合凱文。

☞ suit 雖然是及物動詞，但意思為「（衣服或顏色等）很合適、很搭」時，就不能用被動語態。

單字 museum 博物館 | design 設計 | architect 建築師 | develop 開發 | scientist 科學家 | area 地區 | advise 建議 | suit 搭配

B 基本題型

❶ 被動語態基本句型

1. The temperature _____ at 20°C. 溫度被維持在攝氏20度。

(A) are maintaining   (B) is being maintain

(C) maintain   (D) was maintained

解析 溫度是被維持的對象，所以正確的被動語態選項（D）是答案。

單字 temperature 溫度 | maintain 維持

❷ 進行式和完成式被動語態

2. Many employees _____ by robots. 很多員工都被機器人取代了。

(A) replace　(B) was replacing　(C) are being replaced　(D) are replace

解析 這個句子表示了正在發生的被動變化，所以答案是被動語態進行式選項（C）。
及物動詞 replace 可接介系詞 by，也可以不接，不接 by 時是表示前者代替後者。

單字 replace 取代

3. That fact _____ to the engineers. 工程師一向都了解那項事實。

(A) have known　　　　　(B) has known
(C) having known　　　　(D) had been known

解析 事實被工程師所知道，所以要用過去完成式被動語態，答案是選項（D）。
選項（C）是不符文法的。

單字 engineer 工程師

❸ 不定詞的被動語態

4. The visitors _____ to enter the laboratory. 訪客被允許進入實驗室。

(A) were allowing　　　　(B) were allowed
(C) allows　　　　　　　(D) is allowed

解析 若 allow 要用被動語態的話，必須是「be 動詞＋ allowed ＋ to」的句型。所以答案是選項（B）。
若把選項（D）的 is 改成 are 也是答案。

單字 visitor 訪客　|　enter 進入　|　laboratory 實驗室

5. The price of the new model _____ to go up. 新型號的價格被預期會上漲。

(A) are expecting　　　　(B) is expected

(C) were expected　　　　(D) was expects

解析 若 expect 要用被動語態的話，必須是「be 動詞＋ expected ＋ to」的句型。所以答案是選項（B）。
若把選項（C）的 were 改成 was 也是答案。

單字 expect 預期　|　go up 上漲

C 題型練習

Select the best answer to complete the sentence.

1. Several cars _____ in a fire.

    (A) is destroyed

    (B) are destroying

    (C) were destroyed

    (D) destroying

2. The patient _____ by a famous doctor.

    (A) are treated

    (B) was being treated

    (C) were treating

    (D) was treat

3. The method _____ by designers.

    (A) have explored

    (B) explore

    (C) being explore

    (D) has been explored

4. The intern _____ to work overtime.

    (A) were asked

    (B) ask

    (C) was asked

    (D) asking

5. They _____ to try the new Thailand restaurant.

    (A) were invited

    (B) was inviting

    (C) invite

    (D) inviting

答案和解析

1. (C)

解析 車輛被破壞，所以要用被動語態。因此正確的被動語態選項（C）是答案。

翻譯 有數輛車遭到燒毀。

單字 destroy 摧毀

---

2. (B)

解析 患者被醫師治療，所以答案是選項（B）。選項（A）要將 are 換成 is 才是答案。

翻譯 病患正由一位知名醫生治療。

單字 patient 病患 ｜ treat 治療 ｜ famous 知名的

---

3. (D)

解析 不是方法去探究什麼，而是被探究，所以答案是選項（D）。選項（C）不符合文法。

翻譯 設計人員已經探索過那個方法。

單字 method 方法 ｜ explore 探索

4. (C)

解析 實習生是被要求，動詞 ask 後要加 to，答案是選項（C）。

翻譯 這位實習生被要求加班。

單字 intern 實習生 ｜ work overtime 加班

---

5. (A)

解析 人們是被邀請，所以答案是選項(A)。

翻譯 他們被邀請去嘗試那間新泰國餐廳。

單字 invite 邀請 ｜ try 嘗試

D 應用練習

▶ 解析 P. 518

Select the best answer to complete the sentence.

1. Experts say that such accidents can _____.
   (A) was preventing
   (B) being prevent
   (C) be prevented
   (D) prevent

2. This book should _____ to the professor.
   (A) be sent
   (B) being send
   (C) be sending
   (D) sent

3. The lunch _____ by the housemaid.
   (A) were served
   (B) was being served
   (C) serve
   (D) was serve

4. The tables _____ in a unique manner.
   (A) decorate
   (B) being decorate
   (C) decorated
   (D) were being decorated

5. Her Internet access _____ by her parents.
   (A) have block
   (B) has been blocked
   (C) blocked
   (D) block

6. These buildings _____ by our company.
   (A) have been constructed
   (B) constructed
   (C) to construct
   (D) have construct

7. Anne _____ to be the brightest student in the country.
   (A) believe
   (B) was believed
   (C) were believed
   (D) believing

8. The interns _____ to work harder.
   (A) were encouraged
   (B) encourage
   (C) encouraging
   (D) to encourage

9. You _____ to attend all staff meetings.
   (A) requires
   (B) be require
   (C) be requiring
   (D) are required

10. He _____ to be the greatest inventor in history.
    (A) were thinking
    (B) think
    (C) was thought
    (D) will thought

題型 **05** 假設語氣

Ⓐ 輕鬆上手

◉ 假設法是用 **if** 表達猜測、願望、假設或可能性等，分為與現在事實相反，以及與過去事實相反兩種。

> 與現在事實相反

> If + 子句主詞 + 過去式（were/did），
>   if 子句
>
> + 主句主詞 + would/might/could/should + 原型動詞
>   主要子句

If I **could** afford it, I **would** travel around the world.
如果我負擔得起，我會環遊世界。

☞ 與現在事實相反的假設語氣，對現在無法去環遊世界表達可惜之情，if 子句和主要子句的動詞都要用過去式。

> 與過去事實相反

> If + 子句主詞 + 過去完成式，
>   if 子句
>
> + 主句主詞 + might/could/should/ would have + 過去分詞
>   主要子句

If it **had not been** for her efforts, the company **would have** failed.
如果不是她的努力，公司早就倒閉了。

☞ 與過去事實相反的假設語氣，因為有她的努力，所以公司才沒有倒閉，if 子句和主要子句的動詞都要用過去完成式。

If they **had completed** the project earlier, they **could** enjoy their free time now.
如果他們更早完成案子，他們現在就可以享受空閒時間了。

☞ 因為他們沒有完成案子，所以現在無法休息。混合假設法，主要子句會有 now、today 類似的字詞。

對未來做假設

If + 子句主詞 + should/were + to 不定詞，
　　　　　　　if 子句

+ 主句主詞 + will/would/may/might/can/could + 原型動詞
　　　　　　主要子句

Should you have any questions, call me at 755-8925.
如果你有任何問題，打 755-8925 給我。

☞ 本句的 if 子句本來是 If you should have any questions，用了省略法，
　將 if 省略，並將 you 和 should 倒裝。

◉ 表命令（order）、建議（suggest、propose）、請求（demand、request）、
主張（insist）的動詞，它後接的 that 子句，要用「（should）＋原型動詞」的
句型。要注意，這些動詞即使是用過去式，that 子句的動詞也要用原型。

The CEO **ordered** that Mary **be** promoted to senior manager.
執行長下令讓瑪莉晉升為高級經理。

☞ 雖然本句的 ordered 是過去式，但 that 子句不能用 was promoted，
　要用 be promoted。

單字 afford 負擔 ｜ effort 努力 ｜ fail 失敗 ｜ order 下令 ｜ promote 晉升

Ⓑ 基本題型

❶ 與現在事實相反

1. _____ smarter, I would invent something completely new.
要是我更聰明些，我會發明完全嶄新的東西。

(A) I was　　(B) If I was　　(C) Were I　　(D) If were I

解析 這是與現在事實相反的句子。用省略法，將 if 刪除，主詞和動詞對調。原來是
If I were，省略後變成 Were I，所以答案是選項（C）。選項（B）看起來像是
假設句，但不符文法，所以一定是誤答，不用考慮。

單字 smart 聰明 ｜ invent 發明 ｜ completely 完全

❷ 與過去事實相反

2. _____ for his advice, I would have made a terrible mistake.
要不是他的建議，我早已犯下嚴重的錯誤。

(A) If not be　　(B) If been not　　(C) Has it been　　(D) Had it not been

解析 本句 if 子句的原來型式是 If it had not been for his advice。用省略法將 if 刪除，it 和 had 倒裝，所以答案是選項 (D)。

單字 advice 建議　|　terrible 嚴重的

❸ 混合假設法

3. If we had been more careful, we _____ no problem today.
如果我們更小心一些，今天就不會出問題了。

(A) will have　　(B) have　　(C) would have　　(D) would had had

解析 if 子句是過去完成式，主要子句有 today，所以本句是用混合假設法。因此答案是選項 (C)。

❹ 對未來做假設

4. If you _____ meet him, tell him to be kind to his neighbors.
萬一你碰到他，告訴他對鄰居要和善。

(A) had　　(B) have　　(C) having　　(D) should

解析 本句能放進空格的選項，只有選項 (D)。其他的選項都不符文法。本句的 if 子句，也可以換成 Should you meet him。

❺ 表命令／建議／請求／主張的動詞

5. They suggested that the price of the product _____ reduced.
他們建議降低產品價格。

(A) were　　(B) be　　(C) was be　　(D) was having

解析 suggest 表「建議」之意時，後接的 that 子句一定要用「(should)＋原型動詞」。所以答案是選項 (B)。

單字 suggest 建議　|　product 產品　|　reduce 降低

C 題型練習

Select the best answer to complete the sentence.

1. If I _____ you, I would turn down that job offer.
   (A) am   (B) are
   (C) were   (D) was

2. _____ harder, I could have made more friends.
   (A) If I have tried   (B) If I try
   (C) Had I trying   (D) Had I tried

3. If she had published her novel earlier, I _____ reading it today.
   (A) will enjoy   (B) would enjoy
   (C) would enjoyed   (D) will enjoyed

4. If we _____ South Korea, we would enjoy eating kimchi.
   (A) to visit   (B) be to visit
   (C) are visit   (D) were to visit

5. She proposed that the new medicine _____ tested on animals.
   (A) be   (B) were
   (C) was be   (D) were be

答案和解析

1. (C)

解析 因為主要子句用了 would，所以 if 子句是要表達與現在事實相反，if 子句中的 be 動詞，要用 were，所以答案是選項 (C)。

翻譯 如果我是你，我會婉拒那份工作邀約。

單字 **turn down** 拒絕 | **job offer** 工作邀約

---

2. (D)

解析 主要子句是與過去事實相反的型式，所以 if 子句原來應該是 If I had tried harder，但本句使用省略法，省略 if 然後 had 和 I 倒裝，答案是選項 (D)。

翻譯 如果我更努力一點，我應該可以交到更多朋友。

---

3. (B)

解析 if 子句是過去完成式，主要子句中有 today，所以是混合假設法，答案是選項 (B)。

翻譯 如果她的小說能早點出版，我今天就可以好好拜讀。

單字 **publish** 出版 | **novel** 小說

4. (D)

解析 If 子句使用 were to 對未來做假設，所以答案是選項 (D)。
選項 (C) 不符文法。

翻譯 如果我們到南韓旅遊，就可以好好享用泡菜。

單字 **kimchi** 泡菜

---

5. (A)

解析 表「提議」之意的動詞 propose 後接 that 子句，要用「(should)＋動詞原型」，答案是選項 (A)。
選項 (C) 和 (D) 不符文法。

翻譯 她提議這種新藥物要進行動物測試。

單字 **propose** 提議 | **medicine** 藥物 | **test** 測試

D 應用練習　　　　　　　▶ 解析 P. 519

Select the best answer to complete the sentence.

1. _____ more money, I would
   move to Canada.
   (A) If I has
   (B) If I have
   (C) Had I
   (D) Have I

2. If she _____ more adventurous,
   she would take more risks.
   (A) were
   (B) was be
   (C) were being
   (D) being

3. If she _____ there, she wouldn't
   have been hurt.
   (A) has not being
   (B) has being
   (C) had not been
   (D) have been

4. If they _____ more careful, they
   could have avoided the crisis.
   (A) have been
   (B) having been
   (C) has being
   (D) had been

5. If you _____ him to me, we
   would be good friends by now.
   (A) having introduced
   (B) to introduce
   (C) had introduced
   (D) introducing

6. If the company _____ that risk,
   it would have more money today.
   (A) has taken
   (B) had taken
   (C) have taking
   (D) has taking

7. _____ our college, don't hesitate
   to contact our president.
   (A) Should you visit
   (B) Visit
   (C) If should you visit
   (D) If visit

8. If you _____ smoking, your health
   would improve.
   (A) was stop
   (B) were stop
   (C) to be stopped
   (D) were to stop

9. The committee demanded that
   more time _____ allowed to solve
   the problem.
   (A) be
   (B) were
   (C) being
   (D) was

10. The expert insisted that companies
    _____ employees to be more
    imaginative.
    (A) to encourage
    (B) encourage
    (C) encourages
    (D) encouraging

Quick Test for **Parts 5 & 6**   ▶ 解析 P. 520

Choose the one word or phrase that best completes the sentence.

1. Few _____ willing to challenge the CEO.
   (A) was
   (B) being
   (C) were
   (D) to be

2. Half of the students _____ been learning English for eight years.
   (A) has
   (B) have
   (C) having
   (D) to have

3. The city government is making _____ to improve road safety.
   (A) efforts
   (B) asset
   (C) laboratory
   (D) protection

4. Universities _____ a major role in society.
   (A) plays
   (B) play
   (C) playing
   (D) to play

5. The company _____ big profits last year.
   (A) make
   (B) has made
   (C) have made
   (D) made

6. If it _____ cloudy, the machine will not work properly.
   (A) is
   (B) will be
   (C) was
   (D) were

7. You should report to your supervisor on a(n) _____ basis.
   (A) important
   (B) international
   (C) regretful
   (D) regular

8. Greg _____ a guest when the phone rang.
   (A) greets
   (B) was greeting
   (C) has greeted
   (D) is greeting

9. This time tomorrow, we _____ to Los Angeles.
   (A) drove
   (B) will driven
   (C) will be driving
   (D) driving

10. Our company _____ with the city government since 2002.
    (A) worked
    (B) has worked
    (C) will working
    (D) had been worked

11. The college _____ a new report yesterday.
(A) released
(B) looked
(C) flew
(D) arrived

12. These kinds of mistakes can _____ .
(A) were avoided
(B) avoid
(C) be avoid
(D) be avoided

13. They should _____ of that change.
(A) were informing
(B) inform
(C) be informed
(D) are informing

14. The event _____ by a local church.
A) has organized
(B) organized
(C) was organized
(D) has organizing

15. _____ you have any complaints, send a letter to the mayor.
(A) Should
(B) Were
(C) To
(D) Do

16. If we can _____ costs, we will be successful.
(A) enjoy
(B) invent
(C) reduce
(D) offer

Questions 17–20 refer to the following information.

Thank you _____ buying our washing machine. Our washing machines
      17.
_____ by thousands of Americans since 2010. _____ Visit our website for
 18.   19.
more information _____ this washing machine.
               20.

17. (A) of
(B) by
(C) on
(D) for

18. (A) was used
(B) have been used
(C) were using
(D) are using

19. (A) The first washing machine was produced in 1865.
(B) Few people understand how washing machines work.
(C) Many people enjoy washing the dishes.
(D) Just like those customers, you will be pleased with this washing machine.

20. (A) about
(B) because
(C) although
(D) despite

題型 **01** 不定詞

 A 輕鬆上手

◉ 不定詞就是指「to＋原型動詞」。它可以在句子中依不同的用法，表達名詞「做某事」、形容詞「做某事的」、副詞「為了要去做某事地」等意思。使用不定詞的原因，是因為不定詞能表現單一名詞、形容詞、副詞無法表現的複雜目的。

■ 不定詞當名詞用法的意思是「做某事」，可以在句中當主詞、受詞、補語。

To serve the community is our mission. 服務社區是我們的使命。

☞ to serve the community 是句子的主詞，因為「服務社區」無法用一個字表現，所以用不定詞。

They agreed **to discuss the matter the next day**. 他們同意隔天再討論這件事。

☞ to discuss the matter the next day 是句子的受詞，也是因為「隔天討論」無法用一個字表現，所以用 to 不定詞。

Their aim was **to make good products**. 他們的目標是製作優良產品

☞ to make good products 是句子的補語，因為「製作優良產品」無法用一個字表現，所以用不定詞。

■ 不定詞當形容詞用法的意思是「做某事的、要去做某事的」，可以修飾放在它前面的名詞或代名詞。

They had nothing **to sell**. 他們無貨可賣。

☞ to sell 用來修飾 nothing。無論含意是否複雜，都可以用不定詞來表現。

■ 不定詞當副詞用法的意思是「為了要去做某事」、「……地去做某事」，
可當句子的副詞以表現單一副詞無法表現的複雜含意。

Interestingly, Jane went to London **to learn French**. 有意思地是，珍到倫敦學習法文。
☞ to learn French 是本句的副詞，用單一副詞無法表現這種複雜含意。

單字 serve 服務 ∣ community 社區 ∣ agree 同意 ∣ matter 事情 ∣ aim 目標 ∣
product 產品 ∣ interestingly 有意思地 ∣ learn 學習

Ⓑ 基本題型

❶ 不定詞當名詞用

1. _____ about technology is a wise thing to do. 學習技術是明智之舉。

(A) Learn　　(B) Learned　　(C) Learns　　(D) To learn

解析 從空格到 technology 是本句的主詞，所以空格要放名詞「做某事」的字詞，
答案是選項(D)。動詞若不改成不定詞或動名詞型式，就不能當作主詞來用。

單字 technology 技術

2. We decided _____ a branch in New York. 我們決定在紐約開設分店。

(A) opening　　(B) to open　　(C) open　　(D) opens

解析 本句是「決定要去做某事」的意思，在 decide 後要接不定詞，所以答案是
選項(B)。decide 不能接動名詞，所以選項(A)是錯的。

單字 decide 決定 ∣ branch 分店

3. Our mission is _____ people stay healthy. 我們的使命是幫助大家保持健康。

(A) helps　　(B) helped　　(C) to help　　(D) to helping

解析 具「做某事」之意的不定詞，也可以當句子的補語。所以答案是選項(C)。

單字 mission 使命 ∣ stay healthy 保持健康

❷ 不定詞當形容詞用

4. She has the ability _____ quick decisions. 她有快速下決定的能力。

    (A) to make   (B) makes   (C) making   (D) make

解析「去做某事的能力」可以用「the ability ＋不定詞」來表現，
所以答案是選項 (A)。
本句的片語是由「be able ＋不定詞（能做……）」演變而來。

單字 **ability** 能力 ｜ **quick** 快速的 ｜ **decision** 決定

❸ 不定詞當副詞用

5. We are pleased _____ with you. 我們和你合作感到很愉快。

    (A) work   (B) works   (C) to work   (D) to working

解析「……地去做什麼」可以用 to 不定詞來表現，所以答案是選項 (C)。
不定詞當副詞使用時，可以表現情感的原因、判斷的根據、結果等。

單字 **pleased** 愉快的

Select the best answer to complete the sentence.

1. _____ in a foreign country is not easy.
   (A) Live   (B) Lives
   (C) To live   (D) Lively

2. The company expects _____ the project in May.
   (A) complete   (B) to complete
   (C) to completing   (D) completing

3. Their goal was _____ a new dictionary.
   (A) to publish   (B) to publishing
   (C) published   (D) publishes

4. They regretted their decision _____ him.
   (A) hire   (B) hires
   (C) to hire   (D) hired

5. In order _____ well, we should understand what makes us happy.
   (A) living   (B) lived
   (C) to living   (D) to live

1. (C)

解析 to 不定詞在本句當主詞,答案是選項(C)。選項(D)是形容詞,原則上是不能當主詞的。

翻譯 在國外居住並不容易。

單字 foreign 國外的 | lively 活潑的

---

2. (B)

解析 從空格到 May 是 expects 的受詞。因為 expect 要用不定詞當受詞,所以答案是選項(B)。當受詞是未來的事時,通常會用不定詞當受詞,但並非總是如此。

翻譯 公司預定在五月完成專案。

單字 expect 預定 | complete 完成

---

3. (A)

解析 不定詞在本句當補語,答案是選項(A)。若將動詞的型態轉變成不定詞,它的意思和功能也會不同。

翻譯 他們的目標是出版一本新字典。

單字 goal 目標 | publish 出版

4. (C)

解析 「做某事的決定」要用「decision ＋不定詞」來表現,答案是選項(C)。

翻譯 他們對僱用他的決定感到後悔。

單字 regret 後悔 | decision 決定 | hire 僱用

---

5. (D)

解析 若要表現「為了……而做」之意,可用片語「in order ＋不定詞」,答案是選項(D)。
本句也可以直接用 To live well 開頭,但較不正式。

翻譯 為了生活幸福,我們應該了解是什麼讓我們感到快樂。

D 應用練習　　　　　　　▶ 解析 P. 522

Select the best answer to complete the sentence.

1. _____ a new language calls for time.
   (A) Learn
   (B) To learn
   (C) Learned
   (D) Learns

2. _____ a new machine requires imagination.
   (A) To invent
   (B) Invented
   (C) Invents
   (D) Invent

3. They planned _____ Seoul soon.
   (A) visiting
   (B) to visit
   (C) visited
   (D) visits

4. We want _____ our city.
   (A) improving
   (B) improve
   (C) to improve
   (D) improves

5. In the 1960s, the trend was _____ cheap clothes.
   (A) produced
   (B) to produce
   (C) produces
   (D) to producing

6. The purpose of the report is _____ new ways to protect the environment.
   (A) to discuss
   (B) discussed
   (C) with discussing
   (D) discusses

7. There is no way _____ the future.
   (A) predict
   (B) predicts
   (C) to predicting
   (D) to predict

8. There are plans _____ more parks.
   (A) to build
   (B) build
   (C) built
   (D) to building

9. His instructions were too difficult _____.
   (A) follow
   (B) to follow
   (C) follows
   (D) followed

10. The task was easy enough _____.
    (A) complete
    (B) completes
    (C) to complete
    (D) completed

題型 02　to 不定詞和不含 to 的不定詞

Ⓐ 輕鬆上手

● 因為 to 不定詞和動詞後加 -ing 的動名詞，能表現用單一單字無法表現的含意，所以 to 不定詞和動名詞出現在許多片語中。

● 和未來的事有關的動詞，一般來說要接 to 不定詞。

She **hoped** to travel to Thailand. 她希望到泰國旅遊。

☞ 因為 hope 是含未來的動詞，所以要接 to 不定詞，而不是動名詞。
表具有推測含意的動詞，也要後接 to 不定詞。

Her statement **appeared** to be false. 她的說法似乎並不正確。

☞ 「appear to . . .」是「看似」的意思。

● 「**be about + to 不定詞**」表「即將要做」的意思。

The factory **was about to be** inspected by them. 工廠即將被他們檢查。

☞ 在「be about ＋ to 不定詞」這片語中，可以透過 be 動詞的改變來表示時態。
to 不定詞，也可以使用「to be ＋ p.p.」的型式。

● to 不定詞也可以當**受詞補語以補充說明**。

This program **allows** you **to store** more data. 這個程式可以讓你儲存更多資料。

☞ allow 是能接受詞和受詞補語的動詞。本句用 to 不定詞當受詞補語，表示 to 不定詞這件事有可能發生。

● 表「指使別人去做某事」的使役動詞，還有表「看、聽什麼」的感官動詞，它們的受詞補語要用不含 to 的不定詞。不含 to 的不定詞將 to 省略，所以看起來和動詞原型一樣。

They let the police officer **search** their house. 他們讓警官搜查他們的房子。

☞ 使役動詞 let、make、have 要用不含 to 的不定詞當受詞補語，表示所指的這件事，是真的發生了。

單字 **statement** 說法 ｜ **false** 錯誤的 ｜ **factory** 工廠 ｜ **inspect** 檢查 ｜
store 儲存 ｜ **search** 搜查

B 基本題型

❶ 不定詞片語

1. Most Americans should learn _____. 多數美國人應該學習開車。

　(A) to driving 　(B) to drive 　(C) drove 　(D) driven

解析 表「學習某事」的意思可以用「learn + to 不定詞」來表現，答案是選項（B）。這樣的句型表示 to 不定詞是未來要去做的事。

2. Many people seem _____ the Internet to television.
很多人似乎喜歡網路勝於電視。

　(A) preferring 　(B) prefer 　(C) preferred 　(D) to prefer

解析 seem 表「似乎、好像要去做某事」的推測含意，一般都要後接 to 不定詞，答案是選項（D）。在這樣的句型中，to 不定詞表不太確定的意思。

3. A lot of people are likely _____ for the position.
很多人可能會應徵這個職位。

　(A) to apply 　(B) applied 　(C) apply 　(D) applies

解析 「可能會」的意思，可用不定詞片語「be likely + to」表現，答案是選項（A）。

單字 **be likely to** 可能會 ｜ **apply** 應徵 ｜ **position** 職位

❷ to 不定詞當受詞補語

4. Their bad decision caused their company _____.
他們的錯誤決策導致公司關門。

(A) fail　　(B) failed　　(C) to fail　　(D) to failing

解析 動詞 cause 用 to 不定詞當受詞補語，答案是選項（C）。

單字 decision 決策 ｜ cause 導致

❸ 不含 to 的不定詞當補語

5. Her mother made her _____ in business administration.
她的母親要她主修企業管理。

(A) to major　　(B) majored　　(C) to majoring　　(D) major

解析 具「要求別人做某事」意思的 make，它的受詞補語通常要用沒有 to 的不定詞，答案是選項（D），表示她已經主修企管了。

單字 major 主修 ｜ business administration 企業管理

C 題型練習

Select the best answer to complete the sentence.

1. They refused _____ the building.
   (A) leaving   (B) to leave
   (C) leave   (D) leaves

2. Mary and Kevin happened _____ the same college.
   (A) attend   (B) attending
   (C) to attend   (D) attended

3. We are eager _____ the Asian market.
   (A) to enter   (B) enter
   (C) entered   (D) enters

4. We don't expect them _____ their minds.
   (A) change   (B) changed
   (C) to changing   (D) to change

5. She had them _____ the table.
   (A) to paint   (B) paint
   (C) painted   (D) to painting

1. (B)

解析 「拒絕（之後）去做……」的意思可以用「refuse ＋ to 不定詞」表現，答案是選項（B）。在這個片語中，to 不定詞表未來的事。

翻譯 他們拒絕離開這棟大樓。

單字 refuse 拒絕

---

2. (C)

解析 「巧合」的意思可以用「happen ＋ to 不定詞」表現，所以答案是選項（C）。

翻譯 瑪莉和凱文碰巧上了同一間大學。

單字 attend ……（學校）就學

---

3. (A)

解析 「渴望（之後）去做……」的意思可以用「be eager ＋ to 不定詞」表現，答案是選項（A）。在這個片語中，to 不定詞表未來的事。

翻譯 我們很渴望能進入亞洲市場。

單字 eager 渴望 ｜ enter 進入

4. (D)

解析 動詞 expect 要用 to 不定詞當受詞補語，答案是選項（D）。在這個片語中，to 不定詞表未來的事。

翻譯 瑪莉和凱文碰巧上了同一間大學。

單字 change one's mind 改變想法

---

5. (B)

解析 使役動詞 have 的受詞補語通常要用沒有 to 的不定詞，答案是選項（B），表示他們實際上已經漆好桌子了。

翻譯 她要他們為桌子上漆。

單字 paint 上漆

D 應用練習　　　　　　　　　► 解析 P. 523

Select the best answer to complete the sentence.

1. We wish ＿＿＿＿ our business in this city.
   (A) continuing
   (B) continued
   (C) to continue
   (D) continues

2. We would like ＿＿＿＿ for our mistake.
   (A) to apologize
   (B) apologizing
   (C) apologized
   (D) apologize

3. He can afford ＿＿＿＿ a new smartphone.
   (A) buy
   (B) bought
   (C) to buy
   (D) to buying

4. We can't afford ＿＿＿＿ abroad.
   (A) traveling
   (B) traveled
   (C) to traveling
   (D) to travel

5. These consumers are willing ＿＿＿＿ more money on entertainment.
   (A) to spend
   (B) spent
   (C) spending
   (D) spends

6. Unfortunately, the company is sure ＿＿＿＿.
   (A) to fail
   (B) failed
   (C) failing
   (D) fails

7. The manager reminded them ＿＿＿＿ off the lights.
   (A) turn
   (B) to turn
   (C) turned
   (D) to turning

8. We want our workers ＿＿＿＿ more time with their families.
   (A) spend
   (B) spent
   (C) to spending
   (D) to spend

9. Paul watched his children ＿＿＿＿ golf.
   (A) to play
   (B) play
   (C) plays
   (D) to playing

10. They heard the machine ＿＿＿＿ strange sounds.
    (A) to make
    (B) to made
    (C) to making
    (D) make

題型 **03** 動名詞

Ⓐ 輕鬆上手

- 所謂的動名詞，就是「原型動詞＋ing」。但動名詞和能在句中能擔任多種功能的 to 不定詞不同，動名詞只能當名詞使用。

- 動名詞在句中可以**當作主詞或補語使用**。

  Building a new bridge will cost a lot of money. 建造新橋會有很多花費。
  ☞ 動名詞 building 在本句中當作主詞，引導 Building a new bridge。

- 和名詞一樣，動名詞也可當句子的受詞，一般表示已經發生或未來一定會發生的事。

  Luckily, he **avoided** <u>**getting**</u> hit by the train. 幸運地是，他避開了火車的追撞。
  ☞ 動詞 avoid 要用動名詞當受詞，不能用 to 不定詞當受詞。

  They **considered** <u>**moving**</u> to another country. 他們考慮搬到另一個國家。
  ☞ consider 是「考慮」的意思，一定要用動名詞做受詞，表示是未來的事。

  She made a lot of money by **becoming** a famous writer.
  她靠成為暢銷作家賺了很多錢。
  ☞ 介系詞 by 後接動名詞表「以……為手段（方法）」之意。介系詞絕對不能接 to 不定詞。

- 和 to 不定詞一樣，動名詞也用在許多片語中。

  The cook is used to **working** on weekends. 這位廚師已習慣在週末工作。
  ☞ 「**be used to ＋動名詞**」是「習慣……」之意，這時的 to 不是不定詞而是介系詞，所以要接動名詞。

B 基本題型

❶ 動名詞當主詞和補語

1. _____ the quality of your life is not easy. 改善生活品質並不容易。

(A) Improve   (B) Improved   (C) To improving   (D) Improving

解析 動名詞表「做……這件事」之意，可以當主詞，答案是選項（D）。
若要用 to 不定詞當主詞，要用 to improve 才對，所以選項（C）是錯誤答案。

❶ 動名詞當受詞

2. Our company enjoys _____ the needs of college students.
我們公司很樂意滿足大學生的需求。

(A) to meet   (B) meeting   (C) meet   (D) meets

解析 enjoy 要接動名詞當受詞，不能用 to 不定詞當受詞，答案是選項（B）。

3. They delayed _____ the items to the company.
他們延遲將物品送至公司的時間。

(A) deliver   (B) to deliver   (C) delivered   (D) delivering

解析 delay 要接動名詞當受詞，不能接 to 不定詞，所以答案是選項（D）。

單字 delay 延遲 | deliver 送貨 | item 物品

4. We should be careful in _____ this issue. 我們應該小心處理這個問題。

(A) to approach   (B) approaching   (C) approach   (D) approached

解析 「in ＋動名詞」表「做……時」或「做……方面」的意思，答案是選項（B）。
因為 in 是介系詞，所以要接動名詞，不能接 to 不定詞。

單字 approach 處理 | issue 問題

❸ 動名詞片語

5. The engineers are devoted to _____ technology.
工程師致力於改良技術。

(A) in improve　　　(B) improves　　　(C) improve　　　(D) improving

解析 「be devoted to ＋動名詞」表「致力於」或「奉獻於」的意思。所以答案是選項 (D)。

在這個片語中，to 是介系詞。

單字 **be devoted to** 致力於 ｜ **improve** 改良

C 題型練習

Select the best answer to complete the sentence.

1. _____ the law is a wise thing to do.
   (A) Obey   (B) Obeyed
   (C) Obeying   (D) Obeys

2. The factory stopped _____ cars last month.
   (A) produced   (B) to producing
   (C) produce   (D) producing

3. We recommend _____ the latest software.
   (A) use   (B) using
   (C) to use   (D) used

4. On _____ in New York, he called an old friend of his.
   (A) arriving   (B) arrive
   (C) arrived   (D) to arrive

5. We look forward to _____ with you.
   (A) worked   (B) working
   (C) in working   (D) in works

1. (C)

解析 動名詞可以當主詞用,答案是選項 (C)。用 to 不定詞當主詞的話,要寫成 To obey 才對。

翻譯 守法是明智之舉。

單字 **obey** 遵守 ∣ **law** 法律

2. (D)

解析 stop 要接動名詞當受詞,答案是選項(D)。
stop+V-ing 的意思是「停止……的動作」;**stop to + 動詞原形**的意思是「停下目前的動作而去做……」。

翻譯 工廠上個月停止生產汽車。

單字 **factory** 工廠 ∣ **produce** 生產

3. (B)

解析 recommend 是「推薦」的意思,要用動名詞當受詞,答案是選項(B)。

翻譯 我們推薦使用最新軟體。

4. (A)

解析 「on＋動名詞」表「一……就……」的意思,答案是選項(A)。因為 on 是介系詞,所以要接動名詞。

翻譯 一抵達紐約,他就聯絡了他的一位老朋友。

5. (B)

解析 「**look forward to ＋動名詞**」表「期待做……」的意思,答案是選項(B)。因為片語中的 to 是介系詞,所以要後接動名詞。

翻譯 我們期待與你合作。

▶ 解析 P. 524

D 應用練習

Select the best answer to complete the sentence.

1. The main goal of the charity is _____ care of poor children.
   (A) takes
   (B) taken
   (C) taking
   (D) took

2. The function of education is _____ good citizens.
   (A) produced
   (B) to producing
   (C) produces
   (D) producing

3. The mechanic finished _____ my car.
   (A) to repair
   (B) repairing
   (C) repair
   (D) repairs

4. Keep _____ in yourself, and you'll succeed.
   (A) to believe
   (B) believe
   (C) believing
   (D) to believing

5. Clara suggested _____ with the client in Toronto.
   (A) to meet
   (B) met
   (C) to meeting
   (D) meeting

6. Would you mind _____ for a second?
   (A) waiting
   (B) to wait
   (C) waited
   (D) to waited

7. In addition to _____ stress, good music makes you feel happy.
   (A) reduce
   (B) in reducing
   (C) to reduced
   (D) reducing

8. Instead of _____ surprised, they welcomed our decision.
   (A) be
   (B) being
   (C) to be
   (D) were

9. We will have no difficulty _____ you back.
   (A) paying
   (B) to pay
   (C) pay
   (D) paid

10. Every day, she spends two hours _____ out.
    (A) worked
    (B) to worked
    (C) to working
    (D) working

題型 **04** 分詞

A 輕鬆上手

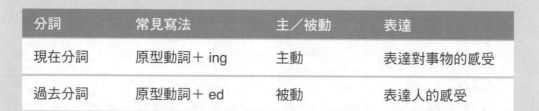

分詞	常見寫法	主／被動	表達
現在分詞	原型動詞＋ing	主動	表達對事物的感受
過去分詞	原型動詞＋ed	被動	表達人的感受

◉ 分詞同時具有動詞和形容詞的性質，和前面學習過的動名詞不同，
現在分詞和過去分詞在句子中是作形容詞用。

The **amazing** thing is that every worker is friendly.
令人驚奇的是每位員工都很友善。

☞ 現在分詞 amazing 的意思是「令人驚訝的」。在英文中，表「事物令人產
生某種感覺」時，要用 V-ing 來表現，不能用 amazed 代替。

In a **booming** economy, people can find good jobs easily.
在經濟蓬勃發展時，人們很容易可以找到好工作。

☞ 現在分詞 booming 的意思是「正蓬勃發展的」，不能用 boomed 代替。

Unfortunately, there was nothing to keep the guests **amused.**
遺憾地是，沒有什麼可以讓客人保持新奇感。

☞ 過去分詞 amused 的意思是「某人覺得有趣的」，是被動的，
且是形容人的感受，不能用 amusing 代替。

There are many ways to reuse **broken** things.
有很多方式可以重新利用損壞的物品。

☞ 過去分詞 broken 的意思是「破掉的、損壞的」，因為是遭受到損壞，
所以要用過去分詞 broken。

The workers have had astonishing experiences in Tokyo.
員工們在東京有著驚人的經驗。

☞ 同樣的動詞，後面加 ing 或 ed 就會完全改變意思。astonishing 是「對事物感覺感覺驚訝」，astonished 是「人感覺驚訝」，彼此不能互換。

單字 **booming** 蓬勃發展的 | **economy** 經濟 | **guest** 客人 | **reuse** 重新利用

Ⓑ 基本題型

❶ 現在分詞

1. The professor was not popular because his lectures were very _____.
這位教授並不受歡迎，因為他的講課很無聊。

(A) bored　　(B) boring　　(C) to boring　　(D) to bored

解析 現在分詞 boring 的意思是「事物使人感覺無聊」，答案是選項（B），主動、積極的含意。

單字 **professor** 教授 | **lecture** 講課

2. A _____ number of students are majoring in earth science.
主修地球科學的學生越來越少。

(A) to decrease　(B) decrease　(C) to decreased　(D) decreasing

解析 現在分詞 decreasing 表示的意思是「正在減少的」，答案是選項（D），表事情正在進行。

單字 **major** 主修 | **earth science** 地球科學

❷ 過去分詞

3. A large number of workers are _____ with their jobs.
為數眾多的勞工覺得他們的工作很無趣。

(A) boring   (B) bore   (C) bored   (D) to bore

解析 過去分詞 bored 的意思是「人覺得無聊的」，答案是選項（C）。人的感受要用過去分詞。

4. We ate _____ vegetables and rice.
我們吃了煮熟的蔬菜和米飯。

(A) cooked   (B) to cooking   (C) cooks   (D) to cook

解析 過去分詞 cooked 的意思是「煮熟的」，答案是選項（A）。因為米是被煮的，所以要用被動語態的過去分詞 cooked。

❸ 現在分詞 vs. 過去分詞

5. Everyone was _____ by the test results. 所有人都對測驗結果感到很驚訝。

(A) astonish   (B) to astonish   (C) astonished   (D) astonishing

解析 過去分詞 astonished 的意思是「人覺得震驚的」，答案是選項（C）。因為是人的感受，所以要用過去分詞。

Select the best answer to complete the sentence.

1. Young people generally prefer to have _____ jobs.
   (A) to challenging   (B) challenging
   (C) to challenged   (D) challenges

2. All _____ members can get a 20 percent discount.
   (A) existed   (B) exist
   (C) exists   (D) existing

3. Michael got _____ because there were too many
   things to understand.
   (A) confused   (B) confusing
   (C) to confused   (D) to confusing

4. Unfortunately, staff meetings do not end at _____ times.
   (A) to fix   (C) fixed
   (B) fixes   (D) to fixing

5. The company reported _____ profits last month.
   (A) disappointing   (B) disappointed
   (C) disappoint   (D) disappoints

答案和解析

1. (B)

解析 現在分詞 challenging 的意思是「有挑戰性的」，答案是選項(B)，主動且描寫事物的分詞要用現在分詞。

翻譯 年輕人一般來說比較喜歡有挑戰性的工作。

---

2. (D)

解析 現在分詞 existing 的意思是「已經存在的」，答案是選項(D)。

翻譯 所有現行會員都可以打八折。

單字 discount 打折

---

3. (A)

解析 過去分詞 confused 的意思是「令人覺得疑惑的」，答案是選項(A)，表示人有什麼感受，要用過去分詞。

翻譯 麥可感到疑惑因為有太多事情要理解了。

4. (C)

解析 過去分詞 fixed 的意思是「固定的」，答案是選項(C)。表示時間被固定下來，所以要用過去分詞。

翻譯 遺憾地是，員工會議不會在固定時間結束。

單字 staff 員工 | fixed time 固定時間

---

5. (A)

解析 現在分詞 disappointing 的意思是「事物使人失望的」，答案是選項(A)。因為利潤讓人失望，所以要用現在分詞。

翻譯 公司上個月的利潤報告讓人失望。

單字 profit 利潤

▶ 解析 P. 523

D 應用練習

Select the best answer to complete the sentence.

1. Mary gave a(n) _____ speech at the conference.
   (A) to inspiring
   (B) inspire
   (C) inspiring
   (D) to inspire

2. For Jennifer, acting is a _____ job.
   (A) to reward
   (B) rewards
   (C) to rewarding
   (D) rewarding

3. All _____ things depend on the sun.
   (A) living
   (B) to lived
   (C) lives
   (D) to live

4. The _____ guests were entertained by the clown.
   (A) remained
   (B) to remain
   (C) remaining
   (D) remain

5. No one was _____ with the results.
   (A) pleased
   (B) please
   (C) to please
   (D) pleasing

6. _____ customers continue to buy products from us.
   (A) Satisfying
   (B) To satisfied
   (C) To satisfying
   (D) Satisfied

7. Teachers should help students discover their _____ talents.
   (A) to hiding
   (B) hidden
   (C) hid
   (D) to hide

8. This area is _____ for its good soil.
   (A) knowing
   (B) knows
   (C) to knowing
   (D) known

9. We were _____ with the service.
   (A) to disappoint
   (B) disappointed
   (C) disappoint
   (D) disappointing

10. The facts about the organization were _____.
    (A) shocking
    (B) to shocked
    (C) shocks
    (D) shocked

題型 05 分詞構句

A 輕鬆上手

◉ 由分詞引導而兼含連接詞和動詞功用的片語，稱為分詞片語或分詞構句。
分詞片語可區分為現在分詞（V-ing）和過去分詞兩種。一般來說，現在分詞
表主動，過去分詞表被動，和時態無關。

分詞構句的重點在於將**副詞子句**改為分詞片語。將副詞子句的連接詞和主詞
省略，動詞主動時改為現在分詞，被動時改為過去分詞。

若副詞子句和主要子句的主詞不同，副詞子句的主詞就不能省略。

Feeling a little tired, Kevin decided to take a 15-minute break.
由於覺得有點累，凱文決定休息 15 分鐘。

☞ 原來是副詞子句 Because he felt a little tired，將其中的連接詞和主詞省
略，將動詞改成 V-ing，就變成分詞構句了。

Announcing the agreement, the mayor felt proud of herself.
市長宣布這項協議，對自己感到很自豪。

☞ 將原來的副詞子句 As she announced the agreement 改成分詞構句。
分詞構句會表示出時間或原因。

◉ 若分詞片語表現的時間和主要子句相同，分詞片語要用現在分詞 V-ing；
若兩個時間不一樣，分詞片語就要用 Having p.p. 來起始。

Walking along the beach, they were approached by a reporter.
他們走在沙灘上時，被一位記者接近交涉。

☞ 他們在海邊散步的時間，跟記者接近他們的時間一樣，所以分詞構句要用
V-ing，用 Walking 起始分詞構句。

Having graduated from college, Paul went back to his hometown.
保羅大學畢業後就回到家鄉。

☞ 畢業先發生，之後 Paul 才回鄉，所以分詞構句要用 Having graduated 來
起始分詞構句。

◉ 轉換成分詞構句的副詞子句若是被動語態，分詞構句要以 Being p.p. 或 Having been p.p. 來起始。這時 Being 或 Having been 可省略，分詞構句變成由 p.p. 起始。

Being praised for her acting, Alice eventually became a famous actress.
由於演技受到讚揚，艾莉斯終於成為一位知名女演員。

☞ 由 Being p.p. 起始，所以是被動語態的分詞構句。可以推知，它原來是 As she was praised for her acting。

單字 **decide** 決定 ｜ **announce** 宣布 ｜ **agreement** 協議 ｜ **mayor** 市長 ｜ **approach** 接近 ｜ **graduate** 畢業 ｜ **praise** 讚揚

Ⓑ 基本題型

❶ 表原因／時間的分詞構句

1. _____ at her own mistake, Mary reminded herself of her strengths.
   瑪莉想起自身的優勢，對自己的錯誤一笑置之。

   (A) Laugh　　(B) To laughed　　(C) Laughing　　(D) To laughing

解析 這是分詞構句的基本型態。原來的副詞子句和主要子句的時間相同，所以用 V-ing 來起始分詞構句。答案是選項（C）。

單字 **remind** 想起 ｜ **strength** 優勢

❷ 簡單式／完成式分詞構句

2. Tears _____ down her face, she felt really sad.

她感到非常憂傷，眼淚直流。

(A) running　　(B) runs　　(C) to run　　(D) ran

解析 做成分詞構句的副詞子句，其原來的主詞是 tears，然而主要子句的主詞是 she，主要子句和副詞子句主詞不同。這時副詞子句的主詞不能省略，只要將動詞改成 V-ing 型就可以了，答案是選項(A)。

3. _____ the company, Jane started her own business.

離開公司後，珍開始自行創業。

(A) Left　　(B) Had left　　(C) Having left　　(D) Has left

解析 珍先離開公司，之後才開始了自己的事業。所以要用 Having left 這完成式來起始分詞構句。答案是選項(C)。

❸ 主動／被動的分詞片語

4. _____ cheerfully, they enjoyed themselves.

他們開心地歡唱，自得其樂

(A) Singing　　(B) To singing　　(C) Sings　　(D) Sang

解析 因為他們唱歌是主動，不能用被動語態，要用一般的 V-ing 開頭，答案是選項(A)。

單字 cheerfully 開心地　｜　enjoy oneself 自得其樂

5. _____ in 1653, it was the oldest church in the country.

這座教堂建於 1653 年，在國內歷史最悠久。

(A) Building　　　　　　(B) Having built
(C) Having building　　(D) Having been built

解析 教堂是被建造的，所以要用被動語態。形成分詞構句的副詞子句，是更早發生的事，所以要用完成式，答案是選項(D)。也可以將 having been 省略改成用 Built 開頭。

C 題型練習

Select the best answer to complete the sentence.

1. _____ the office, I noticed that something was wrong
   with the door.
   (A) Being left   (B) Leaving
   (C) Having leaving   (D) To had left

2. With the operation _____ over, the doctor felt relieved.
   (A) be   (B) was
   (C) were   (D) being

3. _____ her several times, we recognized her easily.
   (A) Met   (B) Having met
   (C) To had met   (D) Had met

4. _____ with another company, our company is now much bigger.
   (A) Having merged   (B) To have merge
   (C) Merge   (D) Merged

5. His computer _____, Jack expected to complete the
   report in time.
   (A) fixing   (B) having fixed
   (C) be fixed   (D) having been fixed

答案和解析

1. (B)

解析 這是分詞構句的基本型態。原來的副詞子句和主要子句發生的時間都相同。所以要用 V-ing 來起始分詞構句，答案是選項（B）。

翻譯 我離開辦公室時，注意到門出問題。

單字 notice 注意

---

2. (D)

解析 形成分詞構句的副詞子句主詞，和主要子句的主詞不同，這時留下原來的副詞子句主詞即可。因為幾乎是相同時間發生的事，所以要用 -ing 型來起始分詞構句，答案是選項（D）。

翻譯 手術結束後，醫生覺得鬆了一口氣。

單字 operation 手術 ｜ relived 放鬆的

---

3. (B)

解析 形成分詞構句的副詞子句，比主要子句更早發生，所以要用 Having p.p. 來起始分詞構句，答案是選項（B）。

翻譯 因為和她有數面之緣，我們很輕易就認出她。

單字 recognize 辨認

4. (A)

解析 形成分詞構句的副詞子句和主要子句的內容，是在不同時間發生的事，所以要用 Having V-ed 來起始分詞構句，答案是選項（A）。

翻譯 我們公司和另一家公司合併後規模變大很多。

單字 merge 合併

---

5. (D)

解析 電腦是被修理的，所以要用被動語態的分詞構句。另外分詞構句和主要子句發生的時間不同，所以要用完成式。答案是選項（D）。

翻譯 傑克的電腦修復後，他預期可以及時完成報告。

單字 fix 修復 ｜ complete 完成 ｜ in time 及時

D 應用練習

▶ 解析 P. 526

Select the best answer to complete the sentence.

1. _____ to wake her up, they quietly walked out of the room.
   (A) Not want
   (B) Wanted not
   (C) Not wanting
   (D) Having wanted not

2. _____ that he hadn't eaten much, he prepared a meal for himself.
   (A) Realizing
   (B) Having realizing
   (C) To realizing
   (D) Realize

3. His daughter _____ in the hospital, he couldn't concentrate on his work.
   (A) was
   (B) were
   (C) has been
   (D) being

4. _____ the street, the man saw a truck approaching him.
   (A) Cross
   (B) Having crossing
   (C) Crossing
   (D) Crossed

5. _____ abroad before, he volunteered to transfer to London.
   (A) Having been
   (B) Be
   (C) To having been
   (D) Was

6. The error _____, her supervisor put the blame on her.
   (A) been identified
   (B) identifying
   (C) identify
   (D) having been identified

7. _____ the movie, they went to a Korean restaurant.
   (A) Watched
   (B) Having watched
   (C) Watch
   (D) Having watching

8. _____ the problem, we faced another one.
   (A) Solved
   (B) Been solved
   (C) Having solved
   (D) Solve

9. _____ by a true expert, the book is a must for every parent.
   (A) Written
   (B) Wrote
   (C) Writing
   (D) Write

10. _____ to only a few people, the recipe remained a secret.
    (A) Knowing
    (B) Knows
    (C) To having known
    (D) Known

Quick Test for **Parts 5 & 6** ▶ 解析 P. 528

Choose the one word or phrase that best completes the sentence.

1. _____ the right thing requires courage.
   (A) Do
   (B) Done
   (C) To do
   (D) To doing

2. Everyone wants _____ a happy life.
   (A) to live
   (B) living
   (C) live
   (D) lives

3. Our _____ is to protect the environment.
   (A) branch
   (B) efforts
   (C) imagination
   (D) mission

4. They can't afford _____ expensive products.
   (A) buy
   (B) to buy
   (C) buying
   (D) buys

5. The company was willing _____ the matter with the mayor.
   (A) to discuss
   (B) discussing
   (C) discussed
   (D) discuss

6. All parents want their children _____ happy.
   (A) are
   (B) to being
   (C) are being
   (D) to be

7. We saw them _____ with each other.
   (A) argue
   (B) to argue
   (C) to arguing
   (D) to argued

8. The project is _____ to bring more jobs to the city.
   (A) false
   (B) likely
   (C) disappointed
   (D) true

9. They finished _____ the new computer network.
   (A) to install
   (B) installed
   (C) installing
   (D) to installing

10. We suggested _____ more eco-friendly products.
    (A) to develop
    (B) developed
    (C) develops
    (D) developing

11. If you don't _____ the rules, you'll be in trouble.
(A) stay
(B) obey
(C) regret
(D) ignore

12. The _____ of the air in China is a serious problem.
(A) statement
(B) data
(C) mistake
(D) quality

13. In the past, collecting stamps was a _____ hobby.
(A) satisfying
(B) satisfied
(C) satisfy
(D) to satisfy

14. We are _____ to announce the launch of our new website.
(A) please
(B) pleasing
(C) pleased
(D) to pleasing

15. The _____ state of the US economy is very good.
(A) confused
(B) astonished
(C) current
(D) cooked

16. One of his _____ is his ability to predict market changes.
(A) discounts
(B) losses
(C) errors
(D) strengths

Questions 17–20 refer to the following email.

Dear Mr. Park,

My brother and I will be _____ China on a business trip from March 1st
                              17.
to April 2nd. _____ our visit to Beijing, we would like _____ with you to
              18.   **19.**
discuss possible projects in China _____.
                                    20.

17. (A) visit
(B) visiting
(C) visited
(D) to visiting

18. (A) When
(B) Although
(C) Despite
(D) During

19. (A) to meet
(B) meeting
(C) meets
(D) meet

20. (A) We don't believe that China will grow economically.
(B) We look forward to working with you and making big profits.
(C) We've heard that you are moving to Australia.
(D) Unfortunately, your Chinese is not adequate.

題型 **01** 形容詞

 A 輕鬆上手

形容詞的用法：	1）修飾名詞
	2）當補充說明主詞或受詞的補語

◉ 形容詞要放在名詞前修飾名詞。

　Coaching is a stressful job. 指導是一項壓力很大的工作。

　☞ 形容詞 stressful 修飾名詞 job。若將修飾名詞的形容詞刪除，
　　句子仍是完整句。

◉ 形容詞可以當補充說明主詞或受詞的補語，當補語使用時不能省略。

　Those customers looked pleased. 那些顧客看起來很高興。

　☞ 形容詞 pleased 補充說明主詞 Those customers，不能將 pleased 刪除。

◉ 要熟知多益常考的形容詞。

　Visit our website for additional information. 請上我們的網站了解更多資訊。

　☞ 形容詞 additional 是用來修飾名詞 information，意思是「額外的」，是
　　常考的形容詞，要熟記用法。

◉ 形容詞搭配介系詞或 to 不定詞形成的片語也很常考。

We are not capable of processing that order. 我們無法處理那份訂單。

☞ 形容詞 capable 搭配介系詞 of 的意思是「有能力的」。因為 of 是介系詞，
所以後面的動詞一定要用動名詞。

We haven't been able to collect the data yet. 我們一直無法收集到資料。

☞ 形容詞 able 搭配 to 不定詞的意思是「有能力的」。
這時的 to 不是介系詞而是不定詞。

單字 coach 指導 ｜ customer 顧客 ｜ order 訂單 ｜ data 資料

B 基本題型

❶ 形容詞的功能

1. _____ ideas are not always useful. 創意並不總是有用處。

(A) Creation　　(B) Create　　(C) Creative　　(D) Creatively

解析 因為空格後接名詞 ideas，所以要找能修飾名詞的形容詞，答案是選項（C）。選項（A）是名詞，選項（B）是動詞，選項（D）是副詞，這些詞類都不能修飾名詞。

單字 creative 有創意的 ｜ useful 有用的 ｜ creation 創造物 ｜ create 創造 ｜ creatively 有創意地

2. This apple pie tastes very _____. 這塊蘋果派非常可口。

(A) well　　(B) goodness　　(C) goodnesses　　(D) good

解析 連綴動詞 tastes 要後接形容詞。因為連綴動詞的意思是「嚐起來」，所以要接意思相符的形容詞，答案是選項（D）。選項（A）也可當形容詞，但因為意思是「健康的」不符句意；選項（B）是名詞。答案是選項（D）。

單字 taste 嚐起來 ｜ well 健康的 ｜ goodness 善良

❷ 重要的必會形容詞

3. The _____ chapter deals with the failure of the company.
以下章節要說明的是公司的失敗。

(A) following (B) follow (C) to follow (D) follower

解析 空格後接名詞，所以空格要放能修飾名詞的形容詞。答案是選項（A）。
選項（D）是名詞，雖然有些名詞也可以修飾名詞，但是這兩個名詞沒辦法形成這樣的名詞詞組，所以是錯誤選項。

單字 following 接下來的 ｜ chapter 章節 ｜ deal with 說明 ｜ failure 失敗 ｜ follower 追隨者

❸ 和形容詞有關的片語

4. There are many problems _____ with the new policy.
新政策有很多相關問題。

(A) connect (B) connection (C) connectedness (D) connected

解析 形容詞 connected 搭配介系詞 with 的意思是「和……有關」。答案是選項（D）。

單字 connected 相關的 ｜ policy 政策 ｜ connect 聯絡 ｜ connection 連結

5. You are _____ to chat with the guest speaker. 你可以隨意與演講嘉賓聊天。

(A) freedom (B) free (C) to free (D) with freely

解析 形容詞 free 搭配 to 不定詞，意思是「自由地」，所以答案是選項（B）。

單字 free 自由的 ｜ chat 聊天 ｜ guest speaker 演講嘉賓 ｜ freedom 自由

Select the best answer to complete the sentence.

1. _____ investors do not make careless decisions.
   (A) Wisdom   (B) With Wisely
   (C) At wisdom   (D) Wise

2. The weather became _____.
   (A) coldness   (B) colder
   (C) coldly   (D) to coldly

3. Acting has long been her _____ source of income.
   (A) principal   (B) principle
   (C) with principally   (D) principally

4. The stadium was _____ to capacity.
   (A) filler   (B) with fill
   (C) filled   (D) to filling

5. Many young people are _____ to serve the country.
   (A) ready   (B) to readily
   (C) at readiness   (D) readiness

答案和解析

1. (D)

解析 因為空格後是名詞，所以要放修飾名詞的詞類，答案是選項(D)。

翻譯 明智的投資人不會草率做決策。

單字 investor 投資人 | careless 草率的 | decision 決策 | wisdom 智慧

---

2. (B)

解析 become 是需要主詞補語的動詞，所以要在選項中找能當補語的詞類，可以考慮選項(A)的名詞和選項(B)的形容詞。形容詞選項(B)較符合句意所以是答案。

翻譯 天氣變得更冷了。

單字 coldness 寒冷 | coldly 寒冷地

---

3. (A)

解析 因為空格接名詞 source，空格要放形容詞，答案是選項(A)。
選項(B)是名詞，是「原則」的意思，不要和選項(A)弄混了。

翻譯 表演一直都是她的主要收入。

單字 acting 表演 | principal 主要的 | source of income 主要收入 | principally 主要地 | principle 原則

4. (C)

解析 動詞 was 一般會接主詞補語，所以空格可以放名詞或形容詞。答案是選項(C)。選項(A)的意思和本句不符。

翻譯 體育館座無虛席。

單字 stadium 體育館 | be filled to capacity 座無虛席 | filler 填充物

---

5. (A)

解析 動詞 are 一般會接主詞補語，答案是選項(A)，形容詞 ready 搭配 to 不定詞是「準備」的意思。

翻譯 許多年輕人都準備報效國家。

單字 ready 準備 | serve 服務 | readiness 準備 | readily 準備地

(D) 應用練習

▶ 解析 P. 530

Select the best answer to complete the sentence.

1. There are many ways to maintain a _____ body.
   (A) healthy
   (B) health
   (C) healthily
   (D) to health

2. Sadly, we don't have all the _____ information about it.
   (A) necessarily
   (B) necessity
   (C) necessary
   (D) with necessity

3. I find it _____ to learn foreign languages.
   (A) useful
   (B) usefully
   (C) at usefully
   (D) usefulness

4. The weather made it _____ for us to enjoy ourselves.
   (A) difficulty
   (B) at difficulty
   (C) with difficult
   (D) difficult

5. His supervisor gave him _____ instructions.
   (A) specifically
   (B) specificity
   (C) specific
   (D) with specifically

6. The _____ cause of the country's success was the diligence of its people.
   (A) chiefly
   (B) with chief
   (C) to chiefly
   (D) chief

7. These results are _____ to those in our report.
   (A) similarly
   (B) similar
   (C) similarity
   (D) at similarly

8. Hotel rates are _____ to change without notice.
   (A) at subjected
   (B) with subjecting
   (C) subjected in
   (D) subject

9. Few citizens are _____ to pay higher taxes.
   (A) willingness
   (B) willing
   (C) to willingness
   (D) willingly

10. The patient was _____ to explain the situation to the nurse.
    (A) inability
    (B) to unable
    (C) unable
    (D) at inability

題型 **02**　副詞

Ⓐ 輕鬆上手

◉ 副詞可以修飾動詞、形容詞和副詞，某些副詞還可以修飾整個句子。

The Asian markets **are growing rapidly**. 亞洲市場正快速成長。

☞ 副詞 rapidly 修飾動詞 are growing，副詞一般都是用來修飾動詞。

◉ 重要的副詞有**頻率副詞**和**表否定含意的副詞**。頻率副詞表達事物發生的頻率。

In this country, too many people have **never** been treated by doctors.
在這個國家，太多人未曾接受過醫生的診治。

☞ 頻率副詞 never 指某事從未發生過；相反的，
頻率副詞 always 指某事總是一直發生。

◉ 否定含意的副詞，最常用的是 **not**。不過具「**很少、幾乎不**」之意的 barely、
hardly、seldom 也可當副詞使用。

These American students can **barely** understand Korean.
這些美國學生幾乎不懂韓語。

☞ 副詞 barely 讓整個句子的含意幾乎相反。考試時要特別注意這種用法。

◉ **連接副詞**也是重要的副詞。連接副詞不能將兩個句子連成一句，所以不是連接詞。
連接副詞只清楚地表明兩個句子之間的關係。

Hiking helps me feel better. **Moreover**, it's the only hobby I can afford now.
健行讓我感覺更好；而且，這是我唯一能負擔的嗜好。

☞ 連接副詞 moreover，並沒有將上述兩個句子合為一個句子的功能，
它只是補充說明兩個句子間的關係。

◉ 副詞中有一種和時間相關且經常使用的副詞，一定要正確熟記用法。

We have **already** reserved a hotel in Seoul. 我們已經預訂了首爾酒店的房間。

☞ 副詞 already 表某事比預期的時間更早發生，通常會和現在完成式或過去完成式搭配使用。

單字 **market** 市場 | **grow** 成長 | **treat** 診治 | **reserve** 預訂

Ⓑ 基本題型

❶ 副詞的功能

1. The CEO _____ chose which words to include in her summary.
執行長仔細挑選她要寫進摘要的字眼。

(A) careful   (B) care   (C) carefulness   (D) carefully

解析 首先，本句若沒有空格也是完整句，這種情況下，空格的詞類通常是副詞，答案是選項（D）。

單字 **include** 包括 | **summary** 摘要 | **carefulness** 謹慎

❷ 頻率副詞和否定副詞

2. We _____ visit local hospitals to cheer up patients.
我們有時拜訪當地醫院為病患打氣。

(A) usual   (B) sometimes   (C) regular   (D) regularity

解析 本句沒有空格仍是完整句，所以空格要放副詞，答案是選項（B）。
選項（A）和（C）是形容詞，選項（D）是名詞，都不是答案。

單字 **local** 當地的 | **cheer up** 打氣 | **patient** 病患 | **usual** 通常 |
regular 規律的 | **regularity** 規律性

3. Jack could _____ believe what he heard from his coworker.

傑克幾乎不敢相信他從同事那裡聽到的話。

(A) negative　　(B) hard　　(C) difficult　　(D) hardly

解析 本句沒有空格仍是完整句。選項（B）可以當副詞使用，但是因為意思是「努力地」，和句意不符，所以答案是選項（D）。

單字 hardly 幾乎不 ｜ coworker 同事 ｜ negative 負面的 ｜ hard 努力地 ｜ difficult 困難的

❸ 連接副詞和重要的副詞

4. Melanie is a good worker. _____, she does not get along with the other workers. 梅蘭妮是位好員工。然而，她和其他同事處不來。

(A) Although　　(B) However　　(C) Despite　　(D) Unless

解析 選項（A）和（D）是連接詞，將兩個句子連接起來。但是例句是獨立的兩個句子，所以不能選。
選項（C）是介系詞，一定要接名詞，所以也不對。所以答案是連接副詞選項（B）。

單字 get along with 相處融洽 ｜ although 即使 ｜ despite 雖然 ｜ unless 除非

5. The manager has _____ finished writing his memo.

經理幾乎快完成撰寫他的備忘錄。

(A) most of　　(B) all of　　(C) near　　(D) almost

解析 本句沒有空格仍是完整句，所以空格要放副詞，答案是選項（D）。
選項（A）和（B）是介系詞片語，要後名詞或代名詞，所以都不是答案。

單字 manager 經理 ｜ finish 完成 ｜ memo 備忘錄 ｜ near 接近

C 題型練習

Select the best answer to complete the sentence.

1. Racism is a _____ dangerous idea.
   (A) really   (B) reality
   (C) realize   (D) to realize

2. Amy _____ meets with her client to discuss investment options.
   (A) frequent   (B) frequency
   (C) often   (D) to frequent

3. This dialect is _____ spoken in most parts of the country.
   (A) rare   (B) rarely
   (C) rarity   (D) too rare

4. They didn't buy the old house. _____, they decided to rent a new house.
   (A) Instead of   (B) Even though
   (C) In spite of   (D) Instead

5. The publisher earned _____ $5 million last year.
   (A) approximate   (B) approximately
   (C) approximation   (D) too approximate

答案和解析

1. (A)

解析 本句沒有空格仍是完整句，空格要放副詞，答案是選項（A）。名詞的選項（B）和動詞的選項（C），是句中必要的成分，無論如何都不能省略，所以不能選。

翻譯 種族歧視是一種非常危險的想法。

單字 racism 種族歧視 | reality 現實 | realize 了解

---

2. (C)

解析 本句沒有空格仍是完整句，空格要放副詞，答案是選項（C）。就像這句一樣，副詞通常都不是非有不可的詞類。

翻譯 艾美經常和客戶會面討論投資選項。

單字 client 客戶 | investment 投資 | frequent 經常的 | frequency 頻率

---

3. (B)

解析 本句沒有空格仍是完整句，空格要放副詞，答案是選項（B）。除了那些非要和動詞搭配的副詞外，其他的副詞都不是句中非有不可的

翻譯 這種方言在國內大多數區域幾乎很少使用。

單字 dialect 方言 | rarely 幾乎很少 | part 部分 | rare 很少的 | rarity 稀有

4. (D)

解析 不是將兩個句子合成一句，所以要選連接副詞，選項（D）是答案。
選項（A）和（C）是介系詞，要接名詞或代名詞，所以都不是答案。

翻譯 他們沒有買那棟舊屋。相反地，他們決定去租一棟新屋。

單字 rent 租 | instead of 取而代之地 | even though 即使 | in spite of 即使

---

5. (B)

解析 本句沒有空格仍是完整句，空格要放副詞，答案是選項（B）。

翻譯 這家出版社去年賺了約五百萬美元。

單字 publisher 出版社 | approximately 大約地 | approximate 大約的／接近 | approximation 接近

D 應用練習

▶ 解析 P. 531

Select the best answer to complete the sentence.

1. Everyone enjoyed the party
   _____ much.
   (A) great
   (B) greatness
   (C) very
   (D) large

2. _____, no one was injured in
   the accident.
   (A) Fortunate
   (B) Fortune
   (C) Fortunes
   (D) Fortunately

3. It _____ takes us two days to
   process an international order.
   (A) usual
   (B) usually
   (C) regularity
   (D) average

4. Laughing has _____ been
   considered a good way to
   reduce stress.
   (A) constant
   (B) recent
   (C) always
   (D) regular

5. This method can _____ be
   considered traditional.
   (A) scarcity
   (B) scarce
   (C) lack
   (D) scarcely

6. The CEO _____ spends time with
   his family.
   (A) rare
   (B) usual
   (C) seldom
   (D) regular

7. The price of clothes went down last
   month. _____, oil prices fell, too.
   (A) Similar
   (B) Similarly
   (C) Similarity
   (D) Similar to

8. She was born and raised in Paris.
   _____, French is her native language.
   (A) Therefore
   (B) Thanks to
   (C) Even though
   (D) Result

9. The tour guide was _____ confused
   that he couldn't think clearly.
   (A) such
   (B) so
   (C) many
   (D) few

10. We haven't decided _____ whether
    to acquire the company.
    (A) yet
    (B) present
    (C) fair
    (D) current

題型 **03** 比較級和最高級

A 輕鬆上手

◉ 形容詞和副詞可以用**比較級**和**最高級**,來表現比較的含意。

	寫法	比較對象
比較級	• 後加 -er • 前面加 more	兩者間做比較
最高級	• 前面加 the,後加 -est • 前面加 the most	三者以上之間做比較

◉ 若兩者某種特性一樣,表示方式是:「as ＋形容詞／副詞＋ as」

Our methods are **as effective as** theirs. 我們的方法和他們的一樣有效。
☞ 比較我們和他們的方法哪個比較有效。

◉ 比較某者比一者擁有更多某種特性時,表示方式是:
「形容詞／副詞的比較級＋ than」

In many ways, printed books are **better than** e-books.
就許多方面來說,紙本書比電子書好。
☞ 比較紙本書和電子書哪種比較好。good 的比較級是 better,
和一般比較級的規則不同,要記下來。

◉ 比較級的強調用法可用以下的單字:**even**、**much**、**still**、**far**、**a lot** 等。

Your job is **still** more demanding than mine. 你的工作還是比我的更吃力。
☞ still 位在比較級 more demanding 前,用來強調比較級。
比較級的強調不能用 very。

◉ 最高級是在形容詞或副詞的原型前加 **the**,後加 -est;或直接在前面加 **most**。

We are **the** oldest publisher in Japan. 我們是日本最古老的出版公司。
☞ 形容詞 old 的最高級 oldest,它前面加了 the,因為最老的出版社就是那一家,
所以要在前面加 the。

◉ 接受最高級修飾的名詞，可以接關係代名詞引導的子句。

That was the **most important decision** <u>that the company had ever made</u>.
那是公司做過最重要的決策。

☞ 形容詞 important 的最高級 most important 修飾名詞 decision，名詞後又接關係代名詞 that 引導的子句。

單字 method 方法 | effective 有效的 | demanding 吃力的 | publish 出版 |
decision 決策

Ⓑ 基本題型

❶ 兩者相同

1. They tried to produce as _____ cars as possible.
他們試圖盡可能地製造汽車。

(A) more   (B) most   (C) many   (D) much

解析 本句用 as . . . as，表兩個對象程度相同。因為 as 要接形容詞或副詞的原型，所以答案是選項（C）。

單字 produce 製造

❷ 比較兩者

2. Good health is _____ than wealth.
良好的健康比財富更重要。

(A) more important   (B) as important
(C) the most important   (D) important

解析 因為句中有 than，所以是形容詞或副詞的比較級。答案是選項（A）。因為 than 的意思「比⋯⋯」，所以要搭配比較級。

單字 health 健康 | wealth 財富

3. The results were _____ more disappointing than we had expected.

結果比我們預期的還更令人失望。

(A) very   (B) such   (C) even   (D) most

解析 比較級的強調用法，可用 even、much、still、far、a lot。所以答案是選項（C）。絕對不能用選項（A）來強調。

單字 result 結果 ｜ disappointing 失望

---

❸ 和形容詞有關的片語

4. Jane is the _____ medical expert in Finland. 珍是芬蘭能力最好的醫學專家。

(A) more competent   (B) a competent

(C) to competently   (D) most competent

解析 首先，因為句子中沒有 than，所以選項（A）絕對不會是答案。
因為「the a」不能連在一起，所以選項（B）也不能選。
選項（C）是副詞，副詞不能修飾名詞，是錯誤答案。所以答案是形容詞最高級的選項（D）。

單字 competent 有能力的 ｜ medical 醫學 ｜ expert 專家

---

5. She was the youngest woman _____ a major insurance company.

她是大型保險公司最年輕的女性管理人。

(A) ran   (B) to run   (C) runs   (D) to running

解析 接受形容詞最高級修飾的名詞，可以接 to 不定詞，答案是選項（B）。
選項（A）、（C）、（D）是不能放進句中空格的型式。

單字 run 管理 ｜ major 大型的 ｜ insurance company 保險公司

Select the best answer to complete the sentence.

1. The charity tried to raise as _____ money as possible.

   (A) much   (B) most

   (C) many   (D) more

2. Computers can work _____ faster than average workers.

   (A) very   (B) much

   (C) more   (D) most

3. Flying is far _____ than taking the bus.

   (A) as expensive   (B) most expensive

   (C) expensive   (D) more expensive

4. For many people, Wikipedia is the _____ website on the Internet.

   (A) as useful   (B) more useful

   (C) most useful   (D) usefully

5. The computer is one of the most creative _____ in history.

   (A) invention   (B) an invention

   (C) the inventions   (D) inventions

答案和解析

1. (A)

解析 用「as . . . as」表兩者的某種特性是一樣的。因為 as 要接形容詞或副詞的原型，所以答案是選項(A)。money 是不可數名詞，所以前面不能加 many。

翻譯 慈善機構試圖盡可能地多募集資金。

單字 charity 慈善機構 | raise 募集

---

2. (B)

解析 表強調比較級的副詞有 even、much、still、far、a lot，答案是選項(B)。
選項(C)「more + -er」的方式是錯誤的。

翻譯 電腦工作的速度比一般人力更快。

單字 average 一般的

---

3. (D)

解析 因為例句中有 than，所以空格一定要放形容詞或副詞的比較級，答案是選項(D)。
不能用選項(A) as expensive than 的型式，因為 as 表同等，than 表不同等的比較，互相矛盾。

翻譯 坐飛機比搭乘巴士昂貴多了。

單字 flying 飛行 | expensive 昂貴的

4. (C)

解析 選項(A)要變成 as useful as 才對，但它只有 as useful，所以是錯誤答案。
選項(C)要和 than 搭配使用。
選項(D)是副詞，不能用來修飾名詞，所以也不對。答案是選項(C)，最高級前要加 the。

翻譯 對許多人來說，維基百科是網路上最有助益的網站。

單字 useful 有助益的

---

5. (D)

解析 one of 後一定要加名詞的複數形，所以答案是選項(D)。
空格放選項(A)、(B)、(C)會變成文法錯誤的句子。

翻譯 電腦是史上最有創意的發明之一。

單字 creative 有創意的 |
invention 發明

▶ 解析 P. 532

D 應用練習

Select the best answer to complete the sentence.

1. Please inform us of your decision as _____ as possible.
   (A) soon
   (B) sooner
   (C) more soon
   (D) most soon

2. This smartphone costs twice as _____ as my digital camera.
   (A) more
   (B) most
   (C) much more
   (D) much

3. Sometimes, high school teachers are _____ than college professors.
   (A) as efficient
   (B) most efficient
   (C) more efficient
   (D) efficient

4. The more you practice, the _____ prepared you are for an interview.
   (A) good
   (B) well
   (C) best
   (D) better

5. Generally speaking, these workers are _____ busier than we are.
   (A) very
   (B) a lot
   (C) most
   (D) best

6. The company is now in a _____ better position to appeal to American consumers.
   (A) very
   (B) more
   (C) much
   (D) good

7. Michael is the _____ student of them all.
   (A) smartest
   (B) smarter than
   (C) a smart
   (D) much smart

8. She is the _____ entrepreneur in Japan.
   (A) more famous
   (B) famously
   (C) more famously
   (D) most famous

9. This is _____ the most effective method for reducing pollution.
   (A) as
   (B) than
   (C) by far
   (D) as than

10. It was one of the most important _____ of the 1970s.
    (A) discoveries
    (B) discovery
    (C) a discovery
    (D) the discoveries

Quick Test for **Parts 5 & 6** ▶ 解析 P. 533

Choose the one word or phrase that best completes the sentence.

1. This book _____ basic accounting principles.
   (A) deals with
   (B) takes after
   (C) pulls over
   (D) gets along with

2. We have already sent all the _____ documents.
   (A) necessity
   (B) necessary
   (C) necessarily
   (D) with necessary

3. I find it _____ to achieve my goals.
   (A) difficulty
   (B) to difficult
   (C) at difficulty
   (D) difficult

4. Our _____ interest is to help companies succeed financially.
   (A) at chief
   (B) chief
   (C) so chiefly
   (D) chiefly

5. Their Thanksgiving traditions are _____ to ours.
   (A) similarity
   (B) similarly
   (C) similar
   (D) with similar

6. Our refund policy is _____ to change without notice.
   (A) with subjected
   (B) subjected with
   (C) subject
   (D) at subjecting

7. The _____ function of business is to satisfy the needs of customers.
   (A) careless
   (B) pleased
   (C) rapid
   (D) principal

8. They _____ wanted to build a public library for children.
   (A) always
   (B) recent
   (C) regularity
   (D) constant

9. The new employee could _____ understand what we wanted from him.
   (A) scarce
   (B) negative
   (C) hardly
   (D) lack

10. They _____ visited the museum because it was far away from their house.
    (A) rare
    (B) rarity
    (C) at rare
    (D) rarely

11. The lake was _____ beautiful that it attracted a lot of tourists.
(A) such
(B) so
(C) a few
(D) many

12. The price _____ hotels and guides.
(A) includes
(B) rents
(C) realizes
(D) exports

13. Julie is _____ than her coworker.
(A) as competent
(B) most competent
(C) competent
(D) more competent

14. Our products are _____ more popular than theirs.
(A) very
(B) far
(C) as
(D) most

15. This is the _____ book ever written about marketing.
(A) better
(B) well
(C) more better
(D) best

16. Being an entrepreneur is a(n) _____ job because it requires a lot of effort.
(A) safe
(B) effective
(C) demanding
(D) dangerous

Questions 17–20 refer to the following paragraph.

Do you want to taste something from a _____ country? _____ This year,
          17.   **18.**
you can taste French food and Korean food. Come to our festival and _____ if
                                                        19.
Korean food tastes _____ than French food.
          20.

17. (A) the foreign
(B) foreigners
(C) some foreign
(D) foreign

18. (A) Then, we can fly to France and Germany in March.
(B) Then, come to our annual food festival on March 3!
(C) Therefore, you cannot stay healthy.
(D) Instead, you should eat healthy food.

19. (A) decide
(B) disappoint
(C) import
(D) surprise

20. (A) as good
(B) as well
(C) better
(D) best

題型 **01** | 介系詞

A 輕鬆上手

◉ 介系詞放在名詞前，表時間、場所或因果關係。和連接詞不同，介系詞沒辦法將兩個句子連接成一個。

■ 表時間的介系詞

The train leaves for Paris **at** <u>nine o'clock</u>. 火車在九點前往巴黎。

☞ 表時間的介系詞 at，指某一個時間點。相反的，in 是指較長的一段時間。

They have been living in New York **since** <u>1997</u>. 他們從 1997 年就住在紐約。

☞ since 一般都和現在完成式搭配使用。因為 since 的意思是「從過去某個時間點開始一直到現在」。

■ 表地點的介系詞

The bus doesn't stop **at** <u>the post office</u>. 這輛巴士不會停靠在郵局。

☞ 表地點的介系詞 at，指「在特定的某個地點」。in 表「在較廣闊的空間中」；on 表「在某物的表面」。

■ 表因果關係的介系詞（片語）

The outdoor party was cancelled **because of** bad weather.
由於天氣不佳，戶外派對取消了。

☞ because of 表「因為」，和連接詞 because 不同，它不能連接兩個句子。

She was admitted to the college **despite** her low test scores.
儘管她的成績不高，還是被錄取進大學。

☞ 介系詞 despite 表「儘管」的意思。意思相近的還有 although，但 although
是連接詞，所以和 despite 的用法不同。

單字 **cancel** 取消 | **weather** 天氣 | **admit** 允許進入

Ⓑ 基本題型

❶ 表時間的介系詞

1. We offer driving lessons ＿＿＿ the morning. 我們提供早上的駕訓課。

(A) and　　(B) in　　(C) on　　(D) with

解析 表「在早晨」之意的介系詞要用 in，答案是選項（B）。
選項（A）不是介系詞是連接詞，不能放進空格中。

單字 **offer** 提供 | **driving** 駕駛

2. We have been waiting for them ＿＿＿ nearly two hours.
我們已經等了他近兩小時。

(A) during　　(B) on　　(C) by　　(D) for

解析 表「花多少時間」的介系詞要用 for，答案是選項（D）。
選項（A）的 during，也是表「在……期間」之意的介系詞，但是它的重點是
放在「這段時間內發生的事」，和介系詞 for 不同。

❷ 表地點的介系詞

3. The artist has been living _____ New York since last year.
這位藝術家從去年就一直住在紐約。

(A) yet　　(B) in　　(C) though　　(D) because

解析 表「在較寬廣的範圍中」的介系詞是 in，答案是選項（B）。
選項（A）是副詞，選項（C）和（D）是連接詞，都不能放進空格裡。

❸ 重要的介系詞

4. His company lost a lot of money _____ his bad choices.
由於他選擇錯誤，他的公司虧了很多錢。

(A) because　　(B) since　　(C) due to　　(D) unless

解析 首先，因為空格後不是子句「主詞＋動詞」，所以空格不能放連接詞的選項（A）、（B）、（D），答案是選項（C）。雖然選項（B）也可以當介系詞用，但因為 since 要接一個時間點，所以不能是答案。

單字 choice 選擇 ｜ unless 除非

5. We enjoyed the performance _____ the noise.
雖然有噪音，我們仍很享受這次表演。

(A) in spite of　　(B) even though　　(C) in spite　　(D) although

解析 因為空格後不是子句「主詞＋動詞」，而是名詞，所以空格不能放是連接詞的選項（B）和（D）。沒有選項（C）這樣的片語。
答案是選項（A），in spite of 是「儘管」的意思。

C 題型練習

Select the best answer to complete the sentence.

1. We will be meeting with the client _____ Wednesday.
   (A) while   (B) at
   (C) on   (D) in

2. He worked as an intern for the company _____ the summer.
   (A) as   (B) and
   (C) at   (D) during

3. Your hat is _____ the table over there.
   (A) on   (B) and
   (C) while   (D) in spite

4. _____ her donations, we helped a lot of poor children.
   (A) Because   (B) Since
   (C) Although   (D) Thanks to

5. _____ being disappointed, they seemed satisfied.
   (A) Instead   (B) Instead of
   (C) During   (D) Either or

答案和解析

1. (C)

解析 特定的星期和日期要和介系詞 on 搭配，答案是選項（C）。選項（A）是連接詞，通常要接「主詞＋動詞」。

翻譯 我們將在週三和客戶會面。

單字 client 客戶

---

2. (D)

解析 during 的焦點是放在「某事是在什麼期間發生」，所以答案是選項（D）。

翻譯 他曾在夏季擔任該公司的實習生。

單字 intern 實習生

---

3. (A)

解析 空格要放表地點的介系詞，答案是選項（A）。選項（B）和（C）是連接詞，不能放進空格中。沒有選項（D）這樣的片語，所以也不能選。

翻譯 你的帽子在那邊的桌子上。

單字 over there 那邊

4. (D)

解析 空格後是名詞片語 her donations，所以空格要放介系詞，答案是選項（D），「拜……所賜」的意思。

選項（A）、（B）、（C）都是連接詞，不能放進空格。選項（B）也可以當作介系詞，但要接表特定時間的名詞，所以不是答案。

翻譯 多虧她的捐獻，我們幫助了許多貧困的孩童。

單字 donation 捐獻 ｜ poor 貧困的

---

5. (B)

解析 因為空格後接動名詞，所以空格要放介系詞。從內容來看，是「他們並沒有失望，而是滿足」之意，答案是選項（B）。instead of 是「取而代之」的意思。

翻譯 他們並不失望，反而感到很滿意。

單字 disappointed 失望的 ｜ satisfied 滿意的

D 應用練習　　　▶ 解析 P. 535

Select the best answer to complete the sentence.

1. Your application should be submitted _____ Friday.
   (A) by
   (B) in
   (C) with
   (D) and

2. Your tourist visa is valid _____ the end of this month.
   (A) although
   (B) until
   (C) or
   (D) but

3. Concerts will be held every weekend _____ the month of March.
   (A) when
   (B) while
   (C) throughout
   (D) yet

4. You are allowed to return faulty items _____ ten days.
   (A) unless
   (B) within
   (C) however
   (D) although

5. The post office is located _____ the bank and the bakery.
   (A) while
   (B) because
   (C) in spite
   (D) between

6. Several American tourists were walking _____ the beach.
   (A) along
   (B) despite
   (C) though
   (D) thanks

7. He retired at the age of 45 _____ his poor health.
   (A) on account
   (B) because
   (C) on account of
   (D) unless

8. The CEO answered questions _____ the safety of the company's products.
   (A) although
   (B) however
   (C) yet
   (D) concerning

9. The museum is open every day _____ Thursdays.
   (A) in spite
   (B) except
   (C) on account
   (D) due

10. _____ being convenient, ebooks are less expensive than printed books.
    (A) In addition
    (B) Instead
    (C) In spite
    (D) In addition to

題型 **02** | 對等連接詞

A 輕鬆上手

- 連接詞是用來連接兩個字詞或句子，大致可分作對等連接詞和從屬連接詞兩種。

- 對等連接詞就是將兩個性質相同的單字、片語、子句或句子連接起來的連接詞。

  They went to the market **and** bought some bananas.
  他們去市場並買了一些香蕉。

  ☞ and 就是當對等連接詞使用的字。在本句中，and 將兩個性質相同的片語 went to the market 和 bought some bananas 連接起來。

  You can have tuna **or** ham on your sandwich.
  你可以在三明治加上鮪魚或火腿。

  ☞ or 也是對等連接詞，本句的 tuna 和 ham 都是 have 的受詞，or 將它們連接起來。

- 若對等連接詞由兩個部分組成，又稱為相關連接詞。

  Both his brother **and** his sister live in the United States.
  他的哥哥和姊姊都住在美國。

  ☞ 「both A and B」是「A 和 B 兩者都」的意思，是相關連接詞。因為是對等連接詞，所以 A 和 B 必須是相同性質的詞類，在句中具有相同的文法功能。本句的 his brother 和 his sister 都是句子的主詞，具有相同的文法功能。

We can stay **either** at a hotel **or** in an apartment. 我們可以住在飯店或公寓。

☞ 「either A or B」是「不是 A 就是 B」的意思，是相關連接詞。
   本句的 at a hotel 和 in an apartment 都是副詞片語，具有相同的文法功能，
   可以用對等連接詞連接。

Both Jennifer **and** her sister enjoy playing golf.
珍妮佛和她的妹妹都很享受打高爾夫球。

◉ 當句子用相關連接詞連接起來的字詞當主詞時，要依主詞來決定動詞的單複數形。
   ☞ 因為主詞是「both A and B」，所以動詞要用複數形，因為主詞是兩個以上。

Ⓑ 基本題型

❶ 重要的對等連接詞

1. Amy never exercises, _____ she is quite athletic.
   艾咪從不運動，但是她的運動表現很好。

   (A) despite   (B) at   (C) but   (D) in spite

解析 but 是重要的對等連接詞，答案是選項（C）。
   沒有選項（D）這種片語，選項（A）和（B）是介系詞，不能將兩個句子連接
   在一起。

單字 despite 雖然 | athletic 擅長運動的

2. We can stay at home for dinner _____ go out to eat.
   我們可以待在家吃晚餐，或是外出吃飯。

   (A) in   (B) for   (C) on   (D) or

解析 or 也是重要的對等連接詞，答案是選項（D）。選項（A）、（B）、（C）
   都是介系詞，所以不能選。雖然選項（B）也可以當作連接詞使用，但 for 要
   後接「主詞＋動詞」。

❷ 相關連接詞

3. Our goal is not to sell a lot of items _____ to satisfy our customers.
我們的目標不是販賣很多商品，而是讓客戶滿意。

(A) but   (B) for   (C) neither   (D) or

解析 重要的相關連接詞有 not A but B，是「不是 A 而是 B」的意思。答案是選項（A）。

單字 goal 目標 ｜ item 品項 ｜ satisfy 滿意 ｜ customer 客戶

4. They can either follow _____ ignore the rules. 他們可以遵守或忽視規定。

(A) both   (B) nor   (C) or   (D) and

解析 重要的相關連接詞還有 either A or B，是「不是 A 就是 B」的意思。答案是選項（C）。

單字 follow 遵守 ｜ ignore 忽視 ｜ rule 規定

❸ 單複數一致

5. Not the professor but her assistant _____ invited to the conference.
受邀參加研討會的不是教授而是她助理。

(A) were   (B) have   (C) has   (D) was

解析 用 not A but B 連接主詞的話，動詞要由 B 決定。因為本句的 B 是 her assistant，所以答案是選項（D）。
若選擇選項（B）和（C），invited 就要有受詞，但因為例句中沒有受詞，所以都不是答案。

單字 professor 教授 ｜ assistant 助理 ｜ conference 研討會

ⓒ 題型練習

Select the best answer to complete the sentence.

1. Mary knocked on the door _____ Kevin answered it.
   (A) at   (B) during
   (C) and   (D) both

2. Watch out, _____ you'll spill the milk.
   (A) despite   (B) within
   (C) nor   (D) or

3. Both the CEO _____ her secretary agreed to the plan.
   (A) nor   (B) or
   (C) neither   (D) and

4. The new medicine is neither safe _____ effective.
   (A) both   (B) nor
   (C) and   (D) either

5. Not only Paul but also his sister _____ taking driving classes.
   (A) have   (B) being
   (C) to be   (D) is

1. (C)

解析 空格要放能連接兩個句子的字詞，所以答案是連接詞選項（C）。
選項（A）和（B）是介系詞，沒辦法連接句子。

翻譯 瑪莉敲了門，而凱文來應門。

單字 knock 敲（門） | answer 應（門）

2. (D)

解析 本題要將兩個句子連在一起，所以空格要放連接詞，答案是選項（D）。
因為選項（A）和（B）是介系詞，所以不是答案。
選項（C）的 nor，要用「neither A nor B」的型式，表「不是A也不是B」之意，與本句不合。

翻譯 當心，不然你會打翻牛奶。

3. (D)

解析 本句要用相關連接詞「both A and B」的型式，答案是選項（D）。

翻譯 執行長和她的秘書都同意計劃。

單字 CEO 執行長 | secretary 秘書 | agree 同意

4. (B)

解析 本句考相關連接詞「neither A nor B」的正確型式，答案是選項（B）。

翻譯 新藥既不安全也不有效。

單字 medicine 藥物 | effective 有效的

5. (D)

解析 「not only A but also B」連接本句的主詞，動詞要依據B來決定。his sister 是單數，所以答案是選項（D）。選項（B）和（C）不能當動詞使用。

翻譯 不只有保羅，連他的妹妹都在上駕訓班。

D 應用練習　　　　　▶ 解析 P. 536

Select the best answer to complete the sentence.

1. They worked for many hours
   _____ became tired.
   (A) at
   (B) during
   (C) and
   (D) while

2. We invited John to the party,
   _____ he decided not to come.
   (A) despite
   (B) within
   (C) in spite
   (D) but

3. Bring your coat, _____ you
   might feel cold.
   (A) both
   (B) or
   (C) in
   (D) due to

4. We can't decide what to do,
   _____ we don't have all the
   necessary information.
   (A) during
   (B) thanks to
   (C) either
   (D) for

5. Children can both play games
   _____ learn important things
   at the same time.
   (A) and
   (B) either
   (C) or
   (D) neither

6. The new product is not only
   innovative _____ affordable.
   (A) nor
   (B) but also
   (C) either
   (D) both also

7. Successful candidates should know
   how to speak either English
   _____ French.
   (A) or
   (B) both
   (C) not only
   (D) but also

8. Neither Brian _____ his brother
   can speak English well.
   (A) nor
   (B) and
   (C) either
   (D) for

9. Either the new employee or her
   supervisor _____ allowed to
   attend the meeting.
   (A) are
   (B) being
   (C) have
   (D) is

10. Neither Emma nor her sister _____
    able to convince him to stay.
    (A) were
    (B) had
    (C) was
    (D) have

題型 **03** 從屬連接詞

A 輕鬆上手

◉ 和對等連接詞不同，從屬連接詞從一個句子，導引出另一個相關的句子，
由它導引出來的句子稱為從屬子句。

■ 由從屬連接詞引導的從屬子句：在句中當**副詞子句**和**名詞子句**使用
■ 由關係代名詞引導的從屬子句：在句中當**形容詞子句**使用

◉ 副詞子句表時間或條件等關係。

When he was in the navy, he worked with American officers.
他在海軍時和美國軍官共事。

☞ When he was in the navy 是表時間的副詞子句，he worked with American
officers 則是主要子句。像副詞子句這樣的從屬子句，不是完整句，
因此 When he was in the navy 不是完整句。

If you need any help, just ask any librarian.
如果你需要任何協助，只要詢問任何一位圖書館員。

☞ If you need any help 是表條件的副詞子句，這樣的從屬子句不是完整句，
一定要有主要子句的幫忙。

A lot of people enjoy eating kimchi <u>because</u> it is delicious.
許多人很喜歡吃韓國泡菜，因為很美味。

☞ because it is delicious 是表原因的副詞子句。

◉ 引導名詞子句的從屬連接詞中，有 that、if/whether 等。
-ever 型式的複合關係代名詞，也可以引導名詞子句。

We believe <u>that</u> everyone should be respected. 我們相信所有人都應該受到尊重。

☞ that everyone should be respected 是名詞子句，是 believe 的受詞。名詞子句
也是從屬子句，所以 that everyone should be respected 不是完整句。

<u>Whoever</u> **makes such mistakes** will be in trouble.
不論是誰犯了這樣的錯誤都會惹上麻煩。

☞ Whoever makes such mistakes 是由 whoever 引導的名詞子句,是本句主詞。

單字 navy 海軍 ｜ officer 辦公室人員 ｜ librarian 圖書館員 ｜ delicious 美味的 ｜ respect 尊重 ｜ mistake 錯誤 ｜ trouble 麻煩

Ⓑ 基本題型

❶ 副詞子句

1. _____ she graduated from college, Mary became a nurse.
瑪莉大學畢業後成了一名護士。

(A) Despite　　(B) However　　(C) At　　(D) After

解析 本題要將兩個句子連接成一句,空格要放連接詞,答案是選項(D)。
選項(A)和(C)是介系詞,選項(B)是副詞,沒辦法連接句子。

單字 graduate 畢業

2. You're welcome to stay and have a cup of tea _____ you're in a hurry.
除非你趕時間,不然很歡迎你留下來喝杯茶。

(A) during　　(B) in spite of　　(C) instead　　(D) unless

解析 本題要將兩個句子連接成一句,空格要放連接詞,答案是選項(D)。
選項(A)和(B)是介系詞。選項(C)是連接副詞。連接詞 unless 是「除非」
的意思,要引導副詞子句。

單字 in a hurry 趕時間

3. _____ it was too expensive, we looked for something cheaper.
因為它太貴了,所以我們要找便宜一點的。

(A) Since　　(B) Because of　　(C) Or　　(D) Due to

解析 空格要放能將兩個句子連接成一句的連接詞,答案是選項(A)。
選項(B)和(D)是表「因為」之意的介系詞片語。選項(C)是對等連接詞,
不能放進空格。

❷ 名詞子句

4. Susan was sure _____ she would succeed as a lawyer.
蘇珊很確定她會成為成功的律師。

(A) despite   (B) in spite of   (C) that   (D) during

解析 空格之後都是 sure 的受詞，也就是名詞子句。所以引導名詞子句的連接詞選項（C）是答案。選項（A）、（B）、（D）全都是介系詞（片語），沒辦法將兩句連接成一句。

5. _____ is interested in history will find this book insightful.
對歷史有興趣的人都會發現這本書見解精闢。

(A) Those   (B) Anyone   (C) Those who   (D) Whoever

解析 首先，因為空格後的動詞是 is，所以不用考慮選項（A）和（C），若要用those，要寫成 those (who are) interested in history . . .。
選項（B）要寫成 anyone (who is) interested . . .。所以答案是選項（D）。

單字 insightful 見解精闢的

C 題型練習

Select the best answer to complete the sentence.

1. We have been good friends _____ we met in college.
   (A) since
   (B) because of
   (C) however
   (D) during

2. Nothing will change _____ you complain.
   (A) despite
   (B) at
   (C) in spite of
   (D) unless

3. _____ it was already late, Kevin decided not to go to the beach.
   (A) Due to
   (B) As
   (C) Because of
   (D) In spite

4. It seems certain _____ they will acquire the company.
   (A) despite
   (B) instead of
   (C) that
   (D) nor

5. _____ needs to learn English is advised to take this course.
   (A) Anyone
   (B) Whoever
   (C) However
   (D) Those who

答案和解析

1. Answer (A)

解析 since 也能當引導時間副詞子句的連接詞來使用，答案是選項（A）。一般來說，since 引導的副詞子句時態是過去式，而主要子句的時態是現在完成式。
選項（B）和（D）是介系詞，所以不會是答案。選項（C）是連接副詞，不能將兩個句子連接成一句。

翻譯 我們從在大學認識後就一直是很好的朋友。

單字 college 大學

---

2. Answer (D)

解析 連接詞 unless，引導表「除非」之意的條件副詞子句，答案是選項（D）。
選項（A）、（B）、（C）全都是介系詞，不能代替連接詞。

翻譯 除非你投訴不然什麼事都不會改變。

單字 complain 抱怨

---

3. Answer (B)

解析 首先，選項（A）和（C）是表「因為」之意的介系詞，且沒有選項（D）這種片語，所以都不是答案。答案是選項（B）。

翻譯 因為已經很晚了，凱文決定不去海灘。

單字 decide 決定 ｜ beach 海灘

4. Answer (C)

解析 可以知道，本句的 it 是虛主詞，空格後才是真主詞。連接詞 that 引導真主詞的名詞子句，答案是選項（C）。像選項（A）和（B）這樣的介系詞，一定要和連接詞區分清楚。

翻譯 很肯定的是，他們將會收購這家公司。

單字 acquire 收購

---

5. Answer (B)

解析 空格要放「任何做⋯⋯的人」之意的字，答案是選項（B）。
選項（A）必須寫成 Anyone who needs to learn . . .；選項（D）要寫成 Those who need to learn . . .。

翻譯 建議需要學習英語的學生參加本課程。

單字 advise 建議

D 應用練習　　　▶ 解析 P. 537

Select the best answer to complete the sentence.

1. Someone opened the door
   _____ we were having a meeting.
   (A) during
   (B) at
   (C) while
   (D) in

2. We won't make a decision
   _____ we hear from them.
   (A) despite
   (B) instead
   (C) instead of
   (D) until

3. _____ it rains tomorrow, the CEO
   will call off her visit.
   (A) Whatever
   (B) If
   (C) Nor
   (D) Whichever

4. She worked over the weekend _____
   she could finish writing the report.
   (A) due to
   (B) concerning
   (C) instead of
   (D) so that

5. We did our best, _____ we knew it
   would be difficult for us to win.
   (A) although
   (B) in spite
   (C) during
   (D) despite

6. _____ he was strongly criticized,
   Paul decided not to resign.
   (A) Despite
   (B) Instead
   (C) And
   (D) Though

7. No one knew _____ the
   new product would appeal to
   consumers.
   (A) since
   (B) if
   (C) from
   (D) during

8. We wondered _____ we could
   help them achieve their goals.
   (A) whether
   (B) both
   (C) either or
   (D) with that

9. Choose _____ is better for
   your health.
   (A) those who
   (B) anyone
   (C) whichever
   (D) those

10. Take advantage of _____ is
    offered to you.
    (A) whatever
    (B) anything
    (C) something
    (D) that

題型 **04** 關係代名詞

Ⓐ 輕鬆上手

◉ 關係代名詞同時在句中擔任代名詞，同時連接兩個句子。位在關係代名詞前的名詞叫先行詞，關係代名詞會依據先行詞是人或事物而有不同。

◉ 當先行詞是「人」，關係代名詞用「**who**」，可以在句中當主詞或受詞使用，其所有格的關係代名詞是 whose。

They decided to hire the candidate who could speak three different languages.
他們決定僱用可以說三種不同語言的求職者。
☞ 本句的 who 把 They decided to hire the candidate，和 who (the candidate) could speak three different languages 連接起來。
另外 who 是它自己引導的子句的主詞。

They had a chance to meet the lawyer who(m) they admired.
他們有機會去和他們欽佩的律師會面。
☞ 本句的 lawyer 可接 who 或 whom。另外，因為 **who(m)** 也是後接句子的受詞，所以可以省略。先行詞是「人」時，關係代名詞可以在它所引導的句子中，依它所擔任的角色，使用 who、whom 或 whose。

◉ 可以省略在句中當及物動詞受詞的關係代名詞。

The students we talked with were quite interested in our research.
之前與我們談過的學生對我們的研究很有興趣。
☞ 本句原來是 The students who(m) we talked with were quite interested in our research.，但因為 who(m) 是介系詞 with 的受詞，所以可以省略。

◉ 當關係代名詞只對先行詞**補充說明**時，這稱作關係代名詞的非限定用法。這時，在句子中，關係代名詞前會出現逗點。

They invited the <u>doctor, who</u> was an internationally famous author.
他們邀請的醫生是國際知名的作家。

☞ who 所引導的形容詞子句，只是補充說明先行詞 doctor，並不是限定 doctor。這種用法稱作關係代名詞的非限定用法。

◉ 關係代名詞 **what** 包含先行詞在內，所以這時 what 前面**不能**再有名詞。

What they did was wrong. 他們的做法是錯誤的。

☞ 雖然 what 前什麼字都沒有，但因為 what 是包含先行詞在內的關係代名詞，表「他們所做的某事」。

單字 hire 僱用 ｜ admire 欽佩 ｜ research 研究 ｜ internationally 國際地

Ⓑ 基本題型

❶ 關係代名詞的格

1. We rented the office _____ was more spacious than we had expected.
我們租下的辦公室比預期的更寬敞。

(A) who　　(B) whom　　(C) whose　　(D) which

解析 因為先行詞是物，所以可以考慮選項(C)和(D)。選項(C)是當所有格使用的關係代名詞，答案是可當主格使用的選項(D)。

單字 rent 租 ｜ spacious 寬敞地

2. This is the book _____ I can personally recommend.
這是一本我可以親自推薦的書。

(A) who　　(B) which　　(C) whose　　(D) when

解析 因為先行詞是事物，所以不能用選項(A)。選項(C)只能當所有格關係代名詞使用。答案是選項(B)，which 因為是受詞，可換成 that 或省略。

單字 personally 親自 ｜ recommend 推薦

❷ 關係代名詞的省略

3. ＿＿＿ in flying can take these free courses.
對飛行有興趣的人可以上這些免費的課程。

(A) Those are interested   (B) interesting

(C) Interested   (D) Those interested

解析 可以將「關係代名詞＋ be 動詞」省略，變成分詞片語。本來的句子是 Those who are interested in flying can take these free courses.，句中的 who are 可以省略，所以答案是選項 (D)。

---

❸ 關係代名詞的非限定用法 / what

4. The reporter interviewed Jennifer, ＿＿＿ he liked personally.
這位記者訪問了珍妮佛，他個人很喜歡她。

(A) whose   (B) that   (C) what   (D) whom

解析 先行詞是人，且關係代名詞是受詞。另外，因為關係代名詞前有逗點，所以可以知道是非限定用法。答案是選項 (D)。
選項 (A) 可以在關係代名詞是所有格時使用。選項 (B) 和 (C) 不能使用關係代名詞的非限定用法。

單字 reporter 記者 ｜ personally 個人

5. ＿＿＿ we need to do is to do our best. 我們需要做的就是盡力而為。

(A) That   (B) What   (C) Which   (D) Who

解析 空格中要放能表「我們需要做什麼」之意的詞，關係代名詞中能表這意思的只有 what，答案是選項 (B)，選項 (A)、(C)、(D) 全都是句子裡要有先行詞才能使用的關係代名詞，所以都是錯的。

Select the best answer to complete the sentence.

1. We get along with the people _____ live next door.
   (A) who
   (B) what
   (C) whose
   (D) which

2. We once worked with a coworker _____ name was Akina.
   (A) that
   (B) whom
   (C) which
   (D) whose

3. This is a _____ my grandfather founded in 1962.
   (A) company who
   (B) company what
   (C) company
   (D) company whose

4. They worked for a German company, _____ produced farming machines.
   (A) that
   (B) which
   (C) what
   (D) whose

5. Nobody believed _____ he said at the interview.
   (A) of which
   (B) whose
   (C) of that
   (D) what

1. (A)

解析 因為先行詞是人,所以可以考慮選項(A)和(C)。選項(C)是所有格,答案是可當主格用的選項(A)。

翻譯 我們和住在隔壁的鄰居相處愉快。

單字 get along with 相處愉快

---

2. (D)

解析 先行詞 coworker 是人,而且因為空格後接名詞 name,所以空格要放所有格關係代名詞,答案是選項(D)。

關係代名詞 whose 可以將 We once worked with a coworker. 和 The coworker's name was Akina 這兩個句子連在一起。

翻譯 我們曾有一位同事叫阿基娜。

---

3. (C)

解析 本句是將「This is a company.」和「My grandfather founded the company in 1992.」兩句合起來的句子。

本來是 This is a company which/that my grandfather founded in 1992. ,因為關係代名詞是受詞,所以可以省略。答案是選項(C)。

翻譯 這是一家我祖父在 1962 年創建的公司。

單字 found 創建

4. (B)

解析 因為空格前有逗點,所以可以知道這是關係代名詞的非限定用法。因為關係代名詞是主格不是所有格,答案是選項(B)。
選項(A)和(C)是不能使用非限定用法的關係代名詞。

翻譯 他們曾在一家德國公司工作,那公司生產農業機具。

單字 produce 生產 | farming 農業的

---

5. (D)

解析 空格要放能表「他說的事」之意的關係代名詞,答案是選項(D)。

翻譯 沒有人相信他在面試時的說法。

單字 interview 面試

Select the best answer to complete the sentence.

1. She prefers to read books _____ can teach her new things.
   (A) who
   (B) which
   (C) whose
   (D) what

2. There are many things _____ you need to learn to be an expert.
   (A) that
   (B) who
   (C) whom
   (D) what

3. The product _____ John had developed did not sell well.
   (A) whose
   (B) that
   (C) whom
   (D) what

4. They had a son _____ dream was to be a professor.
   (A) that
   (B) which
   (C) whose
   (D) what

5. He was a successful _____ everybody wanted to work with.
   (A) businessman what
   (B) at businessman
   (C) businessman with
   (D) businessman

6. The _____ by our chief engineer does not work anymore.
   (A) machine using
   (B) machine used
   (C) machine that
   (D) machine which

7. Jack bought a house, _____ many people thought was too expensive.
   (A) that
   (B) what
   (C) whose
   (D) which

8. The start-up company was struggling, _____ was understandable.
   (A) which
   (B) what
   (C) who
   (D) that

9. Gambling is not _____ I want to do.
   (A) of which
   (B) whose
   (C) what
   (D) whom

10. She took good care of _____ she had borrowed from her friends.
    (A) that
    (B) which
    (C) what
    (D) whose

題型 05 關係副詞

A 輕鬆上手

◉ 關係副詞同時在句中擔任副詞，並連接兩個句子。和關係代名詞不同，關係代名詞的先行詞是人或事物，關係副詞前的詞，是表時間、地點或原因。關係副詞有 when、where、how、why 等。

- when 前要接表**時間**的詞
- where 前要接表**地方**的詞

There was a time **when** everything went smoothly. 有一度一切都很順利。
☞ 原本的句子是：
There was a time. At that time, everything went smoothly.
用 when 將兩句連成一句。

- why 前只能接表原因的名詞（reason）
- how 可以單獨使用，或換成 the way in which，不能用 the way how。

This is the reason **why** I prefer Canada to the United States.
這就是我喜歡加拿大勝於美國的原因。
☞ 原本的句子是：This is the reason. For that reason. I prefer Canada to the Unites States.，用關係副詞 why 將兩句連成一句。

◉ 當先行詞是**表地點**的詞時，先行詞隨著關係詞在句中擔任的角色，可以用關係代名詞也可以用關係副詞。

London was the city **where** they grew up together.
倫敦是他們一起長大的城市。
☞ 本句的關係詞接完整句 they grew up together，所以不能用關係代名詞，要用關係副詞 where。

◉ 關係副詞可以換成「介系詞＋關係代名詞」。

This is the factory where they produce belts. 這就是他們生產皮帶的工廠。

☞ they produce belts 也是完整句，所以要用關係副詞，這時的 where 可以換成 in which。

◉ **whenever** 和 **wherever** 稱為複合關係副詞。

Whenever I visit Toronto, I feel relaxed. 無論何時我造訪多倫多都讓我覺得很放鬆。

☞ whenever 表「任何時候」的意思。

單字 **smoothly** 順利地 │ **factory** 工廠 │ **produce** 生產

Ⓑ 基本題型

❶ 關係副詞

1. The office _____ they work is located near the bank.
他們工作的辦公室離銀行很近。

(A) when　　(B) which　　(C) why　　(D) where

解析 空格後接的 they work 是完整句，所以空格不能放關係代名詞，要放關係副詞。因為先行詞是場所，答案是選項(D)。
選項(B)若改成 in which 就是答案。

單字 **locate** 座落於

2. The engineer described the way _____ the machine operated.
工程師描述機器操作的方式。

(A) how　　(B) in which　　(C) which　　(D) on which

解析 空格後接的 the machine operated 是完整句，所以要放關係副詞。先行詞是 the way，所以關係副詞不能用 how，但用 the way in which 就可以，答案是選項(B)。另外，若把本句改成 The engineer described how the machine operated. 也可以。

單字 **describe** 描述 │ **operate** 操作

❷ 關係副詞和關係代名詞

3. London was the city _____ they visited on business.
倫敦是他們出差的城市。

(A) which   (B) where   (C) how   (D) whom

解析 空格後接的 they visited on business 不是完整句，因為及物動詞 visited 沒有受詞，所以空格要放關係代名詞當受詞，答案是選項（A）。
要注意，雖然空格前有表場所的詞，但不一定要用關係副詞 where。

單字 on business 出差

4. This is the factory _____ they produce belts. 這就是他們生產皮帶的工廠。

(A) which   (B) how   (C) in which   (D) whose

解析 句子跟上一題類似，空格後的 they produce belts 是完整句，所以空格要放關係副詞 where，但選項中並沒有 where，所以要找和關係副詞一樣功能的「介系詞＋關係代名詞」，答案是選項（C）。

單字 factory 工廠 ｜ produce 生產

❸ 複合關係副詞

5. _____ you live, you can use our services conveniently.
無論你住在何處，你都可以便利地使用我們的服務。

(A) Wherever   (B) Whoever   (C) What   (D) That

解析 空格要放能將兩個句子連接成一句的詞。如果放選項（B）Whoever you live 會意思不通，是錯誤的句子，所以不能選。答案是選項（A）。

C 題型練習

Select the best answer to complete the sentence.

1. That was the year _____ we established the company.
   (A) which   (B) when
   (C) how   (D) whom

2. There are several reasons _____ we should try harder.
   (A) which   (B) how
   (C) whose   (D) why

3. Seattle was the city _____ Starbucks was founded.
   (A) which   (B) why
   (C) where   (D) whom

4. That was the year _____ he was appointed as chairperson.
   (A) which   (B) how
   (C) on which   (D) in which

5. _____ you look at it, it is a great opportunity.
   (A) However   (B) Which
   (C) What   (D) Why

答案和解析

1. (B)

解析 空格後的 we established the company 是完整句，所以空格要放關係副詞，答案是選項（B）。

當先行詞是表時間的詞時，就可以用關係副詞 when。本句用 when 將「That was the year.」和「In that year, we established the company.」這兩句話連接成一句。

翻譯 那年就是我們成立公司的時間。

單字 establish 成立

---

2. (D)

解析 空格後接的 we should try harder 是完整句，而且因為空格前有 reasons，所以最合適的關係副詞只有 why，答案是選項（D）。

翻譯 有數個原因所以我們應該更努力嘗試。

---

3. (C)

解析 關係代名詞接不完整句，因為關係代名詞一般都在句中當主詞或受詞用。相反的，關係副詞要接完整句，因為副詞不是句子必備的元素。Starbucks was founded 是完整句，所以答案是選項（C）。

選項（B）的先行詞要是 reason 才行。

翻譯 西雅圖是星巴克創立的城市。

單字 found 創立

4. (D)

解析 空格後的 he was appointed as chairperson 是完整句，所以空格可以放關係副詞 when，但若要讓句子更正式，可以用 in which 代替 when，所以答案是選項（D）。

本句用 in which 將「That was the year.」和「In that year, he was appointed as chairperson.」這兩句話連接成一句。

翻譯 那一年就是他被任命為主席的時間。

單字 appoint 任命 ｜ chairperson 主席

---

5. (A)

解析 空格要放能將兩句連接成一句的詞，而選項（A）是複合關係副詞 However，所以答案是選項（A）。

翻譯 不管你怎麼看，那都是絕佳的機會。

D 應用練習　　　▶ 解析 P. 539

Select the best answer to complete the sentence.

1. They arrived at 10:00 a.m., _____ the tour of the factory began.
   (A) which
   (B) that
   (C) when
   (D) what

2. She was guided to the hall, _____ she gave a moving speech.
   (A) whom
   (B) whose
   (C) which
   (D) where

3. That was the reason _____ he was promoted.
   (A) why
   (B) how
   (C) which
   (D) what

4. That was _____ they succeeded as a start-up company.
   (A) the way how
   (B) whom
   (C) whose
   (D) how

5. Seattle was the city _____ they moved to.
   (A) which
   (B) where
   (C) what
   (D) how

6. The place _____ she worked looked amazing.
   (A) how
   (B) where
   (C) whose
   (D) which

7. That was the day _____ he was appointed as chairperson.
   (A) when
   (B) which
   (C) what
   (D) who

8. This is the office _____ they worked together for a long time.
   (A) which
   (B) what
   (C) who
   (D) where

9. _____ there is a problem, Susan can fix it.
   (A) What
   (B) Whenever
   (C) Whom
   (D) Whose

10. _____ you work, you should learn to stay positive.
    (A) Who
    (B) Which
    (C) Wherever
    (D) What

Quick Test for **Parts 5 & 6** ▶ 解析 P. 540

Choose the one word or phrase that best completes the sentence.

1. The final version needs to be ready _____ next Monday.
   (A) until
   (B) although
   (C) when
   (D) by

2. We completed the project successfully _____ Mary's hard work.
   (A) on account of
   (B) even though
   (C) because
   (D) on account

3. You can ask me any question _____ this matter.
   (A) therefore
   (B) already
   (C) concerning
   (D) still

4. Jack has been teaching science _____ nearly 20 years.
   (A) during
   (B) while
   (C) since
   (D) for

5. This device is not only cheap _____ easy to use.
   (A) neither
   (B) but also
   (C) either or
   (D) either

6. You can discuss the matter either with me _____ with Susan.
   (A) and
   (B) nor
   (C) or
   (D) also

7. Both the boss and the employee _____ going to sign the contract.
   (A) is
   (B) are
   (C) has
   (D) have

8. Neither he _____ his wife can play golf.
   (A) both
   (B) either
   (C) nor
   (D) among

9. Eric called the TV station just to _____ his curiosity about the accident.
   (A) satisfy
   (B) succeed
   (C) depend
   (D) arrive

10. She decided to buy the truck, _____ her husband tried to discourage her.
    (A) despite
    (B) although
    (C) in spite
    (D) because of

11. They couldn't tell _____ she was telling the truth or not.
(A) during
(B) at
(C) since
(D) whether

12. Many large corporations wanted to _____ the start-up company.
(A) decide
(B) complain
(C) acquire
(D) graduate

13. The company _____ she worked for was entering the Asian market.
(A) whom
(B) where
(C) what
(D) which

14. We had a special department _____ role was to support customers in every way possible.
(A) why
(B) which
(C) whose
(D) what

15. Can you _____ a good company to invest in?
(A) recommend
(B) fall
(C) regret
(D) spend

16. In 2012, she moved to Singapore, _____ she started her own business.
(A) which
(B) where
(C) that
(D) what

Questions 17–20 refer to the following advertisement.

Do you want to _____ your own business? But did you know _____
        17.   **18.**
most start-up companies fail within five years? That's _____ you need to
                                           19.
call us today at 555-7388 _____.
                     20.

17. (A) start
(B) decrease
(C) reduce
(D) finish

18. (A) since
(B) that
(C) due to
(D) on account of

19. (A) what
(B) which
(C) why
(D) whose

20. (A) Your start-up company is having a lot of problems.
(B) We don't advise you to start your own business.
(C) That was the year when we started our unique services.
(D) With our excellent support, your start-up company will succeed!

Practice Test

▶ 解析 P. 543

Part 5

Directions: A word or phrase is missing in each of the sentences below. Four answer choices are given below each sentence. Select the best answer to complete the sentence. Then mark the letter (A), (B), (C), or (D) on your answer sheet.

---

1. In order to succeed, we should _____ with each other.
   (A) produce
   (B) beautify
   (C) cooperate
   (D) construct

2. The _____ of a new model can be risky.
   (A) develop
   (B) development
   (C) developmental
   (D) developmentally

3. We _____ our employees to be creative.
   (A) asks
   (B) to ask
   (C) ask
   (D) asking

4. It was a good _____ to hire the candidate.
   (A) decision
   (B) decide
   (C) to decide
   (D) decided

5. The atmosphere was _____.
   (A) pleasantly
   (B) to pleasant
   (C) in pleased
   (D) pleasant

6. It doesn't _____ whether you are old or not.
   (A) cause
   (B) popularize
   (C) matter
   (D) celebrate

7. They asked for _____ to build a new college campus.
   (A) permissive
   (B) permitted
   (C) permission
   (D) permissively

8. The _____ was published by a famous publisher.
   (A) novel
   (B) a novel
   (C) these novels
   (D) novels

9. They greeted _____ with open arms.
   (A) us
   (B) we
   (C) our
   (D) ourselves

10. _____ of the students knew the answer to the question.
   (A) Other
   (B) None
   (C) An
   (D) Every

11. The _____ of the environment is important to everyone.
   (A) asset
   (B) candidate
   (C) laboratory
   (D) protection

12. Some of the furniture _____ used by her neighbor.
   (A) were
   (B) was
   (C) to be
   (D) been

13. A lot of things _____ last week.
   (A) happened
   (B) have happened
   (C) will happen
   (D) has happened

14. They _____ in France for nearly 30 years.
   (A) has lived
   (B) have living
   (C) was living
   (D) have lived

15. The wall _____ by a friend of hers.
   (A) was painted
   (B) have been painted
   (C) painted
   (D) have painted

16. His _____ to speak Chinese helped his business.
   (A) vacation
   (B) issue
   (C) ability
   (D) loss

17. We are planning _____ a new website.
   (A) creating
   (B) created
   (C) creates
   (D) to create

18. She finished _____ the washing machine.
   (A) fixing
   (B) to fix
   (C) fixed
   (D) fixes

19. Everyone was _____ with that decision.
   (A) disappointing
   (B) disappointed
   (C) disappoint
   (D) to disappointed

20. _____ by the CEO, the proposal was met with positive responses.
   (A) Supporting
   (B) Supports
   (C) Supported
   (D) Having supported

21. Many teachers still believe that books are a _____ tool for students.
(A) following
(B) useful
(C) free
(D) careless

22. You can learn a lot from _____ people.
(A) success
(B) in success
(C) to success
(D) successful

23. The club's rules are _____ to change without notice.
(A) subject
(B) to subjecting
(C) from subjected
(D) subjected from

24. She was _____ creative that she could invent a lot of things.
(A) such
(B) much
(C) little
(D) so

25. Experts say that praises are _____ than punishment for children.
(A) as effective
(B) most effective
(C) effective
(D) more effective

26. We attended a(n) _____ held in Seoul.
(A) success
(B) conference
(C) secretary
(D) effect

27. _____ being healthy, kimchi is tasty for most people.
(A) In spite
(B) In addition to
(C) In addition
(D) Instead

28. Neither John nor his brother _____ able to run the race.
(A) have
(B) had
(C) were
(D) was

29. They entered the contest for their company, _____ they were not good at singing.
(A) in spite
(B) during
(C) although
(D) despite

30. The officials visited the company, _____ was quite unusual.
(A) which
(B) that
(C) who
(D) what

Part 6

Directions: Read the texts that follow. A word, phrase, or sentence is missing in parts of each text. Four answer choices for each question are given below the text. Select the best answer to complete the text. Then mark the letter (A), (B), (C), or (D) on your answer sheet.

Questions 31–34 refer to the following email.

To: robert@digilog.com

From: xenon@email.com

Date: June 12

Subject: Thank you letter

Dear Robert,

I am so happy _____ from you. I know that you _____ too hard lately.
         31.   32.

_____ Yes, work is important, but you need to take good care of _____.
  33.   34.

31. (A) heard
    (B) to hear
    (C) to hearing
    (D) hears

32. (A) has worked
    (B) having worked
    (C) have been working
    (D) works

33. (A) I'm sorry to say this, but you're too lazy.
    (B) That's why I have been worried about you.
    (C) You're so rich that you don't have to work at all.
    (D) We should help the poor in every way possible.

34. (A) himself
    (B) your
    (C) yourself
    (D) our

Questions 35–38 refer to the following passage.

Korea's History Drama

These days, a lot of people are interested _____ Korea's history. _____
35. 36.
They are not only _____ but also good for _____ about
37. 38.
Korea's history.

---

35. (A) in spite
(B) on account
(C) in
(D) despite

37. (A) interest
(B) interested
(C) interesting
(D) to interested

36. (A) If you are one of them, you are kindly advised to watch Korean dramas.
(B) You can't benefit from learning about Korea's history.
(C) Korea does not have a good relationship with Japan.
(D) These days, history is not popular among Koreans.

38. (A) learning
(B) to learn
(C) learn
(D) learned

Questions 39–42 refer to the following advertisement.

Visit Our Website!

Do you want _____ new people? Do you enjoy _____ good food? Then,
39. 40.
join our website. _____ In addition, we recommend good restaurants so
41.
that you and your new friends _____ enjoy good food together.
42.

---

39. (A) meeting
(B) to meet
(C) met
(D) meets

40. (A) to eat
(B) ate
(C) eaten
(D) eating

41. (A) It is not a good idea to meet new people.
    (B) These days, we can't trust anybody.
    (C) Our website allows you to make friends with interesting people.
    (D) There are too many bad people out there.

42. (A) should
    (B) can
    (C) must
    (D) shall

Questions 43–46 refer to the following post on a website.

Investing in a start-up company is _____. But with the help of this
                                   43.
website, I was able _____ a lot of money. This website allowed me
                    44.
_____ good start-up companies to invest in. _____
   45.   46.

43. (A) useless
    (B) willing
    (C) impossible
    (D) risky

45. (A) find
    (B) to find
    (C) found
    (D) finding

44. (A) earning
    (B) earned
    (C) earn
    (D) to earn

46. (A) If I had not spent money on entertainment, I would be richer now.
    (B) I don't understand why people want to found a start-up company.
    (C) If I had not used this website, I wouldn't have made so much money.
    (D) You have to think again before starting your own business.

Notes

PART

7

閱讀單篇文／多篇文章

類型 **01** 綜合資訊

Ⓐ 輕鬆上手

多益閱讀測驗解題的過程，可以分為三個階段：

階段一 找出訊息的位置 ⇒ 綜合資訊考題是考文章的主題或目的，這類試題的資訊，通常會出現在文章開頭地方。

I am writing this email **to thank you for all your help.**
我寫這封電子郵件想感謝您的一切幫助。

☞ 在電子郵件開始的地方，表示寫信的目的。

資訊有時也會出現在**文章的最後。**

. . . Find that information and get back to me. ……找到那些資訊再回覆給我。

☞ 顯示出寫電子郵件的目的，是要對方進一步連絡以便知道更多訊息。

階段二 理解訊息的內容 ⇒ 是指將文章內容換句話說（paraphrasing）並試圖理解。

. . . to thank you for all your help. ……感謝您的幫助。

☞ . . . to appreciate all your assistance. ……感謝您的協助。

☞ 把「thank you for all your help」這句話換成「to appreciate all your assistance」。

階段三 找出正確答案時 ⇒ 要在選項中找出正確的改寫說法，因為正確答案不會照著文中的句子寫出來。同時也要注意，不要將肯定的含意誤認是否定的含意。

單字 information 資訊 │ appreciate 感謝 │ assistance 幫助

B 基本題型

❶ 主題或目的在文章的前半部

Question 1 refers to the following advertisement.

Christina's Resort Celebrates Its 10th Anniversary

To celebrate our 10th anniversary, we are offering special discounts from October 9 through November 8. Book your stay at our resort during this period, and you'll get a 20% discount. Yes, it's a 20% discount! Don't miss this rare opportunity. Call us today at 955-2121.

克莉絲汀娜渡假村歡慶十週年

為了慶祝我們十週年，我們將在 10 月 9 日到 11 月 8 日提供特價優惠。若在這段期間於我們的渡假村訂房住宿，可以獲得八折優惠。沒錯，八折優惠！別錯過這次難得的機會。現在就打電話到 955-2121。

What is mainly being advertised?

(A) A special resort for teenagers

(B) A resort's reduced rates

廣告的主要內容是什麼？

(A) 特別替青少年打造的渡假村

(B) 渡假村的折扣

解析 這是廣告文章，第一句話顯示出文章的主題是慶祝十週年慶，提供打折優惠，答案是選項（B）。選項（A）是利用廣告中的 special 這個字，還有利用 tenth 而聯想的 teenagers 這個字做成的誤答陷阱。

單字 resort 渡假村 ┃ celebrate 慶祝 ┃ anniversary 週年 ┃ offer 提供 ┃ discount 折扣 ┃ book 預訂 ┃ rare 難得的 ┃ opportunity 機會 ┃ teenager 青少年 ┃ reduced 減少的 ┃ rate 價格

❷ 主題或目的在文章後半部

Hi Eric,

How is everything? I'm sure you're doing well in your new role as project manager.

As you already know, the National Manufacturing Association's Conference will be held in New York on July 15. Unfortunately, I can't go to the event because I'll be having a meeting with an important client that day. So, I would like you to attend the conference on behalf of our company.

艾瑞克你好：

一切可好？我相信你把擔任專案經理的新角色扮演得很好。

如你所知，全國製造協會研討會將在 7 月 15 日於紐約舉行。遺憾地是，我無法出席這個活動，因為當天我要和一位重要的客戶會面。所以我想請你代表我們公司參加大會。

What is the purpose of this email?

(A) To ask a favor of the recipient

(B) To congratulate the recipient on his promotion

這封電子郵件的目的是什麼？

A. 請收件者幫忙

B. 恭喜收件者升官

解析 在這封電子郵件一開始的地方，提到收件者有新工作，但不要以為答案是選項（B），因為寫電郵的目的出現在後半部。寄件者自己沒辦法出席會議，拜託收件者代替他去參加，答案是選項（A）。

單字 role 角色 ｜ project 專案 ｜ manager 經理 ｜ national 全國的 ｜ manufacturing 製造 ｜ association 協會 ｜ conference 研討會 ｜ event 活動 ｜ client 客戶 ｜ attend 參加 ｜ on behalf of 代表 ｜ favor 幫忙 ｜ recipient 收件者 ｜ congratulate 恭喜 ｜ promotion 升官

C 題型練習

Question 1 refers to the following letter.

To Whom It May Concern:

I am writing this letter to apply for a position as editor for MG Publishing House. As you can see from my résumé, I am an experienced editor. During my six years with SW Publishers, I edited many different books, which turned out to be best-sellers. Therefore, I am sure I will help your company a lot.

1. Why was this letter written?
   (A) To apply for a job with SW Publishers
   (B) To ask MG Publishing House to consider the writer's application

Question 2 refers to the following article.

TORONTO (15 January) - Jane Eastwood, a native of Toronto, is famous for being an "interesting" cook. She does not follow traditional recipes. Instead, she tries to invent new ways to cook food. Eastwood says, "Cooking is my passion, and I really want to cook something special." She will open her own restaurant next month and invite everyone to taste her special food.

2. What is the main topic of the article?
   (A) Special restaurants for natives of Toronto
   (B) A cook's unique cooking styles

答案和解析

1. Answer (B)

翻譯 敬啟者：

我寫這封信的目的是要應徵 MG 出版社的編輯職位。您可從我的履歷表看出，我有當編輯的經驗。在 SW 出版社六年的任職期間，我編輯了許多不同類型的書籍，最後都成為暢銷書。因此，我相信我會為貴公司提供很大的幫助。

....

這封信的撰寫動機是什麼？
(A) 應徵在 SW 出版社的工作
(B) 請求 MG 出版社考慮寄件者的應徵。

解析 寫這封信的原因在一開始的地方有提到，是為了要應徵 MG 出版社而寫信。雖然選項（A）把信的第一句話前半部照樣寫了出來，但後面卻錯了，不是應徵 SW 出版社，所以是錯誤答案。選項（B）把應徵者想說的話正確地換了一種說法，所以是答案。

單字 concern 相關 | apply 應徵 | position 職位 | editor 編輯 | publishing house 出版社 | résumé 履歷表 | experienced 有經驗的 | edit 編輯 | best-seller 暢銷書 | consider 考慮 | application 應徵

2. Answer (B)

翻譯 多倫多（1 月 15 日）──多倫多本地人珍・伊斯特伍德頗為知名，因為她是位「有意思的」廚師。她不採用傳統食譜，相反地，她嘗試發明烹調食物的新方法。伊斯特伍德說：「烹飪是我的熱情所在，而我真的很想做出特別的菜色。」她自己成立的餐廳將在下個月開幕，並邀請所有人去品嚐她的特色料理。

....

這篇文章的主題是什麼？
(A) 為多倫多當地人開設的餐廳
(B) 一位廚師與眾不同的烹飪風格

解析 文章的主題沒辦法用一句話清楚說明，要思考整篇文章內容才能解題，屬於較難的試題。因為整篇文章都是在講 Jane Eastwood 獨特的料理方式，答案是選項（B）。這篇報導不是要介紹餐廳，選項（A）是錯的。

單字 native 本地人 | famous 知名的 | cook 廚師 | traditional 傳統的 | recipe 食譜 | invent 發明 | passion 熱情 | invite 邀請 | unique 特別的 | style 風格

D 應用練習　　▶ 解析 P. 548

Question 1 refers to the following advertisement.

Are you planning to visit an English-speaking country? Do you want to make yourself understood in English? Then, download our Easy Interpretation app now! Just speak to this app in your native language. Then, Easy Interpretation will translate it into English and speak for you. What are you waiting for? Download this amazing app right now!

1. What is mainly being advertised?
   (A) An effective way to learn a foreign language
   (B) An app that translates the user's language into English

Question 2 refers to the following memo.

To: All Staff
From: Alice Tannen, CEO
Date: March 25
Subject: Our Family-Friendly Polices

We are a family-friendly company. So, we pursue family-friendly policies. But not many workers benefit from these policies. This is because they do not know what our policies are. Therefore, we have decided to publish a pamphlet to explain all our family-friendly policies.

2. Why was the memo written?
   (A) To say that the company is a family-run business
   (B) To explain why the company will publish a pamphlet

類型 **02** 細節訊息

 A 輕鬆上手

細節訊息題型，通常都是由**疑問詞**起始句子，經由詢問想得到特定的答案。
透過此試題，了解細節訊息試題的解題方法。

Experts say that stress can be bad for workers. If workers suffer from stress, they can have difficulty focusing on their work. Then, the workers cannot do their work properly. Therefore, employers need to think about ways to reduce stress in the workplace.

Q What will happen when workers are under stress according to the paragraph?
(A) They will be more productive.
(B) They will be less efficient.

專家說壓力可能會對勞工造成不良影響。如果勞工因壓力受苦，他們可能無法專心工作。然後，勞工就無法順利完成工作。所以，僱主都需要思考在職場減壓的方式。

Q 根據此段文字，勞工承受壓力時會發生什麼事？
(A) 他們會更有生產力
(B) 他們會比較沒效率

文中提到，勞工若感到壓力，就無法好好工作。若將這句話換個說法就是選項（Ｂ）。efficient 的意思是「有效率的」，所以答案是選項（Ｂ）。

細節訊息類型和綜合資訊類型一樣，答案會改寫文章內的句子。等到確認需要的訊息在文中何處，再找出將該訊息正確改寫的選項。

單字 expert 專家 | suffer from 受苦於 | focus on 專心於 |
properly 適當地 | employer 僱主 | reduce 減少 |
workplace 職場 | productive 有生產力的 | efficient 有效率的

Ⓑ 基本題型

❶ 有關人的細節資訊

Question 1 refers to the following article.

Mary is an interesting person in many ways. For starters, she makes "small" things, such as paper roses. After she has made them, Mary gives them away. She believes that by giving away her works of art, she can create happiness. A lot of people feel that her belief is worth spreading.	瑪莉在許多方面都是很有趣的人。首先,她製作「小」玩意,像是紙玫瑰。當她做完這些小玩意後,瑪莉就把那些成品送人。她相信把她的藝術品送人,就可以創造快樂。很多人覺得她的信念值得散播。
What kind of person is Mary? (A) She is selfish. (B) She is generous.	瑪莉是什麼樣的人? (A) 她很自私 (B) 她很慷慨

解析 介紹人物也是多益重要的出題類型。看到文章可以知道,製作小藝術品的瑪莉將自己的作品免費送人,目的是為了散播快樂。答案是選項(B)。

單字 **for starters** 首先 | **give away** 送人 | **work of art** 藝術品 | **spread** 散播 | **selfish** 自私的 | **generous** 慷慨的

❷ 有關事務的細節資訊

Question 2 refers to the following email.

Dear Mr. Parker,

Thank you for your order. It usually takes two business days for us to process orders placed online. Therefore, you will probably receive your order by March 3. If you have any questions about your order, feel free to call me at 623-8989. You can also call my secretary at 623-8987. Again, thank you for your order. We really appreciate it.

親愛的帕克先生：

感謝您的訂購。我們通常要花兩個工作天處理線上訂單，因此，您大概會在三月三日前收到貨品。如果您對訂單有任何問題，請打 623-8989 隨時和我聯繫，您也可以打 623-8987 和我的秘書聯絡。再次感謝您的訂購。我們真的很感激。

By when will Mr. Parker's order arrive?

(A) March 3
(B) March 2

帕克先生的貨品在哪一天前會送到？

A. 三月三日
B. 三月二日

解析 這是一封帕克先生向訂購商品的收件者表達感謝的信。題目問細節資訊，信中說三月三日前會收到商品，答案是選項（A）。

參考：時常被譯作「大約、可能」的 probably，意思同等於「幾乎是確定地（almost certainly）」。

單字 **order** 訂單 | **business day** 工作天 | **process** 處理 | **probably** 大概 | **receive** 收到 | **appreciate** 感激

C 題型練習

Question 1 refers to the following notice.

Julie's Language Institute has been in business for almost 10 years. We have served thousands of language learners from all over the world. We are currently looking for competent language teachers. Successful candidates must speak at least two languages. If you are interested in this full-time position, email your résumé and cover letter to sean_smith@julieslang.com.

1. Who can apply for this full-time position?
    (A) Someone who is proficient in at least two languages
    (B) Someone who wants to learn at least two languages

Question 2 refers to the following article.

Traveling in South Korea can be fun. It can also be "insightful." Susan Black has been traveling throughout South Korea for three years. She says that there are so many temples in the country where you can relax. At the same time, in these wonderful temples, you can reflect on life, which can give you new insights into your life. So, traveling in South Korea may change how you look at your life.

2. What can you do in temples in South Korea?
    (A) You can think carefully about your life.
    (B) You can meet interesting people.

1. Answer (A)

翻譯 茱莉語言學院已經經營了近十年。我們已服務了來自世界各地數千名的語言學習者。我們目前正在尋找合格的語言老師,成功的候選人必須至少會說兩種語言。如果你對此全職職位有興趣,請將你的履歷和求職信寄到 sean_smith@julieslang.com。

誰可以應徵此全職職位?
(A) 至少嫻熟兩種語言的人
(B) 想要學習至少兩種語言的人

解析 這是徵求語言老師的廣告。先介紹語言學校,再表示應徵語言學校老師的資格。因為應徵條件是至少要會說兩種語言,答案是選項(A)。

單字 in business 經營 | serve 服務 | currently 目前 | competent 合格的 | candidate 候選人 | full-time position 全職職位 | cover letter 求職信 | proficient 嫻熟

2. Answer (A)

翻譯 在南韓旅行可以很有趣,也可以很有「深度」。蘇珊・布雷克在南韓全國旅遊已有三年。她說南韓有許多可以讓你放鬆的廟宇。同時,在這些美麗的廟宇中,你可審視生活,那可以讓你對自己的人生有全新的洞察。所以,在南韓旅遊可能會改變你對自己人生的看法。

你可以在南韓的廟宇中做什麼?
(A) 你可以好好審視自己的生活
(B) 你可以認識有趣的人

解析 這是詢問事物細節資訊的試題。因為文章中出現了「深度、洞察」這樣的字眼,答案是選項(A)。
選項(B)並沒有出現在文章中。完全沒出現在文章中的內容,在細節資訊的試題中,絕對不會是答案。

單字 insightful 有深度的 | relax 放鬆 | reflect on 審視 | insight 洞察 | interesting 有趣的

▶ 解析 P. 549

D 應用練習

Question 1 refers to the following text message chain.

Paul Smith   2:00 p.m.

Clara, can you go to the airport to pick up Julia Lawrence?

Clara Garner   2:05 p.m.

Hi, Paul. You mean the CEO of the new clothing company?

Paul Smith   2:10 p.m.

Yes. Although her company is new, it is highly successful.

1. Who is Ms. Lawrence?

(A) An executive of a successful company

(B) Someone who wants to start a clothing company

Question 2 refers to the following online chat discussion.

Adams, Jane   9:30 a.m.

Hi. Can we meet in the afternoon to discuss the quarterly report?

Johnson, Kevin   9:31 a.m.

Hi. I'm having a meeting with a new client in the afternoon. She wants to advertise her products on TV.

Adams, Jane   9:32 a.m.

OK. Can you advise her to advertise on the Internet? Maybe we can meet tomorrow.

2. What does Ms. Adams want Mr. Johnson to do?

(A) To advertise some products on TV

(B) To ask a client to change her mind

類型 03 插入式句子

 輕鬆上手

插入句子的類型是新試題類型，要將題目中的句子，放進文章某個空格中。

找出答案的方式，分成利用字彙和利用文法兩種。

利用字彙	找出空格前一句話中所使用的字彙，並看看有沒有和提示句相似的字彙。

In order to succeed, we need to **satisfy the needs of** our customers. To **serve** them, we should be more creative.
為了成功，我們要滿足顧客的需求。為了服務他們，我們應該更有創意。

☞ satisfy the needs of 和 serve 是相似的意思。利用相似的字彙，就能知道這句話應該放進文章的哪個位置。

利用文法	利用像 therefore 這樣的連接副詞，或利用像 they 這樣的代名詞來解題。

A lot of customers are complaining about our service. We have to do everything to make sure that **this** doesn't happen again.
很多顧客對我們的服務產生抱怨。我們必須盡全力確保這種情況不會再發生。

☞ 第二句的 this 就是在指前句的內容。像這樣利用 this 就能知道提示句適合放進哪個位置。

在實際的考試中，因為要將提示句放進較長的文章中難度較高，所以除了利用上述兩種方法外，還要思考文章內容的來龍去脈以挑選答案。

單字 succeed 成功 ｜ satisfy 滿足 ｜ need 需求 ｜ customer 顧客 ｜ creative 有創意的 ｜ complain 抱怨 ｜ make sure 確保

Ⓑ 基本題型

❶ 利用字彙的方法

Question 1 refers to the following article.

Lakeview Public Library says that used books can help students in developing countries. Many of these students are eager to learn English. – [1] – Give your used books to the library. They will be used to help students master English. – [2] –

湖景公立圖書館表示，二手書可以幫助開發中國家的學生。那裡有許多學生渴望學英文。
– [1] – 把二手書捐給圖書館，它們將被用來幫助學生學好英文。
– [2] –

In which of the positions marked [1] and [2] does the following sentence best belong?
"But they don't have many books written in English."

(A) [1]

(B) [2]

[1] 和 [2] 哪一個位置最適合插入以下句子？
「但他們並沒有很多英文書籍。」

(A) [1]

(B) [2]

解析 將提示句直接放進文章的〔1〕和〔2〕中就知道哪個比較通順。若放〔1〕的話，它前面有片語 learn English，因為這個片語能夠和 written in English 連接，答案是選項（A）。放進〔2〕的話，意思就不通順。

單字 used 使用過的 | developing country 開發中國家 | eager 渴望 | master 精通

❷ 利用文法的方法

Question 2 refers to the following letter.

Dear Barry, Thank you so much for the quick reply. I'm so happy we can meet in Seoul. – [1] –Are you interested in Korea's history? Then, we can visit Joseon Dynasty royal tombs in the city. – [2] –	親愛的貝瑞： 非常感謝您的快速回覆。我很高興我們可以在首爾見面。– [1] – 你對韓國的歷史有興趣嗎？那麼，我們可以參觀首爾的朝鮮王朝皇陵。– [2] –

In which of the positions marked [1] and [2] does the following sentence best belong? "These tombs will allow us to understand the rich history of Korea." (A) [1] (B) [2]	[1] 和 [2] 哪一個位置最適合插入以下句子？ 「這些陵墓可以讓我們了解韓國的豐富歷史。」 (A) [1] (B) [2]

解析 提示句的主詞是 these tombs，其中的 these 是指前面出現的事物，所以前一句話中要有 tombs，答案是選項 (B)，也就是放進〔2〕中。
若放進〔1〕，因為前面沒有 tombs，所以不適合。

單字 reply 回覆 | dynasty 王朝 | royal 皇家的 | tomb 陵墓 | rich 豐富的

C 題型練習

Question 1 refers to the following email.

Dear Clara,

– [1] – I'm having a meeting with a local homeless charity tomorrow. Because the CEO really cares about the homeless, I'm sure she'll support the charity's event next month. – [2] – This event will help our citizens better understand homeless people.

1. In which of the positions marked [1] and [2] does the following sentence best belong?

"The organization will invite everyone to talk with homeless people."

(A) [1]

(B) [2]

Question 2 refers to the following article.

Riding a bicycle has many benefits. – [1] – Bicycles do not burn fossil fuels, which cause global warming. – [2] – So, if you ride a bicycle instead of driving, you can help slow down global warming. At the same time, you can also get some exercise.

2. In which of the positions marked [1] and [2] does the following sentence best belong?

"For starters, it is good for the environment."

(A) [1]

(B) [2]

答案和解析

1. Answer (B)

翻譯 –[1]–我明天要和當地的街友慈善機構會談。因為執行長真的很關心街友,我相信她會支持慈善機構在下個月的活動。–[2]–這個活動將會幫助我們的市民更了解街友。

....

[1] 和 [2] 哪一個位置最適合插入以下句子?

「這個組織會邀請所有人和街友聊天。」

(A) [1]
(B) [2]

解析 提示句要放進〔2〕才通順,可以很自然地說明前面的 the charity's event next month,答案是選項(B)。放進〔1〕會突然出現團體(The organization),但卻沒人知道這是什麼,很怪。

單字 **homeless** 無家可歸的 |
charity 慈善機構 | **support** 支持 |
citizen 市民

2. Answer (A)

翻譯 騎腳踏車有很多優點。–[1]–腳踏車不會燃燒石化燃料造成全球暖化。–[2]–所以,如果你放棄開車而改騎腳踏車,就可以幫助減緩全球暖化。同時,你也可以保護環境。

....

[1] 和 [2] 哪一個位置最適合插入以下句子?

「首先,那對環境很友善。」

A. [1]
B. [2]

解析 提示句放進〔1〕才通順,答案是選項(A)。提示句中的 it 是指前一句的 Riding a bicycle,用代名詞 it 代替它。這題要用文法知識來解題。

單字 **benefit** 優點 |
fossil fuel 石化燃料 |
global warming 全球暖化 |
slow down 減緩 | **protect** 保護

D 應用練習　　　　　　▶ 解析 P. 550

Question 1 refers to the following email.

> Dear Paul,
>
> I've just read your article about the danger of eating meat. – [1] – But experts say that we need to eat some meat. If we don't eat meat at all, we cannot stay healthy. – [2] – So, I think you should rewrite your article.

1. In which of the positions marked [1] and [2] does the following sentence best belong?
   "Eating too much meat may not be good for our health."
   (A) [1]
   (B) [2]

Question 2 refers to the following announcement.

> We are a company that really cares about our customers.
> – [1] – Are they satisfied with them? Are they disappointed with them? We invite our customers to visit our special website www.yourvoicematters.com to tell us their opinions. – [2] –

2. In which of the positions marked [1] and [2] does the following sentence best belong?
   "So, we really want to know what they think about our products."
   (A) [1]
   (B) [2]

類型 **04** 掌握目的

A 輕鬆上手

掌握目的類型是新題型，會針對閱讀試題中顯示簡訊或線上聊天的文字內容出題。
此題型大致分為「理解和肯定」以及「疑問和否定」兩種。

Eric Parker   3:19 p.m.
We need to remind everybody that the party
has been cancelled.

Julia Bauer   3:24 p.m.
Got it. I'll take care of the marketing
department.

艾瑞克・帕克　下午 3:19
我們要提醒大家，派對已
經取消了。

茱莉亞・伯爾　下午 3:24
收到。我會負責傳達給行
銷部門。

Q At 3:24, what does Ms. Bauer mean when
she writes, "Got it"?
(A) She wants to go to the party.
(B) She understands what Mr. Parker said.

Q 在下午 3:24 時，伯爾小姐
說「收到」是什麼意思？
(A) 她想去參加派對
(B) 她了解帕克先生說的話

☞ 「got it」是「了解、知道」的意思。看前後句脈絡，可以知道這句話是伯爾聽
帕克說派對取消之後說的，所以答案是選項（B）。本題可以視為理解和肯定
的類型。

單字 remind 提醒 ｜ cancel 取消

B 基本題型

❶ 理解和肯定

Question 1 refers to the following text message chain.

Cindy White 1:05 p.m. Jack, how did the conference in Seoul go?	辛蒂・懷特 下午 1:05 傑克，首爾的研討會進行得 如何？
Jack Smith 1:10 p.m. It went smoothly. Each presentation gave me new insights.	傑克・史密斯 下午 1:10 進行得很順利。每場簡報都給 我許多新的見解。
Cindy White 1:20 p.m. That's great. Can you tell me more about your new insights?	辛蒂・懷特 下午 1:20 太棒了。可以告訴我更多你的 新的見解嗎？

At 1:20, what does Ms. White mean when she writes, "That's great"?

(A) She is happy to learn that the conference was satisfactory.

(B) She doesn't want to attend the conference herself.

在下午 1:20，懷特小姐說「太棒了」是什麼意思？

(A) 她很高興知道大會令人滿意。

(B) 她不想親自參加大會。

解析 看到前後句脈絡可以知道，懷特說很棒，表示對首爾會議的結果很滿意，答案是選項(A)。從內容推測，懷特這麼關心這個會議，應該也想出席，所以選項(B)是錯誤答案。

單字 conference 研討會 | smoothly 順利地 | presentation 簡報 | insight 見解 | satisfactory 令人滿意的

❷ 疑問和否定

Question 2 refers to the following online chat.

10:20 a.m. **Monroe, Mary** Richard, have you talked to Mr. James Collins?	早上 10:20 瑪莉・蒙羅 理察，你和詹姆斯・柯林斯先生談過了嗎？
10:21 a.m. **Parker, Richard** Yes, I have. But I still don't understand why he's complaining.	早上 10:21 理查・帕克 對，我已經談過了。但我還是無法理解他為何抱怨。
10:22 a.m. **Monroe, Mary** Me neither. But he's an important customer, so we need to satisfy him.	早上 10:22 瑪麗・蒙羅 我也不懂。但他是一位重要的客戶，所以我們要滿足他的需求。

At 10:22, what does Ms. Monroe mean when she writes, "Me neither"?

(A) She doesn't think Mr. Parker should get along with Mr. Collins.

(B) She doesn't understand what makes Mr. Collins disappointed.

早上 10:22 時，蒙羅小姐說「我也不懂」是什麼意思？

(A) 她不認為帕克先生和柯林斯先生處得來。

(B) 她不理解什麼讓柯林斯先生失望。

解析 看到前後句脈絡，可以知道蒙羅小姐也不知道柯林斯先生為何抱怨，所以答案是選項（B）。

單字 customer 客戶 ｜ satisfy 滿足 ｜ get along with 處得來 ｜ disappointed 失望的

C 題型練習

Question 1 refers to the following text message chain.

Dominic Johnson	2:20 p.m.

Dominic Johnson   2:20 p.m.
Amy, where are you going to stay in Seoul?

Amy Gradin   2:25 p.m.
I'm going to stay in the Roberts Hotel. I think it's the best hotel in the city.

Dominic Johnson   2:32 p.m.
I couldn't agree more. I'll stay there when I visit Seoul next month.

1. At 2:32, what does Mr. Johnson mean when he writes,

   "I couldn't agree more"?

   (A) He doesn't agree with Ms. Gradin because the hotel is disappointing.

   (B) He thinks the Roberts Hotel is the best hotel in Seoul.

Question 2 refers to the following online chat.

2:15 p.m.   **Park, Rachel**
             Daniel, are you flying to New York?

2:16 p.m.   **Smith, Daniel**
             I'm thinking about driving there. What do you think?

2:17 p.m.   **Park, Rachel**
             I don't think that's a good idea. Flying will save you a lot of time.

2. At 2:17, what does Ms. Park mean when she writes,

   "I don't think that's a good idea"?

   (A) She doesn't think driving to New York is a good idea.

   (B) She doesn't think flying to New York will be convenient.

答案和解析

1. Answer (B)

翻譯　多米尼克 · 強森　　　　下午 2:20
艾美，你在首爾時要住哪裡？

艾梅 · 格拉丁　　　　下午 2:25
我會住羅勃茲飯店，我認為那是首爾最棒的飯店。

多米尼克 · 強森　　　　下午 2:32
我非常同意，我下個月造訪首爾時也會住那裡。

⋯⋯⋯⋯⋯⋯⋯⋯⋯⋯⋯⋯⋯⋯⋯⋯

在下午 2:32 時，強森先生說「我非常同意」是什麼意思？
(A) 他不同意格拉丁小姐，因為飯店讓人失望
(B) 他認為羅勃茲飯店是首爾最棒的飯店

解析　片語「I couldn't agree more」是對某見解表示完全同意，答案是選項(B)。因為片語中有 not，所以很容易誤認為是否定含意，要小心。

單字　agree 同意 |
disappointing 令人失望的

2. Answer (A)

翻譯　　下午 2:15　　　　瑞秋 · 帕克
丹尼爾，你要搭飛機到紐約嗎？

下午 2:16　　　　丹尼爾 · 史密斯
我考慮開車過去。你有什麼想法？

下午 2:17　　　　瑞秋 · 帕克
我認為那不是個好點子，搭飛機會讓你節省很多時間。

⋯⋯⋯⋯⋯⋯⋯⋯⋯⋯⋯⋯⋯⋯⋯⋯

在下午 2:17 時，帕克小姐說「我認為那不是個好點子」是什麼意思？
(A) 她不認為開車到紐約是好點子
(B) 她不認為坐飛機到紐約很方便

解析　從對話內容來看，可以知道帕克小姐對「開車去」是抱持否定看法的。所以答案是選項(A)。

單字　save 節省 | convenient 方便的

374

D 應用練習　　　　　　　　　　　　　▶ 解析 P. 550

Question 1 refers to the following text message chain.

> **Melanie McLean**　　　　　　　　　　3:15 p.m.
> James, have you taken a look at the cover of Amy's book?
>
> **James Smith**　　　　　　　　　　　3:25 p.m.
> Yes, I have. I think it will appeal to children.
>
> **Melanie McLean**　　　　　　　　　　3:27 p.m.
> I'm happy to hear that. Her book is aimed at children.

1. At 3:27, what does Ms. McLean mean when she writes,

   "I'm happy to hear that"?

   (A) She is happy to hear that Mr. Smith has already read Amy's book.

   (B) She is pleased to learn that the cover of Amy's book will attract children.

Question 2 refers to the following online chat.

> 4:30 p.m.　**Rice, Susan**
> 　　　　　Scott, what do you think of the CEO's proposal?
>
> 4:31 p.m.　**Boyle, Scott**
> 　　　　　To tell you the truth, I don't think employees will support it.
>
> 4:32 p.m.　**Rice, Susan**
> 　　　　　What makes you think so? I expect a lot of employees will like the proposal.

2. At 4:32, what does Ms. Rice mean when she writes,

   "What makes you think so?"?

   (A) She does not agree with Mr. Boyle.

   (B) She wants to discuss the proposal with the CEO.

類型 **05** 推測題

 A 輕鬆上手

推測的類型，分成「對全文綜合資訊的意圖作推測」和「對文章內容引導的細節資訊作推測」兩種。

本文要由全文綜合資訊來作推測。

A lot of people say that a college education is too expensive. Yes, it is. But in order to earn more money, your children must go to college. You may not have enough money for your children. Don't worry. We have a lot of financial aid programs for your children.	很多人說大學教育太昂貴了。確實如此。然而為了賺更多錢，您的孩子一定要上大學。您可能沒有足夠資金準備孩子的學費。別擔心。我們有很多財務援助計劃可以幫助您的子女。
Q At whom is the advertisement aimed? (A) Parents who want their children to go to college (B) Parents who have recently graduated from college	**Q** 這個廣告的訴求對象是誰？ (A) 希望孩子上大學的父母 (B) 最近剛從大學畢業的父母

☞ 本廣告鎖定的目標沒辦法單從一句話得知，不過從內容看來，可以推測廣告的對象是希望子女上大學的父母，答案是選項（A）。

單字 **in order to** 為了 | **financial** 財務的 | **aid** 援助 | **recently** 最近 | **graduate** 畢業

Ⓑ 基本題型

❶ 對全文綜合資訊的意圖作推測

Question 1 refers to the following guideline.

A lot of college students want to submit their articles to our magazine.	很多大學生想投稿到我們的雜誌。
The submission guidelines are as follows.	以下為投稿準則。
• The title of your article: Up to 20 characters	• 文章標題：最多 20 字
• The length of your article: Up to 1,000 words	• 文章長度：最多 1,000 字
• The topic of your article: College life	• 文章主題：大學生活

What is suggested about the magazine?	以下關於雜誌的推測何者為真？
(A) It is popular among general readers.	(A) 受到一般讀者的歡迎
(B) It is mainly aimed at college students.	(B) 主要訴求大學生

解析 首先，文章並無直接提到這本雜誌鎖定的讀者群，但是想到是大學生投稿，投稿的主題是大學生活，就可以推測這本雜誌主要的閱讀對象是大學生，答案是選項 (B)。

選項 (A) 因無法確知，所以不能選。

單字 submit 繳交 ｜ article 文章 ｜ submission 投稿 ｜ guideline 準則 ｜ title 標題 ｜ length 長度 ｜ popular 受歡迎的 ｜ mainly 主要地

❷ 對文章內容引導的細節資訊作推測

Question 2 refers to the following online chat.

2:20 p.m. **Collins, Michael** Jane, can you translate this document into Korean?	下午 2:20 麥可・柯林斯 珍，你可以把這份文件翻譯 成韓文嗎？
2:21 p.m. **Foster, Jane** Yes, I can. Oh, didn't you know? I was born in Seoul.	下午 2:21 珍・福斯特 好，我可以。對了，你不知 道嗎？我是在首爾出生的。
2:22 p.m. **Collins, Michael** Oh really? So, you can speak both English and Korean.	下午 2:22 麥可・柯林斯 真的嗎？所以你會說英語和 韓語。

What is suggested about the document?　　以下關於這份文件的推測何者為真？

(A) It is written in English.　　(A) 文件以英文撰寫

(B) It was written by a college professor.　　(B) 是由大學教授撰寫

解析 珍會說英語和韓語，並負責將英文譯成韓文，所以文件應該是用英文寫的，答案是選項(A)。
選項(B)是完全無法推測得知的內容，所以是錯誤答案。

單字 translate 翻譯 ｜ professor 教授

C 題型練習

Question 1 refers to the following text message chain.

Donald Johnson	10:15 a.m.

Willow, are you ready to interview the best-selling author?

Willow Snow	10:19 a.m.

Yes, I am. Interviewing famous people is my job, after all.

Donald Johnson	10:23 a.m.

I just want to make sure that everything is ready.

1. What is suggested about Ms. Snow?

   (A) She does not get along with Mr. Johnson.

   (B) She is probably a reporter.

Question 2 refers to the following advertisement.

A lot of people worry about their washing machines, which is understandable. Most washing machines use too much water. This means that they also use too much electricity. So, we've decided to produce our new Slim Washing Machine. You don't have to worry about water or electricity when using our new washing machine.

2. What is suggested about the washing machine?

   (A) It is more expensive than other washing machines.

   (B) It uses less electricity.

答案和解析

1. Answer (B)

翻譯
唐納德・強森　　早上 10:15
葳蘿，你準備好要訪問暢銷作家嗎？

葳蘿・史諾　　早上 10:19
嗯，我準備好了。畢竟訪問名人是我的工作。

唐納德・強森　　早上 10:23
我只是想確認一切已經就緒。

⋯⋯⋯⋯⋯⋯⋯⋯⋯⋯⋯⋯⋯⋯⋯⋯⋯

以下關於史諾小姐的暗示何者為真？
(A) 她和強森先生處不來
(B) 她可能是記者

解析 史諾小姐提到訪問名人是她的工作，由此看來，可以推測她是記者的可能性很高，答案是選項（B）。選項（A）無法從文章中得知。

單字 best-selling author 暢銷作家｜
famous 知名的｜after all 畢竟｜
make sure 確認｜reporter 記者

2. Answer (B)

翻譯
很多人擔心他們的洗衣機，那是可以理解的。多數洗衣機使用太多水，這表示它們也使用太多電力。所以，我們決定生產新型的節能洗衣機。當您使用我們的新洗衣機時，就不用擔心水或電的問題。

⋯⋯⋯⋯⋯⋯⋯⋯⋯⋯⋯⋯⋯⋯⋯⋯⋯

在以下關於這款洗衣機的暗示何者為真？
(A) 這款洗衣機比其他洗衣機更貴
(B) 它使用較少的電力

解析 這題要推測洗衣機的細節資訊。雖然文中並沒有直接提到，但是可以推測使用這台洗衣機可以節省水和電，答案是選項（B）。選項（A）完全無法從內容中得知。

單字 washing machine 洗衣機｜
understandable 可以理解的｜
electricity 電力｜produce 生產

Ⓓ 應用練習　　　　　　　▶ 解析 P. 551

Question 1 refers to the following text message chain.

_ □ ×

To	erica@yaho.com
From	robert@solute.com
Subject	CEO meeting
Date	June 2

Dear Erica,

In response to your question, I would like to meet with the CEO of your company on Friday. As you may know, I'm giving a speech to some college students on Wednesday. The CEO may be interested in the topic of my speech. It's about how to be more competitive in this globalized world.

1. What is suggested about the CEO?

(A) She has been working with Erica since she founded her company.

(B) She may be interested in improving competitiveness.

Question 2 refers to the following online chat.

Cooper, Amanda　　　　　　　3:15 p.m.
Jack, can you come to my office to repair my computer?

Palmer, Jack　　　　　　　3:16 p.m.
Not now. I'm dealing with an urgent matter.

Cooper, Amanda　　　　　　　3:17 p.m.
I see. Then, let me know when you can come to my office.

2. What is suggested about Mr. Palmer?

(A) He is Ms. Cooper's supervisor.

(B) He can fix computer problems.

類型 06　字彙題

Ⓐ 輕鬆上手

字彙試題是要考生找出與題目意思相同的字彙，可以把它想成是考同義字的試題。解字彙題的訣竅不是要一味地背誦，而是要思考它在句中的用法。

Question 1 refers to the following email.

Dear Michael,

I'm sorry to learn that you haven't achieved what you wanted to this week. But there is still time to finish what you started. I know you're a very diligent person, so I'm sure you'll try harder to achieve what you want.

Good luck with your work.

Ⓠ The word "achieved" in line 2 is closest in meaning to

　(A) reached a goal
　(B) arrived in a city

親愛的麥可：

我得知你在本週並未達成你要的目標而感到遺憾，但你還有時間可以完成未盡之志。我知道你是個非常勤奮的人，因此我相信你會更努力完成你的目標。

祝你順利成功。

Ⓠ 第二行中的「達成」最接近什麼意思？

　(A) 完成目標
　(B) 抵達一個城市

☞ 文章脈絡很清楚，所以很容易找出答案。文章中的 achieved 是「完成了、成就了」的意思，答案是選項（A）。

單字 achieve 達成 │ diligent 勤奮的 │ goal 目標

Ⓑ 基本題型

❶ 同義字 (1)

Question 1 refers to the following email.

Dear Mr. Jack Summers,

We're pleased to learn that you've decided to work with us. We know that you are an excellent graphic designer. We also know that you could have chosen another graphic design company. Therefore, your decision to choose us means a lot to us. We won't let you down. And we're sure you won't disappoint us either.

親愛的傑克‧桑瑪斯先生：

我們很高興得知您已決定要與我們共事合作。我們知道你是一位優秀的平面設計師。我們也知道您也可以選擇另一家平面設計公司。因此，您決定挑選我們對我們來說意義重大。我們不會讓您失望。而且我們也確信您不會讓我們失望。

The word "excellent" in line 4 is closest in meaning to

(A) very busy
(B) very good

第四行中的「優秀的」最接近什麼意思？

(A) 非常忙碌
(B) 非常好

解析 某平面設計師決定到這家公司工作，因此這封信就是歡迎這位平面設計師的信。從內容來看，可以知道這位平面設計師非常優秀，答案是選項 (B)。

單字 pleased 很高興的 ｜ excellent 優秀的 ｜ graphic designer 平面設計師 ｜ let down 使人失望 ｜ disappoint 使人失望

❷ 同義字 (2)

Question 1 refers to the following information.

Thank you for choosing our latest smartphone. Our smartphones are aimed at young people, and our latest model is no exception. The world is changing fast, and our latest smartphone allows young people to prepare themselves for this rapidly changing world. For more information, visit our website www.youngsmart.com.

感謝您挑選我們的最新款智慧手機。我們的智慧手機針對年輕人的需要而設計,我們最新的型號也不例外。世界的變化很快,而我們最新款的智慧手機讓年輕人可以為這個瞬息萬變的世界做好準備。請上我們的網站 www.youngsmart.com 瀏覽更多資訊。

The word "rapidly" in line 6 is closest in meaning to

(A) gradually
(B) quickly

第六行中的「瞬息」最接近什麼意思?

(A) 慢慢地
(B) 迅速地

解析 提到單字 rapidly 的句子前半部,說到世界變化很快,所以要選出同樣含意的字,答案是選項(B)。充分理解前後文,是解字彙試題的秘訣。

單字 **latest** 最新的 | **aim at** 目標為 | **exception** 例外 | **prepare** 準備 | **rapidly** 快速地

C 題型練習

Question 1 refers to the following paragraph.

Too many experts believe that technology is the secret to the success of a company. Nothing could be further from the truth. Those experts don't understand that companies deal with people. The true secret to the success of a company is how companies treat these people. If they treat them well, they will succeed. If they don't treat them well, they will fail.

1. The word "secret" in line 1 is closest in meaning to
    (A) the best way to do something
    (B) something that people know

Question 2 refers to the following notice.

The city government has announced that Oceanview Park will be renovated. As a result, citizens won't be allowed to enter the park from February 21 through July 23. A lot of things will change. The park will plant more trees so that citizens can get fresh air. The park will also allow bears to interact with visitors in a safe manner. For more information, visit the website www.oceanviewrenovation.org.

2. The word "renovated" in line 2 is closest in meaning to
    (A) preserved
    (B) changed

答案和解析

1. Answer (A)

翻譯 太多專家相信科技是公司成功的秘訣，那絕對是背離事實的觀念。那些專家不了解公司要處理的問題是人。公司成功的真正秘訣在於公司如何對待這些人。如果他們對待得當就會成功。如果他們應對失當就會失敗。

....

第一行中的「秘訣」最接近什麼意思？
(A) 執行的最佳方式
(B) 人們知道的事

解析 看前後文脈絡可以知道 secret 不是「秘密」，而是「秘訣」的意思。答案是選項(A)。

單字 expert 專家 ｜ technology 科技｜ secret 秘訣 ｜ success 成功 ｜ deal with 處理 ｜ succeed 成功

2. Answer (B)

翻譯 市政府已宣布海景公園將改建，因此市民在 2 月 21 到 7 月 23 日將不得進入公園。改建將會帶來許多改變。公園會種植更多樹木讓市民可以呼吸新鮮空氣。公園也會讓熊與參觀民眾透過安全的方式互動。請上網站 www.oceanviewrenovation.org 瀏覽更多資訊。

....

第二行中的「改建」最接近什麼意思？
(A) 保存
(B) 變動

解析 文章中出現了很多線索，提到要種更多樹，很多事物將會改變，答案是選項(B)。

單字 government 政府 ｜ renovate 改建 ｜ citizen 市民 ｜ plant 種植 ｜ fresh 新鮮的 ｜ interact 互動 ｜ preserve 保存

D 應用練習 ▶ 解析 P. 552

Question 1 refers to the following email.

To	jennifer@sunwto.com
From	robert@sunwto.com
Subject	About transferring
Date	May 3

Dear Jennifer,

We've heard that you will be transferring to our London office. Unfortunately, some of the people in that branch are not very nice. We hope you'll prepare yourself for such employees. Of course, there are kind and thoughtful employees there as well. You'll be able to tell which employees are kind. Get along with them, and you'll work better at the London branch.

---

1. The word "tell" in line 6 is closest in meaning to
   (A) dislike
   (B) know

Question 2 refers to the following announcement.

We are pleased to announce that we are holding a naming contest for a new public library. As some citizens may know, this new library can have millions of books and magazines in it. In addition, it allows its users to access other public libraries through the Internet. What would you like us to call this amazing library? Email your suggestions to chean@lakecity.library.org.

---

2. The word "access" in line 4 is closest in meaning to
   (A) break
   (B) use

Quick Test for **Part 7**

▶ 解析 P. 552

Question 1 refers to the following advertisement.

Moving Internationally

Moving to another country is a big decision. It also means that you have a lot of things to take care of. But don't worry! Fun Moving International is here to help you every step of the way. In fact, our customer-friendly service will make you feel that moving to another country is a lot fun. So, what are you waiting for? For more information, visit our website www.funmovinginternational.com.

1. What is mainly being advertised?

   (A) A company helping people have fun while traveling to another country

   (B) A company helping people move to a foreign country

Question 2 refers to the following online chat.

Johnson, Melanie	10:20 a.m.
Paul, have you finished rewriting the budget report?	
Adams, Paul	10:21 a.m.
Not yet. I don't have much time. I have too much work to do.	
Johnson, Melanie	10:22 a.m.
I see. I'll try to find a way to ease the burden for you.	

2. Why hasn't Mr. Adams completed his work?

   (A) He hasn't had enough time to do his work.

   (B) He hasn't had any coworkers to help him.

Question 3 refers to the following email.

To	lawrence@empul.com
From	evans@schospital.org
Subject	Volunteer guide
Date	December 11

Dear Ms. Lawrence,

Thank you for contacting us about volunteering at one of our hospitals. You seem to care about children very much. – [1] – Please email Sarah Black at sarah_black@schospital.org. She'll give you more information about what you can do for our young patients at the hospital. – [2] –

3. In which of the positions marked [1] and [2] does the following sentence best belong?

"So, we think you might want to volunteer for Sunny Children's Hospital."

(A) [1]

(B) [2]

Question 4 refers to the following text message chain.

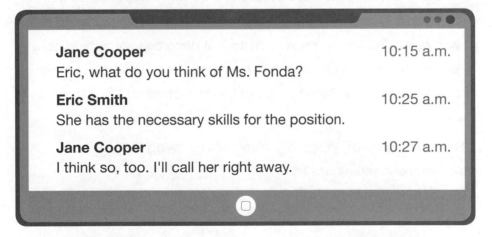

Jane Cooper   10:15 a.m.
Eric, what do you think of Ms. Fonda?

Eric Smith   10:25 a.m.
She has the necessary skills for the position.

Jane Cooper   10:27 a.m.
I think so, too. I'll call her right away.

4. At 10:27, what does Ms. Cooper mean when she writes, "I think so, too"?

(A) She believes that Ms. Fonda can fill the position being discussed.

(B) She believes that Ms. Fonda needs to look for another company.

Mary Parker has been a recruitment agent for over 10 years. Parker says that a lot of companies do not know what kind of worker they want to employ. She believes that to become a good recruitment agent, you should interact patiently with different companies. According to her, this is because understanding the goals of a company takes a lot of time.

5. What is suggested about recruitment agents?

(A) They are supposed to travel to many different countries.

(B) They should try to understand a company at a deeper level.

Question 6 refers to the following announcement.

Importance of Recycling

The city government knows that the environment is important to everyone. That is why the government advises every citizen to recycle and reuse. When you recycle an item, it becomes something else. When you reuse an item, it is not wasted. Whether you recycle or reuse an item, you help to protect the environment.

6. The word "protect" in line 5 is closest in meaning to

(A) make something useless

(B) keep something safe

Notes

類型 **01** 信件和電子郵件

Ⓐ 輕鬆上手

信件試題要閱讀一篇正式的書信並回答問題。因為是正式的書信,所以一定會符合英文書信的型式,並標示出日期和收件者。在信件的本文中,有時也會提到檢附的文件。電郵也會標示出寄信者、收件者、主題和寄信日期。

信件和電郵的閱讀文章,不會考掌握目的類型試題,其他所有類型的試題都會出。掌握目的類型試題,只會在簡訊和線上聊天文中出現。

Dear Ms. Adams,

Please accept my apologies for this late response to your proposal. I've just come back from my vacation, so I haven't had much time. However, I'm sure it includes a lot of creative ideas, since you're one of the most creative writers I know. I'll get back to you as soon as I finish reviewing your proposal.

Ⓠ Who most likely is Ms. Adams?

(A) An author

(B) An editor

親愛的亞當斯小姐:

關於我對你的提案延遲回覆,請接受我的道歉。我才剛休假回來,所以一直沒時間。但我相信裡面有很多有創意的想法,因為你是我見過最有創意的作家。我會在看完你的提案後會盡快回覆你。

Ⓠ 亞當斯小姐最有可能是誰?

(A) 作家

(B) 旅遊業者

☞ 因為信中說亞當斯小姐是有創意的作者(writer),所以答案是選項(A)。選項(B)應該是受信者。

單字 accept 接受 | apology 道歉 | response 回覆 | vacation 休假

B 基本題型

❶ 信件

Question 1 refers to the following letter.

Dear Ms. Kidman,

My name is Sarah Jones, and I'm one of your biggest fans. You've appeared in so many good films, and I'm fascinated by your acting skills. As a high school teacher, I'm sure my students would love to hear your speak. Can you come to my high school and share your thoughts with us?

親愛的基曼小姐：

我叫莎拉・瓊斯,是您最忠實的粉絲之一。您曾出現在很多優秀的電影中,而我對您的演技著迷不已。我是位高中老師,我相信我的學生會非常想聽您演講。您可以到我的高中和我們分享您的想法嗎？

Who most likely is Ms. Kidman?

(A) A science teacher

(B) A popular actress

基曼小姐最有可能是誰？

(A) 科學教師

(B) 受歡迎的女演員

解析 從信件的內容,可以知道基曼小姐演出過許多電影,並且有很多影迷,所以答案是選項 (B)。

單字 appear 出現 | fascinated 著迷的 | acting 演出 | popular 受歡迎的

❷ 電子郵件

Dear Nicole,

I know that you've been working very hard to organize the office party. If we held the event, all the employees would be happy. Unfortunately, however, the CEO has decided to cancel the office party. This is because the deadline for the research project has been changed. Therefore, all of us must work harder. I hope you understand the situation.

親愛的妮可：

我知道你一直很努力籌劃辦公室派對。如果我們舉辦活動，所有員工都會很開心。然而，遺憾的是，執行長決定取消辦公室派對。因為研究案的截止日期改變了。所以，我們所有人都應該更努力工作。我希望你理解這個情況。

Why was the email written?

(A) To inform Nicole that the CEO wants to meet with her

(B) To inform Nicole that the office party has been called off

這封電子郵件的撰寫動機是什麼？

(A) 通知妮可執行長想見她

(B) 通知妮可辦公室派對已被取消

解析 從電子郵件的內容，可以知道妮可籌劃的公司派對被取消了，答案是選項（B）。選項（A）在電子郵件中並沒有提到，所以是錯誤答案。

單字 organize 籌劃 ｜ event 活動 ｜ cancel 取消 ｜ deadline 截止日期 ｜ research 研究 ｜ inform 通知 ｜ call off 取消

C 題型練習

Question 1 refers to the following letter.

Dear Employees,

I am writing this letter to thank all of you for your hard work. Thanks to your efforts, our sales have continued to increase. As you may know, our competitors have been failing, while we have been successful over the past six months. I would like to say that I really appreciate your efforts. Therefore, all of you may take the day off tomorrow.

1. The word "competitors" in line 4 is closest in meaning to

   (A) companies that are cooperating

   (B) companies that are competing

Question 2 refers to the following email.

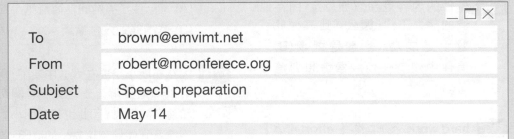

To	brown@emvimt.net
From	robert@mconferece.org
Subject	Speech preparation
Date	May 14

Dear Ms. Erica Brown,

I'm really pleased to learn that you have agreed to give a speech at our annual conference. I think you are an exceptional speaker. So, I'm sure that your speech will inspire all the participants. Your travel and accommodations have already been arranged. For detailed information, email Bill Murray at bill_murray@mconference.org.

2. Why would Ms. Brown email Mr. Murray?

   (A) To learn more about her accommodations

   (B) To invite him to give a speech at the conference

1. Answer (B)

翻譯 親愛的全體員工：

我寫這封信是要感謝你們辛勤的工作。多虧你們的努力，我們的銷售業績持續增長。如你們所知，我們的競爭對手節節敗退，而我們在過去六個月大獲成功。我想說我真的很感謝你們的付出。因此，你們明天都可以放假一天。

．．．．．．．．．．．．．．．．．．．．．．．．

第四行中的「競爭對手」最接近什麼意思？
(A) 合作的公司
(B) 競爭的公司

解析 信件的內容是在感謝員工，因為他們的努力工作，讓公司比其他競爭對手更成功，答案是選項(B)。信件中沒有任何線索會想到選項(A)。

單字 hard work 辛勤工作 ｜ effort 努力 ｜ sales 銷售業績 ｜ competitor 競爭對手 ｜ appreciate 感謝 ｜ cooperate 合作 ｜ compete 競爭

2. Answer (A)

翻譯 收件者：brown@emvimt.net
寄信者：robert@mconference.org
主旨：演講準備事項
日期：5 月 14 日

親愛的艾瑞卡・布朗小姐：

我很高興得知您已同意在我們的年度大會中演講，我認為您是位非凡的演說家，所以我確信您的演講會鼓舞所有的與會者。你的旅行和住宿已經安排妥當。欲知詳細資訊，請寄信到 bill_murray@mconference.org 和比爾・莫瑞聯繫。

．．．．．．．．．．．．．．．．．．．．．．．．

布朗小姐為何要寄信給莫瑞先生？
(A) 進一步了解她的住宿資訊
(B) 邀請他到大會演講

解析 因為布朗小姐要在大會中演講，所以可以知道莫瑞先生有更多有關交通和住宿的訊息，因此也是布朗小姐要寄電子郵件給莫瑞先生的原因，答案是選項(A)。

單字 agree 同意 ｜ speech 演講 ｜ annual 年度的 ｜ exceptional 非凡的 ｜ inspire 鼓舞 ｜ participant 與會者 ｜ accommodation 住宿

D 應用練習

▶ 解析 P. 554

Question 1 refers to the following letter.

April 3

Dear Mr. Hoffman,

I am a regular customer at your coffee shop. I love the atmosphere. I also love everyone that works there, except for one employee. I don't want to tell you who he or she is, but you must have heard similar complaints from other customers. I would like you to encourage that employee to be more friendly toward customers. That is the employee's job, after all.

1. The word "complaints" in line 6 is closest in meaning to

   (A) statements in which you praise someone for something they did

   (B) statements in which you say that you are unhappy about something

Question 2 refers to the following email.

To	employees@alrado.net
From	representative@alrado.net
Subject	Retirement party
Date	July 13

Dear Employees,

As some of you may know, Ms. Alice Lynch is retiring next month. She has been with us for almost 20 years. She has introduced innovative methods to improve worker productivity. Thanks to her methods, our company has been highly successful. We would like to thank her, and we'll hold a retirement party for her. I would like all the employees to attend the party and thank her for her hard work.

2. Why will a party be held for Ms. Lynch?

   (A) Because her company wants to thank her for her hard work

   (B) Because her company wants to lay her off

類型 **02** 廣告

Ⓐ 輕鬆上手

廣告大致分為徵求員工的**求才廣告**，和提供商品或服務的**宣傳廣告**兩種。廣告試題中，有時會出現單篇廣告文，有時也會出現雙篇甚至三篇廣告相關文章。出題類型不僅有綜合資訊和細節資訊類型，其他試題類型也會出現。但掌握目的類的題型不會出現。

Too many people believe that it is almost impossible to learn to write clearly. But great writers tell us that writing is a skill anyone can learn. Unfortunately, however, not everyone can learn from the best writers. That's why we have decided to offer online writing classes. All the classes are interactive, and you'll learn to write clearly within two months. Visit our website www.writingclearly.com for more information.	太多人認為要寫出立論清楚的文章近乎不可能。然而優秀的作家告訴我們，寫作是任何人都可以學習的技能。不過，遺憾地是，不是每個人都可以向優秀作家學習，因此我們決定提供線上寫作課程。所有課程都是互動式的，而且你可以在兩個月內學會寫出條理分明的文章。請上我們的網站 www.writingclearly.com 瀏覽更多資訊。
Ⓠ Which is true about the online writing classes? (A) People can take the classes free of charge. (B) People can find additional information on the website.	Ⓠ 關於線上寫作課程何者為真？ (A) 民眾可以免費上課 (B) 民眾可以上網找到額外的資訊

☞ 這是細節資訊類型。因為選項（A）在廣告中沒有清楚說明，所以無法知道正不正確。選項（B）有在廣告的最後部分提到，所以是答案。

單字 **clearly** 清楚地 ｜ **skill** 技能 ｜ **unfortunately** 遺憾地是 ｜
interactive 互動式的 ｜ **free of charge** 免費的 ｜ **additional** 額外的

B 基本題型

❶ 廣告（1）

Question 1 refers to the following advertisement.

Volunteering for Senior Citizens	銀髮族照護志工隊

The needs of senior citizens are different from those of young people. That's why not everyone is qualified to take care of them. We, at Volunteering for Senior Citizens, make sure that only qualified volunteers look after senior citizens. As a result, you may feel that our selection process is too difficult. However, once you are allowed to join us, you'll find your work very rewarding. To learn more about our selection process, visit our website www.volunteeringforelderly.com.

銀髮族的需求和年輕人不一樣。因此，並非每個人都有資格照顧他們。我們「銀髮族照護志工隊」確保只有合格的志工才能照顧銀髮族。因此，你可能會覺得我們的甄選過程太困難。然而，只要你獲選加入我們，你會發現你的工作很有收穫。請上我們的網站 www.volunteeringforelderly.com 了解更多甄選過程的資訊。

What is suggested about Volunteering for Senior Citizens?

(A) It employs only senior citizens.

(B) It fully understands the needs of the elderly.

關於「銀髮族照護志工隊」的推測何者為真？

(A) 它只雇用銀髮族

(B) 它完全了解銀髮族的需求

解析 這是推測類型。單看廣告，無法知道這個單位是不是只僱用老人，答案是可以從廣告中清楚了解的選項（B）。

單字 need 需求 ｜ senior citizen 銀髮族 ｜ qualified 合格的 ｜ volunteer 志工 ｜ selection process 甄選過程 ｜ rewarding 有收穫的 ｜ fully 完全地

❷ 廣告 (2)

Question 2 refers to the following advertisement.

For Rent by Owner

A two-bedroom apartment is available for rent. It is conveniently located near Oak Subway Station. There are three huge shopping malls near the apartment. The two bedrooms are spacious. With a kitchen and a large lounge, this apartment is convenient and comfortable. We can discuss whether you can keep pets in the apartment. If you are interested in renting this apartment, email me at mary_jones@hmail.com.

屋主出租

兩臥室公寓可供出租。近橡樹地鐵站，交通便利，公寓附近有三間大型購物中心。兩間臥室都很寬敞。包括一間廚房和大間休息室，這間公寓既方便又舒適。我們可以討論您是否可以在公寓內養寵物。如果您對承租這間公寓有興趣，請寄信到 mary_jones@hmail.com 與我聯繫。

What is suggested about the apartment?

(A) It has recently been renovated.

(B) You may keep a dog as a pet in this apartment.

關於這間公寓的推測何者為真？

(A) 最近經過改建

(B) 你可能可以在這間公寓養狗

解析 這是推測類型的試題。選項 (A) 沒有出現在廣告中，所以答案是選項 (B)。選項 (B) 中的 may，表示不一定可以，因為廣告中提到要討論看看是否能養寵物，意思是也有可能不能養。

單字 available 可使用的 ｜ rent 出租 ｜ conveniently 便利地 ｜ huge 大的 ｜ spacious 寬敞的 ｜ renovate 改建

C 題型練習

Question 1 refers to the following advertisement.

> Yoga has been around for thousands of years. – [1] – Forget about strange movements. You need to understand that yoga is aimed at accessing the deepest part of your mind. For this month only, we offer free yoga classes. – [2] – So, what are you waiting for? Just call us today at 755-3882 or email us at <u>alice_yoga@ internationalyoga.org.</u>

1. In which of the positions marked [1] and [2] does the following sentence best belong?

   "It has helped millions of people relax and stay healthy."

   (A) [1]

   (B) [2]

Question 2 refers to the following advertisement.

> **Challenge Network, Your Professional HR Partner**
>
> We, at Challenge Network, have been helping employees to develop their abilities to the fullest. – [1] – At the same time, we have been making every effort to make each employee happy. – [2] – Do you want to be happy and help others? Then, feel free to email our human resources department at <u>H_R@challenge_network.com</u>.

2. In which of the positions marked [1] and [2] does the following sentence best belong?

   "This is because we believe that only happy people can make a difference in other people's lives."

   (A) [1]

   (B) [2]

答案和解析

1. Answer (A)

翻譯 瑜珈已流傳了數千年。– [1] – 別以為瑜珈只是做奇怪的動作。你要了解瑜珈著重在連結心靈最深層的部分。我們只在本月提供免費的瑜珈課程。– [2] – 所以，你還在等什麼？今天就打 755-3882 或寄電子郵件到 alice_yoga@internationalyoga.org 和我們聯絡。

....

[1] 和 [2] 哪一個位置最適合插入以下句子？
「瑜珈已幫助了數百萬人放鬆並維持健康。」
(A) [1]
(B) [2]

解析 看一下前後文脈絡，會發現〔2〕不是好位置。因為〔1〕的前句是「瑜珈有數千年歷史」，後接提示句「幫助很多人」的意思比較合適，答案是選項（A）。

單字 relax 放鬆 ｜ movement 動作 ｜ aim at 著重於 ｜ access 連結

2. Answer (B)

翻譯 挑戰網絡公司，你的專業人力資源夥伴

我們「挑戰網絡公司」一直幫助員工們將他們的能力發展到極致。– [1] – 同時，我們也一直盡一切努力讓每一位員工快樂。– [2] – 你想要快樂並幫助別人嗎？那麼，隨時寄電子郵件到 H_R@challenge_network.com 和我們的人力資源部門聯繫。

....

[1] 和 [2] 哪一個位置最適合插入以下句子？
「因為我們相信只有快樂的人，才可以讓別人的生活變得不一樣。」
(A) [1]
(B) [2]

解析 想一想前後文脈絡，會發現答案是選項（B）。因為〔2〕的前句是「盡力讓員工快樂」，若後接提示句就剛好表示出要讓員工快樂的原因。

單字 develop 發揮 ｜
to the fullest 到極限 ｜ effort 努力 ｜
human resources department
人力資源部門

Question 1 refers to the following advertisement.

Smart Digital Cam

Too many people believe that digital cameras are not useful anymore. They say that smartphones can replace them. Try using our latest digital camera, and you'll find it much more useful than ordinary smartphones. You'll also find out that taking pictures of different things is very rewarding. For more information, visit our website www.smartdigitalcam.com.

1. The word "replace" in line 2 is closest in meaning to
   (A) take the place of
   (B) make use of

Question 2 refers to the following advertisement.

Sally's Kitchen,
NOT AN ORDINARY RESTAURANT
739-9932

Sally's Kitchen is not an ordinary restaurant. Of course, we serve tasty food. At the same time, we'll help you to cook your favorite dish. Just let us know what you want to cook before you come. Then, we'll prepare all the ingredients for the dish. Our friendly cook will help you cook the food of your choice. For this amazing experience, call us today at 739-9932!

2. The word "ordinary" in line 1 is closest in meaning to
   (A) exceptional
   (B) usual

類型 **03**　簡訊和通訊軟體

A 輕鬆上手

簡訊和線上通訊是新的文章類型，內容是有關工作的聯絡訊息，多半是對話，所以十分口語。有關簡訊和線上通訊的出題型式，**特別會出掌握主題的試題**。
另外，也會針對簡訊和線上通訊，出一些綜合資訊類型或細節資訊類型的試題。

David Johnson　9:25 a.m. I'm going to be late for the meeting.	大衛・強森　　上午 9:25 我開會將會遲到。
Kate Snow　9:27 a.m. What? You're supposed to give a presentation at the start of the meeting.	凱特・史諾　　上午 9:27 什麼？但你在會議一開始就要簡報耶。
David Johnson　9:33 a.m. I'm stuck in a traffic jam. I don't know what to do.	大衛・強森　　上午 9:33 我塞在車陣中，我也不知該如何是好。

Q What is suggested about Mr. Johnson?

(A) He has difficulty communicating with Ms. Snow.

(B) He is unlikely to give his scheduled presentation.

Q 關於強森先生的推測何者為真？

(A) 他跟史諾小姐溝通困難

(B) 他不太可能照原定計劃報告

☞ 這是推測類型的試題。因為強森先生現在正卡在車陣中，所以可以推測會出席會議的可能性很低，答案是選項（B）。看到簡訊可以判斷出溝通上是沒有問題的，所以選項（A）是錯誤答案。

單字 be late for 遲到某事 ｜ be supposed to 應該要…… ｜ presentation 簡報 ｜ stuck 卡住的 ｜ traffic jam 塞車 ｜ communicate 溝通

Ⓑ 基本題型

❶ 簡訊

Question 1 refers to the following text message chain.

Adam Smith 9:25 a.m. Lisa, I think there's something wrong with my security software.	亞當‧史密斯　　上午 9:25 麗莎，我認為我的防毒軟體有問題。
Lisa Snow 9:28 a.m. Oh really? Maybe it's time you replaced it with the latest version.	麗莎‧史諾　　上午 9:28 真的嗎？或許你現在應該要改換最新的版本。
Adam Smith 9:35 a.m. I'm not sure. I'll contact the Technical Support Team.	亞當‧史密斯　　上午 9:35 我不確定。我會聯絡技術支援團隊。

At 9:35, what does Mr. Smith mean when he writes, "I'm not sure"?

(A) He thinks that security software is too expensive.

(B) He thinks he may not need to replace his software.

早上 9:35 時，史密斯先生說「我不確定」是什麼意思？

(A) 他認為防毒軟體太貴了

(B) 他認為他也許不需要更換他的軟體

解析 史諾小姐説要把防毒軟體換成最新版，對此，史密斯先生回答我不確定，所以可以推測他可能不認為有更換的必要，答案是選項(B)。

單字 security 安全 ｜ replace 更換 ｜ technical 技術的

❷ 線上聊天

Question 2 refers to the following online chat.

Austen, Jane 2:23 p.m. Kevin, I've heard you drew up a product proposal.	珍・奧斯登 上午 2:23 凱文，我聽說你擬定了一份產品提案。
Jackson, Kevin 2:31 p.m. Yes, I did. I hope the CEO supports my proposal.	凱文・傑克森 上午 2:31 沒錯，我完成了。希望執行長會支持我的提案。
Austen, Jane 2:32 p.m. Well, she doesn't like taking risks.	珍・奧斯登 上午 2:32 嗯，她不喜歡冒風險。

At 2:32, what does Ms. Austen mean when she writes, "Well, she doesn't like taking risks"?

(A) She doesn't think the CEO will support Mr. Jackson's proposal.

(B) She doesn't think Mr. Jackson can meet with the CEO today.

下午 2:32 時，奧斯登小姐說「嗯，她不喜歡冒風險」是什麼意思？

(A) 她認為執行長不會支持傑克森先生的提案

(B) 她認為傑克森先生今天沒辦法和執行長會面

解析 這是掌握目的的試題類型。傑克森先生寫好了新產品提案書，但是奧斯登小姐認為執行長是不喜歡冒險的人，所以可以推測，執行長小姐認為她可能不會支持新的產品提案。答案是選項(A)。

單字 draw up 擬定 ｜ product 產品 ｜ proposal 提案 ｜ support 支持 ｜ take a risk 冒險

C 題型練習

Question 1 refers to the following text message chain.

Donald Cooper	3:25 p.m.
Buffy, do you know when we're having lunch?	
Buffy Adams	3:29 p.m.
At one o'clock, as far as I know. Why?	
Donald Cooper	3:36 p.m.
I just want to make sure we have enough time to discuss the quarterly report before lunch.	

1. What is suggested about Mr. Cooper?

   (A) He has an important matter to take care of after lunch.

   (B) He wants to discuss something thoroughly before lunch.

Question 2 refers to the following online chat discussion.

11:20 a.m.	**Baker, Jane** Paul, when are you arriving at the airport?
11:21 a.m.	**Smith, Paul** I'm supposed to be there at 2:00 p.m. But my flight has been delayed.
11:22 a.m.	**Baker, Jane** I see. Let me know as soon as you arrive.

2. What is suggested about Ms. Baker?

   (A) She has been waiting for Mr. Smith.

   (B) She will have a meeting with Mr. Smith at 1:00 p.m.

答案和解析

1. Answer (B)

翻譯　唐納德・庫柏　　　下午 3:25
巴菲，你知道我們何時吃午餐嗎？

巴菲・亞當斯　　　下午 3:29
就我所知是一點。有問題嗎？

唐納德・庫柏　　　下午 3:36
我只是想確認我們在午餐前有足夠時間討論季報。

....

關於庫柏先生的推測何者為真？
(A) 他在午餐後有一件重要的事要處理
(B) 他想在午餐前詳細討論某件事

解析　這是推測類型的試題。庫柏先生詢問午餐的時間，因為他想要知道討論的時間是否足夠，所以可以推測答案是選項(B)。

單字　**as far as I know** 就我所知 |
make sure 確認 |
quarterly 一季的 |
thoroughly 詳細地

2. Answer (A)

翻譯　珍・貝克　　　早上 11:20
保羅，你何時抵達機場？

保羅・史密斯　　　早上 11:21
我應該在下午兩點抵達。但我的航班延誤了。

珍・貝克 早上 11:22
了解。你到了就馬上通知我。

....

關於貝克小姐的推測何者為真？
(A) 她一直在等待史密斯先生抵達
(B) 她將在下午一點和史密斯先生開會

解析　貝克小姐請史密斯先生一到就通知她，所以可以知道貝克小姐在等史密斯先生，答案是選項（A）。因為預定下午兩點到達，下午一點開會是不可能的，選項（B）是錯誤答案。

單字　**arrive** 抵達 |
be supposed to 應該要 |
delay 延誤

D 應用練習　　　　　　　▶ 解析 P. 556

Question 1 refers to the following text message chain.

Jack Smith	2:45 p.m.
Willow, have you talked to Mr. Green?	
Willow Bauer	2:48 p.m.
Not yet. I have urgent matters to take care of.	
Jack Smith	2:55 p.m.
Then, I think I can talk to him about his order. Just give me his number.	

1. What is suggested about Mr. Smith?

   (A) He has met with Mr. Green before.

   (B) He wants to take care of Mr. Green's order.

Question 2 refers to the following online chat discussion.

11:20 a.m.	**Grant, Amy** I'm happy that we completed the project ahead of schedule.
11:21 a.m.	**Johnson, Eric** Everybody worked really hard. I think we're a great team.
11:22 a.m.	**Grant, Amy** I think so, too. Together, we can do anything.

2. At 11:22, what does Ms. Grant mean when she writes, "I think so, too"?

   (A) She believes that her team is efficient.

   (B) She believes that her team needs to work harder.

類型 **04** 備忘錄和公告

Ⓐ 輕鬆上手

所謂的備忘錄文章類型，就是指公司內部給員工傳閱的文件。上面記載了公司的方針或人事變動等訊息。

公告的內容可能是給顧客的說明事項或活動介紹等。在多益考試中，一般都將備忘錄稱作 memo，公告稱作 notice。備忘錄和公告不會考掌握目的的試題，但其他類型的試題都會考。

I'm pleased to announce that Ms. Amy Summers will be promoted to vice president. Ms. Summers has been with us for almost five years. She has been dedicated to helping us enter the European market. Thanks to her efforts, our sales have increased dramatically in Europe. I'm sure that as vice president, Ms. Summers will take our company to the next level.

Ⓠ Which is true about Ms. Summers?

(A) She has been working for the company for nearly five years.

(B) She is going to leave the company next year.

我很高興宣布艾美・桑瑪斯小姐將晉升為副總裁。桑瑪斯小姐和我們共事已近五年。她一直致力於幫助我們進入歐洲市場。多虧她的努力，我們在歐洲的業績大幅成長。我相信擔任副總裁的桑瑪斯小姐，將會帶領我們邁向更高的巔峰。

Ⓠ 關於桑瑪斯小姐何者為真？

(A) 她已經在公司服務近五年

(B) 她將在明年離開公司

☞ 這是細節資訊類型試題。在備忘錄中提到和桑瑪斯小姐一起工作五年，所以答案是選項（A）。
選項（B）在備忘錄中並沒有出現，所以是錯誤答案。

單字 **announce** 宣布 | **promote** 晉升 | **dedicate** 致力於 | **effort** 努力 | **dramatically** 大幅地

B 基本題型

❶ 備忘錄

Question 1 refers to the following memo.

Dear Employees,	親愛的全體同仁：
A lot of companies don't allow employees to use their private emails during business hours. Their policy is aimed at getting workers to focus on their work. However, we need to understand that we are not machines. We need to take a break from time to time. That's why I have decided to allow our employees to use their private emails during business hours.	很多公司不讓員工在工作時使用私人電子郵件。他們的政策是為了讓員工專注於自己的工作。然而，我們要了解我們不是機器。我們偶爾需要休息。因此我決定讓我們的員工在工作時使用私人電子郵件。

Why was the memo written?	撰寫這份備忘錄的動機是什麼？
(A) To encourage employees to work harder	(A) 鼓勵員工更努力工作
(B) To explain a company's policy	(B) 解釋公司的政策

解析 就像這樣，很多備忘錄都是在說明公司的方針。答案是選項（B），因為備忘錄也提到休息的重要性，選項（A）是錯誤答案。

單字 private 私人的 ｜ business hours 上班時間 ｜ policy 政策 ｜ focus 專注 ｜ take a break 休息 ｜ encourage 鼓勵

Question 2 refers to the following notice.

Julia Language Institute is moving to another location! We have been extremely popular among Asian students. In order to better serve their needs, we've decided to move closer to them. Our new location is right in the center of Brooklyn. We've also decided to offer online courses for all levels. For detailed information, visit our website www.julialanguageinstitute.com.

茉莉亞語言學院將搬至新址！我們一直非常受亞洲學生的歡迎。為了針對他們的需求提供更好的服務，我們決定搬到離他們更近的地點。我們的新址就在布魯克林中心。我們也決定為各程度學生提供線上課程。請上我們的網站 www.julialanguageinstitute.com 瀏覽詳細資訊。

The word "serve" in line 4 is closest in meaning to

(A) ignore
(B) to satisfy

第四行的「服務」最接近什麼意思？

(A) 忽視
(B) 滿足

解析 這是字彙試題，要看前後文脈絡。文中提到，這是亞洲學生喜愛的語言學校，為了服務他們，語言學校將要搬到更靠近學生的地方，所以答案是選項（B）。選項（A）剛好跟 serve 的意思相反，和文意不符。

單字 location 地點 ｜ extremely 非常地 ｜ offer 提供 ｜ detailed 詳細的

C 題型練習

Question 1 refers to the following memo.

As you may know, Cynthia Library Book Club is the most popular book discussion group in Chicago. This book club has been led by Cynthia Lennon, who is a dedicated librarian. Unfortunately, Ms. Lennon is moving to South Korea, and we are looking for someone who can replace her. To recommend a qualified librarian for the position, please email me at dorothy_kim@cl_bookclub.org.

1. Why was the memo written?
   (A) To ask members to recommend good books to read
   (B) To ask members to help the club find a good librarian

Question 2 refers to the following notice.

Carlston University has always respected the political rights of students. However, the primary role of our university is to produce well-educated citizens. Therefore, we have decided not to allow demonstrations on campus. This decision does not mean that our students cannot take part in demonstrations. It just means that they are not allowed to hold demonstrations on campus.

2. The word "primary" in line 2 is closest in meaning to
   (A) most important
   (B) most dangerous

答案和解析

1. Answer (B)

翻譯 如你所知,辛西亞圖書館讀書俱樂部是芝加哥最受歡迎的讀書會。這個讀書俱樂部一直由辛西亞・藍能領導,她是一位盡職的圖書管理員。遺憾地是,藍能小姐將搬到南韓,因而我們要尋找替代人選。如要推薦適合這個職位的優良圖書館員,請寄信到 dorothy_kim@cl_bookclub.org 與我聯繫。

撰寫這份備忘錄的動機是什麼?
(A) 要求成員推薦可供閱讀的優良書籍
(B) 要求成員協助俱樂部尋找一位優良的圖書館員

解析 帶領讀書會的圖書館員要搬去南韓,所以正在找人代替她,答案是選項(B)。
選項(A)不是備忘錄中的內容,所以是錯誤答案。

單字 **book club** 讀書俱樂部 |
dedicated 盡心盡力的 |
librarian 圖書館員 | **replace** 代替 |
recommend 推薦

2. Answer (A)

翻譯 查爾斯頓大學一直尊重學生的政治權利。然而,大學的主要角色是培養有良好教育的公民,所以,我們決定不允許在校園內進行示威活動。這個決定不代表我們的學生不能參與示威活動。那只表示他們不能在校園內舉辦示威活動。

第二行的「主要」最接近什麼意思?
(A) 最重要
(B) 最危險

解析 這是大學的公告。看前後文脈絡,可以知道 primary 的意思是「主要的、最重要的」,所以答案是選項(A)。

單字 **political** 政治的 | **right** 權利 |
role 角色 | **produce** 創造 |
demonstration 示威活動

D 應用練習　　　　　　　▶ 解析 P. 556

Question 1 refers to the following memo.

Attention

It has been reported that our company fired Steve Lee. They said that he was angry over our decision to let him go. Nothing could be further from the truth. Mr. Lee was a dedicated employee. Because his wife was seriously ill, he told us that he wanted to spend more time with her. So, he has left our company, but we are still on good terms with him.

1. Why was the memo written?
   (A) To encourage employees to have a better relationship with Mr. Lee
   (B) To explain why Mr. Lee left the company

Question 2 refers to the following notice.

Important Notice

We are a company with a philosophy of serving those in need. As a new employee, you may wonder if serving those in need has anything to do with a clothing company. Our experiences have taught us that clothing companies can succeed only when they serve those in need. In an effort to help you learn that lesson, we ask you to find someone who is in need. For further details, contact the Human Resources Department.

2. The word "philosophy" in line 1 is closest in meaning to
   (A) Ideas that define an organization's behavior
   (B) Ideas that are too difficult to understand

類型 **05** 報導和介紹

Ⓐ 輕鬆上手

多益中出現的**報導**刊登於新聞或雜誌，內容多半是探討當地公司的人物、事業體或介紹地區活動等。**介紹文**多半是對產品的說明或說明活動的行程。

報導和介紹文除了掌握目的的試題外，會出其他類型的試題。平常多閱讀英文報紙或雜誌，對考試會有很大的幫助。

When Sally Wayles moved to New York at the age of seven, she didn't know her life would change forever. In that city, the young girl came across Betty Jefferson, who was an established singer. Jefferson realized that Wayles had a unique voice. She gave her free private music lessons. Before long, Wayles became the youngest singer to win the Best Singer Award.

Ⓠ Which is true about Ms. Wayles, according to the article?

(A) She came across Ms. Jefferson before moving to New York.

(B) Ms. Jefferson helped her become a great singer.

莎莉・威爾斯在七歲搬到紐約時，她不知道她的人生會永遠改變。在那個城市，這位年輕女孩遇上了貝蒂・傑佛森，她是一位有豐富資歷的歌手。傑佛森意識到威爾斯有副獨特的歌喉，她給她上了免費的私人音樂課程。不久後，威爾斯成為贏得最佳歌手獎的最年輕歌手。

Ⓠ 根據這篇文章，關於威爾斯小姐何者為真？

(A) 她在搬到紐約前遇到傑佛森小姐

(B) 傑佛森小姐幫助她成為一名優異的歌手

☞ 這是細節資訊試題。威爾斯小姐和傑佛森小姐相遇是威爾斯搬到紐約以後的事，不是之前，所以選項（A）是誤答。答案是和報導內容一致的選項（B）。

單字 **come across** 遇到 | **established** 有成就的 | **unique** 特別的 | **private** 私人的

B 基本題型

❶ 報導

Question 1 refers to the following article.

A Famous Chocolate Company's Closure

Melanie's Chocolate Company has announced that it will close its factory in Edgewater. The company has been having financial difficulties. By closing the Edgewater factory, it hopes that it gets better financially. However, experts predict that Melanie's Chocolate Company is likely to fail. Some even say that the company will go out of business.

一家知名巧克力公司關閉廠房

梅蘭妮巧克力公司已宣布它將關閉在艾格華特的工廠。這家公司一直有財務困難，藉由關閉艾格華特工廠，它希望能紓緩財務壓力。然而，專家預測梅蘭妮巧克力公司很可能會走下坡。有些專家甚至說這家公司會結束營業。

Which is true about Melanie's Chocolate Company?

(A) It has not made any efforts to improve its financial situation.

(B) Experts don't expect that its financial situation will get better.

關於梅蘭妮巧克力公司何者為真？

(A) 它一直沒有努力改善財務困境

(B) 專家並不期望它的財務困境會好轉

解析 這是細節資訊試題。和報導內容一致的選項（B）是答案。選項（A）說公司沒有努力改善財務，但是要關閉艾格華特工廠就是改善財務的方式，所以選項（A）是錯的。

單字 financial 財務的 ｜ predict 預測 ｜ go out of business 結束營業

❷ 引介文

Question 1 refers to the following article.

Thank you for purchasing this mechanical pencil. – [1] – All our mechanical pencils are popular among office workers, and this 700 line is no exception. As you may know, we have the 800 line, which is more expensive than the 700 line. – [2] – For detailed information about these offices, visit our website www.mettmechanical.com.

感謝您購買這一款自動鉛筆。– [1] –我們所有的自動鉛筆都很受辦公室員工的歡迎，而這一款 700 系列也不例外。如你所知，我們也有比 700 系列更貴的 800 系列。– [2] –請上我們的網站 www.mettmechanical.com 瀏覽這些辦公室的進一步資訊。

In which of the positions marked [1] and [2] does the following sentence best belong?

"If you want to upgrade your pencil to the 800 line, bring it to one of our customer service offices."

(A) [1]
(B) [2]

[1] 和 [2] 哪個位置最適合插入以下句子？

「如果您想將鉛筆升級到 800 系列，請帶鉛筆到我們任何一間客服中心。」

(A) [1]
(B) [2]

解析 要看前後文脈絡，找出最適合放進提示句的位置。答案是選項（B）。前一句要提到可以前往客服中心（offices），後一句才會有 these offices。

單字 purchase 購買 ｜ mechanical pencil 自動鉛筆 ｜ exception 例外 ｜ detailed 詳細的

Question 1 refers to the following article.

Andy Griffith is an exceptional novelist in many ways. Most novelists often base their stories on real events in their lives. Griffith is different. His first novel, *The Ghost*, is about a ghost who explores a strange world called Liara. The world of Liara is quite different from our world. Griffith explains that he bases his stories on his imagination, and he is extremely popular among children.

1. Which is true about Mr. Griffith?
   (A) He has written many best-sellers.
   (B) He does not base his stories on real events.

Question 2 refers to the following notice.

Thank you for choosing our service. We'll help you write an impressive résumé and cover letter. – [1] – Of course, we don't write your résumé or cover letter for you. What we do is help you find your own voice. – [2] – In order to do that, you need to give us some personal information. For more details, call Michael Green at 833-2931.

2. In which of the positions marked [1] and [2] does the following sentence best belong?
   "When you find your own voice, you can impress your potential employer."
   (A) [1]
   (B) [2]

答案和解析

1. Answer (B)

翻譯 安迪葛瑞芬斯以許多方面來看都是一位傑出的小說家。多數小說家經常以自己生活中的真實事件為故事藍本。葛瑞芬斯另闢蹊徑，他的首部小說《鬼怪》講了一個鬼的故事，那個鬼探索了叫做萊拉的世界。萊拉和我們的世界不太相同。葛瑞芬斯解釋，他的故事都基於自己的想像力，而他非常受到孩童愛戴。

……………………………………………

關於葛瑞芬斯先生何者為真？
(A) 他寫了許多暢銷書
(B) 他的故事並非基於真實事件

解析 這是一篇關於暢銷作家的報導。報導提到他和其他作者不同，他的故事都是想像出來的，答案是選項(B)。選項(A)單從報導的內容來看無法確認是否為真，所以不是答案。

單字 exceptional 傑出的 |
novelist 小說家 | base 根據 |
explore 探索 | imagination 想像力

2. Answer (B)

翻譯 感謝您選擇我們的服務，我們會協助您寫出讓人印象深刻的履歷和求職信。–[1]–當然，我們不會幫您寫簡歷或求職信，我們要做的是幫您找到自己的聲音。–[2]–為了達到那個目標，您需要提供我們一些個人資訊。請打 833-2931 給麥可・葛林取得更多資訊。

……………………………………………

[1] 和 [2] 哪一個位置最適合插入以下句子？
「你找到了自己的聲音後，就能讓潛在的僱主對你留下深刻印象。」
(A) [1]
(B) [2]

解析 要看前後文脈絡，找出最適合放進提示句的位置，答案是選項(B)。重複前一句話的內容，是為了提高文章的一貫性，這是很常使用的手法。

單字 impressive 印象深刻的 |
résumé 履歷 | cover letter 求職信 |
potential 潛在的

C 應用練習

▶ 解析 P. 557

Question 1 refers to the following article.

> The Cardiff Museum has announced that it will hold an exhibition of South Korean artists. South Korea is not a familiar country for most Americans. The museum hopes that the exhibition will help Americans better understand Korean art. The exhibition is open to the general public from 10:00 a.m. to 6:00 p.m. between March 2 and April 1. Admission is free to Cardiff residents.

1. Which is true about the Cardiff Museum?
   (A) It was founded by a South Korean immigrant.
   (B) It wants Americans to familiarize themselves with Korean art.

Question 2 refers to the following information.

> Thank you for choosing Charlie's hamburgers. By eating our hamburgers, you help other people stay healthy. – [1] – This is because we make our suppliers raise chickens without using drugs. If chickens are raised with drugs, they can cause public health problems. – [2] – Share this amazing story with your friends by clicking the link below.

2. In which of the positions marked [1] and [2] does the following sentence best belong?
   "Because our suppliers don't use drugs when raising chickens, we can prevent such problems."
   (A) [1]
   (B) [2]

類型 06　網頁

A 輕鬆上手

多益也會用網頁來出題。這些網頁通常是產品或服務的使用心得，或線上徵人啟事。此類試題除掌握目的試題外，其他所有類型的試題都會出。

I had always wanted to stay in shape, but fitness training seemed too demanding. When a friend of mine recommended Alice's Fitness Center, I didn't expect the center would change my fitness level. But after working out at the center for two months, everything changed. More than anything else, I felt confident! I highly recommend this fitness center to anyone interested in staying in shape.

Q What is suggested about the writer?

　(A) Her fitness level has improved.

　(B) She does not have many friends.

我一直想保持身材。但健身訓練實在太耗體力。我的一位朋友推薦艾麗絲健身中心時，我沒有期望健身中心會改變我的體能程度。然而在健身中心運動兩個月後，一切都改變了。最重要的是，我覺得充滿自信！對保持身材有興趣的人，我衷心推薦這家健身中心給你。

Q 關於作者的推測何者為真？

　(A) 她的體能程度改善了

　(B) 她沒有很多朋友

☞ 這是使用服務後的心得。因為是推測類型的試題，所以要排除無法從文章中知道的內容，選項（B）完全無法從文章中得知，所以答案是選項（A）。因為文中提到，所有事都改變了，可以推測她的體能水準也改變了。

單字 stay in shape 保持身材 │ demanding 吃力的 │ confident 有自信的 │ recommend 推薦

Ⓑ 基本題型

❶ 信件

Question 1 refers to the following web page.

```
┌─────────────────────────────────────── _ □ ✕ ┐
│  http://www.pbinterpreter.net                 │
```

Frequently Asked Questions

Thank you for choosing our service. We recommend that you check these Frequently Asked Questions before contacting our customer service department.

常見問題

感謝您選擇我們的服務。我們建議您在連絡我們的客服部門前先檢視這些常見問題。

Can I meet with my interpreter before the conference?

Yes, you can. Your interpreter will contact you because he or she needs detailed information about your conference.

我可以在研討會前和我的口譯員見面嗎？

可以，您可以和他見面。您的口譯員會和您聯絡，因為他或她需要關於您研討會的詳細資訊。

What is suggested about the service?

(A) Customers are not allowed to contact the customer service department.

(B) It is aimed at conference participants.

關於這項服務的暗示何者為真？

(A) 客戶不被允許和客服部門聯繫

(B) 服務是針對研討會的與會者

解析 這是推測類型的試題。從文章內容可以知道，這項服務的對象是參加會議的人，答案是選項(B)。因為並沒有禁止與會者聯絡客服，所以選項(A)是錯誤答案。

單字 interpreter 口譯員 | detailed 詳細的 | participant 與會者

❷ 網頁 (2)

Question 1 refers to the following web page.

```
                                              _ □ ✕
   http://www.cstm-stationery.net
```

Recommended Items for Ms. Susan Jones

You have been our customer since 2012. Based on what you have purchased so far, we recommend these items for you.

- Mett Color Brush Pen, Black
- Sattel Charcoal Jar,
- Diron Pencil, Black

推薦給蘇珊・瓊斯小姐的商品

您自 2012 年就一直是我們的顧客。根據您到目前為止的購買記錄，我們要向您推薦下列商品：

- 黑色麥特毛筆
- 賽托木炭罐
- 黑色迪朗鉛筆

What is suggested about Ms. Jones?

(A) She is an internationally famous artist.

(B) She may be interested in drawing pictures.

關於瓊斯小姐的推測何者為真？

(A) 她是國際知名的藝術家

(B) 她可能對繪畫有興趣

解析 這是推測類型的試題。推薦的物品主要是繪畫時的必備品，答案是選項 (B)。選項 (A) 無法從本文中清楚得知，所以這種選項是錯誤答案。

單字 recommend 推薦 ｜ purchase 購買 ｜ brush 筆刷 ｜ charcoal 木炭

C 題型練習

Question 1 refers to the following web page.

---

http://www.tdrsites.net/login-help

Password Assistance

Have you forgotten your password?

Option 1: Do you remember the email address connected with your
TDR account?

Enter the email address:

Option 2: Do you remember the cellphone number connected with your
TDR account?
Enter the cellphone number:

---

1. The word "connected" in line 2 is closest in meaning to

   (A) disconnected

   (B) associated

Question 2 refers to the following web page.

Order Placed:	December 29, 2017
Total:	$20.91
Ship To:	David Johnson
	Order # 100-720082-0311327
Delivered:	January 16, 2018

Click Invoice for order details.

---

2. Which is true about Mr. Johnson?

   (A) He received his shipment in January, 2018.

   (B) He placed an order by phone in January, 2018.

答案和解析

1. Answer (B)

翻譯 **密碼協助**

你忘記密碼了嗎?

選項一:你記得你連結 TDR 帳戶的
　　　　電子信箱嗎?
　　　　輸入電子信箱地址:

　　　　_____

選項二:你記得你連結 TDR 帳戶的
　　　　手機號碼嗎?
　　　　輸入手機號碼:

　　　　_____

第二行的「連結」最接近什麼意思?
(A) 斷開的
(B) 關聯的

解析 這是忘記密碼時可以使用的網頁。從
前後文脈絡看來,答案是選項(B)。

單字 assistance 協助 |
connected 連結 | account 帳戶

2. Answer (A)

翻譯 訂購日期:2017 年 12 月 29 日
總價:20.91 美元
收貨人:大衛・強森
訂購編號 100-720082- 0311327
運送日期:2018 年 1 月 16 日

點選收據查詢訂購細節。

關於強森先生何者為真?
(A) 他在 2018 年 1 月收到他的訂
　　購品
(B) 他在 2018 年 1 月以電話下訂單

解析 這是細節資訊類型試題。從文章中可以
清楚看到選項(A)的內容,所以是答案。
沒辦法知道選項(B),所以是錯誤
答案。

單字 order 訂購 | deliver 運送 |
shipment 貨品

D 應用練習   ▶ 解析 P. 558

Question 1 refers to the following web page.

http://www.xenacss.net/form-sell

If you want to sell your item to other Xena customers, just fill out the following form.

Item Type:

Item Purchased on

Item Condition:

Asking Price:

International Shipping: Yes   No

1. What is suggested from the web page?

　　(A) Customers cannot sell their books to other Xena customers.

　　(B) Foreigners can be Xena customers.

Question 2 refers to the following web page.

Make a Complaint

If you want immediate assistance, you can call us anytime at 080-7552-8282. Or you can fill out the following online form to make a complaint. We'll contact you as soon as we can to resolve your issue.

Your Full Name: _____

Your Phone Number: _____

What is the issue that you want us to address?

_____

Complaint Details

_____

_____

2. Which is true about the phone number 080-7552-8282?

　　(A) Only privileged customers can call the phone number.

　　(B) It is accessible 24 hours a day, 7 days a week.

類型 **07** | 雙篇文章

A 輕鬆上手

所謂的雙篇文章類型，就是要連接、活用兩篇文章的訊息才能解題。可能會同時出現一篇報導和一封電郵，也可能同時出現一篇廣告和一封信。

雙篇文章類型因為文章數量增加，所以是比較困難的類型。在多益初期的學習階段，要以單篇文章為主來學習，熟悉後，再逐漸學習雙篇和三篇文章，循序漸進。

The following question refers to the following article and email.

There are several things to consider when buying a car. Do you want a brand-new car or a used car? A used car is usually cheaper, but remember that it might need repairs later. What style of car do you want? You can choose from many different models, but some cars are more expensive to maintain than others.	買車時有幾項事情要考慮。您想要全新汽車或是中古車？中古車通常比較便宜，但請記得中古車之後可能需要修理。您想要什麼款式的汽車？您可以從許多不同車型中選擇，然而有些款式的車比其他車要花更多錢保養。

Dear Ms. Buffy Smith, Thank you for telling me about all the cars you sell. As you may know, I'm just a college student. So, I can't afford expensive cars. I like the TX200 model, although I know it might need repairs later.	親愛的巴菲・史密斯小姐： 感謝你告訴我你所有要銷售的汽車的相關訊息。如你所知，我只是一名大學生，所以我買不起昂貴的汽車。我喜歡 TX200 車型，雖然我知道以後可能需要維修。

Q What is most likely the TX200 model?

(A) A brand-new car

(B) A used car.

Q TX200 車型最有可能是什麼？

(A) 全新汽車

(B) 中古車

☞ 在報導中提到，雖然中古車較便宜，但是以後會需要修理。此外，因為電子郵件也提到，TX200 型更便宜，但以後會需要修理，所以可以知道它是中古車，答案是選項（B）。

單字 **several** 一些 ｜ **consider** 考慮 ｜ **used** 二手的 ｜ **repair** 修理 ｜ **maintain** 保養

Notes

❶ 雙篇文章

Question 1 refers to the following notice and email.

The music club

The music club is a new club for every student who likes music. Music club meetings take place in the student hall after class every day. On Mondays, Wednesdays, and Fridays, members listen to CDs that they bring to the meetings. The members can also talk about their favorite musicians.

音樂社

音樂社是個全新的社團，適合每個喜歡音樂的學生。音樂社每天課後在學生大廳集會。在週一、週三和週五的集會，成員會聆聽他們帶來聚會的音樂光碟。成員也可以討論他們最喜歡的音樂家。

Dear Paul,

I'm a new member of the music club. I've always been in love with music. I especially like Enya's music. It is so mysterious. On Wednesday, I'll bring one of my CDs, which contains her music. I'm sure everyone will like Enya!

親愛的保羅：

我是音樂社的新成員。我一直都很喜歡音樂，我尤其喜歡恩雅的音樂，她的音樂聽起來很有神秘感。在週三，我會帶一片我的音樂光碟，裡面有她的音樂。我相信所有人都會喜歡恩雅！

About whom will the music club talk on Wednesday?

(A) Paul

(B) Enya

音樂社將在週三會討論誰？

(A) 保羅

(B) 恩雅

解析 這是雙篇文章類型。提到成員在週一、週三、週五都可以帶 CD 來聽，並聊聊喜歡的音樂家。電子郵件提到，會帶恩雅的音樂光碟來，答案是選項 (B)。

單字 student hall 學生大廳 ｜ especially 特別地 ｜ mysterious 神祕的

C 題型練習

Question 1 refers to the following text message chain.

To	andrew@yahouniv.net
From	amysmith@miaminews.net
Subject	Interview request
Date	May 15

Dear Mr. Andrew Mills,

My name is Amy Smith. I'm a reporter for The *Miami Times*.
I know you're not an ordinary teenager. Can you tell me more about
yourself? I think your story will inspire many students in Miami. Let
me know when I can interview you. I really look forward to meeting
you in person.

About Andrew Mills

Andrew Mills is not a typical teenager. He is a gymnast who dreams
of competing in the Olympics. He wakes up at five every morning to
practice before school. He jogs to the National Gymnasium, and he
practices gymnastics for two hours. Then, he goes to school from
8:30 a.m. until 3:00 p.m. After school, he returns to the gymnasium for
special classes with his coach.

1. What will Mr. Mills tell Ms. Smith in an interview?
   (A) That he wants to be a famous athlete
   (B) That he wants to compete in the Olympics

1. Answer (B)

翻譯

收件者	andrew@yahouniv.net
寄件者	amysmith@miaminews.net
主旨	訪問請求
日期	5 月 15 日

親愛的安德魯・米爾斯先生：

我是艾美・史密斯，是《邁阿密時報》的記者。我知道您不是普通的青少年。您可以多告訴我關於您的事嗎？我認為您的故事會鼓舞邁阿密許多的學生。請告訴我何時可以訪問您，我真的很期待可以親自和您見面。

關於安德魯・米爾斯

安德魯・密爾斯不是位普通的年輕人。他是一位夢想可以在奧運比賽的體操選手。他每天早上五點起床練習後再去上學。他慢跑到到國家體育館，並且練習體操兩小時。然後，從早上八點半到下午三點在學校上課。放學後，他回到體育館和他的教練上特別課程。

米爾斯先生會在訪問中向史密斯小姐說什麼？
(A) 他想成為知名運動員
(B) 他想參加奧運比賽

解析 電子郵件提到史密斯小姐想採訪收件者，並談談他自己。報導提到他的夢想是參加奧運，所以答案是選項（B）。
選項（A）因為並沒有清楚在文內提到，所以不是答案。

單字 **ordinary** 普通的 ｜ **inspire** 鼓舞 ｜ **in person** 親自 ｜ **typical** 典型的 ｜
gymnast 體操選手 ｜ **compete** 比賽

D 應用練習 ▶ 解析 P. 558

Question 1 refers to the following letter and article.

_ □ ×

November 15

Dear Sally,

I'm having a great time here in London. There are so many fascinating things to see. I have also met some great people here: Danny, Ivy, and Leo. Danny is British, and I met him when I got lost. He kindly showed me the way to my hotel. I was able to get back safely thanks to his help. Ivy and Leo are Chinese-Americans traveling together.

When Erica visited London for the first time, she just wanted to have fun. But she got lost and didn't know what to do. Luckily, Danny came across her and showed her the way to her hotel. Thanks to Danny's kindness, Erica came to love London. She's announced that she and Danny will be getting married this summer.

1. What is suggested about Sally?
   (A) She met Ivy and Leo in the United States.
   (B) She is a friend of Erica's.

類型 **08** 三篇文章

A 輕鬆上手

三篇文章類型的考題，因為要了解三篇文章的資訊才能解題，所以是非常困難的類型。不過，在解多益閱讀試題時，具備以下能力是最重要的：

1. 找出必要訊息的位置
2. 理解它的意思
3. 找出符合問題的答案。

培養出了這樣的能力，無論是解兩或三篇文章類型題目都很容易。

The following question refers to the following article and emails.

Having a private life is becoming more and more difficult. Today, everything we do is recorded on computers. With one touch of a key, a total stranger can know everything about your life. That is the price we pay as the world embraces technology.

擁有私生活變得越來越困難。現今，我們做的一切都會紀錄在電腦上。只要在點擊一下，一個全然的陌生人就可以知道你的全部生活。那是我們生活在擁抱科技的世界所要付出的代價。

Dear Kevin,

I've just read an interesting article about privacy. This article makes me think a lot about my private life. In today's world, nobody has a private life. What do you think? Can we meet to discuss this issue?

親愛的凱文：

我剛讀了一篇有關個人隱私的有趣文章。這篇文章讓我對自己的私生活想了很多。在現今的世界裡，沒有人擁有私生活。你有什麼看法？我們可以見面聊聊這個議題嗎？

▭ ▢ ✕

Dear Jane, Yesterday, I read the article you mentioned in your email. I'm available on Friday.	親愛的珍： 我在昨天讀了你在電子郵件提到的文章。我週五有空。

Q What will Jane and Kevin discuss when they meet?

(A) Whether famous people should enjoy private lives

(B) Why it is difficult to have a private life in today's world

Q 珍和凱文見面時會聊什麼？

(A) 名人是否該享受私生活

(B) 為何在現今的世界很難擁有私生活

☞ 珍想和凱文見面聊聊第一篇文章，內容是關於在現代的科技世界擁有個人隱私很困難，因此答案是選項（B）。因為在文中沒有提到關於名人的事，所以選項（A）是錯誤答案。

單字 private 私人的 ｜ record 紀錄 ｜ embrace 擁抱 ｜ technology 科技 ｜ privacy 隱私 ｜ discuss 討論 ｜ issue 議題 ｜ mention 提到

B 基本題型

❶ 三篇文章

Question 1 refers to the following advertisement and emails.

Kennywood is located between the beautiful Monga River and the towering Kanah Mountain Range. It is the finest traditional amusement park in the West. The park features 25 major rides, including roller coasters, two water rides, and 20 kinds of land rides. There are also 35 games, two video arcades, and four souvenir shops throughout the park.	肯尼伍德座落於美麗的孟加河與高聳的迦納山脈之間。它是西部最棒的傳統遊樂園。這個遊樂園的特色在於 25 種主要遊樂設施，包括雲霄飛車、兩種水上遊樂設施，和 20 多種陸上遊樂設施。整個樂園還有 35 種遊戲、兩個電玩遊戲廳和四間紀念品商店。

To	david@coolmail.net	收件者：david@coolmail.net
From	buffy@yaho.com	寄件者：buffy@yaho.com
Subject	Kennywood Park	主旨：肯尼伍德遊樂園
Date	June 3	日期：六月三日

Dear David,

I'm thinking about going to Kennywood. There are so many fun things to do. I want to ride the roller coasters. What do you think? Do you want to come with me?

親愛的大衛：

我在考慮去肯尼伍德。那裡可以做很多有趣的事。我想去坐雲霄飛車。你有什麼想法？你想跟我去嗎？

To	buffy@yaho.com	收件者：buffy@yaho.com
From	david@coolmail.net	寄信人：david@coolmail.net
Subject	RE: Kennywood Park	主旨：回覆：肯尼伍德遊樂園
Date	June 4	日期：六月四日

Dear Buffy,

Riding roller coasters sounds like fun. I'd like to come. I also want to buy some souvenirs when we visit Kennywood.

親愛的巴菲：

坐雲霄飛車聽起來很好玩，我也想去。我們到肯尼伍德遊覽時，我也想買一些紀念品。

Who will buy some souvenirs in Kennywood?

(A) David

(B) Buffy

誰會在肯尼伍德買一些紀念品？

(A) 大衛

(B) 巴菲

解析 透過報導可以知道肯尼伍德有紀念品店，而且可以推測，巴菲和大衛要一起去肯尼伍德。因為 Buffy 沒有提到要買禮物，而大衛有提到他會買，所以選項（A）是答案。

單字 towering 高聳的 ｜ range 山脈 ｜ feature 特色 ｜ souvenir 紀念品

(C) 題型練習

Question 1 refers to the following article and emails.

Chocolate is a food made from cacao beans. These beans are actually the seeds of a tropical tree called the cacao. These trees flourish in warm, moist climates and grow to be about 7.5 meters high.

They produce leaves, flowers, and fruit in all seasons of the year.

Cacao trees grow in equatorial regions around the world.

— □ ✕

To	Sally Russell <sally@pitamo.net>
From	Jack Baker <jack@coolmail.com>
Subject	Chocolate from cacao beans
Date	November 3

Dear Sally,

I've just read an interesting article about chocolate. I didn't know chocolate was made from cacao beans.

— □ ✕

To	Jack Baker<jack@coolmail.com>
From	Sally Russell <sally@pitamo.net>
Subject	RE: Chocolate from cacao beans
Date	November 4

Dear Jack,

The article you mentioned in your email contains interesting information. We may visit the regions where cacao trees grow.

1. Which regions will Jack and Sally visit to learn more about chocolate?

(A) Polar regions

(B) Equatorial regions

答案和解析

1. Answer (B)

翻譯 巧克力是由可可豆製作的食物。這種豆子是一種叫可可亞的熱帶樹的種子。這些樹在溫暖潮濕的氣候生長茂盛,而且可以長到 7.5 公尺左右。它們全年四季都可以長出葉子、花和果。可可樹在全世界的赤道地區生長。

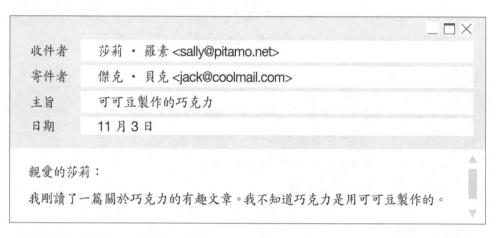

收件者　莎莉・羅素 <sally@pitamo.net>
寄件者　傑克・貝克 <jack@coolmail.com>
主旨　可可豆製作的巧克力
日期　11 月 3 日

親愛的莎莉:

我剛讀了一篇關於巧克力的有趣文章。我不知道巧克力是用可可豆製作的。

收件者　傑克・貝克 <jack@coolmail.com>
寄件者　莎莉・羅素 <sally@pitamo.net>
主旨　回覆:可可豆製作的巧克力
日期　11 月 4 日

親愛的傑克:

你在信中提到的文章資訊很有意思。我們可以到可可樹生長的地區遊覽。

傑克和莎莉要遊覽什麼地區以了解更多關於巧克力的資訊?
(A) 極地地區
(B) 赤道地區

解析 透過兩封電子郵件,可以知道傑克和莎莉要去參觀可可樹生長的地方,而且因為報導提到可可樹生長的地方是赤道地區,所以答案是選項 (B)。

單字 tropical 熱帶的 ｜ flourish 生長茂盛 ｜ moist 潮濕的 ｜ climate 氣候 ｜ produce 生長 ｜ equatorial 赤道地區的 ｜ region 地區

D 應用練習 ▶ 解析 P. 559

Question 1 refers to the following article and emails.

Chris is a very adventurous boy. He always likes to try new things without being afraid of the risks he might face. In particular, he enjoys extreme sports like skydiving and bungee jumping. His parents always worry that their only child might hurt himself.

To	Amy Johnson <johnson@campred.com>
From	Jane Smith <smith@edwardmail.net>
Subject	My adventurous son
Date	April 10

Dear Dr. Johnson,

You may have read a note about my son. He likes extreme sports too much. My husband and I don't know what to do.

To	Jane Smith <smith@edwardmail.net>
From	Amy Johnson <johnson@campred.com>
Subject	RE: My adventurous son
Date	April 11

Dear Ms. Smith,

Your son is really adventurous. But some extreme sports are especially dangerous. I'd like to advise your son not to jump from a plane in the sky.

---

1. What does Dr. Johnson want Chris to stop doing?

    (A) Driving

    (B) Skydiving

Quick Test for **Part 7**

▶ 解析 P. 559

Question 1 refers to the following online chat.

Smith, Erica	10:20 a.m.
Do you think we should invest in Timple Company?	
Garner, Paul	10:22 a.m.
I don't think so. The company is having a lot of difficulties.	

1. At 10:22, what does Mr. Garner mean when he writes, "I don't think so"?

   (A) He doesn't want to invest in the company.

   (B) He doesn't think it's a good idea to raise money for the poor.

Question 2 refers to the following letter.

Dear Ms. Susan Black,

Tomorrow, I'm having a meeting with the CEO I told you about.
I'm going to present my project to her. If she likes it, she'll support
it financially. My project will help children to learn about the past
by visiting museums. I believe that learning about the past is
important to every child.

2. What is suggested about the writer?

   (A) She has visited every museum in her hometown.

   (B) She believes that history is helpful in children's lives.

Question 3 refers to the following article.

> Robert Lee, CEO of Green Company, resigned yesterday. Lee was a successful businessman who was widely respected in the oil industry. The company did not explain why he stepped down. Therefore, a lot of people wonder what is going on in the company.

3. The word "resigned" in line 1 is closest in meaning to
   (A) started his job
   (B) left his job

Question 4 refers to the following email.

To	white@emvimt.net
From	robert@savechildren.org
Subject	Volunteering projects in Malaysia
Date	February 11

Dear Mr. White,

Thank you for your email. I really appreciate it. We have been helping thousands of volunteers to go abroad to help those in need. You seem to be interested in helping poor children in Malaysia. We do have several volunteer projects in that country. Can you come to my office to discuss those projects with me? I'm sure you'll make a difference in the lives of poor children in Malaysia.

4. Why was the email written?
   (A) To encourage Mr. White to help poor children in Europe
   (B) To invite Mr. White to discuss some projects

Marie's Travel Agency

A guided tour is an excellent way to explore a foreign city. The problem is that it is very difficult to find qualified tour guides. However, if you choose Marie's Travel Agency, you have nothing to worry about. All our tour guides really care about you. They will do everything to make your travel experience truly enjoyable. Just call us today at 373-7883 and have an unforgettable travel experience.

To	Marie Brown
From	Susan Lee
Subject	none
Date	March 3

Dear Ms. Brown,

I have recently traveled to Seoul, South Korea. I was worried because I had never been to the city. But Sumi, one of your guides, was so kind and efficient. Thanks to her sincere efforts, I really enjoyed my trip to Seoul. So, I have recommended your agency to Mary Smith, a close friend of mine. She'll call you soon.

5. What will Ms. Smith do in the near future?
   (A) Dial 373-7883
   (B) Travel to Seoul with a friend

Notes

Practice Test

▶ 解析 P. 561

Part 7

Directions: In this part you will read a selection of texts, such as magazine and newspaper articles, letters, and advertisements. Each text is followed by several questions. Select the best answer for each question and mark the letter (A), (B), (C), or (D) on your answer sheet.

Question 1 refers to the following online chat.

Adams, Mary	3:20 p.m.
Donald, do you know how much we've spent on the marketing campaign?	
Johnson, Donald	3:21 p.m.
$3 million. I think it's the money well spent.	
Adams, Mary	3:22 p.m.
I agree. Our sales have improved significantly since the marketing campaign.	

1. At 3:22, what does Ms. Adams mean when she writes, "I agree"?
   (A) She thinks the company needs to spend more than $3 million on marketing.
   (B) She does not understand why the company has wasted so much money.
   (C) She thinks the decision to invest $3 million in the campaign was a wise one.
   (D) She does not believe that Mr. Johnson is telling the truth.

Question 2 refers to the following notice.

All of us at the Aurora Hotel really care about you. We firmly believe that customer satisfaction is the reason why our hotel exists. So, before you leave, be sure to complete our customer satisfaction questionnaire. Any issues you may have with our hotel will be dealt with immediately. At the same time, your responses will help us improve our service.

2. Which is true about the Aurora Hotel?
   (A) It does not think highly of customers.
   (B) It does not want its customers to complain about its service.
   (C) It has been in business for more than five years.
   (D) It wants to improve its service.

Question 3 refers to the following announcement.

We, at Green Motors, believe that safety is the most important aspect of the automobile industry. Therefore, we regret to inform our customers that we'll be recalling some of our SUVs. We'll recall the new 2009 SUV, the new 3010 SUV, and the new 5012 SUV. Unfortunately, these SUVs may not be safe for our customers. Call us at 555-7882 for further details.

3. Why will the new 5012 SUV be recalled?
   (A) Because Green Motors will not produce the SUV anymore.
   (B) Because the SUV may put drivers in danger.
   (C) Because the SUV is not popular among young people.
   (D) Because the SUV is not generating profits.

Question 4 refers to the following web page.

http://www.tdrsites.net/registraion

Online Registration Form for Our Online Services

Please give us the following information so that we can provide you with our online services. We won't share your information with anyone.

Full name:

Date of birth:

SES account number:

Address:

Phone number:

4. What information is NOT required for online registration?

(A) Your last name

(B) Your contact information

(C) Your account number

(D) Your place of birth

Question 5 refers to the following article.

Earth Hour

Earth Hour is a worldwide event organized by the World Wildlife Fund. It is held on the last Saturday of every March. On this day, households and businesses are encouraged to turn off their nonessential lights for one hour, which is meant to raise people's awareness of saving energy. The event first took place in Sydney, Australia, in 2007, when 2.2 million people participated by turning off their lights to save electricity.

5. Which is NOT true about Earth Hour?

(A) It usually lasts for twelve hours.

(B) It takes place on a yearly basis.

(C) It aims to teach people to save energy.

(D) It was first held in Australia.

Question 6 refers to the following information.

Chili Recipe

Chili is an easy dish to prepare. First, cut up two large onions and fry them in a little oil. Then, add some garlic and diced chili peppers. When the onions are soft, add two pounds of ground beef. Stir until the beef turns brown which means it's completely cooked. Sprinkle some red chili powder on top.

6. The word "prepare" in line 1 is closest in meaning to
   (A) organize an event
   (B) train people
   (C) make plans to do something
   (D) make a meal

Question 7 refers to the following article.

When you travel to a new destination with unusual customs and traditions, you can easily experience culture shock. Although culture shock is not a life-threatening disease, it can lead to some serious problems such as sleep deprivation and depression. However, by taking a simple precaution, you can avoid these problems and get full enjoyment out of your trip.

7. Which is NOT true about culture shock?
   (A) It may prevent you from sleeping.
   (B) It may make you unhappy.
   (C) It is generally good for your physical health.
   (D) There is a way to overcome it.

Question 8 refers to the following article.

"Let's go for coffee!" says your American friend. – [1] – All over North America, people like to meet at coffee shops. – [2] – There, people sit and talk about the day's business, news and sports, personal concerns, or simply gossip. – [3] – People go to coffee shops not only to socialize with family and friends but also to discuss business or to treat their employees to a snack. – [4] – Others go there to read the newspaper or their favorite magazines.

8. In which of the positions marked [1], [2], [3], and [4] does the following sentence best belong?

"Coffee shops have an informal atmosphere that encourages conversation."

(A) [1]

(B) [2]

(C) [3]

(D) [4]

Question 9 refers to the following article and email.

Great Britain is famous for sports. Many sports, such as soccer, rugby, and cricket, originated in Britain. The country is also famous for literature, and there have been great writers like William Shakespeare and C. S. Lewis. It is also well known as the home of London, the host of the 2012 Olympic Games. With its unique culture, Great Britain has visitors from all over the world.

_ □ ✕

To	Eric Smith
From	Erica Johnson
Subject	Article about Great Britain
Date	July 3

Dear Mr. Eric Smith,

I have read your article about Great Britain with great interest. I run a small company that manufactures sporting goods. I'd like to know which sport is the most popular in the country. I'm particularly interested in the three sports you mentioned in your article. Please send me an email at erica_johnson@sportstop.com.

9. Which of the following sports is the writer of the email NOT particularly interested in?

(A) soccer

(B) polo

(C) cricket

(D) rugby

A newborn baby panda is a helpless little creature. It is amazingly small, and its eyes remain closed for three weeks. The babies are highly dependent on their mothers. The only food they eat is their mother's milk. Mother pandas are known for being very careful and protective. They carry their babies gently in their mouths when they are on the move.

— ☐ ✕

To	kevin@danomen.net
From	johnson@mconerce.com
Subject	A newborn baby panda
Date	May 14

Dear Mr. Snow,

Welcome aboard! Montgomery Zoo is a good place to work. Since you are responsible for taking care of baby pandas, you need to learn about these little creatures.

— ☐ ✕

To	johnson@mconerce.com
From	kevin@danomen.net
Subject	RE: A newborn baby panda
Date	May 14

Dear Ms. Johnson,

Thank you. Fortunately, I've just read an interesting article about baby pandas. Maybe we can invite the reporter to our zoo.

10. Why does Mr. Snow want to invite the reporter to the zoo?

(A) Because the reporter keeps baby pandas as pets.

(B) Because Mr. Snow reads the newspaper every day.

(C) Because he will write a book about baby pandas.

(D) Because the reporter can help him do his job effectively.

Notes

ANSWER

—— 中譯解析 ——

Part 1
照片描述

① 各類型照片說明

題型 **01** 人物照片

Ⓓ 應用練習　　P. 15 🎧 005

1. (A)

> Script
>
> (A) The man is using a microphone.
> (B) The man is crying.
> (C) The man is reading a magazine.
>
> (A) 男子正在使用麥克風。
> (B) 男子正在哭。
> (C) 男子正在讀一本雜誌。

解析 這是一人照片類型，只要選出客觀的敘述即可。男子手中拿的東西是不是雜誌，並不太清楚，而且從他臉部的表情推斷，他並沒有在看手中的東西。看到男子身前的麥克風和男子的動作，可以判斷男子正透過麥克風在講話，所以答案是選項（A）。

單字 **microphone** 麥克風

2. (B)

> Script
>
> (A) They are standing in front of a store.
> (B) They are holding umbrellas.
> (C) They are lying on the beach.
>
> (A) 他們站在一家商店前。
> (B) 他們撐著雨傘。
> (C) 他們躺在沙灘上。

解析 這是多人照片類型。有兩個小孩蹲在地上，看姿勢就知道選項（A）是錯的。小孩手中都拿著雨傘，這是不能否定的客觀事實，所以答案是選項（B）。

單字 **in front of** 在……之前 | **umbrella** 雨傘 | **beach** 海灘

題型 **02** 以室內為背景的照片

Ⓓ 應用練習　　P. 21 🎧 010

1. (C)

> Script
>
> (A) She is looking out the window.
> (B) There is a child in the laboratory.
> (C) She is holding something.
>
> (A) 她正看向窗外。
> (B) 實驗室裡有一個小孩。
> (C) 她握著某項物品。

解析 這是一人照片類型。可以確認照片中的女子正在看著某物，但不是向窗外看。另外，單從照片無法判斷實驗室裡有沒有小孩。女子手中拿著試管，這是確定的事實，所以答案是選項（C）。

單字 **laboratory** 實驗室

2. (B)

> Script
>
> (A) There are two people in the bedroom.
> (B) She is sleeping in the bed.
> (C) There is no pillow in the bedroom.
>
> (A) 臥室有兩個人。
> (B) 她在床上睡覺。
> (C) 臥室裡沒有枕頭。

解析 這是以室內為背景的一人照片類型。從床可以推測這是臥室，但是單從照片無法看出來房間除了女子還有誰，所以選項（A）錯了。照片中的女子頭枕著枕頭，所以不能說臥室內沒有枕頭。從女子躺在床上閉著眼睛的樣子，說她在睡覺是客觀的事實，所以答案是選項（B）。

題型 03 以室外為背景的照片

Ⓓ 應用練習　　P. 27　　▮▮ 🎧 015

1. (C)

Script

(A) There are no trees along the road.
(B) There is a rabbit on the bench.
(C) A woman is running on the road.

(A) 路旁沒有樹木。
(B) 長椅上有一隻兔子。
(C) 有一位女子正在路上跑步。

解析 這是以室外為背景的照片類型。照片背景是沿路上的路樹，而選項（A）和照片完全相反，所以是錯的。照片左側有貌似長椅的東西，但是沒有兔子，所以選項（B）也是錯的。女子在路中央，頭髮飛揚，雙手擺動，右腿往後踢，毫無疑問是在跑步，所以答案是選項（C）。

單字 bench 長椅

2. (B)

Script

(A) A lot of people are playing in the forest.
(B) The woman is pointing at something.
(C) There are few trees in the forest.

(A) 有很多人在森林裡玩耍。
(B) 女子正指著某樣東西。
(C) 森林裡的樹木很稀少。

解析 這是以室外為背景的照片類型。因為照片中只出現了一名女子，無法知道樹林裡有沒有很多人，所以選項（A）不對。另外，選項（C）說森林裡的樹木很稀少，但照片中我們看到模糊的樹木，可是無法判斷多少，不是一個客觀的描述。我們可以從途中看到女子的手指著一個方向，眼睛也朝著那邊看，所以選項（B）是答案。

單字 forest 森林 ｜ point 指著

Quick Test　　P. 28　　🎧 016

1. (A)　2. (C)　3. (B)　4. (C)

1. (A)

Script

(A) They are smiling.
(B) They are opening the door.
(C) They are wearing glasses.

(A) 她們在微笑。
(B) 她們正在開門。
(C) 她們戴著眼鏡。

解析 這是兩人以上的照片類型。照片中除了人以外，看不到背景所以不知道是室內還是室外，也看不到選項（B）提到的門。另外，兩位女子都沒有戴眼鏡，所以選項（C）是錯的。兩位女子嘴巴都輕鬆地張開，且嘴角上揚，所以不是大笑而是微笑，答案是選項（A）。

單字 glasses 眼鏡

2. (C)

(A) There are books on the floor.
(B) A boy is entering the room.
(C) There are some apples in the basket.

(A) 地板上有書本。
(B) 有一個男孩走進房間。
(C) 籃子裡有一些蘋果。

解析 照片中沒有人物，是以事物為主的照片類型。因為照片中沒有男孩，也沒有書，所以選項（A）和（B）不是答案。竹籃裡裝滿了蘋果，並且是用 some 來表示數量，是最一般且普遍的表示法，所以是對照片客觀的描述，答案是選項（C）。

單字 **floor** 地板 | **enter** 進入 | **basket** 籃子

3. (B)

(A) They are leaving the restaurant.
(B) They are eating some food.
(C) They are using computers.

(A) 她們正在離開餐廳。
(B) 她們正在享用一些食物。
(C) 她們正在使用電腦。

解析 是兩人以上的照片類型。照片中的女子面前都有食物，每個人手中都拿著叉子，左側女子的叉子上有食物，所以可以知道她們正在吃東西。因為她們都坐著，所以沒有正要離開餐廳，選項（A）錯了。照片中並沒有出現電腦，選項（C）也錯了。因為描述她們正在吃東西，是客觀的事實，所以答案是選項（B）。

單字 **restaurant** 餐廳

4. (C)

(A) They are playing chess.
(B) They are singing together.
(C) They are outdoors.

(A) 她們正在下棋。
(B) 她們正在一起唱歌。
(C) 她們在戶外。

解析 這是兩人以上且以室外為背景的混合照片類型。照片中沒看到棋子和棋盤，另外，也沒看到小孩子在唱歌，所以選項（A）和（B）都是錯的。小孩在室外，所以說小孩在戶外（outdoors），是客觀的事實，因此答案是選項（C）。

單字 **outdoors** 戶外

Practice Test　　P. 31　　🎧 017

1. (C)　2. (D)　3. (D)　4. (B)
5. (D)　6. (B)

1. (C)

(A) She is wearing sunglasses.
(B) She is watching TV.
(C) She is holding some balloons.
(D) She is using the Internet.

(A) 她戴著太陽眼鏡。
(B) 她正在看電視。
(C) 她正拿著一些氣球。
(D) 她正在使用網路。

解析 這是一人照片類型，但不知道是室內還是室外。沒看到照片中有太陽眼鏡，所以選項（A）是錯的。完全無法知道女

子是不是在看電視，也沒看到她在用電腦、手機或網路，所以（B）和（D）是錯的。因為女子的手正抓著一束氣球（some balloons），所以答案是選項（C）。

2. (D)

(A) The dog is barking.
(B) They are entering a store.
(C) The girl is playing the piano.
(D) The girl is sleeping.

(A) 狗正在吠叫。
(B) 他們正走進一間商店。
(C) 女孩正在彈鋼琴。
(D) 女孩正在睡覺。

解析 這是人物加上動物的照片類型。照片中出現的狗眼睛是閉著的，好像在睡覺，嘴巴沒有張開，所以不是在吠叫。照片中的人物完全沒有移動的樣子。另外，照片中也沒有出現鋼琴。小女孩臉側躺著，眼睛閉著，所以可以推測她在睡覺，答案是選項（D）。

單字 bark 吠叫 ｜ enter 進入

3. (D)

(A) A woman is using a notebook computer.
(B) A woman is crossing the street.
(C) A woman is driving a truck.
(D) A woman is writing something.

(A) 一名女子正在使用筆電。
(B) 一名女子正在過街。
(C) 一名女子正在駕駛卡車。
(D) 一名女子正在寫東西。

解析 這是以室內為背景的照片類型。照片中出現了好像是筆記本（notebook）的東西，這很清楚地不是筆電。女子也不像在戶外開車或走路。女子手拿著筆正在寫什麼的樣子，所以答案是選項（D）。

單字 cross 穿越（馬路）

4. (B)

(A) They are eating spaghetti.
(B) They are looking at their smartphones.
(C) They are reading newspapers.
(D) They are entering a museum.

(A) 她們正在吃義大利麵。
(B) 她們正在看她們的手機。
(C) 她們正在讀報紙。
(D) 她們正走進一間博物館。

解析 這是兩人以上的照片類型。她們沒有在吃東西，照片中也沒看到報紙。另外，雖然可推測她們所在的地方是室內，但單從照片，無法判斷這裡是不是博物館。她們手中拿著手機，而且各自看著自己的手機，所以選項（B）是答案。

單字 newspaper 報紙 ｜ museum 博物館

5. (D)

(A) A child is playing with his cat.
(B) They are in the library.
(C) They are buying some vegetables.
(D) A man is playing the guitar.

(A) 一個小孩正在和他的貓玩耍。
(B) 他們在圖書館。
(C) 他們正在購買一些蔬菜。
(D) 一名男子正在彈吉他。

解析 這是兩人以上且以室外為背景的照片類型。照片中找不到貓，也沒有正在買東西的樣子。另外，照片以非常空曠的戶外為背景，看不到圖書館，也不像是圖書館前的廣場。照片左側的男子正在彈吉他，照片右側的男子和女子正在拍手，可以推測應該是在打拍子。所以描述一名男子正在彈吉他的選項（D）是答案。

單字 library 圖書館 | vegetable 蔬菜

6. (B)

Script
(A) She is buying some meat.
(B) She is holding a notepad.
(C) She is using a washing machine.
(D) She is writing something.

(A) 她正在買一些肉。
(B) 她正拿著一本記事本。
(C) 她正在使用洗衣機。
(D) 她正在寫一些東西。

解析 這是一人照片類型。照片中的女子手托著下巴正在思考什麼的樣子，背景出現了各式各樣的水果，推測她應該是在商店，不過從照片中無法推測女子有沒有買肉。照片中沒看到洗衣機。另外女子手中雖然有筆，但她並沒有在記事本寫東西。她只是一手拿筆一手拿著類似記事本的東西，所以答案是選項（B）。

單字 meat 肉類 | notepad 記事本 | washing machine 洗衣機

Part 2
應答問題

❶ 一般疑問句

題型 01 Do/Does 疑問句

D 應用練習 　　　P. 41 　　🎧022

1. (C)

Script
Do you like classical music?
(A) My sister is a singer.
(B) I don't like poetry.
(C) I love Mozart.

你喜歡古典音樂嗎？
(A) 我妹妹是歌手。
(B) 我不喜歡詩。
(C) 我喜歡莫札特。

解析 雖然是基本的 Yes/No 疑問句，但省略回答 Yes/No，直接說：「喜歡莫札特的音樂」，也就表示喜歡古典音樂代表作曲家莫札特的作品，所以答案是選項（C）。

單字 classical music 古典音樂

2. (B)

Script
Does he work for a trading company?
(A) He didn't have breakfast.
(B) Not anymore.
(C) I enjoyed your company.

他在貿易公司上班嗎？

(A) 他沒有吃早餐。
(B) 已經沒有了。
(C) 我喜歡你的陪伴。

解析 雖然沒有用 Yes/No 來回答，但用「已經不在了（Not anymore）」來取代否定回答句，因此答案是選項（B）。選項（C）的 company 是利用它其他的意思（陪伴）做成的錯誤答案陷阱。

單字 trading 貿易 ｜ company 公司

3. (C)

Script

Did you play the piano last night?

(A) You're a good pianist.
(B) I sold an old piano last month.
(C) No. I just read some comics.

你昨晚有彈鋼琴嗎？

(A) 你是位優秀的鋼琴家。
(B) 我上個月賣了一台舊鋼琴。
(C) 沒有，我只有看一些漫畫書。

解析 這是用 Yes/No 來回答的疑問句，所以（C）一邊用 no 來回答，一邊說做了其他的事是答案。若將選項（B）的 an old piano 改成 my piano，就可以是答案了。

單字 comic 漫畫

4. (B)

Script

Did they treat you well?

(A) I'm not a child anymore.
(B) They were very kind to me.
(C) I don't want to see you again.

他們對你好嗎？

(A) 我不再是小孩了。
(B) 他們對我很友善。
(C) 我不想再見到你。

解析 雖然是 Yes/No 疑問句，但不用 Yes/No 來回答，直接用有肯定含意的話語來回答的選項（B）是答案。

單字 treat 對待 ｜ anymore 不再

題型 02 Be 動詞疑問句

D 應用練習 P. 47 027

1. (C)

Script

Are you a native speaker of French?

(A) I'm planning to visit France this summer.
(B) My parents went to Paris last month.
(C) Actually, I don't speak French.

你的母語是法語嗎？

(A) 我打算今夏去法國遊覽。
(B) 我爸媽上個月去巴黎。
(C) 事實上，我不說法語。

解析 因為是 Be 動詞疑問句，所以要用 Yes/No 開頭，再接 I am 來回答。但選項（C）否定了問題，並回答：「事實上，我不說法語。」，所以是答案。

單字 native 天生的

2. (B)

Script

Are there any Chinese students in your class?

(A) China is growing rapidly.
(B) Most of the students are Chinese.
(C) I like that Chinese restaurant.

你的班上有中國學生嗎？

(A) 中國正在快速成長。
(B) 多數學生是中國人。
(C) 我喜歡那家中餐廳。

解析 雖然是 Be 動詞疑問句，但選項（B）省略了 Yes／No，並提供了和問句有關的肯定訊息，所以答案是選項（B）。選項（A）和（C）和提問完全無關。

單字 **rapidly** 快速地

3. (B)

Script

Are you reading a magazine?

(A) There is a magazine on the desk.
(B) I'm just watching TV.
(C) That magazine is not popular anymore.

你正在閱讀雜誌嗎？

(A) 書桌上有一本雜誌。
(B) 我只是在看電視。
(C) 那本雜誌不再受歡迎。

解析 雖然是 Be 動詞疑問句，但選項（B）省略了 Yes／No，直接回答正在做別的事，所以是答案。

4. (C)

Script

Was the letter written by your daughter?

(A) We're visiting her next month.
(B) She spends a lot of time drawing pictures.
(C) My son wrote it last night.

信是你女兒寫的嗎？

(A) 我們下個月要探望她。
(B) 她花很多時間繪畫。
(C) 是我兒子昨晚寫的。

解析 雖然是 Be 動詞疑問句，但選項（C）省略了 Yes／No，並回答提問中的行為是其他人做的，所以選項（C）是答案。選項（A）和（B）都是東問西答。

題型 **03** Have／Has 疑問句

Ⓓ 應用練習　　P. 53　‖‖　🎧 032

1. (C)

Script

Have you made up your mind?

(A) Why do you keep changing jobs?
(B) I don't think he'll change his mind.
(C) I'm still debating what to do.

你做好決定了嗎？

(A) 你為什麼要一直換工作？
(B) 我不認為他會改變心意。
(C) 我還在思考要做什麼。

解析 雖然是用 Yes／No 來回答的疑問句，但選項（C）省略了 Yes／No，並提到和提問相反的情況，表示否定了提問，所以選項（C）是答案。

單字 **make up one's mind** 做決定 ｜
debate 思考

2. (B)

Script

Have they booked a hotel yet?
(A) There are a lot of good hotels in Miami.
(B) I don't think they're going to stay in a hotel.
(C) I like the hotel very much.

他們訂飯店了嗎？
(A) 邁阿密有很多不錯的酒店。
(B) 我不認為他們會去住飯店。
(C) 我很喜歡這間飯店。

解析 雖然是用 Yes/No 來回答的疑問句，但選項中沒有 Yes/No。提問詢問他們有沒有訂飯店，選項（B）迂迴地回答說他們應該沒有，所以是答案。提問人並沒有提到特定的旅館，所以選項（C）說 the hotel，是不對的。

單字 book 預訂

3. (A)

Script

Have they cleaned the room yet?
(A) It's still dirty.
(B) We used to know each other.
(C) Have you known them well?

他們清理房間了嗎？
(A) 房間還是髒的。
(B) 我們以前就認識彼此。
(C) 你以前和他們很熟嗎？

解析 雖然是 Yes/No 疑問句，但選項中沒有 Yes/No。若已經打掃房間的話，房間應該是乾淨的，選項（A）說房間仍然很髒，表示還沒掃，所以選項（A）是答案。

4. (C)

Script

Has he stopped smoking?
(A) He was hospitalized yesterday.
(B) Smoking is bad for your health.
(C) He's still a heavy smoker.

他戒菸了嗎？
(A) 他昨天住院。
(B) 抽菸有害你的健康。
(C) 他還是菸癮很重。

解析 雖然是 Yes/No 疑問句，但選項中沒有 Yes/No。選項（C）說他仍然菸癮很重，表示他還是抽很多菸，所以選項（C）是答案。

單字 hospitalize 住院 | heavy smoker 嚴重菸癮者

題型 04 助動詞疑問句

D 應用練習　　P. 59　　🎧 037

1. (C)

Script

Can I send this document to Ms. Cooper?
(A) Do you know my address?
(B) Do you know who wrote it?
(C) She's been waiting for it.

我可以把這份文件寄給庫伯小姐嗎？
(A) 你知道我的地址嗎？
(B) 你知道這份文件是誰寫的嗎？
(C) 她一直在等這份文件。

解析 這是助動詞疑問句，要用 Yes/No 來回答，但選項中沒有 Yes/No。選項（C）說她正在等文件，和提問相關，所以答案是選項（C）。

單字 document 文件 ｜ address 地址

2. (B)

Script

Can I take tomorrow off?
(A) You must have forgotten the keys.
(B) You have a very important meeting tomorrow.
(C) He's not in right now.

我明天可以休假嗎？
(A) 你一定忘了鑰匙
(B) 你明天有一場很重要的會議。
(C) 他現在不在。

解析 這是助動詞疑問句，也要用 Yes/No 來回答，但選項中沒有 Yes/No。詢問「明天可以休假嗎」，選項（B）告知不能休假的理由，間接回答 No，所以是答案。

單字 key 鑰匙 ｜ meeting 會議

3. (C)

Script

Should we lower the price of the product?
(A) The marketing director couldn't attend the meeting.
(B) It was much better than expected.
(C) That is an option we have to consider.

我們該降低這項產品的價格嗎？
(A) 行銷總監無法出席會議。
(B) 那比預期的好多了。
(C) 那是我們該考慮的選項。

解析 這是用助動詞 should 起始的疑問句，但是選項中沒有直接表示肯定或否定的回答。選項（C）回答是個該考慮的選項表示肯定，所以選項（C）是答案。

單字 lower 降低 ｜ expect 預期 ｜ option 選項 ｜ consider 考慮

4. (B)

Script

Would you like something to eat?
(A) I can lend you some money.
(B) I'm starving.
(C) You'd better not skip breakfast.

你想吃點東西嗎？
(A) 我可以借一些錢給你。
(B) 我很餓。
(C) 你最好不要不吃早餐。

解析 詢問說要不要吃東西，選項（B）回答說我很餓，表示想吃東西，所以答案是選項（B）。

單字 starve 很餓

Quick Test　　P. 60　　🎧038

1. (B)　2. (C)　3. (A)　4. (B)
5. (C)　6. (B)　7. (C)　8. (B)

1. (B)

Script

Does she work out every day?
(A) She works for a travel agency.
(B) Not anymore.
(C) She used to be a good cook.

她每天都會健身嗎？
(A) 她在一家旅行社工作。
(B) 已經沒有了。
(C) 她曾是一名優秀廚師。

解析 是 Do/Does 疑問句，但選項中沒有 Yes/No。對提問者所說的行為，選項（B）回答：「已經沒有了」，表示否定，所以是答案。

單字 agency 代辦公司

2. (C)

Script

Do you like your job?
(A) I don't think they'll fire me.
(B) Enjoy yourself.
(C) I find it very rewarding.

你喜歡你的工作嗎？
(A) 我不認為他們會炒我魷魚。
(B) 盡情享受吧。
(C) 我認為這工作令人受益良多。

解析 是 Do/Does 疑問句，但選項中沒有 Yes/No。選項（C）回答令人受益良多，這和喜歡的意思雖然不同，但仍然表示肯定自己的工作，所以答案是選項（C）。

單字 rewarding 受益良多的

3. (A)

Script

Are there any restaurants near the hotel?
(A) There are two Korean restaurants nearby.
(B) I'm going to check out the new hotel.
(C) Chinese food usually tastes good.

飯店附近是否有餐廳？
(A) 附近有兩家韓式餐廳。
(B) 我會去看看那家新飯店。
(C) 中國菜通常很美味。

解析 想詢問附近是否有餐廳，所以有 yes 含意並正面回應的選項（A）是答案。

單字 nearby 附近 | check out 看看

4. (B)

Script

Are you looking for something in particular?
(A) If you need any help, just let me know.
(B) I'm just looking around.
(C) How much do I owe you?

您有特別想找的東西嗎？
(A) 如果您需要任何協助，告訴我一聲。
(B) 我只是四處看看。
(C) 我要付你多少？

解析 通常會在商店聽到類似的詢問，遇到這樣的狀況，若不需要銷售人員的幫忙時，會用選項（B）來回答。選項（A）是銷售人員對客人說的話，選項（C）是結帳時會出現的對話。

單字 in particular 特別 | look around 四處看看 | owe 欠

PART 2 ❶ 一般疑問句

Quick Test

463

5. (C)

Was the contract signed by your wife?

(A) My sister got divorced last year.

(B) I didn't write the contract.

(C) It was my mother who signed it.

那份合約是由你太太簽名的嗎?

(A) 我妹去年離婚了。

(B) 合約不是我寫的。

(C) 是我母親簽的字。

解析 是 be 動詞疑問句,要用 Yes/No 來回答,但選項中沒有 Yes/No。被動式問句中提到了可能動作行使人,選項(C)表示實際狀況中是不同人,所以是答案。

單字 contract 合約 ｜ divorce 離婚

6. (B)

Have you ever learned a foreign language?

(A) She speaks three different languages.

(B) I picked up French when I was in Paris.

(C) Learning a foreign language makes you smart.

你有學過外語嗎?

(A) 她會說三種不同的語言。

(B) 我在巴黎學會了法語。

(C) 學外語會讓你變得聰明。

解析 用完成式詢問有沒有學過外語,要用 Yes/No 來回答。但選項(B)沒有用 Yes/No 回答,直接表示有過類似的學習經驗,所以選項(B)是答案。題目詢問的對象的是「你」,選項(A)回答「她」,講到了不同的人,而選項(C)根本是答非所問,所以都是錯的。

7. (C)

Has she suggested a good solution?

(A) She used to be very happy.

(B) I'm still confused.

(C) Not yet.

她提出萬全之計了嗎?

(A) 她曾經非常快樂。

(B) 我還是很迷惑。

(C) 還沒有。

解析 這是要用 Yes/No 來回答的問句,選項(C)雖是直述句,卻有否定的含意,所以是答案。

單字 solution 解決方式 ｜ confused 迷惑的

8. (B)

Can you help me lift this table?

(A) You should have attended the meeting.

(B) It doesn't look heavy.

(C) It's kind of you to say that.

你可以幫我搬起這張桌子嗎?

(A) 你原本應該出席會議。

(B) 桌子看起來不重。

(C) 你那樣說真好。

解析 詢問能不能幫忙,選項(B)沒有回答可否,直接表示要幫忙的事看起來不難所以是答案。選項(A)和(C)全都答非所問。

單字 lift 搬起來 ｜ attend 參加

單字 pick up (自然地)學會

❷ 疑問詞疑問句

題型 01 Who 疑問句

D 應用練習　　P. 67　🎧 043

1. (C)

Script

Who drew this picture?

(A) Yes, we're seeing each other.
(B) She bought it last week.
(C) A famous artist.

這張圖是誰畫的？

(A) 是的，我們正在交往中。
(B) 是她上週買的。
(C) 一位知名的藝術家。

解析 詢問具體的訊息，選項（C）回答是一位知名藝術家，雖然回應不是很明確，但卻是最合適的回答，所以是答案。因為是疑問詞疑問句，所以用 Yes 回答的選項（A）絕對是錯的。問題詢問這幅畫的創作者，選項（B）卻回答買畫的買家，是陷阱選項。

單字 each other 彼此 ｜ famous 知名的

2. (B)

Script

Who will meet with Mr. Rosenberg?

(A) No, we haven't met before.
(B) You'd better talk to the manager.
(C) I don't know who you are.

誰將和羅森柏格先生見面？

(A) 沒有，我們以前不曾見過。
(B) 你最好和經理談談。
(C) 我不知道你是誰。

解析 用疑問詞 who 詢問具體訊息，但選項中卻沒有明確的答案。選項（B）回答若想知道答案的話，最好去問經理，所以是答案。

3. (B)

Script

Who revised this article?

(A) Yes, it is an insightful article.
(B) What makes you think it was revised?
(C) No, I haven't been there before.

這篇文章是誰修訂的？

(A) 沒錯，這篇文章很有見地。
(B) 你為何認為這篇文章已經被修訂過？
(C) 沒有，我以前從沒去過那裡。

解析 用疑問詞 who 詢問具體訊息，但選項中卻沒有明確的答案。選項（B）反問為何認為文章被修過，和提問內容相關，所以是答案。

單字 insightful 具洞察力的 ｜ revise 修訂

4. (C)

Script

Who should I report to?

(A) No, I haven't read the report yet.
(B) Thank you for your advice.
(C) Ms. Johnson is your immediate supervisor.

我該向誰報告？

(A) 沒有，我還沒讀那篇報告。
(B) 謝謝你的建議。
(C) 強森小姐是你的直屬主管。

因為是詢問具體訊息，所以選項（A）用 No 來回答絕對是錯的。選項（B）是表示感謝，也不符合狀況。選項（C）回答提問，所以是答案。

單字 report 報告 | immediate 直屬 | supervisor 主管

題型 02 When/Where 疑問句

Ⓓ 應用練習　　P. 73　　🎧048

1. (C)

Script

When did you report the problem to your supervisor?

(A) No, we didn't discuss the issue.
(B) At the theater.
(C) Last Wednesday.

你何時向主管報告這個問題？

(A) 不，我們沒有討論這個問題。
(B) 在戲院。
(C) 上週三。

解析 因為是用詢問具體訊息，所以回答時間點的選項（C）是答案。問句不是詢問是或非，所以不用考慮選項（A）。因為是詢問時間，所以回答場所的選項（B）也不用考慮。

單字 issue 問題

2. (B)

Script

Where are you from?

(A) I'm moving to Canada next month.
(B) I'm a native of New York City.
(C) Yes, we met there last week.

你是哪裡人？

(A) 我下個月要搬到加拿大。
(B) 我是紐約市本地人。
(C) 是的，我們上週在那裡見面。

解析 因為是詢問來自何方，所以回答家鄉在何處的選項（B）是答案。

單字 native 本地人

3. (C)

Script

When will the renovation be finished?

(A) No, they haven't started it yet.
(B) I wasn't invited to the party.
(C) It is scheduled to be completed by August.

改建何時會完工？

(A) 不對，他們還沒開工。
(B) 我並沒有受邀參加派對。
(C) 預計在八月前完工。

解析 因為是用疑問詞 when 詢問時間，所以回答具體時間點的選項（C）是答案。因為不能用 Yes／No 回答，所以不用考慮選項（A）。選項（B）是毫無關聯的回答。

單字 renovation 改建

4. (B)

Script

Where will the ceremony be held?

(A) Yes, it went smoothly.
(B) At Harvard University, as far as I know.
(C) Everybody is supposed to attend the event.

典禮會在哪裡舉行？

(A) 沒錯，進行得很順利。

(B) 就我所知，在哈佛大學。

(C) 所有人都應該要參加這個活動。

解析 問題詢問具體的場所，所以回答場所的選項（B）是答案。選項（A）不能用來回答疑問詞疑問句，選項（C）沒有提供與地點相關的回應。

單字 ceremony 典禮 ｜ be supposed to 應該要 ｜ attend 參加

題型 03 How 疑問句

D 應用練習　　P. 79　　🎧 053

1. (C)

Script

How can we increase our sales?

(A) No, we didn't do anything wrong.

(B) The price is already discounted.

(C) We should develop an aggressive marketing strategy.

我們要如何增加業績？

(A) 不對，我們什麼都沒做錯。

(B) 這個價格已經打過折了。

(C) 我們應該研發積極的行銷策略。

解析 這是詢問方式的 how 疑問句，選項中有提到行銷策略的選項（C）是答案。這個問句不能用 Yes／No 回答，不用考慮選項（A）。選項（B）是和提問無關的答案。

單字 increase 增加 ｜ discount 打折 ｜ strategy 策略

---

2. (B)

Script

How do you like the new CEO?

(A) Yes, we went to the same college together.

(B) She seems to be demanding.

(C) I'm not that popular among customers.

你如何看待新執行長？

(A) 是啊，我們曾在同一所大學求學。

(B) 她似乎對員工要求很多。

(C) 我在顧客中不是那麼受歡迎。

解析 問句透過疑問詞 how 詢問喜好程度，有顯露對執行長觀感的選項（B）是最合適的回答。

單字 demanding 要求多的

---

3. (B)

Script

How much did you earn last month?

(A) We had a good time in Italy.

(B) I don't like talking about my income.

(C) No, I didn't mean to hurt your feelings.

你上個月的收入如何？

(A) 我們在義大利玩得很愉快。

(B) 我不喜歡談論我的收入。

(C) 不是，我無意傷害你的情感。

解析 這是疑問詞 how 結合形容詞副詞的疑問句。雖然是詢問具體訊息，但拒絕提供回應，不想談這個話題的選項（B）是最合適的回答。

單字 income 收入 ｜ mean 有意

4. (C)

How long have you been working here?

(A) It's up to you.
(B) Yes, we can improve our financial situation.
(C) For nearly fifteen years, I think.

你在這裡已經工作多久了？

(A) 全由你決定。
(B) 沒錯，我們可以改善我們的財務狀況。
(C) 快 15 年了，我想。

解析 這是疑問詞 how 結合形容詞／副詞的疑問句。直接回應具體訊息的選項（C）是答案。詢問具體訊息，選項（A）卻回答由對方決定，所以不是答案。疑問詞疑問句不能用 Yes／No 來回答，所以選項（B）也不對。

單字 financial 財務的

題型 04 What/Which 疑問句

D 應用練習　　P. 85　　 058

1. (C)

Script

What is the best way to compete in the Asian market?

(A) No, Asia isn't having financial difficulties.
(B) Yes, we'd better cooperate with them.
(C) We should try to understand Asian consumers better.

要在亞洲市場競爭的最佳方式是什麼？

(A) 不對，亞洲並沒有財務困難。
(B) 是啊，我們最好和他們合作。
(C) 我們應該試著更加了解亞洲消費者。

解析 用疑問詞 what 詢問具體訊息，因為是疑問詞疑問句，所以用 Yes／No 來回答的選項（A）和（B）是錯誤答案。提出具體回答的選項（C）是答案。

單字 compete 競爭 ｜ market 市場 ｜ cooperate 合作 ｜ consumer 消費者

2. (A)

Script

Which is more environmentally friendly? Electric cars or hybrid cars?

(A) I think electric cars are better for the environment.
(B) No, they are more expensive than hybrid cars.
(C) Yes, we'd better stop driving cars.

哪一種對環境更友善？電動車或油電混合車？

(A) 我認為電動車對環境比較好。
(B) 不對，它們比油電混合車更貴。
(C) 是啊，我們最好不要再開車。

解析 本題要在對方提出的選項訊息中選一個回答。選項（A）在給予的選項中選了一種來回答，所以是答案。選項（B）和（C）用 Yes／No 回答，不符合疑問詞疑問句的回答方式。

單字 electric 電的 ｜ hybrid 混合而成的

3. (B)

PART
2
❷ 疑問詞疑問句

Script

What issues were discussed at the meeting?

(A) Yes, everybody must attend the meeting.
(B) Unfortunately, I couldn't attend the meeting.
(C) We can discuss that issue later today.

什麼問題在會議中會被討論？

(A) 沒錯，大家都必須要出席會議。
(B) 遺憾的是，我無法出席會議。
(C) 我們今天稍後可以討論那個問題。

解析 疑問詞 what 放在名詞 issues 前，是表限定含意的疑問句。提問想得到具體訊息，但選項中都沒出現。用 Yes 來回答的選項（A）不能用來回答疑問詞疑問句。選項（B）雖然沒有具體訊息，但卻是最適合的回答，所以是答案。

單字 issue 問題 | discuss 討論

4. (C)

Script

Which hotel are you going to stay in?

(A) Yes, the hotel offers the best view.
(B) If I were you, I would listen to her advice.
(C) I haven't made up my mind yet.

你會住在哪一家飯店？

(A) 是啊，那家飯店有最棒的景觀。
(B) 如果我是你，我會聽從她的勸告。
(C) 我還沒決定。

解析 疑問詞 which 放在名詞 hotel 前，是表限定含意的疑問句。選項（C）表示還沒做出選擇，所以是答案。

單字 make up one's mind 做決定

題型 05 Why 疑問句

D 應用練習　　P. 91　　🎧 063

1. (C)

Script

Why do you want to return this item?

(A) No, I don't have the receipt with me.
(B) I'm going to return to my hometown.
(C) Because it is defective.

您為何想退回這項商品？

(A) 不，我身上沒有帶收據。
(B) 我要回到我的家鄉。
(C) 因為它有瑕疵。

解析 這是詢問原因的 why 問句，選項（C）直接表示原因，所以是答案。

單字 receipt 收據 | hometown 家鄉 | defective 有瑕疵的

題型
05
Why 疑問句

2. (B)

Script

Why did you lend the money to her?

(A) Yes, we can improve our lives.
(B) Because I felt sorry for her.
(C) When did you borrow money from her?

你為何要把錢借給她？

(A) 沒錯，我們可以改善我們的生活。
(B) 因為我為她感到難過。
(C) 你何時向她借錢？

解析 這是詢問原因的問句，選項（B）直接表示明確的原因，所以是答案。

單字 improve 改善 | borrow 借

3. (C)

Script

Why are you moving to the United Sates?

(A) No, we haven't been properly introduced.
(B) Nobody told me anything about the conference.
(C) To give my children better opportunities.

你為何要搬到美國？

(A) 我們並沒有被適當地介紹。
(B) 沒有人告訴我關於會議的任何事。
(C) 給我的孩子更好的機會。

解析 這是詢問原因的問句，選項（C）直接闡明目的，所以是答案。選項（A）用 Yes/No 來回答疑問詞疑問句，選項（B）是沒參加會議的原因，都不是答案。

單字 **properly** 適當地 ｜ **conference** 會議 ｜ **opportunity** 機會

4. (B)

Script

Why don't you learn how to drive?

(A) Yes, I drive to school every day.
(B) The idea of driving makes me nervous.
(C) No, I don't think you're driving too fast.

你為何不學開車？

(A) 是啊，我每天開車去學校。
(B) 想到開車就讓我感到緊張。
(C) 不會，我不認為你開太快。

解析 用 why 來表示建議，但仍然是疑問詞疑問句，所以選項（A）、（C）用 Yes/No 來回答都不對。建議對方學開車，選項（B）回答開車會令他緊張，所以是答案。

1. (C)　2. (B)　3. (C)　4. (B)

5. (C)　6. (B)　7. (C)　8. (B)

1. (C)

Script

Who made that decision?

(A) Yes, we respect your choice.
(B) We'll go to the movies tonight.
(C) Ms. Jones, I guess.

誰做了那項決定？

(A) 是啊，我們尊重你的選擇。
(B) 我們今晚會去看電影。
(C) 我想是瓊斯小姐。

解析 以疑問詞 who 起始的疑問句，所以說出具體訊息的選項（C）是答案。選項（B）和提問毫無關聯。

單字 **respect** 尊重 ｜ **choice** 選擇

2. (B)

Script

Where do you want me to put this contract?

(A) Review the document before you sign it.
(B) On the desk, please.
(C) I saw it last night.

你要我把這份合約放在哪裡？

(A) 在你簽名前審查這份文件。
(B) 請放在辦公桌上。
(C) 我昨晚有看到。

解析 這是 where 疑問句，目的要詢問地點。回答具體地點的選項（B）是答案。選項（A）和（C）只提到了合約，但沒有提到和地點有關的訊息，所以是答非所問。

單字 **contract** 合約 | **review** 審查 | **document** 文件

3. (C)

Script

When will your new product be launched?

(A) The concert will start soon.
(B) It will appeal to young consumers.
(C) Hopefully in June.

你的新產品何時會推出？

(A) 音樂會很快就會開始。
(B) 那會吸引年輕顧客。
(C) 希望會在六月。

解析 用疑問詞疑問句來詢問具體的時間訊息，所以提供時間點的選項（C）是答案。選項（A）雖然提供了時間訊息，但卻是講其他活動的時間，選項（B）沒有所需的訊息，所以都是錯誤答案。

單字 **launch** 推出

4. (B)

Script

How can we reduce the noise?

(A) I heard a strange noise.
(B) I think we need professional help.
(C) It was the computer that was making a strange noise.

我們可以怎樣減少噪音？

(A) 我聽到一種奇怪的聲音。
(B) 我認為我們需要專業協助。
(C) 那是電腦發出的奇怪聲音。

解析 這是詢問具體方式的疑問詞疑問句，直接表示做法的選項（B）是答案。

單字 **reduce** 減少 | **strange** 奇怪的 | **professional** 專業的 |

5. (C)

Script

How long have you known Ms. Jackson?

(A) Do you want me to contact her right away?
(B) She lives in a small apartment.
(C) For nearly twenty years.

你認識傑克森小姐有多久了？

(A) 你要我立刻和她聯絡嗎？
(B) 她住在一間小公寓。
(C) 將近 20 年。

解析 How 搭配形容詞，是詢問時間長度的疑問句，因此回答出具體時間長度的選項（C）是答案。

單字 **contact** 聯絡 | **apartment** 公寓

6. (B)

Script

What happened to Eric?

(A) No, he didn't call me yesterday.
(B) He injured himself while helping a stranger.
(C) He has a creative mind.

艾瑞克發生了什麼事？

(A) 不，他昨天沒有打電話給我。
(B) 他在協助一位陌生人時傷到了自己。
(C) 他的想法很有創意。

解析 這是用疑問詞 what 詢問具體訊息的疑問詞疑問句。詳細告知相關訊息的選項（B）是答案。選項（A）不能回答疑問詞疑問句。選項（C）不是回答過去發生的事。

單字 **injure** 使受傷

7. (C)

Which country is better for immigrant workers, Canada or the United States?

(A) Canada exports a lot of things to America.
(B) No, we don't have any branches in the United States.
(C) Definitely Canada.

哪一個國家給移工較佳的待遇，加拿大或美國？

(A) 加拿大出口了很多貨品到美國。
(B) 不，我們在美國沒有任何分公司。
(C) 絕對是加拿大。

解析 用疑問詞 which 當限定詞的選擇疑問句。對此做出明確選擇的選項（C）是答案。

單字 immigrant 移民的 ｜ export 出口 ｜ branch 分公司

8. (B)

Why are you learning English?

(A) Yes, I've been learning it since childhood.
(B) To better understand people from different countries.
(C) Chinese is an interesting language to learn.

你為何在學英語？

(A) 是啊，我從小時候就一直學英語。
(B) 對不同國家的人有更深的了解。
(C) 中文是可以學習的有趣語言。

解析 這是用詢問原因的疑問詞 why 開頭的疑問詞疑問句。表示具體原因的選項（B）是答案。詢問學英文的原因，選項（C）卻提到中文，是錯誤答案。

單字 childhood 小時候

---

1. (C)	2. (A)	3. (C)	4. (A)
5. (C)	6. (B)	7. (C)	8. (B)
9. (C)	10. (B)	11. (C)	12. (B)
13. (C)	14. (B)	15. (C)	16. (A)

1. (C)

Does she write articles for *The New York Times*?

(A) When are you going to meet her?
(B) I don't understand what she's trying to say.
(C) She has been a reporter for that newspaper since 2002.

她有為《紐約時報》撰寫文章嗎？

(A) 你何時會和她見面？
(B) 我不了解她想說什麼。
(C) 她從 2002 年就一直擔任該報記者。

解析 是 Do/Does 疑問句，雖然選項沒有直接回答 Yes/No，但選項（C）提到她是該報社的記者，做了肯定的回應，所以是答案。

單字 article 文章

2. (A)

Was this software developed by a Korean company?

(A) The name of the company is Samsung.
(B) I don't want the program.
(C) Have you ever been to South Korea?

這個軟體是由韓國公司研發的嗎？

(A) 公司的名稱叫三星。
(B) 我不要那個程式。
(C) 你去過南韓嗎？

解析 雖然是 be 動詞疑問句，但選項中都沒有 Yes/No 的回答。詢問是不是韓國公司研發軟體，選項（A）比回答是或否提出更詳細的資訊，所以是答案。

單字 develop 研發

3. (C)

Script

Have you heard from Ms. Summers recently?

(A) Actually, I met him last night.
(B) I'm pleased to see you again.
(C) She called me yesterday.

你知道桑瑪斯女士近來是否安好嗎？

(A) 事實上，我昨晚有和他見面。
(B) 我很高興和你再度見面。
(C) 她昨天打電話給我。

解析 雖然是助動詞 have 疑問句，但選項中都沒有 Yes/No 的回答。詢問她近況如何，選項（C）告知她最近有聯絡，所以是答案。

4. (A)

Script

Should we invite Mr. Jackson to speak at the conference?

(A) He is an inspirational speaker, after all.
(B) Do you know why the event has been canceled?
(C) Are you flying to Miami?

我們該邀請傑克森先生來會議演說嗎？

(A) 畢竟他是位激勵演說家。
(B) 你知道為何活動被取消了嗎？
(C) 你要飛到邁阿密嗎？

解析 助動詞 should 疑問句，要用 Yes/No 回答，但選項中都沒有用 Yes/No 起始的回答句。選項（A）說明邀請他的理由，可以解讀為肯定回答，所以是答案。

單字 inspirational 激勵人心的｜
after all 畢竟｜cancel 取消

5. (C)

Script

Who sent these flowers to me?

(A) Yes, they are beautiful.
(B) You'll be visiting the factory next month.
(C) Mr. Cooper, I guess.

這些花是誰送給我的？

(A) 是啊，這些花很漂亮。
(B) 你將在下個月拜訪那間工廠。
(C) 我想是庫柏先生。

解析 這是疑問詞 who 疑問句。對此直接表示具體訊息的選項（C）是答案。

單字 factory 工廠

6. (B)

Script

When can we discuss your proposal?

(A) No, he hasn't proposed to me yet.
(B) Any time would work for me.
(C) Not that I know of.

我們何時可以討論你的提案？

(A) 不，他還沒跟我求婚。
(B) 任何時間我都可以。
(C) 我沒聽說過那件事。

解析 這是以疑問詞 when 開頭且用來詢問「何時」的疑問句。選項（B）直接回答「任何時間都可以」，是最合適的回答。

單字 proposal 提案

7. (C)

Script

How can we get there faster?

(A) Yes, that's a brilliant idea.

(B) No, I've never been there before.

(C) Maybe we can fly there.

我們要如何更快抵達那裡？

(A) 是啊，那的確是個很棒的點子。

(B) 沒有，我以前從未去過那裡。

(C) 或許我們可以坐飛機去那裡。

解析 用疑問詞 how 來詢問具體方式，選項（C）提出具體方法，所以是答案。

單字 brilliant 很棒的

8. (B)

Script

What is the best way to learn a foreign language?

(A) Yes, I've been learning English since childhood.

(B) You should learn how to think in that language.

(C) No, Chinese won't be an international language.

學習外語最好的方式是什麼？

(A) 是的，我從小就在學英語。

(B) 你應該學習如何用該外語思考。

(C) 不，中文不會成為國際語言。

解析 這是詢問具體資訊的疑問詞疑問句。選項（A）和（C）用 Yes/No 回答，不適合用來回答疑問詞疑問句。選項（B）提出了具體的方式，所以是答案。

9. (C)

Script

Why do you want to work with us?

(A) No, I haven't heard anything from them.

(B) I've always wanted to start my own business.

(C) To help take your company to the next level.

你為何想和我們合作？

(A) 不，我還沒聽到他們的任何消息。

(B) 我一直想開創自己的事業。

(C) 幫助你的公司達到更高的境界。

解析 用疑問詞 why 來詢問目的，選項（C）提出具體的目的，所以是答案。

單字 level 程度

10. (B)

Script

Can I pay by credit card or in cash?

(A) You deserve credit for your hard work.

(B) I'm afraid we accept only cash.

(C) You might want to check out the new restaurant.

我可以用信用卡或現金支付嗎？

(A) 你的辛勤努力值得嘉獎。

(B) 我們恐怕只收現金。

(C) 你可能想看看新的餐廳。

解析 這是包含 or 的選擇疑問句，選項（B）從選擇項目中選一個回應所以是答案。選項（A）的 credit 和信用卡無關，選項（C）的 check 不是支票是查看的意思。

單字 deserve 值得 ｜ credit 嘉獎

11. (C)

Script

Shall we watch a movie or read a novel together?

(A) Yes, we enjoyed the movie.
(B) Who's your favorite actor?
(C) Either would be fine with me.

我們要一起看電影或讀小說？

(A) 沒錯，我們很享受那部電影。
(B) 誰是你最喜歡的演員？
(C) 兩種我都可以。

解析 這是包含 or 的選擇疑問句，三個選項都沒有做出選擇。不過選項（C）放棄選擇，表示都接受，也可以是答案。

單字 either 任何一種

12. (B)

Script

Isn't that Julie's suitcase?

(A) We are close friends.
(B) No, it isn't.
(C) Yes, it belongs to me.

那不是茉麗的手提箱嗎？

(A) 我們是要好的朋友。
(B) 不，那不是。
(C) 沒錯，那是我的。

解析 這是 be 動詞疑問句，同時也是否定疑問句。遇到否定疑問句，回答時要由回答句的內容來決定用 Yes 還是用 No。選項（B）回答說那不是茉麗的（it isn't），所以前面要加 No，選項（B）是答案。

單字 suitcase 手提箱

13. (C)

Script

Haven't you received the parcel?

(A) I'm having dinner with the CEO this evening.
(B) My flight had already left when I arrived at the airport.
(C) Not yet.

你還沒收到包裹嗎？

(A) 我在今晚要和執行長吃晚餐。
(B) 我抵達機場時我的航班已飛走。
(C) 還沒有。

解析 這是用 have 做成的否定疑問句，但是選項中都沒有用 Yes/No 回答。不過即使沒有 No，以 Not 起始的選項（C），直接回答「還沒有」也可以是答案。

單字 flight 航班

14. (B)

Script

Do you know when the next available flight to Toronto will be?

(A) Toronto is a beautiful city.
(B) In about two hours.
(C) I was raised in that city.

你知道下一班到多倫多的航班何時可以出發嗎？

(A) 多倫多是個美麗的城市。
(B) 大約兩小時內。
(C) 我在那個城市長大。

解析 雖然是以 Do 起始，但句中含有疑問詞，是間接疑問句，當然要用 Yes/No 回答。但為了讓對話自然簡潔，直接回答出疑問句所問的資訊也可以，所以回答具體時間的選項（B）是答案。

單字 available 可用的 | raise 養育

15. (C)

I'm here to meet with Ms. Brown.
(A) I placed an order two weeks ago.
(B) Do you know why this computer isn't working properly?
(C) I'm sorry, she's not in right now.

我來和布朗女士會面。

(A) 我在兩週前下了訂單。
(B) 你知道為何這台電腦不能正常運作嗎？
(C) 我很抱歉，她現在不在。

解析 要在選項中找出能回應敘述句的話語。
對方說出到這裡的目的，選項（C）告
知對方目的不能達成，所以選項（C）
是答案。

單字 **place an order** 下訂單 |
properly 正常地

16. (A)

You had a meeting with the client last week, didn't you?
(A) Yes, I did. It was a productive meeting.
(B) Everyone is supposed to attend the staff meeting.
(C) Your proposal sounds promising.

你在上週和那位客戶開會，不是嗎？

(A) 沒錯。那次會議很有成效。
(B) 所有人都應該出席員工會議。
(C) 你的提案聽起來很有希望。

解析 用附加疑問句來詢問對方，對方要用
Yes／No 回答，選項（A）肯定回答
Yes，接著又再附加說明，所以答案是
選項（A）。

單字 **client** 客戶 | **productive** 有成效的 |
be supposed to 應該 | **staff** 員工 |
promising 很有希望的

Part 3
簡短對話

1 各類型試題說明

題型 **01** 掌握主題

D 應用練習　　P. 103　　🎧070

1. (B)

W: Good afternoon. Thank you for calling Orange Hill Restaurant.
M: Hello. I'd like to book a table for two people for six tonight.
W: OK, sir. Which would you prefer, smoking or non-smoking?
M: None-smoking, please.

Q. What is the main topic of the conversation?
(A) The effects of smoking on public health
(B) Reserving a table at a restaurant

女：午安。感謝您致電橙丘餐廳。
男：你好。我想訂位，晚上六點兩位。
女：好的，先生。您想要哪種，吸菸區或非
吸菸區？
男：請給我非吸菸區。

這段對話的主題是什麼？
(A) 抽菸對公眾健康的影響。
(B) 預訂餐廳的席位。

解析 這段對話是打電話到餐廳以預約兩人用
餐，而不是在談吸菸不吸菸的問題，不
要搞混。所以答案是選項（B）。

單字 book 預訂 ┃ prefer 偏好 ┃
public health 公眾健康 ┃
reserve 預訂

2. (A)

> Script
>
> **W:** Ted, how did you do in the singing contest? Did you win a prize?
> **M:** I couldn't even make it to the stage.
> **W:** What happened? You were so confident.
> **M:** I completely forgot it was my turn. I was too focused on practicing backstage.
>
> **Q.** What are the speakers mainly talking about?
> (A) Why the man couldn't sing in the contest
> (B) How confidence leads to success

女：泰德，你在歌唱比賽表現得如何？你有
贏得獎項嗎？
男：我根本連上台比賽都沒辦法。
女：發生了什麼事？你原本很有信心。
男：我完全忘記輪到我了，我在後台練習得
太專心了。

對話者主要在談論什麼？
(A) 為何這名男子無法在比賽中唱歌。
(B) 自信才會帶來成功。

解析 對話中的男子因專注練習而錯過了自己
上台的機會，因此比賽是否成功不是對
話的重點，所以選項（A）是答案。

單字 contest 比賽 ┃ confident 有信心的 ┃
completely 完全 ┃ turn 輪到的機會 ┃
focus on 專心於 ┃ practice 練習 ┃
backstage 後台 ┃ lead to 導致 ┃
success 成功

題型 02 掌握目的

D 應用練習   P. 109   075

1. (B)

> Script
>
> **W:** Hi, I'd like to cash this check, please.
> **M:** Can I see some ID?
> **W:** Here is my driver's license.
> **M:** OK. I'll make a copy of it. Would you like to look at our savings program in the meantime?
>
> **Q.** Why is the woman talking to the man?
> (A) To find out more information about the man's bank
> (B) To ask the man to cash her check

女：嗨，請幫我兌換這張支票。
男：可以讓我看您的證件嗎？
女：這是我的駕照。
男：好，我要拿去影印。在此期間您想參閱
我們的存款方案嗎？

女子為何與男子對話？
(A) 需要男子工作銀行更多的資訊。
(B) 要求男子幫她兌現支票。

解析 女子和男子打完招呼後，提到要將支票
兌換成現金。之後，女子提到要影印證
件以便辦理手續，接著男子交給女子一
本手冊，讓她在他辦理手續時閱覽，但
這些都不重要。重要的是女子一開始提
出的要求，所以答案是選項（B）。

單字 cash 兌現 ┃ check 支票 ┃ ID 證件 ┃
license 駕照 ┃ copy 影印副本 ┃
savings 存款 ┃ meantime 同時 ┃
information 資訊

2. (B)

Script

M: Are you doing your homework now?

W: No. I'm just reading some books. What's up?

M: I'm wondering if you can go to a graduation party with me this Saturday.

W: I'd love to, but my family is moving into a new place that day.

Q. Why is the man talking to the woman?

(A) To promise to help her move into a new place

(B) To ask her to go with him to a party

男：你正在寫作業嗎？

女：沒有。我只是在讀幾本書。有什麼事？

男：我想問你本週六是否可以和我去畢業派對。

女：我很樂意去，但我家人那天要搬家到新地點。

男子為何要和女子對話？

(A) 答應幫她搬新家。

(B) 邀她跟他一起去派對。

解析 男子先跟女子說話，目的是要邀請女子去參加畢業派對。搬家是女子不能去參加派對的原因，而且男子也沒答應要幫女子搬家，所以答案是選項（B）。

單字 wonder 想知道 | graduation 畢業 | promise 答應

題型 **03** 掌握細節資訊（1）

Ⓓ 應用練習　　　P. 115　　‖‖　080

1. (B)

Script

W: I'd like to exchange my California license for an international driver's license.

M: You can apply for that only if your license is not going to expire in the next three months.

W: That's not a problem. Is there any way that I can apply online?

M: Of course. Please go to our website and download an application form.

Q. Which is true about the woman?

(A) She has been living in Florida for the past three years.

(B) Her driver's license will not expire in the next three months.

女：我想把我的加州駕照換成國際駕照。

男：您可以申請，但前提是您的駕照不會在三個月內到期。

女：那沒有問題。有什麼方式可以在線上申請嗎？

男：當然有。請到我們的網站並下載申請表。

關於女子何者為真？

(A) 她過去三年都住在佛羅里達州。

(B) 她的駕照在三個月內不會過期。

解析 女子要換國際駕照。男子說到期前三個月內就不能申請，女子表示那不是問題，並透露出她想利用網路申請，所以可以知道女子的駕駛執照距到期期限最少有三個月，所以答案是選項（B）。

單字 license 駕照 | international 國際 | apply for 申請 | expire 失效 | download 下載 | application form 申請表

2. (B)

Script

M: I eat what I want to eat. In fact, I often eat fast food.

W: Well, you should be careful of what you eat.

M: But I exercise a lot. I think that's enough.

W: Your daily diet is really important. You are what you eat.

Q. Which is true about the man?

(A) He has been working out for the past six years.

(B) He does not feel that he should restrict his diet.

男：我吃我想吃的東西。事實上，我常吃速食。

女：嗯，你應該要小心飲食。

男：不過我經常運動。我認為那就夠了。

女：你的日常飲食真的很重要。你的飲食會從身心表現出來。

關於男子何者為真？

(A) 他過去六年都有一直在健身。

(B) 他不認為他需要控制飲食。

解析 男子說他做很多運動，所以對飲食不注重也沒關係。不過男子並沒有提到他運動了多久，所以選項（A）是錯的。女子說要注意飲食，但男子並不同意，所以可以知道男子不會控制飲食，答案是選項（B）。

單字 in fact 事實上 | be careful of 小心 | daily 每日的 | diet 飲食 | work out 健身 | restrict 控制

題型 04 掌握細節資訊（2）

D 應用練習　　P. 121　　085

1. (B)

Script

W: None of my friends seems to remember my birthday.

M: You may feel excluded from your friends.

W: I'm so disappointed. I don't think they're really my friends.

M: Don't think like that. Maybe they're very busy.

Q. Which is true about the woman?

(A) She doesn't want her friends to remember her birthday.

(B) She may feel lonely.

女：我的朋友似乎沒人記得我的生日。

男：你可能覺得被你的朋友排擠。

女：我很失望，我不認為他們是我真正的朋友。

男：別那樣想。或許他們很忙。

關於女子何者為真？

(A) 她不想讓她的朋友記得她的生日。

(B) 她可能覺得寂寞。

解析 從對話中可以知道女子的朋友中沒人記得她的生日，她非常失望，她還說他們不是她的朋友，她感受到沒有朋友的孤單，所以答案是選項（B）。因為對話顯露出女子希望朋友記得她的生日，所以選項（A）是不對的。

單字 exclude 排擠 | disappointed 失望的 | lonely 寂寞的

2. (A)

Script

W: I'm glad you could make it.
M: What are friends for? Wow, this place is awesome!
W: Thank you. I really like this house.
M: Who was your real estate agent? Maybe I need her help.

Q. Which is true about the man?

(A) He may be looking for a new house.
(B) He can't afford to buy a new house.

女：我很高興你能趕來。

男：誰叫我們是朋友呢？這地方太棒了！

女：謝謝你。我真的很喜歡這間房子。

男：誰是你的房仲？我可能需要她的協助。

關於男子何者為真？

(A) 他在找新房子。
(B) 他買不起新房子。

解析 男子拜訪女子新家，並讚美房子很漂亮，接著詢問房仲是誰，說也許會請她幫忙。從這裡可以推測男子可能也在找房子，所以答案是選項（A）。

單字 glad 高興 | make it 趕來 | awesome 很棒的 | real estate agent 房仲 | afford 負擔

題型 **05** 掌握意圖

D 應用練習　　P. 127 　　090

1. (B)

Script

W: How may I help you, sir?
M: I bought this coat last week and found a hole in it.

W: I'm very sorry. If you have the receipt, you can exchange it for a new one.
M: I threw it away. Is there any way you can fix it?

Q. What does the man mean when he says, "Is there any way you can fix it"?

(A) He is usually good at fixing things.
(B) He does not want to exchange his coat for a new one.

女：先生，我可以為您效勞嗎？

男：我上週買了這件外套，發現裡面有一個洞。

女：我很抱歉。如果您有收據，您可以換一件新的。

男：我把收據丟了。你有其他辦法可以解決嗎？

男子說：「你有其他辦法可以解決嗎？」是什麼意思？

(A) 他通常善於修理東西。
(B) 他不想換一件新外套。

解析 男子發現新買的外套有一個洞，這是他回到購買商店和店員間的對話。女子建議男子換一件新的，並出示之前的收據。但男子將收據弄丟了，並問說有沒有別的修補破洞的辦法。所以可以知道男子不想換一件新的，答案是選項（B）。

單字 hole 洞 | receipt 收據 | exchange 更換 | throw away 丟棄 | fix 解決

2. (B)

Script

M: Is there any problem?
W: My computer isn't working again. Can you take a look at it?
M: I'll drop by at around three. Would that work for you?
W: Yes. Thanks.

Q. What does the man mean when he says, "Would that work for you"?

(A) He wants to check if the computer is working now.

(B) He wants to check if 3:00 would be fine with the woman.

男：有任何問題嗎？

女：我的電腦又當機了。你可以幫我看看嗎？

男：我會在三點左右過去。你覺得時間可能嗎？

女：好的，謝了。

男子說：「你覺得時間可以嗎？」是什麼意思？

(A) 他想要檢查電腦目前是否可以正常運作。

(B) 他想要確定女子是否覺得三點合適。

解析 這段對話中，work 出現兩次，但意思都不同。前面是電腦「運作」的意思，後面是「符合、可行」的意思。男子詢問女子「三點來修理電腦，可以嗎」，要確認女子的時間，所以答案是選項（B）。

單字 take a look at 看看｜
drop by 順道拜訪

Quick Test　　P. 128　　091

1. (B) 2. (B) 3. (A)

4. (B) 5. (A) 6. (A)

【 Questions 1–3 】

Script

W: Thank you for contacting Irvine California Restaurant. How may I help you?

M: Hello. I'd like to book a table for three for seven.

W: All right. Can you give me your name and phone number?

M: My name is David Wood. My phone number is 714-233-0717.

W: OK. Thank you very much.

女：歡迎您致電艾文加州餐廳，有什麼可以為您效勞的嗎？

男：您好。我想訂位，七點三位。

女：沒問題。可以給我您的名字和電話號碼嗎？

男：我的名字是大衛・伍德。我的電話號碼是 714-233-0717。

女：好的。非常感謝您。

單字 contact 聯絡｜book 訂位

1. (B)

Script

What is the purpose of the man's phone call?

(A) To find out if he can fly to California at seven

(B) To book a table at a restaurant

男子打電話來的目的是什麼？

(A) 查詢他是否可以七點飛往加州。

(B) 在一家餐廳訂位。

解析 男子打電話來跟餐廳人員，也就是女子，預約三人的席位。所以男子打電話的目的就是訂位，選項（B）是答案。

單字 purpose 目的

2. (B)

Script

Which is true about the man?

(A) He has never been to California.

(B) He is likely to visit the facility at seven.

關於男子何者為真？

(A) 他從未去過加州。

(B) 他有可能在七點到那家餐廳。

解析 在跟女子的對話中，男子並沒有提到是否去過加州。因為預約好餐廳後，男子可能會和朋友一起來這家餐廳用餐，所以答案是選項（B）。

單字 be likely to 有可能 | facility 設施

3. (A)

Script

Will the man visit the facility by himself?

(A) He will be accompanied by two people.

(B) He does not know whether other people will join him.

男子會獨自到那家餐廳嗎？

(A) 他將會有兩個人陪同。

(B) 他不知道其他人是否會加入。

解析 因為預約三個人的席位，所以男子來餐廳時，還有另外兩人同行，所以答案是選項（A）。因為如果男子不確定其他人來不來，怎麼會預約三人的座位呢？

單字 by oneself 某人獨自 | accompany 陪同 | whether 是否

【 Questions 4–6 】

Script

M: Today I learned about global warming.

W: Yes, it is quite a serious issue.

M: I think we need to recycle a lot more.

W: I couldn't agree more. We should also plant more trees.

M: Exactly! We can protect the environment in a lot of ways.

男：今天我學到有關全球暖化的事。

女：是啊，那是很嚴肅的議題。

男：我認為我們需要多做回收。

女：我非常同意。我們也應該種植更多樹木。

男：沒錯！我們有許多方式可以保護環境。

單字 global warming 全球暖化 | serious 嚴肅的 | issue 議題 | recycle 回收 | plant 種植 | environment 環境

4. (B)

Script

What is the main topic of the conversation?

(A) That the danger of global warming has been exaggerated

(B) The many different ways to preserve the environment

這段對話的主題是什麼？

(A) 全球暖化危機被誇大。

(B) 許多不同保護環境的方法。

解析 男女對話完全沒有提到地球暖化危機，但提到為了保護環境，要資源回收，並要多種樹，所以答案是選項（B）。

單字 danger 危機 | exaggerate 誇大 | preserve 保護

5. (A)

Script

What does the woman mean when she says, "I couldn't agree more"?

(A) She believes that recycling is a good idea.

(B) She does not believe that recycling is good for the environment.

女子說：「我非常同意。」是什麼意思？

(A) 她相信回收是很好的點子。

(B) 她不相信回收對環境有好處。

解析 男子提到要再多做回收，之後女子表示完全同意，也就是她覺得回收再利用是個好點子，所以答案是選項（A）。

6. (A)

Script

Which is true about the man?

(A) He is likely to make efforts to protect the environment.

(B) He wants to be an internationally recognized scientist.

關於男子何者為真？

(A) 他可能會努力保護環境。

(B) 他想成為國際認可的科學家。

解析 男子提出要做回收，所以他應該會去實踐，選項（A）是答案。男子完全沒有提到要成為科學家。

單字 make efforts 努力 | protect 保護 | recognized 受認可的

Practice Test　　P. 130　　🎧 092

1. (C) 2. (D) 3. (C) 4. (D) 5. (D)

6. (C) 7. (B) 8. (C) 9. (D)

【 Questions 1–3 】

Script

M: I'm sorry I missed your concert.

W: You should have come. I played your favorite song.

M: Unfortunately, my sister had an accident that day.

W: Really? Is she OK?

M: Fortunately, yes, but I had to look after her at the hospital.

W: I hope she gets better soon.

男：很抱歉我錯過了你的音樂會。

女：你應該來的。我演奏了你最喜歡的歌曲。

男：遺憾的是，我的妹妹在那天出了意外。

女：真的嗎？她還好嗎？

男：幸運的是，她還好，但我要在醫院照顧她。

女：希望她能早日康復。

單字 miss 錯過 | favorite 最喜歡的 | accident 意外 | look after 照顧

1. (C)

Script

What are the speakers mainly discussing?

(A) Why the woman missed the man's concert

(B) When they can meet to discuss the upcoming concert

(C) The man's sister's hospitalization

(D) The man's disappointing performance

對話者主要在談論什麼？

(A) 為何女子錯過了男子的音樂會。

(B) 他們在何時可以見面討論即將舉行的音樂會。

(C) 男子的妹妹住院治療。

(D) 男子令人失望的表演。

解析 是男子錯過女子的表演，選項（A）和對話內容完全相反。選項（C）提到男子錯過表演的原因和之後的狀況，所以選項（C）是這段對話主要的內容。

單字 upcoming 即將舉行的 | hospitalization 住院 | disappointing 令人失望的 | performance 表演

2. (D)

Script

Why couldn't the man attend the woman's event?

(A) He went to a foreign country that day.

(B) He didn't believe that her music was worth listening to.

(C) He was having a meeting with an important client.

(D) One of his family members was involved in an accident.

男子為何不能參加女子的活動？

(A) 他在那天出國了。

(B) 他不認為她的音樂值得聆聽。

(C) 他和一位重要的客戶開會。

(D) 他的一位親人出了意外。

解析 男子沒有去看女子的表演是因為妹妹發生意外，妹妹是家族成員，所以選項（D）是答案。

單字 attend 參加 | foreign 國外 | worth 值得 | client 客戶 | be involved in 涉及

3. (C)

Script

What does the woman mean when she says, "You should have come"?

(A) She believes that the man was too careless.

(B) She wanted to go to a foreign country with the man.

(C) She's sorry that the man didn't attend her event.

(D) She doesn't like the man's sister.

女子說「你應該來的」是什麼意思？

(A) 她認為男子太不小心了。

(B) 她想和男子到國外。

(C) 她很遺憾男子沒有參加她的活動。

(D) 她不喜歡男子的妹妹。

解析 片語「should have ＋ p.p.」的意思是「應該做什麼但沒做」，在表示遺憾時可以使用。女子說這句話是對男子沒來看她的表演表示遺憾，所以答案是選項（C）。

單字 careless 不小心的

【 Questions 4–6 】

Script

W: Excuse me. My name is Erica Kim. I left my bag on the train.

M: Let me check. What does it look like?

W: It is brown and small.

M: There's nothing like that here right now.

W: Can you call me if you find it? My number is 555-3783.

M: Of course. That's my job.

女：不好意思。我叫艾瑞卡・金姆。我的包包掉在火車上了。

男：讓我查查。包包是什麼樣子？

女：棕色的小型包。

男：目前沒有那樣的失物。

女：如果你找到可以打電話給我嗎？我的電話號碼是 555-3783。

男：沒問題。那是我的職責

單字 leave 掉 | check 查詢

4. (D)

Script

Why is the woman talking to the man?

(A) She believes that the man is hiding something.

(B) She wants to date the man.

(C) She believes that the man is very kind.

(D) She wants to find her missing bag.

女子為何與男子對話？

(A) 她認為男子藏了某樣東西。

(B) 她想和男子約會。

(C) 她認為男子很和善。

(D) 她想找到她遺失的包包。

解析 聽男女的對話，可以推知女子來到失物招領處，選項（D）是答案。

單字 hide 藏 | date 和……約會

5. (D)

Script

Look at the graphic. Which piece of information about the bag does the man not have?

(A) The color of the bag
(B) The size of the bag
(C) The owner's phone number
(D) The owner's address

請看圖表。男子沒有包包的哪一項資訊？

(A) 包包的顏色。
(B) 包包的尺寸。
(C) 失主的電話號碼。
(D) 失主的地址。

解析 女子提供了包包的顏色、大小，還有自己的電話號碼，但沒有說地址，所以答案是選項（D）。

單字 **address** 地址

6. (C)

Script

What does the man mean when he says, "Of course"?

(A) He is not sure if he can find her bag.
(B) He does not care about the woman.
(C) It is his duty to call the woman if he finds her bag.
(D) He thinks that the woman is too difficult to please.

男子說「沒問題」是什麼意思？

(A) 他不確定是否可以找到她的包包。
(B) 他不在乎女子。
(C) 他的責任是在找到包包時打電話給女子。
(D) 他認為女子難以取悅。

解析 女子說找到包包後請打電話通知她，男子回答說當然，並補充說這是他的工作，所以找尋失物以及相關事宜是男子的職責，答案是選項（C）。

單字 **care about** 在乎 | **duty** 職責

【 Questions 7–9 】

Script

M: Where are you going for winter vacation?
W: Somewhere warm. It's too cold here in winter.
M: Check out this weather guide for each country. It might be helpful.
W: Australia seems to be the best choice for me. How about you?
M: I like skiing, so I am deciding between Canada and Switzerland.

男：你寒假要去哪裡？

女：去溫暖的地方。這裡的冬季太冷了。

男：在這查查每個國家的氣象指南，可能會有幫助。

女：對我來說澳洲似乎是最佳選項。那麼你呢？

男：我喜歡滑雪，所以我會選加拿大或瑞士。

單字 **vacation** 假期 | **temperature** 氣溫

7. (B)

Script

What are the speakers mainly talking about?

(A) Whether Australia is better than Canada
(B) Where they will go for winter vacation
(C) When they will travel around the world
(D) The reason why they hate cold weather

對話者主要在談論什麼？

(A 澳洲是否比加拿大更好。
(B) 他們寒假要去哪裡。
(C) 他們何時要環遊世界。
(D) 他們痛恨寒冷天氣的理由。

解析 男女的對話，主要談的是寒假要去哪國玩，所以答案是選項（B）。

單字 travel 旅遊 ｜ winter 冬天

8. (C)

Script

Which is true about the woman?

(A) She has been living in Switzerland for three years.
(B) She has been to Australia.
(C) She is likely to go to Australia this winter.
(D) She enjoys skiing.

關於女子何者為真？

(A) 她曾在瑞士住了三年。
(B) 她曾去過澳洲。
(C) 她在今年冬季有可能去澳洲
(D) 她很喜歡滑雪。

解析 女子提到要去溫暖的地方，好像無法忍受太冷的天氣。男子建議看一下各國溫度資訊，之後女子說澳洲應該是最好的選擇，所以她去澳洲的可能性最大。因此答案是選項（C）。

單字 be likely to 有可能

9. (D)

Script

Which is true about the man?

(A) He has visited Canada many times.
(B) Switzerland is his favorite country.
(C) He prefers hot weather to cold weather.
(D) He is likely to spend time in a foreign country this winter.

關於男子何者為真？

(A) 他去過加拿大很多次。
(B) 瑞士是他最喜歡的國家。
(C) 他喜歡炎熱天氣甚於寒冷天氣。
(D) 他今年冬季有可能在國外待一些時間。

解析 男子和女子都計劃在寒假出國玩。男子說他要去滑雪，但煩惱不知道該選加拿大或瑞士。兩個地方都不是國內是國外，暗示應該會出國。所以答案是選項（D）。

單字 prefer 較喜歡 ｜ foreign 國外

Part 4

獨白

❶ 各類型試題說明

題型 **01** 掌握主題

Ⓓ 應用練習　　P. 139　🎧 097

1. (B)

Script

Hawaii is made up of more than 100 tropical islands, but people only live on 7 of them. Hawaii's population comprises several different ethnic groups. Only 1 percent of the total population is Hawaiian-American. About 40% are Japanese or Filipino, and about 30% are from mainland America. The rest of the people come from many different ethnic backgrounds.

Q. What is the main topic of the talk?

(A) Why Hawaii is popular among tourists

(B) The ethnic makeup of Hawaii

夏威夷由 100 多個熱帶島嶼組成，然而有人居住的只有七座島。夏威夷的人口包括數種不同的族裔。全部人口中只有百分之一是夏威夷裔美國人。大約四成是日本人和菲律賓人，而約有三成來自美國本土。其餘人口來自許多不同的種族背景。

這段獨白的主題是什麼？

(A) 為何夏威夷受到遊客的歡迎。

(B) 夏威夷的種族構成。

解析 獨白一開始提到夏威夷的地理狀況，接著說明夏威夷的人口結構，以及各族裔的人口比重，所以答案是選項（B）。

單字 **be made up of** 由……組成｜**tropical** 熱帶｜**population** 人口｜**comprise** 包括｜**ethnic** 族裔的｜**mainland** 本土大陸｜**rest** 剩下的

2. (B)

Script

It has been reported to us that people in our office have received numerous phishing emails over the past week. Somehow hackers have infiltrated our office network and have sent out fake emails from banks and even some departments of the government. When you open an email that leads you to a bank or government website, make sure that the site can be found in a regular search engine first.

Q. What is the main topic of the talk?

(A) How to report phishing emails to managers

(B) How to deal with phishing emails

我們已經收到一些報告，關於本辦公室有些同事在過去一週收到許多網路釣魚的電子郵件。駭客以某種方法駭入到我們的辦公室網絡，並寄給我們來自銀行甚至政府部門的偽造電子郵件。當你打開將你引導到銀行或政府網站的電子郵件，首先你要確認這個網站可以用一般搜尋引擎找到。

這段談話的主題是什麼？

(A) 如何向經理報告網路釣魚電子郵件。
(B) 如何處理網路釣魚電子郵件。

解析 獨白提到收到很多網路詐騙郵件，但沒提到要向經理報告。只提到收到包含特定網址的郵件時，要確認一下該網站能否用一般的搜尋引擎找到，所以是在說明應對的方法，答案是選項（B）。

單字 **numerous** 許多 | **phishing** 網路釣魚 | **somehow** 某種方法 | **infiltrate** 駭入 | **fake** 偽造的 | **deal with** 處理

題型 **02** 掌握目的

 應用練習　　P. 145　　🎧 102

1. (B)

Script

On my first day at work, I felt extremely nervous. I was a very shy person, and I was overwhelmed by the number of people I would work with. I was not sure if I would survive that day. My boss was Buffy Smith, and she instantly knew why I was so nervous. She approached me with a big smile and invited me to her office. In her office, she told me that she was a shy person, too. Her confession gave strength to me, and I really want to show my appreciation of her kindness.

Q. What is the purpose of the speech?

(A) To claim that shy people can succeed
(B) To thank Ms. Smith for encouraging the speaker

第一天工作時，我覺得非常緊張。我這個人很害羞，而且我要共事的人很多讓我感到震撼。我不確定是否可以撐過那一天。我的老闆是巴菲・史密斯，她立刻就知道我如此緊張的原因。她臉上掛著大大的笑容向我走來，並邀請我到她的辦公室。在她的辦公室裡，她告訴我她也是很害羞的人。她的坦誠帶給我力量，而我真的想對她的善意表達感謝。

這段獨白的目的是什麼？

(A) 宣稱害羞的人可以成功。
(B) 感謝史密斯小姐鼓勵發話者。

解析 發話者回想身為職場新鮮人時的經驗。第一天上班，在極度緊張的狀態下，感受到上司溫暖的鼓勵，並說很想向她表示感謝。所以答案是選項（B）。

單字 **extremely** 非常 | **nervous** 緊張的 | **overwhelm** 震撼 | **instantly** 立刻地 | **approach** 接近 | **confession** 坦言 | **strength** 力量 | **appreciation** 感謝

2. (A)

Script

Hello. This is Kevin Summers, the owner of the building. I'm sorry to hear that your neighbor is constantly making loud noises, even late at night. I'll try to talk to him in person. Unfortunately, however, I must leave for Seoul to address an urgent matter. As soon as I come back, I'll talk to your neighbor. In the meantime, I suggest that you write a kind of agreement between you and your neighbor.

Q. Why is the speaker calling?

(A) To inform the listener that he will make efforts to address a problem

(B) To suggest that the listener write an agreement with the speaker

---

你好。我是凱文・桑瑪斯，這棟建築物的所有人。我很遺憾聽說你的鄰居一直製造很大的噪音，甚至在深夜也是如此。我將會試著親自和他談。然而遺憾的是，我必須到首爾處理一件急事。我一回來就會找你的鄰居談話。同時，我建議你和你的鄰居草擬某種書面協議。

獨白者為何打電話來？

(A) 通知受話者他會努力處理問題。

(B) 建議受話者和發話者擬出某種書面協議

解析 發話者打電話要跟受話者說，他會解決有關住戶製造噪音的事，但是因為他有其他緊急的事情要處理，所以不能立即處理，但是他會盡力，所以答案是選項（A）。

單字 **owner** 所有人 | **neighbor** 鄰居 | **constantly** 一直 | **noise** 噪音 | **address** 處理 | **urgent** 緊急的 | **meantime** 同時 | **agreement** 協議

題型 **03** 掌握細節資訊 (1)

Ⓓ 應用練習　　P. 151　　🎧 107

1. (B)

Script

Welcome aboard! We are pleased to work with every one of you. As a new employee, you have a lot of things to learn about our company. Three speakers will talk about the most important things you'll need to know. Charlie Brown, the first speaker, will

talk about how you will be promoted to a higher position. Mary Smith, the second speaker, will talk about our vacation policy. Finally, Jane Baker will explain your retirement plan.

Q. Who will talk about how the company promotes employees?

(A) Ms. Smith

(B) Mr. Brown

歡迎加入！我們很高興和你們所有人共事。作為新進員工，你們有許多關於公司的資訊

要了解。三位講者將會談論你們最需要知道的重要事項。查理・布朗是第一位講者，他會說明你們要如何晉升到更高的職位。瑪莉・史密斯是第二位講者，她會說明我們的休假政策。最後一位講者是珍・貝克，她會說明你們的退休計劃。

誰會說明公司如何拔擢員工？

(A) 史密斯小姐。

(B) 布朗先生。

解析 這是以新進員工為對象，介紹公司的說明會。有關員工晉升事項，由第一位演講者布朗先生說明，所以答案是選項（B）。

單字 **aboard** 加入（團隊） | **employee** 員工 | **promote** 晉升 | **policy** 政策 | **retirement** 退休

2. (B)

Hello. This is Alice Johnson, at ST Mart. I'm so sorry to hear that one of our employees was not friendly to you. I've talked to the employee, whose name is Jack Smith. Smith is usually a friendly employee. But when you saw him, he was having a problem with his landlord. That was why he appeared unfriendly to you. In any case, he wants to apologize to you in person. Please call him at 555-7833.

Q. Why did Ms. Johnson leave a phone number?

(A) Because she was having a problem with her landlord

(B) Because she wants the listener to call Mr. Smith

您好，我是 ST 超商的艾莉絲‧強森。我很遺憾聽說我們的一位員工對您不友善。我已經和那位員工談過，他的名字是傑克‧史密斯。史密斯通常很友善。然而當您看到他時，他和他的房東剛好出了問題。那就是他看起來對您不友善的原因。無論如何，他想親自向您道歉。請打 555-7833 的電話給他。

為何強森小姐留下電話號碼？

(A) 因為她和她的房東產生糾紛。

(B) 因為她要受話者打電話給史密斯先生。

解析 因為員工不親切想親自向顧客道歉，留下了該員工的電話號碼，所以答案是選項（B）。

單字 **friendly** 友善的 | **landlord** 房東 | **in any case** 無論如何 | **apologize** 道歉

D 應用練習　P. 157　 112

1. (A)

Hello. This is Sarah Taylor, from Tiffany Zoo, returning your call yesterday. Your phone call made me feel very happy. I had been worried about Jack. He is a bear that has been with us for nearly five years. We didn't know what had happened. He had been missing for several days. Fortunately, you came across him and let us know that he was OK. Thank you very much.

Q. How long has the bear been at the zoo?

(A) For almost five years

(B) For almost three years

你好。我是第凡內動物園的莎拉‧泰勒，回覆您昨天的來電。您的電話讓我覺得很高興。我一直很擔心傑克，牠是一隻待在我們這裡近五年的熊。我們不知道發生什麼事，但牠已經失蹤了數天。幸運的是，您碰上了牠，並讓我們知道牠沒事。非常感謝您。

熊在動物園有多久了？

(A) 近五年。

(B) 近三年。

解析 根據電話留言，可以知道名叫傑克的熊，在第凡內動物園已經生活了將近五年。所以答案是選項（A）。

單字 **worry about** 擔心 | **missing** 失蹤的 | **come across** 遇見

2. (B)

Script

David Johnson has been living in Chicago for almost twenty years. He was born in Los Angeles and lived there until he was nineteen. Then, his family moved to Chicago, where Johnson went to Carlston University. After graduating from college, he became a successful banker. But music has always been his passion, and now he is an established pianist. He will be performing next month for poor children in Chicago.

Q. What musical instrument does Mr. Johnson play?

(A) The flute
(B) The piano

大衛・強森住在芝加哥已近 20 年，他在洛杉磯出生長大直到 19 歲。然後，他們全家搬到芝加哥，強森在那裡上了卡爾斯頓大學。大學畢業後，他成為成功的銀行家。然而音樂一直是他的愛好，而現在他已是一位受肯定的鋼琴家。他在下個月將於芝加哥為貧困兒童表演。

強森先生演奏的樂器是什麼？
(A) 長笛。
(B) 鋼琴。

解析 這是一段介紹大衛・強森的獨白，提到他是一位成功的銀行家，也是一位受肯定的鋼琴家，所以答案是選項（B）。

單字 raise 扶養 | graduate 畢業 | successful 成功的 | passion 愛好 | established 受肯定的 | musical instrument 樂器

題型 05 掌握意圖

D 應用練習　P. 163　🎧 117

1. (B)

Script

Hello. This is Eric Smith, at Smith Car Repairs. I am calling because we are having difficulty repairing your car. This is because we need to purchase some parts. One of our suppliers will deliver the parts to us by next Tuesday. I'm so sorry for this delay. I know that you need your car to get around and that this will cause you some inconvenience. Please accept my apologies.

Q. What does the speaker mean when he says, "I know that you need your car to get around"?

(A) He thinks that the listener should think about buying a new car.
(B) He thinks that the listener will use his car often.

您好。我是史密斯汽車修理廠的艾瑞克・史密斯。我打電話來是要說明修理您的汽車遇上了困難。這是因為我們需要購買一些零件，我們的供應商會在下週二前把零件寄給我們。我對拖延到修理時間感到很抱歉。我知道您得開車四處行動，而這會讓您不太方便。請接受我的道歉。

發話者說「我知道您得開車四處行動」是什麼意思？
(A) 他認為受話者應該考慮買一輛新車。
(B) 他認為受話者會常用到他的車。

解析 因為購買零件而延誤時間，讓汽車無法如期修理好，所以修車廠留下了這通電話留言向顧客致歉。電話留言中提到，車主沒辦法使用自己的車，將對修車廠失望，含有對自身延誤相當自責的意思。所以選項（B）是答案。

單字 repair 修理 | purchase 購買 | part 零件 | supplier 供應商 | deliver 寄送 | delay 延誤 | apology 道歉

2. (B)

Script

The Human Resources Department has recently found out that some contact information is not current for some employees. For several employees, contact information is missing. This is unacceptable. We will contact those employees whose contact information is missing. We will also find out why some information is not current. Your contact information is important to us. Help us keep it current.

Q. What does the speaker mean when she says, "This is unacceptable"?

(A) The company does not pay attention to contact information.

(B) The company must have an employee contact information.

人力資源部門最近發現有些員工的聯絡資訊並不是最新的,有幾位員工的聯絡資訊缺漏了。這樣的情況是不被允許的。我們會和缺漏聯絡資訊的員工聯繫。我們也會查看看為何一些資訊沒有更新。你們的聯絡資訊對我們來說很重要。請協助我們更新。

發話者說「這樣的情況是不被接受的」是什麼意思?

(A) 公司不重視聯絡資訊。

(B) 公司一定要有員工聯絡資訊。

解析 人力資源部門發現,他們管理的員工聯絡資訊和目前的不一致,站在公司的立場,這樣的情形是不被允許的,公司必須有員工最新的聯絡方式,所以答案是選項(B)。

單字 Human Resources Department 人力資源部門 | recently 最近 | contact 聯絡 | current 目前的 | unacceptable 無法接受的 | pay attention to 注意

Quick Test   P. 164   🎧 118

1. (B) 2. (A) 3. (B)

4. (B) 5. (B) 6. (B)

【Questions 1–3】

Script

Hello. This is Alice Brown, at Carlston University. I'm so sorry to hear about your car accident last Monday. I know that you're in the hospital. I do know that your health is the most important

thing right now. Unfortunately, however, I must inform you that you have failed Economics 101. Since you had not informed us of your situation, we assumed that you didn't want to take the final exam. You might want to discuss this matter with Professor Bauer after you're discharged from the hospital.

你好。我是卡爾斯頓大學的艾麗絲‧布朗。我很遺憾聽到您在上週一發生車禍,知道你正在醫院。我確實了解現在健康對你來說是真正要緊的事。然而遺憾的是,我必須通知你,你的經濟 101 課程不及格。因為你並沒有通知我們關於你的狀況,我們以為你不想參加期末考。你在出院後也許可以和博爾教授討論此事。

單字 traffic accident 車禍 | matter 要緊的 | inform 通知 | assume 以為 | be discharged 出院

1. (B)

Script

Why is the speaker calling?

(A) To inform the listener that Professor Bauer has left the university

(B) To inform the listener that he has failed a course

發話者為何打電話來？

(A) 通知受話者博爾教授已經離開大學。

(B) 通知受話者他有一科不及格。

解析 推測是學校女職員從學校打來留這通留言，告知發生車禍的學生，因為他沒聯絡學校，以為他不想來考試，所以不及格。答案是選項（B）。

單字 course 課程

2. (A)

Script

Which is true about the listener?

(A) He is a student at Carlston University.

(B) He was hospitalized last Thursday.

關於聽話人何者為真？

(A) 他是卡爾斯頓大學的學生。

(B) 他在上週四住院治療。

解析 內容提到是從卡爾斯頓大學打來的電話，同時告知受話者某科不及格，所以知道來電者是卡爾斯頓大學處理相關業務的人，因此可以推測，受話者應該是卡爾斯頓大學的學生。答案是選項（A）。

單字 hospitalize 住院

3. (B)

Script

What does the speaker mean when she says, "I do know that your health is the most important thing right now"?

(A) She believes that the listener wants to be a medical doctor.

(B) She believes that the listener is making efforts to get better.

發話者說「我確實了解現在健康對你來說是真正要緊的事」是什麼意思？

(A) 她認為受話者想要成為醫生。

(B) 她認為受話者正努力讓身體康復。

解析 學生發生交通意外，且沒有跟學校聯絡，由此推測學生應該受傷很嚴重，所以才會留言說，目前對你來說沒有什麼比恢復健康更重要的了。所以答案是選項（B）。

單字 medical 醫療的 ｜ make efforts to 努力 ｜ get better 康復

【 Questions 4–6 】

Script

Can international politics negatively affect your business? According to Charlie Smith, that is a new reality we are dealing with in this globalized world. Then, what can you do to protect your business? On Friday, Smith will tell you everything you need to know to make sure that your business survives and thrives. You can also buy his latest book at half price. For more information, visit our website www.politicsbusiness.com.

國際政治會對你的企業產生負面影響嗎？根據查理・史密斯的說法，那是我們在全球化時代所面臨的新現況。那麼，你要如何保護自己的企業呢？本週五史密斯將告訴你所有你必須知道的秘辛，確保你的企業可以存續和繁榮。你也可以半價購買他最新出版的書。欲知詳情，請上我們的網站 www.politicsbusiness.com。

單字 **politics** 政治 | **negatively** 負面地 | **affect** 影響 | **reality** 實際 | **deal with** 面臨 | **survive** 存續 | **thrive** 繁榮

4 (B)

Script

Who is the advertisement aimed at?

(A) Diplomats
(B) Business owners

這則廣告的訴求對象是誰？

(A) 外交官。
(B) 企業主。

解析 因為是有關「保護企業不被國際政治所影響」的講座，所以鎖定的目標應該是企業主而不是外交官。選項（B）是答案。

單字 **advertisement** 廣告 | **aim at** 訴求對象 | **diplomat** 外交官

5. (B)

Script

Which is true about Mr. Smith?

(A) He does not believe that international politics can affect business.
(B) He has written more than one book.

關於史密斯先生何者為真？

(A) 他不相信國際政治可能會影響你的企業。
(B) 他曾寫超過一本書。

解析 從史密斯先生提出「國際政治會對企業產生負面影響」這點看來，可以知道他應該相信國際政治會影響企業。從他最新出版的新書半價促銷看來，他之前一定也出版過相關書籍。選項（B）是答案。

6. (B)

Script

When can listeners meet with Mr. Smith?

(A) On Wednesday
(B) On Friday

聽眾可以在何時與史密斯先生見面？

(A) 在週三。
(B) 在週五。

解析 因為提到史密斯先生演講會舉行的日期是星期五，所以答案是選項（B）。

單字 **meet** 見面

Practice Test P. 166   119

1. (D) 2. (B) 3. (C) 4. (C) 5. (D)
6. (B) 7. (C) 8. (D) 9. (B)

【Questions 1－3】

Script

Hello. This is Robert Johnson, at the Best Inventor Awards Committee. Each year, we select the most creative inventor in the world. This year, we have decided to present this award to you. We are certain that you are the most creative inventor in the world. The awards ceremony will be held in Toronto, on March 15, 2017. Your travel and accommodations have already been arranged. Did you know that your award is worth $5 million? Yes, it's $5 million! Congratulations!

您好。我是最佳發明家獎委員會的羅伯特‧強森。每年，我們選出全世界最佳創意發明家，今年我們已經決定由您獲得這個獎項。我們確信您是世界上最有創意的發明家。頒獎典禮將在2017年3月15日於多倫多舉行。我們已經安排好了您的旅行和住宿。您知道您的獎項價值五百萬元嗎？沒錯，就是五百萬元！恭喜！

單字 inventor 發明家｜award 獎項｜
committee 委員會｜ceremony 典禮｜
accommodation 住宿｜
arrange 安排｜congratulation 恭喜

1. (D)

Script

Why is the speaker calling?
(A) To encourage the listener to be more creative
(B) To ask the listener when he will move to the United States
(C) To ask the listener to give a speech at a conference
(D) To inform the listener that he has won an award

發話者為何打電話來？
(A) 鼓勵受話者要更有創意。
(B) 詢問受話者何時會搬到美國。
(C) 請受話者在大會演講。
(D) 通知受話者他獲得一個獎項。

解析 電話留言中提到，受話者獲得最佳創意投資人獎。來電目的是為了告知得獎的消息，同時邀請他參加頒獎典禮，選項（D）是答案。

單字 conference 大會

2. (B)

Script

Which is true about the listener?
(A) He will visit Toronto on May 15, 2017.
(B) He is recognized for his creativity.
(C) He used to be a wealthy man.
(D) He teaches engineering at college.

關於受話者何者為真？
(A) 他將在2017年5月15日前往多倫多。
(B) 他因為創意而獲得肯定。
(C) 他曾是位有錢人。
(D) 他在大學教工程學。

解析 因為留言中提到頒獎典禮是在3月15日，不是5月15日，所以選項（A）錯了。他曾經相當富有或曾經在大學教工程學，留言中都沒有提到。從他獲得最有創意發明人獎看來，可以推知，他非常有創意，所以答案是選項（B）。

單字 recognize 獲得肯定｜
wealthy 富有的｜engineering 工程學

3. (C)

What does the speaker mean when he says, "Did you know that your award is worth $5 million"?

(A) The listener must be wise enough to handle a lot of money.
(B) The listener must be disappointed to learn that he has lost a lot of money.
(C) The listener may be surprised to learn that he will receive a lot of money.
(D) The listener may want to invest his money in medicine.

發話者說「你知道你的獎項價值五百萬元嗎」是什麼意思？

(A) 受話者一定要有足夠的智慧處理龐大的金錢。
(B) 受話者得知他損失一大筆錢一定很失望。
(C) 受話者得知他會收到一大筆錢可能會很驚訝。
(D) 受話者可能將他的錢投資在醫學上。

解析 從發話者告知獎項金額的方式，可以推測獲得獎金的受話者聽到這個金額會非常驚訝。答案是選項（C）。

單字 handle 處理 | disappointed 失望的 | surprised 驚訝的 | invest 投資

【Questions 4–6】

Script

At Griffith International, we offer free language courses. You can learn Chinese, Japanese, French, German, Spanish, or Korean. Every employee must learn at least one foreign language. You are kindly advised to learn at least two foreign languages. Many new employees at Griffith International wonder why a clothing company cares so much about foreign languages. I just want to mention that learning a foreign language makes you more creative.

在葛瑞菲斯國際公司，我們提供免費語言課程。你可以學習中文、日文、法文、德文、西班牙文和韓文。每位員工必須學習至少一種外語。誠摯地建議你至少學習兩種外語。葛瑞菲斯國際公司的許多新員工很好奇，為何一家服飾公司那麼在乎外語。我只想告訴大家，學習外語可以讓你更有創造力。

單字 at least 至少 | kindly 誠摯地 | advise 建議 | mention 提出

4. (C)

Script

Look at the graphic. Who follows the company's advice?

(A) Ms. Smith
(B) Mr. Johnson
(C) Mr. Bauer
(D) Ms. Baker

請看圖表。誰遵循了公司的建議？

(A) 史密斯小姐。
(B) 強森先生。
(C) 博爾先生。
(D) 貝克小姐。

解析 公司建議說最少要學兩種外語，圖表中學兩種以上外語的人只有博爾先生，其他人都只學一種外語。所以答案為（C）。

單字 follow 遵循 | advice 建議

5. (D)

Script

Which is true about Griffith International?

(A) It requires its employees to learn at least two foreign languages.
(B) Its founder was an immigrant from South Korea.
(C) It believes that learning foreign languages is useless.
(D) It is a clothing company.

關於葛瑞菲斯國際公司何者為真？

(A) 公司要求員工學習至少兩種外語。
(B) 公司創始人是來自南韓的移民。
(C) 公司相信學習外語毫無用處。
(D) 這是一家服飾公司。

解析 發話者提到，公司的新進員工好奇為什麼服裝公司那麼在意學習外語。所以由此可知葛瑞菲斯國際公司是服裝公司。答案是選項（D）。

單字 founder 創始人｜ immigrant 移民｜ useless 無用的

6. (B)

Script

What can learning a foreign language help you develop, according to the talk?

(A) Knowledge
(B) Creativity
(C) Social skills
(D) Balance

根據發話者，學習外語可以幫你開發什麼？

(A) 知識。
(B) 創造力。
(C) 社交技巧。
(D) 均衡。

解析 發話者在最後提到新進員工好奇的部分，想提醒大家學習外語能促進創造力。所以答案是選項（B）。

單字 knowledge 知識

【 Questions 7–9 】

Script

Too many people believe that the publishing industry is failing. That is why not many people want to work for publishing companies. But we need to understand that the publishing industry plays a unique role in society. The industry helps us broaden our knowledge. When our knowledge is broadened, we can come up with creative ways to solve problems facing our society. In this sense, our society cannot survive without the publishing industry.

許多人認為出版業正在衰退，因此不是很多人想在出版公司工作。然而我們需要了解出版業在社會中扮演一個獨特的角色，這個行業可以幫助拓展我們的知識。當我們的知識變寬廣了，就可以針對任何社會問題找出有創意的解決辦法。就這個層面而言，我們的社會需要出版業才能存續。

單字 publish 出版｜ industry 行業｜ unique 獨特的｜ play a role 扮演角色｜ broaden 拓展｜ knowledge 知識｜ come up with 找出｜ solve 解決｜ face 面對｜ survive 存續

7. (C)

Script

What is the speech mainly about?

(A) Why the publishing industry is struggling financially

(B) Why the publishing industry is unpopular among college graduates

(C) The importance of the publishing industry in our society

(D) The importance of expanding your knowledge

這段談話的主要目的是甚麼?

(A) 為何出版業經營不善。

(B) 為何出版業不受大學畢業生的歡迎。

(C) 出版業在我們社會中的重要性。

(D) 拓展你的知識有其重要性。

解析 四個選項在演說中都有提到,然而演說重點是,出版事業是讓知識普及以解決社會問題的基石,所以答案是選項(C)。

單字 struggle 受苦 | financially 財務上地 | graduate 畢業生 | expand 拓展

8. (D)

Script

What is true about the speaker?

(A) She believes that the publishing industry is not useful anymore.

(B) She is an internationally recognized novelist.

(C) She runs several publishing companies.

(D) She believes that the publishing industry is essential for the survival of society.

關於發話者何者為真?

(A) 她認為出版業不再有用。

(B) 她是受到國際肯定的小說家。

(C) 她經營數家出版公司。

(D) 她認為出版業對社會的存續很重要。

解析 發話者表示出版社普及知識,是解決社會問題的方式。也就是說,沒有出版社,社會的存續會有困難。所以答案是選項(D)。

單字 run 經營 | essential 重要的 | survival 存續

9. (B)

Script

According to the speaker, why should we expand our knowledge?

(A) Because we want to lead a healthy lifestyle

(B) Because we need to find innovative ways to solve social problems

(C) Because we want to earn a lot of money

(D) Because we need to live peacefully with foreign countries

根據發話者,我們為何要拓展我們的知識?

(A) 因為我們要有健全的生活。

(B) 因為我們要找到解決社會問題的創新方式。

(C) 因為我們要賺很多錢。

(D) 因為我們要和外國和平相處。

解析 發話者提到說,透過知識的普及,能導引出解決社會問題的方案,所以選項(B)是答案。

單字 innovative 創新的 | peacefully 和平地

Parts 5&6
句子填空和段落填空

❶ 句子結構

題型 **01** 主詞和動詞

Ⓓ 應用練習　　P. 175

| 1. (B)　2. (D)　3. (C)　4. (D)　5. (B) |
| 6. (D)　7. (B)　8. (D)　9. (C)　10. (D) |

1. (B)

翻譯 這座橋在 2012 年開始建造。

解析 在片語「the ＋空格＋ of」中，能放進空格的是名詞。選項（A）是動詞，選項（B）是名詞，選項（C）是形容詞，選項（D）是副詞。答案是選項（B）。

單字 construct 建造｜
construction 建造工程｜
constructive 有建設性的｜
constructively 有建設性地

2. (D)

翻譯 操作這台洗衣機毫不費力。

解析 這是片語「the ＋空格＋ of」，所以空格要放名詞。選項（A）是動詞，選項（B）是形容詞，選項（C）是副詞，選項（D）是名詞。答案是選項（D）。

單字 operate 操作｜operational 操作的｜
operationally 操作地｜
operation 操作

3. (C)

翻譯 最終，他提出正式要求。

解析 空格是主詞，故需用主格。選項（A）是受格，選項（B）是所有格＋ be 動詞，選項（C）是主格，選項（D）是反身代名詞。所以答案是選項（C）。

單字 formal 正式的｜request 要求

4. (D)

翻譯 他們終於決定離開首爾。

解析 空格要放表「某人」之意的主詞，故需用主格。選項（A）是所有格，選項（B）是受格，選項（C）是反身代名詞，選項（D）是主格。答案是選項（D）。

單字 eventually 最終｜decide 決定

5. (B)

翻譯 信任他是一件愚蠢的事。

解析 空格要放能代替 to trust him 的虛構主詞。因為只有 it 能當虛構主詞，所以答案是選項（B）。

單字 foolish 愚蠢的｜trust 相信

6. (D)

翻譯 很高興昨天遇見你。

解析 空格要放能代替 to meet you yesterday 的虛主詞。It 是虛構主詞，答案是選項（D）。

單字 pleasure 高興

7. (B)

翻譯 執行長要處理很多公務。

解析 CEO 是第三人稱單數，所以動詞也要符合。答案是選項（B）。

8. (D)

翻譯 甜點很可口。

解析 dessert 是第三人稱單數，所以要用單數動詞（+s）答案是選項（D）。

單字 dessert 甜點 | taste 可口的

9. (C)

翻譯 這些領導人要求工人要受到更好的待遇。

解析 These leaders 是複數，所以要用複數動詞，答案是選項（C）。

單字 leader 領導人 | demand 要求 | treatment 待遇

10. (D)

翻譯 請仔細閱讀這份文件。

解析 這是省略主詞的命令句。命令句要用動詞原形起始句子，答案是選項（D）。

單字 document 文件 | carefully 仔細地

題型 **02** 受詞和補語

Ⓓ 應用練習　　P. 181

1. (C)　2. (A)　3. (D)　4. (A)　5. (B)
6. (D)　7. (D)　8. (B)　9. (D)　10. (B)

1. (C)

翻譯 這兩家公司簽署一份協議。

解析 不定冠詞 a 或 an 後要接名詞。選項（A）是形容詞，選項（B）是副詞，選項（C）是名詞，選項（D）是動詞。所以答案是選項（C）。

單字 company 公司 | sign 簽署 | agreement 協議 | agreeable 一致的 | agreeably 一致地 | agree 同意

2. (A)

翻譯 這間動物園成功飼養了健康的動物。

解析 空格要放具「成功」之意的名詞。選項（A）是名詞，選項（B）是形容詞，選項（C）是副詞，選項（D）是動詞。所以答案是選項（A）。

單字 zoo 動物園 | succeed 成功 | raise 飼養 | successful 成功的

3. (D)

翻譯 這位執行長將失敗怪在他們身上。

解析 空格要放 blamed 的受詞。選項（A）是所有格，選項（B）是主格，選項（C）是反身代名詞，選項（D）是受格。答案是選項（D）。

單字 blame 責怪 | failure 失敗

4. (A)

翻譯 委員會對我們感到高興。

解析 空格要放介系詞 with 的受詞。選項（A）是受格，選項（B）是主格，選項（C）是所有格，選項（D）是反身代名詞。答案是選項（A）。

單字 committee 委員會 | pleased 高興的

5. (B)

翻譯 是梅蘭妮而非他主持了這場活動。

解析 空格要放介系詞 instead of 的受詞。選項（A）是主格，選項（B）是受格，選項（C）是反身代名詞，選項（D）是主格＋ be 動詞。所以答案是選項（B）。

單字 host 主持 | event 活動

6. (D)

翻譯 這棟公寓是由一位知名演員所擁有。

解析 空格要放能和 a 搭配的名詞。選項（A）是形容詞，選項（B）是副詞，選項（C）是動詞或名詞，選項（D）是名詞。根據句意，答案是選項（D）。

單字 belong to 擁有 | actor 演員 | active 活躍的 | actively 活躍地 | act 演戲

7. (D)

翻譯 中文是學習語言的好選擇。

解析 空格要放 a 後接的名詞。選項（A）是動詞，選項（B）是形容詞，選項（C）是不定詞，選項（D）是名詞。所以答案是選項（D）。

單字 Chinese 中文 | choice 選擇 | choose 選擇

8. (B)

翻譯 結果很令人滿意。

解析 空格要放 be 動詞後補充說明主詞的主詞補語，所以只能放名詞或形容詞。又因為「結果」不是「滿意」，是「滿意的」，所以不能用名詞，要用形容詞，答案是選項（B）。

單字 result 結果 | satisfy 滿意 | satisfactory 滿意的 | satisfactorily 滿意地 | satisfaction 滿足感

9. (D)

翻譯 城市生活一般來說很舒適。

解析 空格要放 be 動詞後接補充說明主詞的主詞補語。因為「都市生活」後要用形容詞，答案是選項（D）。

單字 generally 一般來說 | comfortable 舒適的 | comfort 舒適 | comfortably 舒適地

10. (B)

翻譯 時間不足使得完成這個案子困難重重。

解析 空格要放能代替 to complete the project 的虛受詞。因為只有 it 能當虛受詞，所以答案是選項（B）。

單字 lack 缺乏 | complete 完成

題型 **03** 修飾詞

D 應用練習　　P. 187

1. (B)	2. (D)	3. (C)	4. (D)	5. (D)
6. (B)	7. (C)	8. (D)	9. (C)	10. (D)

1. (B)

翻譯 穩定的環境對青少年來說很重要。

解析 選項（A）是副詞，選項（B）是形容詞，選項（C）是名詞，選項（D）是動詞。空格是用來修飾名詞，environment 能修飾名詞的是形容詞，答案是選項（B）。

單字 stable 穩定的 | environment 環境 | stably 穩定地 | stability 穩定度 | stabilize 穩定

2. (D)

翻譯 這位有創意的作家出版了數本小說。

解析 能修飾名詞 writer 的是形容詞。選項（A）是動詞，選項（B）是名詞，選項（C）是副詞，選項（D）是形容詞。答案是選項（D）。

單字 creative 有創意的 | publish 出版 | novel 小說 | create 創造 | creation 創造物 | creatively 有創意地

3. (C)

翻譯 電腦的發明改變了許多事物。

解析 在片語「the ＋空格＋ of」中，能放進空格的是名詞。選項（A）是動詞，選項（B）是形容詞，選項（C）是名詞，選項（D）是副詞。答案是選項（C）。

單字 invention 發明物 | invent 發明 | inventive 發明的 | inventively 發明地

4. (D)

翻譯 她和客戶的關係純粹是專業方面的。

解析 因為空格位在所有格和介系詞之間，所以空格要放名詞。選項（A）是動詞，選項（B）是副詞，選項（C）和（D）是名詞。不過，如果選項（C）是答案，那句子的動詞就要用 were。所以答案是選項（D）。

單字 relationship 關係 | client 客戶 | professional 專業的 | relate 相關 | relatively 相對地 | relation 關係

5. (D)

翻譯 這位醫生想到一種檢測癌症的新方法。

解析 空格要放能修飾前面名詞 way 的字。因為不定詞可作為形容詞，修飾名詞的功能，所以答案是選項（D）。

單字 detect 檢測 | cancer 癌症

6. (B)

翻譯 遵循正確的程序以修改資料。

解析 空格要放能修飾前面名詞 procedure 的字。因為不定詞有這樣的功能，所以答案是選項（B）。

單字 follow 遵循 | correct 正確的 | procedure 程序 | modify 修改

7. (C)

翻譯 新產品賣得很快。

解析 空格要放能修飾動詞 was selling 的字。因為副詞有這樣的功能，所以答案是選項（C）。

單字 product 產品 | sell 賣 | quickly 很快地 | quickness 迅速 | quicken 加快

8. (D)

翻譯 這些昆蟲在南韓非常少見。

解析 空格要放能修飾動詞 were found 的詞類。因為副詞有這樣的功能，所以答案是選項（D）。

單字 insect 昆蟲 | rarely 很少地 | rare 很少的 | rareness 珍貴 | rarity 罕見

9. (C)

翻譯 山姆和其他員工的互動良好。

解析 句子中一定要有動詞。選項（A）是名詞，選項（B）是形容詞，選項（C）是動詞，選項（D）是副詞。所以答案是選項（C）。

單字 interact 互動 ┃ employee 員工 ┃ interaction 互動 ┃ interactive 互動的

10. (D)

翻譯 他的提案帶來驚人的成果。

解析 句子中一定要有動詞，答案是選項（D）。動詞 lead 的過去式是 led。選項（C）不能選是因為主詞是第三人稱單數，動詞是現在式，一定要加 s，變成 leads。

單字 proposal 提案 ┃ lead to 導致 ┃ result 成果

Quick Test	P. 188

1. (A)	2. (B)	3. (C)	4. (A)	5. (D)
6. (B)	7. (D)	8. (B)	9. (A)	10. (C)
11. (B)	12. (A)	13. (B)	14. (D)	15. (C)
16. (D)	17. (C)	18. (D)	19. (B)	20. (D)

1. (A)

翻譯 收到這筆款項讓人驚訝。

解析 在片語「the ＋空格＋ of」中，能放進空格的是名詞。選項（B）是形容詞，選項（C）是動詞的過去式，選項（D）是動詞。
選項（A）是名詞。答案是選項（A）。

單字 receipt 收取 ┃ payment 款項 ┃ receivable 可接受的

2. (B)

翻譯 幸運地是，他們達成妥協。

解析 若句子不是命令句，就一定要有主詞。代名詞當主詞時要用主格。選項（A）是受格，選項（B）是主格，選項（C）是所有格，選項（D）是反身代名詞。答案是選項（B）。

單字 reach 達成 ┃ compromise 妥協

3. (C)

翻譯 對任何事物抱持質疑一直都是很好的想法。

解析 空格要放能代替 to question everything 的虛主詞。因為只有 it 能當虛主詞，所以答案是選項（C）。

單字 question 質疑

4. (A)

翻譯 這位發明家定期創造新發明。

解析 空格要放說明主詞的動詞。因為主詞是第三人稱單數，時態是現在式，所以答案是選項（A）。

單字 inventor 發明家 ┃ create 創造 ┃ on a regular basis 定期

5. (D)

翻譯 請小心遵循這些指示。

解析 因為句子沒有主詞，所以可以知道是命令句，要用動詞原形，答案是選項（D）。

單字 instruction 指示 ┃ carefully 小心地

6. (B)

翻譯 委員會從數名候選人中挑選了一位。

解析 空格只能放名詞。選項（A）是形容詞，選項（B）是名詞，選項（C）是副詞，選項（D）是動詞。答案是選項（B）。

單字 committee 委員會｜selection 挑選｜candidate 候選人｜selective 有選擇的｜selectively 有選擇地｜select 挑選

7. (A)

翻譯 我們針對他們的需求蒐集資訊。

解析 要放能當及物動詞 collect 受詞的名詞，所以答案是選項（A）。

單字 collect 蒐集｜information 資訊｜need 需求｜informative 教育性的

8. (B)

翻譯 保全阻止他們進入辦公室。

解析 空格要放及物動詞 stop 的受詞。代名詞當受詞時要用受格。選項（A）是反身代名詞，選項（B）是受格，選項（C）是主格，選項（D）是所有格。答案是選項（B）。

單字 bodyguard 保全人員｜stop A from V-ing 阻止 A 做……

9. (A)

翻譯 我們的父母以我們為恥。

解析 空格要放介系詞 of 的受詞。代名詞當受詞時要用受格。選項（D）是所有格，選項（B）是主格，選項（C）是反身代名詞，選項（A）是受格。答案是選項（A）。

單字 be ashamed of 以……為恥

10. (C)

翻譯 這案子的成功取決於他們。

解析 空格要放介系詞 on 的受詞，代名詞當受詞時要用受格。選項（A）是所有格，選項（B）是反身代名詞，選項（C）是受格，選項（D）是主格。答案是選項（C）。

單字 success 成功｜depend on 取決

11. (B)

翻譯 湯瑪斯‧愛迪生是位傑出的發明家。

解析 空格要放能和 an 搭配的名詞。選項（A）是動詞，選項（B）是名詞，選項（C）是形容詞，選項（D）是副詞。答案是選項（B）。

單字 outstanding 傑出的｜inventor 發明家｜invent 發明

12. (A)

翻譯 寫作是一個發揮創造力的過程。

解析 空格要放能和 a 搭配的名詞，答案是選項（A）。

單字 creative 有創造力的｜process 過程｜processor 加工者

13. (B)

翻譯 這些房間很寬敞。

解析 空格要放 be 動詞後補充說明主詞的主詞補語，只能放名詞或形容詞。因為本句只能用形容詞當主詞補語，所以答案是選項（B）。

單字 spacious 寬敞的｜spaciously 寬敞地｜spaciousness 寬敞｜space 空間

14. (D)

翻譯 她的預測讓人震驚。

解析 空格要放當作主詞補語使用的形容詞。副詞選項（A）一般不能當補語使用。所以答案是選項（D）。

單字 prediction 預測 | alarming 驚人的 | alarmed 驚恐的 | alarm 警報

15. (C)

翻譯 他的努力使得節約許多能源是有可能的。

解析 空格要放能代替 to conserve a lot of energy 的虛受詞。因為只有 it 能當虛受詞，所以答案是選項（C）。

單字 effort 努力 | conserve 節約

16. (D)

翻譯 很少人過著健康的生活型態。

解析 空格要放能修飾名詞 lifestyle 的形容詞。選項（A）是名詞，選項（B）是副詞，選項（C）是名詞，選項（D）是形容詞。答案是選項（D）。

單字 healthy 健康的 | lifestyle 生活型態

17–20.

翻譯 信任專家並非總是明智的。專家也只是人，他們也會犯下許多錯誤。例如，很少專家預測到全球景氣在 2008 年開始衰退。所以，運用自己的常識很重要，而不要完全仰賴專家。

單字 trust 信任 | expert 專家 | human 人類 | predict 預測 | global recession 全球景氣衰退 | depend on 仰賴

17. (C)

需要能代替 to trust experts 的虛主詞，答案是選項（C）。

18. (D)

空格要放 be 動詞後能補充說明主詞的主詞補語，所以只能放名詞或形容詞，本句只能用名詞，所以答案是選項（D）。

19. (B)

因為要放入專家曾犯錯的例子，所以答案是選項（B）。

20. (D)

介系詞片語 instead of 後要接名詞，所以要將動詞改成動名詞。答案是選項（D）。

❷ 名詞和代名詞

題型 01 名詞的功能

Ⓓ 應用練習 P. 195

1. (D)	2. (B)	3. (A)	4. (C)	5. (D)
6. (B)	7. (C)	8. (D)	9. (B)	10. (C)

1. (D)

翻譯 南韓的經濟拓展顯著擴大。

解析 空格要放接受形容詞 economic 修飾的名詞。選項（A）是動詞，選項（B）是形容詞，選項（C）是副詞，選項（D）是名詞。答案是選項（D）。

單字 economic 經濟 | expansion 拓展 | remarkable 顯著的 | expand 擴大

2. (B)

翻譯 這間博物館的改建由市政府資助。

解析 片語「the ＋空格＋ of」中，能放進空格的是名詞。答案是選項（B）。

單字 renovation 改建 | fund 資助

3. (A)

翻譯 這家公司獲得設立新工廠的許可。

解析 空格要放及物動詞 got 的受詞。能當受詞的只有名詞和代名詞，因為選項（A）是名詞所以是答案。

單字 permission 許可

4. (C)

翻譯 他們延遲一小時出發。

解析 空格要放所有格 their 修飾的名詞，答案是選項（C）。

單字 delay 延遲 | departure 出發

5. (D)

翻譯 我們可以指望他們的善意。

解析 空格要放形容詞 good 修飾的名詞，答案是選項（D）。

單字 count on 指望 | good will 善意 | willing 願意的 | will 意志

6. (B)

翻譯 這些學生開始當志工。

解析 片語 take to 中的 to 是介系詞，所以接動詞時，動詞要改成動名詞 V-ing，答案是選項（B）。

單字 take to 開始 | volunteer 自願 | voluntary 自願的 | voluntarily 自願地

7. (C)

翻譯 他們的表現讓人印象深刻。

解析 所有格 their 後要接名詞。選項（A）是動詞，選項（B）是動詞的過去式或過去分詞，選項（C）是名詞，選項（D）是不定詞。答案是選項（C）。

單字 impressive 印象深刻的 | performance 表現 | perform 表演

8. (D)

翻譯 我們需要的是勤勉盡責。

解析 這題考 be 動詞後的主詞補語。因為主詞是「我們必須具備的東西」，所以補語要用名詞，答案是選項（D）。

單字 diligence 勤勉盡責

9. (B)

翻譯 他的努力使他成為很棒的溝通者。

解析 空格要放能和 a 搭配的名詞。選項（A）是動詞，選項（B）是名詞，選項（C）是形容詞，選項（D）是副詞。答案是選項（B）。

單字 effort 努力 | communicator 溝通者 | communicate 溝通

10. (C)

翻譯 許多專家認為那是很好的投資。

解析 空格要放能和 a 搭配的名詞，答案是選項（C）。

單字 expert 專家 | consider 認為 | investment 投資 | invest 投資

題型 **02** 名詞的種類

D 應用練習　　P. 201

1. (A)	2. (B)	3. (A)	4. (B)	5. (C)
6. (B)	7. (C)	8. (D)	9. (B)	10. (C)

1. (A)

翻譯 這項公告由政府發布。

解析 首先，the 和 these 不能連在一起，因為 these 中已經含有 the 的意思。另外，the 和 a 也不能連在一起，因為所指的東西不同。因為選項（C）是複數名詞，而句子動詞是 was，兩者單複數不一致。答案是選項（A）。

單字 **issue an announcement** 發布公告｜**government** 政府

2. (B)

翻譯 這份報告由知名的教授撰寫。

解析 因為選項（D）是複數名詞，而句子動詞是 was，兩者單複數不一致。所以答案是選項（B）。

單字 **report** 報告｜**professor** 教授

3. (A)

翻譯 那些公告受到市議會的歡迎。

解析 those 要搭配可數名詞的複數形，而且 those 和 the 不能連在一起，所以答案是選項（A）。

單字 **city council** 市議會

4. (B)

翻譯 那些報告是由特委會繳交的。

解析 those 要搭配可數名詞的複數形。選項（D）是錯的，因為 those 和 the 不能連在一起。答案是選項（B）。

單字 **submit** 繳交｜**committee** 委員會

5. (C)

翻譯 城市中可以接觸到新鮮空氣的人很少。

解析 access 是不可數名詞，所以它不能像選項（A）那樣前面加上 an，也不能像選項（B）和（D）那樣是複數形。答案是選項（C）。

單字 **access** 接觸｜**clean** 乾淨的

6. (B)

翻譯 這間工廠沒有太多設備。

解析 equipment 是不可數名詞，答案是選項（B）。

單字 **factory** 工廠｜**equipment** 設備

7. (C)

翻譯 獲取那項資訊途徑被遭到拒絕。

解析 access 是不可數名詞，不可數名詞當主詞時，動詞要用單數，答案是選項（C）。選項（B）和（D）不能當句子的動詞。

單字 **access** 途徑｜**deny** 拒絕

8. (D)

翻譯 所有設備都正常運轉。

解析 equipment 是不可數名詞，當主詞時，動詞要用單數，答案是選項（D）。

單字 **work** 運轉｜**properly** 正常地

9. (B)

翻譯 產品經理的能力很強。

解析 「名詞＋名詞」可以用來表某特定含意，答案是選項（B）。

單字 production 產製｜
competent 能力強的｜produce 製造｜
productively 有效地

10. (C)

翻譯 這項產品無法達到安全標準。

解析 「名詞＋名詞」可以用來表某特定含意，答案是選項（C）。

單字 meet 達到｜safety 安全｜
standard 標準

題型 03 人稱代名詞

D 應用練習 　　　P. 207

| 1. (D) | 2. (B) | 3. (A) | 4. (C) | 5. (B) |
| 6. (D) | 7. (B) | 8. (D) | 9. (A) | 10. (D) |

1. (D)

翻譯 我們正在研發新藥。

解析 這不是命令句，所以句子一定要有主詞。因為空格要放主詞，所以代名詞要用主格。答案是選項（D）。

單字 develop 研發｜medicine 藥品

2. (B)

翻譯 她對政府法規有強烈的意見。

解析 若代名詞是句子的主詞，代名詞要用主格。答案是選項（B）。

單字 opinion 意見｜government 政府｜
regulation 法規

3. (A)

翻譯 他因她聰明的點子而讚美她。

解析 及物動詞 praised 要接受詞。受詞若是代名詞，要用受格，答案是選項（A）。

單字 praise 讚美｜bright 聰明的

4. (C)

翻譯 我們提出不錯的報價和他們商談。

解析 及物動詞 approached 要接受詞。受詞若是代名詞，要用受格，答案是選項（C）。

單字 approach 接觸｜offer 報價

5. (B)

翻譯 我靠他帶領討論。

解析 介系詞 on 要接受詞，受詞若是代名詞，要用受格，答案是選項（B）。
選項（A）反身代名詞也可以當受詞，但是主詞必須是 he，所以不能選。

單字 depend on 仰賴｜lead 帶領

6. (D)

翻譯 這位員工向我們抱怨她的工作環境。

解析 介系詞 to 要接受詞，受詞若是代名詞，要用受格，答案是選項（D）。

單字 working condition 工作環境

7. (B)

翻譯 他們優異的服務讓我們印象深刻。

解析 在本句中,介系詞 by 的受詞是名詞 service。名詞前需用所有格形容,答案是選項(B)。

單字 impress 使印象深刻

8. (D)

翻譯 我們對自家產品的品質感到很自豪。

解析 介系詞 of 的受詞是 products。名詞 products 前必須用所有格形容,答案是選項(D)。

單字 quality 品質 | product 產品

9. (A)

翻譯 他畫作的名氣沒有她的高。

解析 句子將男子和女子的畫來比較,所以空格要放代替「女子的畫」之意的代名詞,答案是選項(A)。

單字 painting 畫作

10. (D)

翻譯 我們的程序不像他們的那麼單純。

解析 句子將我們和他們的程序做比較,具「他們的程序」之意的選項(D)是答案。。

單字 procedure 程序 | simple 簡單

題型 04 反身代名詞

(D) 應用練習　　　P. 213

| 1. (A) | 2. (B) | 3. (C) | 4. (C) | 5. (D) |
| 6. (C) | 7. (B) | 8. (D) | 9. (B) | 10. (A) |

---

1. (A)

翻譯 這家公司為合併做準備。

解析 因為是「公司自己準備」的意思,所以要用反身代名詞,答案是選項(A)。如果 prepare 的受詞是 it,就表示公司不是為自己準備,而是為其他對象準備。

單字 merger 合併

2. (B)

翻譯 他們得保護自己不受歧視。

解析 是「他們要自己保護自己」的意思,所以要用反身代名詞,答案是選項(B)。選項(A)是主格,不能放在受詞的位置。選項(D)是所有格,不能單獨放在受詞的位置。

單字 protect 保護 | discrimination 歧視

3. (C)

翻譯 他因為辜負主管的期望而對自己感到失望。

解析 因為句意是「他對他自己很失望」,所以要用反身代名詞。答案是選項(C)。若空格填 him,表示和主詞 he 是不同的人。

單字 disappointed 失望的 | fail 使失望 | supervisor 主管

4. (C)

翻譯 我因為讓他們失望而對自己感到羞愧。

解析 因為句意是「我對我自己很失望」,所以要用反身代名詞。答案是選項(C)。

單字 be ashamed of 對……感到羞愧 | let . . . down 讓……失望

5. (D)

翻譯 這位醫生親自和新病患打招呼。

解析 這題是考反身代名詞的強調用法。因為可以將 himself 放在主詞 the doctor 之後來強調,答案是選項(D)。

單字 patient 病患

6. (C)

翻譯 經理親自出席大會。

解析 這題是考反身代名詞的強調用法。因為可以將 herself 放在主詞 the manager 之後來強調,答案是選項(C)。

單字 manager 經理 | attend 參加 | conference 大會

7. (B)

翻譯 遺憾地是,這位技師無法獨自修理這輛車。

解析 by oneself 是「獨自地」或「獨力地」的意思,答案是選項(B)。

單字 mechanic 技師 | fix 修理

8. (D)

翻譯 這位主任獨自過節。

解析 by oneself 是「獨自地」或「獨力地」的意思,答案是選項(D)。

單字 director 主任 | holiday 節日

9. (B)

翻譯 吸菸本身對你的健康有害。

解析 in itself 是「就本身而言」或「本質上」的意思,答案是選項(B)。

單字 smoking 吸菸 | harmful 有害的

10. (A)

翻譯 釣魚本身不會破壞環境。

解析 in itself 是「就本身而言」或「本質上」的意思,答案是選項(A)。

單字 fishing 釣魚 | harm 傷害 | environment 環境

題型 **05** 指示代名詞

(D) 應用練習　　P. 219

| 1. (D) | 2. (B) | 3. (A) | 4. (C) | 5. (D) |
| 6. (B) | 7. (D) | 8. (B) | 9. (C) | 10. (A) |

1. (D)

翻譯 我們的策略和主要競爭對手的大為不同。

解析 空格要放能代替「策略」的字,答案是選項(D)。

單字 strategy 策略 | main 主要 | competitor 競爭對手

2. (B)

翻譯 我對該城市的第一印象和我最好朋友的很類似。

解析 空格要放能代替「對該都市第一印象」的字,答案是選項(B)。

單字 impression 印象 | similar 類似的

3. (A)

翻譯 有些人說法國的宮殿比南韓的更大。

解析 空格要放能代替「那些宮殿」的字,答案是選項(A)。

單字 palace 宮殿

4. (C)

翻譯 我們的決策比主要競爭對手的好多了。

解析 空格要放能代替「那些決策」的字,答案是選項(C)。

單字 decision 決策 | chief 主要的

5. (D)

翻譯 有人努力改善我們社區的環境。

解析 空格要放具「……的人」之意的字,答案是選項(D)。

單字 effort 努力 | community 社區

6. (B)

翻譯 想參加大會的人應該和李小姐聯繫。

解析 空格要放具「……的人」之意的字,答案是選項(B)。

單字 attend 參加

7. (D)

翻譯 和意外有關的人可以在醫院幫忙。

解析 空格要放具「……的人」之意的字,答案是選項(D)。

單字 accident 意外

8. (B)

翻譯 想販賣商品的人,應該學習如何與人良好交流。

解析 空格要放具「……的人」之意的字,答案是選項(B)。

單字 product 商品 | communicate 交流

9. (C)

翻譯 對行銷有興趣的人可以上這些課程。

解析 空格要放具「……的人」之意的字,答案是選項(C)。

單字 marketing 行銷 | course 課程

10. (A)

翻譯 想減重的人要規律地運動。

解析 空格要放具「……的人」之意的字,答案是選項(A)。

單字 lose weight 減重 | work out 運動 | regularly 規律地

題型 06 其他代名詞

D 應用練習　　P. 225

| 1. (C) | 2. (A) | 3. (B) | 4. (D) | 5. (C) |
| 6. (D) | 7. (C) | 8. (A) | 9. (C) | 10. (D) |

1. (C)

翻譯 在我們的戲院,你可以買兩張票再送一張。

解析 空格要放具「另一個」之意的字,答案是選項(C)。

單字 theater 戲院

2. (A)

翻譯 他的兩位女兒有一位是醫生,而另一位是律師。

解析 兩者中的其中一個用「one」,兩者其一之外的另一個用「the other」,答案是選項(A)。

3. (B)

翻譯 他們認識彼此有 20 年了。

解析 空格要放具「彼此」之意的字,答案是選項(B)。

單字 each other 彼此

4. (D)

翻譯 家庭成員應該互相幫忙。

解析 因空格要放具「彼此」之意的字,答案是選項(D)。

單字 family member 家庭成員

5. (C)

翻譯 我可以保留任何一個紀念品嗎?

解析 空格要放具「任何一個」之意的字,答案是選項(C)。

單字 souvenir 紀念品

6. (D)

翻譯 員工沒有完成任何任務。

解析 這題考否定句中 any 的用法,答案是選項(D)。其他選項都造成雙重否定,所以都不能選。

單字 staff 員工 | carry out 完成 | task 任務

7. (C)

翻譯 我們的競爭對手都不考慮那個選項。

解析 空格要放表否定含意的代名詞,答案是選項(C)。

單字 competitor 競爭對手 | consider 考慮 | option 選項

8. (A)

翻譯 這些活動沒有一個是由委員會籌辦。

解析 空格要放表否定含意的代名詞。,答案是選項(A)。

單字 event 活動 | organize 籌辦

9. (C)

翻譯 你可以選擇茶或咖啡。

解析 這題考相關連接詞 either A or B,答案是選項(C)。

10. (D)

翻譯 不管是醫生或病患都不對檢查結果感到驚訝。

解析 這題考相關連接詞 neither A nor B,答案是選項(D)。

單字 patient 病患 | result 結果

Quick Test   P. 226

1. (C)	2. (B)	3. (D)	4. (A)	5. (D)
6. (B)	7. (D)	8. (C)	9. (A)	10. (D)
11. (B)	12. (D)	13. (C)	14. (D)	15. (B)
16. (D)	17. (B)	18. (D)	19. (A)	20. (D)

1. (C)

翻譯 新部門的成立是由專家小組建議的。

解析 空格要放表「創立」之意的名詞,答案是選項(C)。

單字 creation 成立 | panel 專門小組 | creative 有創意的

2. (B)

翻譯 我們的公司和大學有發展緊密的關係。

解析 空格要放表「關係」之意的名詞,答案是選項（B）。

單字 develop 發展 ｜ close 緊密的 ｜ relation 關係 ｜ relative 親戚

3. (D)

翻譯 誠實才是最重要的。

解析 空格要放表「誠實」之意的名詞,答案是選項（D）。

單字 matter 重要的 ｜ honesty 誠實

4. (A)

翻譯 這些機器需要特別照護。

解析 空格要放表這些「機器」之意的名詞,答案是選項（A）。

單字 machine 機器 ｜ care 照護

5. (D)

翻譯 他們買了二手家具。

解析 furniture 是不可數名詞,答案是選項（D）。

單字 second-hand 二手的

6. (B)

翻譯 瑪莉不知道她的行李遺失了。

解析 baggage 是不可數名詞,答案是選項（B）。

單字 baggage 行李

7. (D)

翻譯 他們支持這項新政策。

解析 空格要放主格代名詞,答案是選項（D）。

單字 support 支持 ｜ policy 政策

8. (C)

翻譯 她母親從小教她要慷慨大方。

解析 空格要放代名詞的受格,答案是選項（C）。

單字 raise 養育 ｜ generous 慷慨大方的

9. (A)

翻譯 梅蘭妮是他最優秀的學生。

解析 空格要放代名詞的所有格,答案是選項（A）。

單字 best 最好的

10. (D)

翻譯 她向他們自我介紹。

解析 空格要放反身代名詞,答案是選項（D）。

單字 introduce 介紹

11. (B)

翻譯 傑克學會善待自己。

解析 空格要放反身代名詞,答案是選項（B）。

單字 kind 仁慈的

12. (D)

翻譯 快樂這件事對你的健康有好處。

解析 空格要放反身代名詞,答案是選項
（D）。

單字 happiness 快樂 ∣ health 健康

13. (C)

翻譯 日本的消費市場比南韓的大多了。

解析 空格要放能代替「消費市場」的字,答
案是選項（C）。

單字 consumer 消費者 ∣ market 市場

14. (D)

翻譯 美國的傳統和英國的類似。

解析 空格要放能代替「傳統」的字,答案是
選項（D）。

單字 tradition 傳統 ∣ similar 類似的

15. (B)

翻譯 想要成功的人都應該慷慨大方。

解析 空格要放具「任何……的人」之意的字,
答案是選項（B）。

單字 succeed 成功

16. (D)

翻譯 兩者其一的建議會被部門接受。

解析 具「兩個中的任何一個」之意的選項
（D）是答案。

單字 suggestion 建議 ∣
acceptable 可接受的

17–20.

翻譯 感謝您寄的電子郵件。我可以接受您在
月底付款給我,我週二時會將我的銀行
存摺影本傳真給您。祝您在美國有個美
好的假期。

解析

17. (B)

空格要放代名詞的所有格,答案是選項（B）。

18. (D)

動名詞當主詞時,動詞要用單數形,答案是選
項（D）。

19. (A)

空格要放介係詞的受格,答案是選項（A）。

20. (D)

因為空格要放跟付款相關的內容,答案是選項
（D）。

---

❸ 動詞

題型 01 單複數一致

Ⓓ 應用練習　　P. 233

1. (B)	2. (D)	3. (A)	4. (D)	5. (D)
6. (B)	7. (C)	8. (D)	9. (A)	10. (D)

1. (B)

翻譯 很多人擔心那些露營者的安全。

解析 因為 many 是複數代名詞,答案是選
項（B）。

單字 safety 安全 ∣ camper 露營者

2. (D)

翻譯 很少人意識到使用社群媒體的危險。

解析 因為 few 是複數代名詞，答案是選項（D）。

單字 aware 意識到 ｜
social media 社群媒體

3. (A)

翻譯 有半數的蛋糕是由艾蜜莉所烘焙。

解析 「部分＋ of ＋全部」後的動詞要跟「全部」一致，答案是選項（A）。

單字 bake 烘焙

4. (D)

翻譯 有部分的設備由一家加拿大公司研發。

解析 「部分＋ of ＋全部」後的動詞要跟「全部」一致，答案是選項（D）。

單字 equipment 設備 ｜ develop 研發

5. (D)

翻譯 有些建築物無水可用。

解析 因為 a few 通常被視為複數，答案是選項（D）。

單字 leave 留下

6. (B)

翻譯 數名乘客被送到一家當地醫院。

解析 因為 several 通常被視為複數，答案是選項（B）。

單字 passenger 乘客 ｜ local 當地的

7. (C)

翻譯 遺失項鍊的女子看起來不太高興。

解析 因為主詞是第三人稱單數，答案是選項（C）。

單字 necklace 項鍊

8. (D)

翻譯 反對計劃的人們覺得不自在。

解析 因為具「人們」之意的 people 是複數，答案是選項（D）。

單字 against 反對 ｜ plan 計劃

9. (A)

翻譯 被森林圍繞的湖看起來很美。

解析 因為主詞是第三人稱單數 lake，答案是選項（A）。

單字 surround 圍繞

10. (D)

翻譯 問了他很多問題的訪者感到失望。

解析 因為主詞 interviewer 是單數，答案是選項（D）。

單字 interviewer 訪者

題型 02 簡單式

D 應用練習　　P. 239

1. (A)　2. (D)　3. (C)　4. (D)　5. (B)
6. (C)　7. (D)　8. (A)　9. (C)　10. (D)

1. (A)

翻譯 每年有數百萬美國人自願做出改變。

解析 因為主詞是複數，答案是選項（A）。

單字 volunteer 自願｜
make a difference 做出改變

2. (D)

翻譯 瑪莉每天通勤去工作。

解析 因為主詞是第三人稱單數，答案是選項（D）。

單字 commute 通勤

3. (C)

翻譯 銷售在去年上升了 15%。

解析 因為是發生在過去的事，答案是選項（C）。

4. (D)

翻譯 卡列拉在上個月被調到芝加哥辦公室。

解析 因為時態是過去式，主詞是單數，答案是選項（D）。

單字 transfer 調動

5. (B)

翻譯 農業曾是南韓的蓬勃發展的產業。

解析 因為時態是過去式，主詞是單數，答案是選項（B）。

單字 farming 農業｜industry 產業

6. (C)

翻譯 有一次我們考慮與保險公司合併。

解析 因為時態是過去式，答案是選項（C）。

單字 consider 考慮｜merge 合併｜
insurance 保險

7. (D)

翻譯 我們將要發展新策略。

解析 因為主詞是 we，答案是選項（D）。

單字 develop 發展｜strategy 策略

8. (A)

翻譯 要控制這個局勢會很困難。

解析 因為主詞是 it，所以選項中除了選項（A）以外，其他都不符合。

單字 control 控制｜situation 局勢

9. (C)

翻譯 你抵達東京後，立刻打電話給帕克先生。

解析 在表時間或條件的副詞子句中，可以用現在式代替未來式，答案是選項（C）。

單字 arrive 抵達｜immediately 立刻

10. (D)

翻譯 如果下雨，我們會取消活動。

解析 在表時間或條件的副詞子句中，可以用現在式代替未來式，答案是選項（D）。

單字 cancel 取消｜event 活動

題型 **03** 完成式和進行式

D 應用練習　　P. 245

1. (A)　2. (D)　3. (C)　4. (A)　5. (C)
6. (D)　7. (B)　8. (C)　9. (C)　10. (D)

1. (A)

翻譯 根據專家的說法，經濟會持續好轉。

解析 因為主詞是單數，並且正在進行中，答案是選項（A）。

單字 expert 專家｜economy 經濟

2. (D)

翻譯 公立圖書館在五月會搬到新地點。

解析 因為主詞是單數，又要用現在進行式代替未來式，答案是選項（D）。

單字 public library 公立圖書館｜location 地點

3. (C)

翻譯 麥克並沒有出席儀式，因為他正和一位客戶會面。

解析 要用過去進行式，答案是選項（C）。

單字 attend 出席｜ceremony 儀式

4. (A)

翻譯 我們所有人將在下個月加班。

解析 next month 表未來，空格要用未來進行式，答案是選項（A）。

單字 work overtime 加班

5. (C)

翻譯 該地區由高山組成。

解析 主詞是單數，consist 是不能用進行式的動詞，所以答案是選項（C）。

單字 consist of 組成

6. (D)

翻譯 這本小冊子包含了整年度的活動資訊。

解析 因為主詞是第三人稱單數，所以答案是選項（D）。

單字 pamphlet 小冊子｜contain 包含｜annual 年度的

7. (B)

翻譯 他們已經寫完了行銷報告。

解析 前面有 have，要用現在完成式，答案是選項（B）。

單字 already 已經｜marketing 行銷

8. (C)

翻譯 我們公司已經營運了近十年。

解析 要用現在完成式，答案是選項（C）。

單字 in business 營運

9. (C)

翻譯 我們回家時，傑克已經前往機場了。

解析 要用過去完成式，答案是選項（C）。

10. (D)

翻譯 到本週末時，我們會賣超過 500 本。

解析 要用未來完成式，答案是選項（D）。

單字 copy 本

題型 **04** 主動和被動語態

D 應用練習　　P. 251

1. (C)	2. (A)	3. (B)	4. (D)	5. (B)
6. (A)	7. (B)	8. (A)	9. (D)	10. (C)

---

1. (C)

翻譯 專家說那樣的意外可以避免。

解析 因為助動詞後要接被動語態，答案是選項（C）。

單字 expert 專家｜ accident 意外｜ prevent 避免

2. (A)

翻譯 這本書應該要寄給教授。

解析 因為助動詞後要接被動語態，答案是選項（A）。

單字 send 寄｜ professor 教授

3. (B)

翻譯 午餐正由女傭服務。

解析 因為是過去進行式被動語態，答案是選項（B）。

單字 serve 服務｜ housemaid 女傭

4. (D)

翻譯 這些桌子被裝飾成一種獨特的樣貌。

解析 因為是過去進行式被動語態，答案是選項（D）。

單字 table 桌子｜ decorate 裝飾｜ unique 獨特的

5. (B)

翻譯 她的網路連線已經被她爸媽封鎖。

解析 因為是現在完成式被動語態，答案是選項（B）。

單字 access 使用權利｜ block 封鎖

6. (A)

翻譯 這些建築物曾被本公司建造。

解析 因為是現在完成式被動語態，答案是選項（A）。

單字 construct 建造

7. (B)

翻譯 安妮當時被認為是全國最聰明的學生。

解析 因為是過去式被動語態，所以答案是選項（B）。

單字 believe 認為｜ bright 聰明

8. (A)

翻譯 實習生被鼓勵要更努力工作。

解析 因為是過去式被動語態，答案是選項（A）。

單字 intern 實習生｜ encourage 鼓勵

9. (D)

翻譯 你被要求出席所有員工會議。

解析 因為是現在式被動語態,答案是選項（D）。

單字 require 要求 | staff 員工

10. (C)

翻譯 他被公認是史上最傑出的發明家。

解析 因為是過去式被動語態,答案是選項（C）。

單字 inventor 發明家 | history 歷史

題型 05 假設語氣

(D) 應用練習　　P. 257

1. (C)　2. (A)　3. (C)　4. (D)　5. (C)
6. (B)　7. (A)　8. (D)　9. (A)　10. (B)

1. (C)

翻譯 如果我有更多錢,我會搬到加拿大。

解析 是與現在事實相反的假設法,並省略if,此時主詞和動詞要倒置,答案是選項（C）。

2. (A)

翻譯 如果她更有冒險精神,她就會冒更多險。

解析 在與現在事實相反的假設法中,若 if 子句中有 be 動詞,be 動詞一定要用 were。答案是選項（A）。

單字 adventurous 有冒險精神的 |
take a risk 冒險

3. (C)

翻譯 如果當初她不在那裡,就不會受傷。

解析 是與過去事實相反的假設法,答案是選項（C）。

單字 hurt 受傷

4. (D)

翻譯 如果他們更小心一些,就可以避免危機。

解析 是與過去事實相反的假設法,答案是選項（D）。

單字 careful 小心的 | avoid 避免 |
crisis 危機

5. (C)

翻譯 要是你把他介紹給我,我們現在早就是好友了。

解析 是混合假設法,答案是選項（C）。

6. (B)

翻譯 如果公司承擔那個風險,今天早就賺更多錢了

解析 是混合假設法,答案是選項（B）。

單字 take a risk 承擔風險

7. (A)

翻譯 如果你要參訪我們的大學,別猶豫務必聯絡我們的校長。

解析 在使用 should 的假設法中省略 if,主詞和動詞要倒置,答案是選項（A）。

單字 hesitate 猶豫 | president 校長

8. (D)

翻譯 要是你戒菸，你的健康會獲得改善。

解析 是使用 were to 的假設法，答案是選項（D）。

9. (A)

翻譯 委員會要求更多時間去解決問題。

解析 表要求的 demand 若接 that 子句，動詞要用原型或用 should，答案是選項（A）。

單字 committee 委員會 | demand 要求

10. (B)

翻譯 專家強調公司要鼓勵員工發揮想像力。

解析 表主張的 insist 若接 that 子句，動詞要用原型或用 should，答案是選項（B）。

單字 insist 強調 | imaginative 有想像力的

Quick Test   P. 258

1. (C)	2. (B)	3. (A)	4. (B)	5. (D)
6. (A)	7. (D)	8. (B)	9. (C)	10. (B)
11. (A)	12. (D)	13. (C)	14. (C)	15. (A)
16. (C)	17. (D)	18. (B)	19. (D)	20. (A)

1. (C)

翻譯 很少有人願意去質疑執行長。

解析 因為 few 是複數代名詞，答案是選項（C）。

單字 willing to 願意 | challenge 挑戰

2. (B)

翻譯 半數學生學習英文已有八年之久。

解析 「部分＋ of ＋全部」後面接的動詞要跟「全部」一致。因為 students 是複數，答案是選項（B）。

3. (A)

翻譯 市政府正致力於改善公路安全。

解析 這題是字彙試題。從句子內容來看，「市政府正在努力」的句意最適合，答案是選項（A）。

單字 effort 努力 | protection 保護 | asset 資產 | laboratory 實驗室

4. (B)

翻譯 大學在社會中扮演重要角色。

解析 因為主詞是複數，動詞也要用複數形，所以答案是選項（B）。

5. (D)

翻譯 公司在去年賺得豐厚利潤。

解析 因為句子內容很清楚是發生在過去的事情，答案是選項（D）。

單字 profit 利潤

6. (A)

翻譯 如果是陰天，機器就不會正常運轉。

解析 在表條件的副詞子句中，可以用現在式代替未來式，答案是選項（A）。

單字 cloudy 多雲的 | properly 正常地

7. (D)

翻譯 你應該定期向你的主管報告。

解析 這題是字彙題。因為要定期地跟主管做報告，答案是選項（D）。

單字 report 報告 ｜ supervisor 主管 ｜ regretful 遺憾的 ｜ regular 定期的

8. (B)

翻譯 電話響時葛瑞格正在跟客人打招呼。

解析 表在過去的某個時間，因發生了某事而妨礙了另一件事，所以要用過去進行式，答案是選項（B）。

9. (C)

翻譯 明天此時，我們將會開車去洛杉磯。

解析 要用未來進行式，答案是選項（C）。

10. (B)

翻譯 我們公司自 2002 年就與市政府合作。

解析 因為 since 通常要和現在完成式搭配使用，答案是選項（B）。

單字 government 政府

11. (A)

翻譯 這間大學昨天發布了一份新報告。

解析 這題是字彙題。因為報告是要用發布的，答案是選項（A）。

單字 release 發布 ｜ arrive 抵達

12. (D)

翻譯 這樣的錯誤是可以被避免的。

解析 因為助動詞後要接被動語態，答案是選項（D）。

單字 avoid 避免

13. (C)

翻譯 他們應該被告知那項更動。

解析 因為助動詞後要接被動語態，答案是選項（C）。

單字 inform 告知

14. (C)

翻譯 這個活動由一間當地教堂籌辦。

解析 是過去式被動語態，答案是選項（C）。

單字 event 活動 ｜ organize 籌辦

15. (A)

翻譯 如果你有任何不滿，可以寄信給市長。

解析 是使用 should 的假設法。若省略 if，主詞和動詞要倒置，答案是選項（A）。

單字 complaint 不滿 ｜ mayor 市長

16. (C)

翻譯 如果我們可以減少花費，就成功在望。

解析 這題是字彙題。因為節省花費就會成功，所以答案是選項（C）。

單字 cost 花費 ｜ reduce 減少 ｜ invent 發明 ｜ offer 提供

17–20.

翻譯 感謝您購買我們的洗衣機。我們的洗衣機自 2010 年來，已被數千萬名美國人所使用。就像那些消費者一樣，您將會對這台洗衣機感到滿意。請上我們的官網瀏覽這台洗衣機的更多資訊。

解析

17. (D)

Thank you 要後接介系詞 for，答案是選項（D）。

18. (B)

因為 since 通常要搭配現在完成式，同時又是被動語態，所以答案是選項（B）。

19. (D)

因為前句也提到了顧客，所以接選項（D）是最合適的。

20. (A)

information 要接介系詞 about，答案是選項（A）。

④ 動狀詞

題型 01 不定詞

D 應用練習　　P. 265

| 1. (B) | 2. (A) | 3. (B) | 4. (C) | 5. (B) |
| 6. (A) | 7. (D) | 8. (A) | 9. (B) | 10. (C) |

1. (B)

翻譯 學習新語言需要時間。

解析 因為 to 不定詞可以當句子的主詞，答案是選項（B）。

單字 call for 需要

2. (A)

翻譯 發明新機器需要想像力。

解析 因為 to 不定詞可以當句子的主詞，答案是選項（A）。

單字 invent 發明｜require 需要｜imagination 想像力

3. (B)

翻譯 他們計劃很快去首爾遊覽。

解析 plan 要接不定詞當受詞，答案是選項（B）。

單字 plan to 計劃

4. (C)

翻譯 我們想要改善我們的城市。

解析 動詞 want 要用不定詞當受詞，答案是選項（C）。

5. (B)

翻譯 在 1960 年代，生產廉價服飾是當時的潮流。

解析 這個句子用 to 不定詞當主詞補語，答案是選項（B）。

單字 trend 潮流｜produce 生產

6. (A)

翻譯 這份報告的目的是要討論保護環境的新方法。

解析 這個句子用不定詞當主詞補語，答案是選項（A）。

單字 purpose 目的｜protect 保護

7. (D)

翻譯 我們沒有辦法預測未來。

解析 way 接不定詞的意思是「做……的方式」，答案是選項（D）。

單字 predict 預測 | future 未來

8. (A)

翻譯 目前有建立更多公園的計劃。

解析 plan 接不定詞的意思是「計劃去……」，答案是選項（A）。

單字 plan 計劃 | build 建立

9. (B)

翻譯 他的指示令人難以遵循。

解析 「too . . . to . . .」的意思是「太……而不能……」，答案是選項（B）。

單字 instruction 指示 | follow 遵循

10. (C)

翻譯 這項任務足夠簡單可以完成。

解析 本句是 enough 接不定詞片語，答案是選項（C）。

單字 task 任務 | complete 完成

題型 02 to 不定詞和不含 to 的不定詞

(D) 應用練習　P. 271

1. (C)　2. (A)　3. (C)　4. (D)　5. (A)
6. (A)　7. (B)　8. (D)　9. (B)　10. (D)

---

1. (C)

翻譯 我們希望可以在這個城市持續經營企業。

解析 因為 wish 要用 to 不定詞來當受詞，答案是選項（C）。

單字 continue 持續 | business 企業

2. (A)

翻譯 我們要為我們的錯誤道歉。

解析 因為 would like 要用 to 不定詞來當受詞，答案是選項（A）。

單字 apologize 道歉 | mistake 錯誤

3. (C)

翻譯 他買得起一支新的智慧型手機。

解析 因為 can afford 要接 to 不定詞，答案是選項（C）。

單字 afford to 負擔得起

4. (D)

翻譯 我們負擔不起到國外旅遊。

解析 因為 can't afford 要接 to 不定詞，答案是選項（D）。

單字 can't afford to 負擔不起

5. (A)

翻譯 這些消費者願意花更多錢在娛樂上。

解析 因為 be willing 要接 to 不定詞，所以答案是選項（A）。

單字 consumer 消費者 | entertainment 娛樂

6. (A)

翻譯 遺憾地是，這間公司一定會倒閉。

解析 因為 be sure 要接 to 不定詞，答案是選項（A）。

單字 be sure to 一定會

7. (B)

翻譯 經理提醒他們關燈。

解析 因為「remind ＋受詞」要接 to 不定詞，答案是選項（B）。

單字 manager 經理 ｜ remind 提醒

8. (D)

翻譯 我們要員工多花時間陪家人。

解析 因為「want ＋受詞」要接 to 不定詞，答案是選項（D）。

9. (B)

翻譯 保羅看著他的孩子們打高爾夫球。

解析 因為「see ＋受詞」要接原型動詞，答案是選項（B）。

單字 golf 高爾夫球

10. (D)

翻譯 他們聽到機器發出怪聲。

解析 因為「hear ＋受詞」要後接原型動詞，答案是選項（D）。

單字 machine 機器

題型 03 動名詞

Ｄ 應用練習　　　　P. 277

1. (C)	2. (D)	3. (B)	4. (C)	5. (D)
6. (A)	7. (D)	8. (B)	9. (A)	10. (D)

1. (C)

翻譯 這個慈善會的主要目標是照顧貧困的孩子。

解析 因為動名詞可當 be 動詞後的主詞補語，答案是選項（C）。

單字 charity 慈善會

2. (D)

翻譯 教育的功能是培養良好公民。

解析 因為動名詞可當 be 動詞後的主詞補語，答案是選項（D）。

單字 function 功能 ｜ produce 製造

3. (B)

翻譯 技工把我的汽車修復完成。

解析 因為 finish 的受詞一定要用動名詞，答案是選項（B）。

單字 mechanic 技工 ｜ repair 修復

4. (C)

翻譯 始終相信自己，你就會成功。

解析 因為是「繼續」之意，keep 後要接動名詞，答案是選項（C）。

5. (D)

翻譯 克蕾拉建議在多倫多和客戶見面。

解析 雖然是未來的事，若實現的可能很大，要用動名詞當受詞，答案是選項（D）。

單字 suggest 建議 ｜ client 客戶

6. (A)

翻譯 你介意等一下嗎？

解析 因為及物動詞 mind 的受詞要用動名詞，答案是選項（A）。

單字 mind 介意 ｜ for a second 一下子

7. (D)

翻譯 除了減輕壓力，美妙的音樂也會讓你感到愉快。

解析 介系詞片語 in addition to 接動詞時，一定要用動名詞，答案是選項（D）。

單字 reduce 減輕 ｜ stress 壓力

8. (B)

翻譯 他們不但不感到驚訝，反而欣喜接受我們的決定。

解析 介系詞片語 instead of 接動詞時，一定要用動名詞，答案是選項（B）。

單字 decision 決定

9. (A)

翻譯 我們付款給你將不會有困難。

解析 have no difficulty 要接動名詞，答案是選項（A）。

單字 pay back 付款

10. (D)

翻譯 她每天花兩小時健身。

解析 「spend ＋時間」一定要接動名詞，答案是選項（D）。

單字 work out 健身

題型 04 分詞

Ⓓ 應用練習　　P. 283

1. (C)	2. (D)	3. (A)	4. (C)	5. (A)
6. (D)	7. (B)	8. (D)	9. (B)	10. (A)

1. (C)

翻譯 瑪莉在大會發表了激動人心的演說。

解析 因為「演說激動人心」，所以要用現在分詞，答案是選項（C）。

單字 inspiring 激動人心的 ｜ speech 演說 ｜ conference 大會

2. (D)

翻譯 對珍妮佛來說，表演是一份很有意義的工作。

解析 為「表演有回報」，所以要用現在分詞，答案是選項（D）。

單字 acting 表演 ｜ rewarding 有意義的

3. (A)

翻譯 萬物都依賴陽光。

解析 因為是「有生命的」東西，所以要用現在分詞，所以答案是選項（A）。

單字 living things 萬物 ｜ depend on 依賴

4. (C)

翻譯 留下來的賓客都被小丑娛樂。

解析 因為是客人主動「留下來的」,所以要用現在分詞,答案是選項(C)。

單字 remaining 剩餘的 | entertain 娛樂 | clown 小丑

5. (A)

翻譯 沒有人對結果感到高興。

解析 因為是人「感到高興的」,所以要用過去分詞,答案是選項(A)。

單字 result 結果

6. (D)

翻譯 滿意的顧客持續購買我們的商品。

解析 因為是人「感到滿足的」,所以要用過去分詞,答案是選項(D)。

單字 product 商品

7. (B)

翻譯 老師應該幫助學生發掘他們潛在的才能。

解析 因為才能是「被隱藏的」,所以要用過去分詞,答案是選項(B)。

單字 discover 發掘 | talent 才能

8. (D)

翻譯 這個區域以肥沃的土壤而聞名。

解析 因為地區是「被知道的」,所以要用過去分詞,所以答案是選項(D)。

單字 area 區域 | soil 土壤

9. (B)

翻譯 我們對服務感到失望。

解析 因為是人「感到失望的」,所以要用過去分詞,答案是選項(B)。

單字 disappointed 失望的

10. (A)

翻譯 關於這個組織的事實讓人震驚。

解析 因為是「事實讓人震驚」,所以要用現在分詞,答案是選項(A)。

單字 organization 組織

題型 05 分詞構句

D 應用練習　　P. 289

1. (C)	2. (A)	3. (D)	4. (C)	5. (A)
6. (D)	7. (B)	8. (C)	9. (A)	10. (D)

1. (C)

翻譯 他們不想吵醒她,安靜地離開這個房間。

解析 分詞構句副詞子句是主動要用以現在分詞開頭,將分詞片語形成否定句時,要在分詞前加 not,答案是選項(C)。

2. (A)

翻譯 他意識到之前吃得不多,就為自己準備了餐點。

解析 副詞子句是主動且與主要子句同時發生,要以現在分詞開頭,所以答案是選項(A)

單字 realize 意識

3. (D)

翻譯 由於他的女兒在住院，他無法專心工作。

解析 若要將副詞子句改成分詞片語，且副詞子句的主詞和主要子句的主詞不同，要保留副詞子句的主詞，然後將動詞改成現在分詞。答案是選項（D）。

單字 concentrate 專心

4. (C)

翻譯 男子穿越街道時，看到一輛卡車向他駛近。

解析 副詞子句是主動且與主要子句同時發生，要以現在分詞開頭，所以答案是選項（C）

單字 approach 靠近

5. (A)

翻譯 他以前在國外生活過，因此自願轉調到倫敦。

解析 形成分詞構句的副詞子句，比主要子句更早發生，所以要用 Having p.p. 來起始分詞構句。

單字 volunteer 自願 | transfer 轉調

6. (D)

翻譯 錯誤確認後，她的主管把責任歸咎於她。

解析 若要變成分詞構句，且原副詞子句的主詞和主要子句的主詞不同，要用完成式分詞構句。另外，因為錯誤是被發現的，所以要用被動語態，答案是選項（D）。

單字 error 錯誤 | identify 確認 | supervisor 主管 | blame 過錯

7. (B)

翻譯 看過電影後，他們去一家韓國餐廳。

解析 因為看完電影後再去韓國餐廳，所以要用完成式分詞構句。答案是選項（B）。

8. (C)

翻譯 解決了一個問題，我們又碰到另一個。

解析 空格的部分屬於過去較早的時間，所以要用完成式分詞構句。答案是選項（C）。

9. (A)

翻譯 這本書由一位真正的專家撰寫，是每位家長的必看讀物。

解析 因為書是先被撰寫，所以可以刪除原句「Having been written by a true expert」的 Having been，答案是選項（A）。

單字 expert 專家 | must 必要的事物

10. (D)

翻譯 因為只有少數人知道這個食譜，它始終是個秘密。

解析 因為食譜是被知道，所以要用被動語態分詞構句，答案是選項（D）。

單字 recipe 食譜 | secret 祕密

1. (C)	2. (A)	3. (D)	4. (B)	5. (A)
6. (D)	7. (A)	8. (B)	9. (C)	10. (D)
11. (B)	12. (D)	13. (A)	14. (C)	15. (C)
16. (D)	17. (B)	18. (D)	19. (A)	20. (B)

1. (C)

翻譯 做正確的事需要勇氣。

解析 因為 to 不定詞可以當句子的主詞,答案是選項(D)。

2. (A)

翻譯 大家都想擁有快樂的人生。

解析 want 要用 to 不定詞當受詞,答案是選項(A)。

3. (D)

翻譯 我們的使命是保護環境。

解析 這是字彙試題。選項(B)無論是意思還是文法都不符合。選項(D)是最適合的單字,所以是答案。

單字 mission 使命 | protect 保護 | branch 分公司 | effort 努力 | imagination 想像力

4. (B)

翻譯 他們買不起昂貴的商品。

解析 因為 can't afford 要接 to 不定詞,答案是選項(B)。

5. (A)

翻譯 這家公司願意和市長討論這件事。

解析 因為 willing 要接 to 不定詞,答案是選項(A)。

單字 willing to 願意 | mayor 市長

6. (D)

翻譯 所有家長都希望自己的孩子過得快樂。

解析 因為「want +受詞」要接 to 不定詞,所以是選項(D)。

7. (A)

翻譯 我們看到他們相互爭論。

解析 因為「see +受詞」要接原形不定詞,答案是選項(A)。

8. (B)

翻譯 這計劃有可能會為這個城市帶來更多工作。

解析 這是字彙試題。要用表未來可能性的單字,答案是選項(B)。

單字 likely 可能會 | disappointed 失望的

9. (C)

翻譯 他們已經安裝好新的電腦網路。

解析 finish 的受詞要用動名詞,所以答案是選項(C)。

單字 install 安裝

10. (D)

翻譯 我們建議開發更多環保產品。

解析 因為 suggest 的受詞不能用 to 不定詞,要用動名詞,答案是選項(D)。

單字 develop 開發 | eco-friendly 環保的

11. (B)

翻譯 如果你不守規矩，你會惹禍上身。

解析 這是字彙試題。不遵守規矩會產生負面結果，答案是選項（B）。

單字 obey 遵守 | regret 後悔 | ignore 忽略

12. (D)

翻譯 中國的空氣品質是很嚴重的問題。

解析 這是字彙試題。因為「空氣的品質」是最適合的，答案是選項（D）。

單字 statement 聲明 | data 資料

13. (A)

翻譯 集郵在過去是一個令人感到滿足的嗜好。

解析 因為嗜好令人滿足，答案是選項（A）。

14. (C)

翻譯 我們很高興宣布新網站的推出。

解析 因為是人「感到高興的」，所以要用過去分詞，答案是選項（C）。

單字 pleased 高興的 | launch 推出

15. (C)

翻譯 美國經濟現況非常繁榮興盛。

解析 因為「美國經濟的現況」的意思最適合，答案是選項（C）。

單字 current 現在的 | state 聲明 | economy 經濟 | confused 疑惑的 | astonished 震驚的

16. (D)

翻譯 他的優勢之一在於有能力預測經濟變化。

解析 這是字彙試題。最適合的字是「長處、強項」，答案是選項（D）。

單字 strength 優勢 | predict 預測 | discount 折扣 | error 錯誤

17–20.

翻譯 親愛的帕克先生：

我哥哥和我從三月一日至四月二日，將到中國出差。在我們造訪北京的期間，我們想和您商談可能在中國發展的計劃。我們期待與您合作，一起同創造高利潤。

解析

17. (B)

因為是未來進行式，答案是選項（B）。

18. (D)

要放表「期間」之意的介系詞，答案是選項（D）。

19. (A)

因為知道 would like 的受詞要用 to 不定詞，答案是選項（A）。

20. (B)

因為要和前面的 possible projects 連接起來最適合，答案是選項（B）。

單字 profit 利潤 | adequate 適當的

⑤ 形容詞和副詞

題型 **01** 形容詞

D 應用練習　　P. 297

1. (A)　2. (C)　3. (A)　4. (D)　5. (C)
6. (D)　7. (B)　8. (D)　9. (B)　10. (C)

1. (A)

翻譯 維持健康體魄有很多方式。

解析 空格要放修飾名詞 body 的形容詞，答案是選項（A）。

單字 maintain 維持｜healthy 健康的｜healthily 健康地

2. (C)

翻譯 遺憾地是，我們沒有關於它所有的必要資訊。

解析 空格要放修飾名詞 information 的形容詞，答案是選項（C）。

單字 necessary 必要的｜necessarily 必要地｜necessity 必要性

3. (A)

翻譯 我覺得學習外語很有用處。

解析 因為要用形容詞當受詞補語的，答案是選項（A）。

單字 useful 有用的｜usefully 有用地｜usefulness 用處

4. (D)

翻譯 天氣讓我們難以盡情享受。

解析 因為要用形容詞當受詞補語，答案是選項（D）。

5. (C)

翻譯 他的主管給了他具體的指示。

解析 空格要放修飾名詞 instructions 的形容詞，答案是選項（C）。

單字 supervisor 主管｜specific 明確的｜specificity 明確性

6. (D)

翻譯 國家成功的主要原因在於人民的勤奮。

解析 空格要放修飾名詞 cause 的形容詞，答案是選項（D）。

單字 chief 主要的｜cause 原因｜diligence 勤奮｜chiefly 主要地

7. (B)

翻譯 這些結果和我們報告的結果很類似。

解析 因為要用形容詞當主詞補語，答案是選項（B）。

單字 result 結果｜similar 類似的｜similarly 類似地｜similarity 類似

8. (D)

翻譯 飯店價格如有更改，恕不另行通知。

解析 因為要用形容詞當主詞補語，所以答案是選項（D）。

單字 rate 價格｜subject to 受到……的影響

9. (B)

翻譯 願意繳付更高稅額的公民很少。

解析 因為「be willing to . . .」是「願意」的意思,答案是選項(B)。

單字 citizen 公民｜tax 稅｜
willingness 意願｜willingly 樂意地

10. (C)

翻譯 病患無法向護士解釋情況。

解析 因為「be unable to . . .」是「沒辦法……」之意,答案是選項(C)。

單字 patient 病患｜inability 無能

題型 02 副詞

D 應用練習　　P. 303

| 1. (C) | 2. (D) | 3. (B) | 4. (C) | 5. (D) |
| 6. (C) | 7. (B) | 8. (A) | 9. (B) | 10. (A) |

1. (C)

翻譯 所有人都非常享受派對。

解析 副詞可以修飾副詞,答案是選項(C)。

單字 greatness 偉大

2. (D)

翻譯 幸運地是,沒有人在車禍中受傷。

解析 副詞可以修飾整個句子,答案是選項(D)。

單字 injure 受傷｜fortune 財產｜
fortunate 幸運的

3. (B)

翻譯 我們通常花兩天處理國際訂單。

解析 要用頻率副詞,答案是選項(B)。

單字 process 處理｜order 訂單｜
regularity 規則性｜average 平均

4. (C)

翻譯 大笑一直被認為是減輕壓力的好方法。

解析 空格可以放頻率副詞,答案是選項(C)。

單字 reduce 減輕｜constant 不斷的｜
regular 定期的

5. (D)

翻譯 這個方法很少被認為是傳統的方式。

解析 空格只能放副詞,答案是選項(D)。

單字 method 方法｜scarcely 很少｜
traditional 傳統的｜scarcity 缺乏｜
scarce 缺乏的

6. (C)

翻譯 執行長很少花時間陪家人。

解析 空格只能放副詞,答案是選項(C)。

單字 CEO 執行長｜seldom 很少

7. (B)

翻譯 上個月服飾價格下跌。同樣地,油價也下跌。

解析 空格要放表「兩個句子意思相似」的連接副詞,答案是選項(B)。

單字 price 價格｜oil price 油價｜
similarly 同樣地｜similar 同樣的

PARTS
5&6

⑤
形容詞和副詞

題型
02
副詞

8. (A)

翻譯 她在巴黎出生長大。因此，法語是她的母語。

解析 空格要放表因果關係的連接副詞，答案是選項（A）。

單字 raise 養育 | therefore 因此 | native language 母語

9. (B)

翻譯 導遊很困惑，以至於無法思考清楚。

解析 因為要放片語「so . . . that」，所以答案是選項（B）。

單字 tour guide 導遊 | confused 困惑

10. (A)

翻譯 我們還未決定是否要收購該公司。

解析 空格只能放副詞，答案是選項（A）。

單字 decide 決定 | acquire 收購

題型 **03** 比較級和最高級

D 應用練習　　P. 309

1. (A)	2. (D)	3. (C)	4. (D)	5. (B)
6. (C)	7. (A)	8. (D)	9. (C)	10. (A)

1. (A)

翻譯 請盡快通知我們您的決定。

解析 片語「as . . . as」中間要用原型形容詞，答案是選項（A）。

單字 inform 通知 | decision 決定

2. (D)

翻譯 這支手機的價格比我的數位相機多一倍。

解析 片語「as . . . as」中間要用原型形容詞，答案是選項（D）。

單字 digital 數位的

3. (C)

翻譯 有時高中老師比大學教授更有效率。

解析 因為有 than，所以要用比較級，答案是選項（C）。

單字 efficient 有效率的 | professor 教授

4. (D)

翻譯 你練習越多，面試準備的就越好。

解析 因為是片語「the + 比較級 , the + 比較級」，答案是選項（D）。

單字 practice 練習 | prepared 準備好的

5. (B)

翻譯 一般來說，這些工人比我們忙碌得多。

解析 選項中有強調比較級的副詞 a lot，答案是選項（B）。

單字 generally 普遍地

6. (C)

翻譯 這家公司現在處於更好的狀況，可吸引美國消費者。

解析 選項中有強調形容詞比較級 better 的副詞 much，答案是選項（C）。

單字 appeal to 吸引 | consumer 消費者

7. (A)

翻譯 麥可是他們之中最聰明的學生。

解析 空格要放最高級形容詞，答案是選項（A）。

8. (D)

翻譯 她是日本最知名的企業家。

解析 空格要放最高級形容詞，答案是選項（D）。

單字 entrepreneur 企業家

9. (C)

翻譯 這是目前減少汙染最有效的方式。

解析 空格要放強調最高級的用語，答案是選項（C）。

單字 reduce 減少 | pollution 汙染

10. (A)

翻譯 這是 1970 年代最重要的發現之一。

解析 空格要放名詞的複數形，答案是選項（A）。選項（D）不能放進空格裡。

單字 discovery 發現

Quick Test　　　　　　P. 310

1. (A)	2. (B)	3. (D)	4. (B)	5. (C)
6. (C)	7. (D)	8. (A)	9. (C)	10. (D)
11. (B)	12. (A)	13. (D)	14. (B)	15. (D)
16. (C)	17. (D)	18. (B)	19. (A)	20. (C)

1. (A)

翻譯 這本書探討基本會計原則。

解析 這是字彙試題。空格要放「探討某主題」的字，答案是選項（A）。

單字 deal with 探討 | basic 基本的 | accounting 會計 | principle 原則

2. (B)

翻譯 我們已寄出所有的必要文件。

解析 空格要放修飾名詞的形容詞，所以答案是選項（B）。

單字 necessary 必要的 | necessity 必要性 | necessarily 必然地

3. (D)

翻譯 我覺得要達成我的目標很困難。

解析 空格要放當受詞補語用的形容詞，答案是選項（D）。

單字 achieve 達成 | goal 目標

4. (B)

翻譯 我們的首要興趣是幫助企業在財務上取得成功。

解析 空格要放修飾名詞的形容詞，答案是選項（B）。

單字 chief 首要的 | financially 財務地

5. (C)

翻譯 他們的感恩節傳統和我們的很類似。

解析 空格要放當主詞補語用的形容詞，答案是選項（C）。

單字 tradition 傳統 | similar 類似 | similarity 相似處 | similarly 類似地

6. (C)

翻譯 我們的退款政策如有更改，恕不另行通知。

解析 「subject to . . .」是「受到……影響」的意思，答案是選項（C）。

單字 refund 退款 | policy 政策

7. (D)

翻譯 企業的主要功能是滿足客戶的需求。

解析 這是字彙試題。空格要放能讓句子意思最完整的單字，所以答案是選項（D）。

單字 principal 主要的 | function 功能 | satisfy 滿足 | rapid 迅速的

8. (A)

翻譯 他們一直想要為孩童建造一座公共圖書館。

解析 空格只能放副詞，答案是選項（A）。

單字 regularity 規則性 | constant 持續不斷的

9. (C)

翻譯 這位新員工幾乎不了解我們對他的要求。

解析 空格只能放副詞，答案是選項（C）。

單字 employee 員工 | hardly 幾乎不 | scarce 缺乏的 | negative 負面的

10. (D)

翻譯 他們很少參觀這間博物館，因為離他們的房子很遠。

解析 空格只能放副詞，答案是選項（D）

單字 rarely 很少地 | rare 很少的 | rarity 稀罕之物

11. (B)

翻譯 這個湖是如此美麗，吸引了很多遊客。

解析 片語「so . . . that」表結果，所以答案是選項（B）。

單字 attract 吸引 | tourist 遊客

12. (A)

翻譯 價格包括飯店和導遊費用。

解析 最適合放進空格的字是選項（A）。

單字 rent 租借 | export 出口

13. (D)

翻譯 茱莉亞比她的同事更有能力。

解析 因為空格後接 than，空格要放比較級，答案是選項（D）。

單字 competent 有能力的

14. (B)

翻譯 我們的產品比他們的受歡迎多了。

解析 空格要放強調比較級的副詞，答案是選項（B）。

單字 product 產品

15. (D)

翻譯 這本是關於行銷寫得最棒的書。

解析 空格要放形容詞最高級，所以答案是選項（D）。

單字 marketing 行銷

16. (C)

翻譯 做為企業家是要求很高的工作，因為要付出很大的努力。

解析 空格要放能表「because 造成的結果」的形容詞，所以答案是選項（C）。

單字 entrepreneur 企業家｜demanding 要求很高｜effective 有效率的

17–20.

翻譯 您想嚐嚐異國美食嗎？那麼請來參加我們在三月三日的年度美食節！今年，您可以品嚐到法式和韓式料理。來參加我們的美食節，並評判韓式料理是否比法式料理美味。

解析

17. (D)

空格要放形容詞，答案是選項（D）。

18. (B)

因為後面有一句提到 Come to our festival，所以可以知道是在 festival 發生的事，故答案是選項（B）能合句子的脈絡。

19. (A)

從前後句脈絡來看，要放「決定」之意的字，答案是選項（A）。

20. (C)

因為空格接 than，空格要放比較級，答案是選項（C）。

單字 annual 年度的｜festival 節慶

❻ 介系詞和連接詞 / 關係代名詞
題型 **01** 介系詞

Ⓓ 應用練習　　P. 317

1. (A) 2. (B) 3. (C) 4. (B) 5. (D)
6. (A) 7. (C) 8. (D) 9. (B) 10. (D)

1. (A)

翻譯 你要在週五前提出申請。

解析 要放有「在……前」之意的介系詞 by，答案是選項（A）。

單字 application 申請｜submit 提出

2. (B)

翻譯 你的觀光簽證到月底前都還有效。

解析 要放有「直到……」之意的介系詞 until，答案是選項（B）。

單字 visa 簽證｜valid 有效

3. (C)

翻譯 音樂會將在整個三月的週末舉行。

解析 要放有「整個……期間」之意的介系詞 throughout，答案是選項（C）。

單字 concert 音樂會｜hold 舉行

4. (B)

翻譯 您可以在十天內將瑕疵商品退貨。

解析 因為是「在一定期間內」的意思，答案是選項（B）。

單字 return 退貨｜faulty 瑕疵的｜item 品項

5. (D)

翻譯 郵局位在銀行和烘焙店之間。

解析 因為要由具「在兩個對象之間」之意的 between 來表現，答案是選項（D）。

單字 be located 位於

6. (A)

翻譯 一些美籍遊客沿著海灘漫步。

解析 因為要由具「沿著……」之意的 along 來表現，答案是選項（A）。

單字 tourist 遊客 | beach 海灘

7. (C)

翻譯 由於健康不佳，他45歲就退休了。

解析 因為要由具「因為……」之意的 on account of 來表現，答案是選項（C）。

單字 retire 退休

8. (D)

翻譯 執行長針對公司的產品安全回答提問。

解析 因為要由具「關於……」之意的 concerning 來表現，答案是選項（D）。

單字 safety 安全 | product 產品

9. (B)

翻譯 除了週四，博物館每天開放。

解析 因為要由具「除……之外」之意的 except 來表現，答案是選項（B）。

單字 museum 博物館

10. (D)

翻譯 電子書除了便利，還比紙本書更便宜。

解析 因為要由具「此外」之意的 in addition to 來表現，答案是選項（D）。

單字 print 印刷

題型 **02** 對等連接詞

Ⓓ 應用練習　　P. 323

1. (C)	2. (D)	3. (B)	4. (D)	5. (A)
6. (B)	7. (A)	8. (A)	9. (D)	10. (C)

1. (C)

翻譯 他們工作了好幾個小時，然後就變得疲倦。

解析 空格要放對等連接詞 and，答案是選項（C）。

2. (D)

翻譯 我們邀請約翰加入派對，但他決定不參加。

解析 因為兩個句子的意思是相反的，答案是選項（D）。

3. (B)

翻譯 帶你的外套，不然你會覺得很冷。

解析 命令句後加具「否則」之意的 or，答案是選項（B）。

4. (D)

翻譯 我們無法決定要做什麼，因為我們沒有所有的必要資訊。

解析 for 當連接詞時表「原因」，答案是選項（D）。

單字 decide 決定 | necessary 必要的

5. (A)

翻譯 孩童可以玩遊戲同時學習重要的事物。

解析 「both A and B」是常見的相關連接詞，答案是選項（A）。

6. (B)

翻譯 新產品不僅創新，而且也不貴。

解析 「not only A but also B」也是很重要的相關連接詞，答案是選項（B）。

單字 innovative 創新的｜
affordable 付得起的

7. (A)

翻譯 成功的候選人應該會說英語或法語。

解析 「either A or B」也是很重要的相關連接詞，答案是選項（A）。

單字 candidate 候選人

8. (A)

翻譯 布萊恩和他的哥哥英文都說不好。

解析 「neither A nor B」也是很重要的相關連接詞。答案是選項（A）。

9. (D)

翻譯 新員工或她主管都被允許出席會議。

解析 「either A or B」動詞要由靠近動詞的名詞決定，所以本句是由 B 決定，答案是選項（D）。

單字 employee 員工｜ supervisor 主管

10. (C)

翻譯 不管是艾瑪或她妹妹，都無法說服他留下來。

解析 「neither A nor B」動詞要由靠近動詞的名詞決定，所以本句是由 B 決定。答案是選項（C）。

單字 convince 說服

題型 **03** 從屬連接詞

D 應用練習　　P. 329

1. (C)	2. (D)	3. (B)	4. (D)	5. (A)
6. (D)	7. (B)	8. (A)	9. (C)	10. (A)

1. (C)

翻譯 有人在我們開會時把門打開。

解析 空格要放具「當……的時候」之意的連接詞 while，答案是選項（C）。

單字 while 當……的時候

2. (D)

翻譯 我們聽到他們的消息才會做決定。

解析 空格要放具「直到……」之意的連接詞 until，答案是選項（D）。

3. (B)

翻譯 如果明天下雨，執行長會取消她的拜會。

解析 因為表條件，答案是選項（B）。

單字 call off 取消

4. (D)

翻譯 她在週末工作，以便能寫完報告。

解析 空格要放具「以便……」之意的連接詞 so that，答案是選項（D）。

單字 due to 由於

5. (A)

翻譯 儘管我們知道要獲勝不容易，但我們盡力而為。

解析 空格要放具「雖然」之意的連接詞，答案是選項（A）。

6. (D)

翻譯 儘管受到強烈批評，保羅還是決定不辭職。

解析 空格要放具「雖然」之意的連接詞，答案是選項（D）。

單字 strongly 強烈地｜criticize 批評｜resign 辭職

7. (B)

翻譯 沒有人知道新商品是否吸引消費者。

解析 空格要放具「是否」之意的連接詞，答案是選項（B）。

單字 appeal to 吸引｜consumer 消費者

8. (A)

翻譯 我們想知道是否可以幫助他們達成目標。

解析 空格要放具「是否」之意的連接詞，答案是選項（A）。

單字 achieve 達成｜goal 目標

9. (C)

翻譯 挑選對你的健康比較好的選擇。

解析 空格要放具「無論哪一個」之意的連接詞 whichever，答案是選項（C）。

10. (A)

翻譯 充分利用提供給你的任何事物。

解析 空格要放具「任何」之意的連接詞 whatever，答案是選項（A）。

單字 take advantage of 利用｜offer 提供

題型 04 關係代名詞

D 應用練習　　P. 335

| 1. (B) | 2. (A) | 3. (B) | 4. (C) | 5. (D) |
| 6. (B) | 7. (D) | 8. (A) | 9. (C) | 10. (C) |

1. (B)

翻譯 她比較喜歡閱讀可以教她新事物的書。

解析 空格要放先行詞是事物的主格關係代名詞，答案是選項（B）。

單字 prefer 比較喜歡

2. (A)

翻譯 你要學習許多事物才能成為專家。

解析 空格要放先行詞是事物的受格關係代名詞，答案是選項（A）。

單字 expert 專家

3. (B)

翻譯 約翰研發的商品賣得並不好。

解析 空格要放先行詞是事物的受格關係代名詞，答案是選項（B）。

單字 product 商品｜develop 研發

4. (C)

翻譯 他們曾有一個兒子夢想成為教授。

解析 空格要放先行詞是人的所有格關係代名詞，答案是選項（C）。

5. (D)

翻譯 他曾是人人都想與之共事的成功商人。

解析 省略受格關係代名詞也可以，答案是選項（D）。

6. (B)

翻譯 我們總工程師使用的機器不能再運作了。

解析 本來是 The machine which had been used 或 The machine which was used，此時省略 which had been 或 which was，答案是選項（B）。

單字 chief 主要的｜ work 運作

7. (D)

翻譯 傑克買了一棟很多人認為很貴的房子。

解析 是關係代名詞的補充說明用法。因為先行詞是事物，答案是選項（D）。關係代名詞 that 或 what，不能當補充說明使用。

8. (A)

翻譯 這家新創公司經營維艱是可以理解的。

解析 能代表整個前句，並能使用補充說明用法的關係代名詞只有 which，答案是選項（A）。

單字 start-up company 新創公司｜
struggle 掙扎

9. (C)

翻譯 賭博不是我想從事的活動。

解析 空格要放包含先行詞在內的關係代名詞，答案是選項（C）。

單字 gamble 賭博

10. (C)

翻譯 她小心保管向朋友借來的東西。

解析 空格要放包含先行詞在內的關係代名詞，答案是選項（C）。

題型 05 關係副詞

D 應用練習 P. 341

1. (C) 2. (D) 3. (A) 4. (D) 5. (A)
6. (B) 7. (A) 8. (D) 9. (B) 10. (C)

1. (C)

翻譯 他們在早上十點抵達開始參觀工廠。

解析 先行詞是時間時，要用關係副詞 when。關係副詞 when 可以當補充說明用，答案是選項（C）。

2. (D)

翻譯 她被引導到大廳，做了一場感動人心的演講。

解析 先行詞是地點時，要用關係副詞 where。關係副詞 where 可以當補充說明用，答案是選項（D）。

單字 guide 引導｜ hall 大廳｜
moving 感動人心的

3. (A)

翻譯 那就是他獲得拔擢的原因。

解析 先行詞是 reason 時，能使用的關係副詞是 why，答案是選項（A）。

單字 promote 拔擢

4. (D)

翻譯 那是他們這個新創公司成功的方式。

解析 先行詞是 the way 時，關係副詞不能使用 how。本句要用 the way in which，或 how 來表現，答案是選項（D）。

單字 start-up 新創的

5. (A)

翻譯 西雅圖是他們移居的城市。

解析 要記住，本句的空格不能放選項（B）。因為 where 已經含有介系詞 in 或 to 的意思在內，所以不能和介系詞搭配使用。答案是選項（A）。

6. (B)

翻譯 她工作的地方看起來很棒。

解析 因為 she worked 之後沒有像 in 這樣的介系詞，所以空格可以放關係副詞，答案是選項（B）。

7. (A)

翻譯 那就是他被任命為主席的那一天。

解析 因為先行詞是時間，所以用關係副詞 when。答案是選項（A）。

單字 appoint 任命 | chairperson 主席

8. (D)

翻譯 這就是他們共事很久的辦公室。

解析 因為先行詞是場所，所以用關係副詞 where。答案是選項（D）。

9. (B)

翻譯 無論何時出了問題，蘇珊都能解決。

解析 空格要放具「任何時候」之意的 whenever，答案是選項（B）。

單字 fix 解決

10. (C)

翻譯 無論在何處工作，你都應該學會保持積極態度。

解析 空格要放具「任何地方」之意的 wherever，答案是選項（C）。

單字 positive 積極的

Quick Test P. 342

1. (D)	2. (A)	3. (C)	4. (D)	5. (B)
6. (C)	7. (B)	8. (C)	9. (A)	10. (B)
11. (D)	12. (C)	13. (D)	14. (C)	15. (A)
16. (B)	17. (A)	18. (B)	19. (C)	20. (D)

1. (D)

翻譯 最後的版本要在下週一前準備好。

解析 因為是「到某個特定的時間點以前要完成」的意思，所以要放介系詞 by，提醒到期的時間，這樣句意比較順。

單字 version 版本

2. (A)

翻譯 多虧瑪莉的努力，我們順利完成這個案子。

解析 選項（A）on account of 是「拜……所賜、因為……」的意思，是當介系詞用的片語，可放在名詞片語前，答案是選項（A）。

單字 on account of 多虧

3. (C)

翻譯 關於這件事，你可以問我任何問題。

解析 concern 是動詞，但這裡將 concerning 當介系詞來用。concerning 和 about 一樣，是「關於」的意思。這題可以將名詞 his matter 當受詞用的字只有選項（C）介系詞 concerning。

4. (D)

翻譯 傑克已經教授科學近 20 年。

解析 能在現在完成進行式中表期間的介系詞只有選項（A）和（D）。選項（A）要用在不明確的數字期間前，選項（D）可以放在日期、月、年等明確的數字期間前，所以答案是選項（D）。

單字 science 科學

5. (B)

翻譯 這項裝置不只便宜，而且容易使用。

解析 考相關連接詞「not only …but also …」，答案是選項（B）。

單字 device 裝置 | cheap 便宜

6. (C)

翻譯 你可以和我或蘇珊討論這件事。

解析 考相關連接詞「either . . . or . . . 」，答案是選項（C）。

單字 matter 事情

7. (B)

翻譯 老闆和員工都會去簽署合約。

解析 考相關連接詞「both . . . and . . . 」的單複數一致性。和其他相關連接詞不同，「both . . . and . . . 」的動詞要用複數，答案是選項（B）。

單字 contract 合約

8. (C)

翻譯 他和他太太都不會打高爾夫球。

解析 考相關連接詞「neither . . . nor . . . 」。通常 neither 出現在句首，並且也不是副詞的話，它就是相關連接詞的 neither。答案是選項（C）。

單字 golf 高爾夫球

9. (A)

翻譯 艾瑞克打電話到電視台只為了滿足對這次意外的好奇心。

解析 考找出能和 curiosity 搭配使用的動詞。「滿足」好奇心，意思上是很合適的，答案是選項（A）。

單字 satisfy 滿足

10. (B)

翻譯 儘管她丈夫試圖勸阻她,她還是執意要買卡車。

解析 選項中能當連接詞使用的,只有選項(B)。因為要連接子句和子句,所以要放連接詞選項(B)。

單字 discourage 勸阻

11. (D)

翻譯 他們無法判斷她的說法是否真實。

解析 考連接詞 whether 的用法,表「不知道是或不是」的意思。答案是選項(D)。

單字 tell 判斷 | truth 真相

12. (C)

翻譯 許多大企業想要收購新創公司。

解析 考及物動詞/不及物動詞的用法。除了選項(C)是及物動詞,其他選項都是不及物動詞,要加介系詞才能接受詞。及物動詞 acquire 是「獲得」的意思。答案是選項(C)。

單字 corporation 企業 | star-up 新創的

13. (D)

翻譯 她那時服務的公司正要進入亞洲市場。

解析 考掌握關係詞子句中表地點的介系詞和關係詞的關係。worked 後若沒有接 for,選項(B)就可以是正確答案;關係詞子句裡有 for,空格就要放能當介系詞 for 的受詞的關係代名詞 which。所以答案是選項(D)。

14. (C)

翻譯 我們有個特殊部門,它的角色是盡可能滿足顧客的需求。

解析 考掌握先行詞和關係詞子句之間的關係。先行詞 department 和起始關係詞子句的 role 之間是所有格的關係,所以要用選項(C)的關係代名詞 whose。

單字 department 部門 | role 角色 | support 支援 | customer 顧客

15. (A)

翻譯 你可以推薦績優公司給我投資嗎?

解析 因為「推薦」一家可投資的公司的句意最合適,答案是選項(A)。

單字 recommend 推薦 | invest 投資

16. (B)

翻譯 她在 2012 年移居新加坡,並在那裡創業。

解析 因為空格要連接前後兩個子句,但選項中沒有連接詞,這樣要看子句和子句間的關係。因為女子在前一子句有提到地點,所以選項(B)的關係副詞 where 是答案。

17-20.

翻譯 你想創業嗎?然而你知道多數的新創公司會在五年內失敗嗎?這就是你今天得打 555-7388 和我們聯繫的原因。有我們優秀智囊團的協助,你的新創公司將會邁向成功!

解析

17. (A)

從句意上來看，不是結束或減少事業，而是開始事業，才是人們值得關注的內容。所以答案是選項（A）。

18. (B)

因為需要一個引導名詞子句的連接詞，所以選項（B）的連接詞 that 是答案。因為連接詞 that 引導當作受詞的子句，所以也可以省略。

19. (C)

因為之前都是在講打電話來的「原因」，所以要放關係副詞 why。用 the reason 代替 why 也可以。

20. (D)

打電話來的話，會告知想開立新企業的人，成功的方法。所以可以知道，打電話來會幫助新公司走上成功的道路，選項（D）是答案。

單字 within ……之內｜
on account of 因為

Practice Test				P. 344

1. (C)	2. (B)	3. (C)	4. (A)	5. (D)
6. (C)	7. (C)	8. (A)	9. (A)	10. (B)
11. (D)	12. (B)	13. (A)	14. (D)	15. (A)
16. (C)	17. (D)	18. (A)	19. (B)	20. (C)
21. (B)	22. (D)	23. (A)	24. (D)	25. (D)
26. (B)	27. (B)	28. (D)	29. (C)	30. (A)
31. (B)	32. (C)	33. (B)	34. (C)	35. (C)
36. (A)	37. (C)	38. (A)	39. (B)	40. (D)
41. (C)	42. (B)	43. (D)	44. (D)	45. (B)
46. (C)				

---

1. (C)

翻譯 為了成功，我們應該彼此合作。

解析 從句意上來看，是要大家相互合作。因為沒有受詞，所以動詞是不及物動詞。完全符合的是選項（C）cooperate。

單字 cooperate 合作｜beautify 美化｜
construct 建造

2. (B)

翻譯 新型號的開發可能會有風險。

解析 能放進主詞位置的是名詞或相當於名詞的片語。選項中只有選項（B）是名詞，答案是選項（B）。

單字 development 開發｜
developmental 研發的

3. (C)

翻譯 我們要求員工要有創意。

解析 主詞是複數 we，空格是動詞的位置，所以選項（C）ask 是答案。

4. (A)

翻譯 僱用這位求職者是明智的決定。

解析 這題要找出能當補語的選項。因為空格前有修飾詞和不定冠詞，所以要放當作補語的名詞，答案是選項（A）。

單字 decision 決定｜hire 僱用｜
candidate 候選人｜decide 決定

5. (D)

翻譯 氣氛很愉悅。

解析 主詞補語的位置能放形容詞或名詞，答案是選項（D）。

單字 atmosphere 氣氛｜ pleasant 愉悅的｜ pleasantly 愉悅地

6. (C)

翻譯 無論你年紀大小都無關緊要。

解析 因為空格後的 whether 子句是真正的主詞，所以空格要放不後接受詞或補語的完全不及物動詞，答案是選項（C）

單字 matter 有關係｜ cause 原因｜ popularize 使普及｜ celebrate 慶祝

7. (C)

翻譯 他們請求允許建造新的大學校園。

解析 因為空格要放介系詞的受詞，所以空格要放 to 不定詞之外的名詞或相當於名詞的片語。答案是選項（C）。

單字 permission 允許｜ permissive 許可的

8. (A)

翻譯 這本小說是由一家知名出版社出版。

解析 因為空格位在定冠詞後，所以空格要放名詞。且空格後是單數形的 be 動詞 was，名詞的部分要放可數名詞單數形或不可數名詞，答案是選項（A）。

單字 novel 小說｜ publish 出版

9. (A)

翻譯 他們張開雙臂迎接我們。

解析 因為空格位在及物動詞 greet 之後，所以要放受格代名詞，答案是選項（A）。

單字 greet 迎接

10. (B)

翻譯 沒有一位學生知道問題的答案。

解析 因為空格接受介系詞 of 的修飾，所以空格要放名詞或代名詞。答案是選項（B）。

11. (D)

翻譯 環境保護對每個人來說都很重要。

解析 空格位在定冠詞和介系詞 of 之間，所以空格可以放名詞。介系詞 of 的受詞須合乎句意，因此介系詞和前面名詞之間的關係很重要。答案是選項（D）。

單字 protection 保護｜ environment 環境｜ asset 資產｜ laboratory 實驗室

12. (B)

翻譯 有些家具曾被他的鄰居使用過。

解析 由片語 some of 起始，動詞要和它後接的名詞單複數一致。furniture 是不可數名詞，所以動詞要用單數，單數且適合放進空格中的選項，只有選項（B）。

單字 furniture 家具

13. (A)

翻譯 上週發生了很多事。

解析 句尾的 last week 是特定的過去時間，所以不能用完成式或未來式。答案是選項（A）。

14. (D)

翻譯 他們已經住在法國近 30 年了。

解析 因為主詞是複數，且後面有表示期間，所以空格放複數形現在完成式最適合。答案是選項（D）。

15. (A)

翻譯 牆是由她的一位朋友所彩繪的。

解析 主詞是第三人稱單數，空格後有表行為者的介系詞 by，所以空格要放單數形被動語態。答案是選項（A）。

16. (C)

翻譯 他說中文的能力對他的事業有幫助。

解析 這不是考文法的試題，是要找出符合句意的字彙。說語言的「能力」最適合放進空格中，答案是選項（C）。

單字 vacation 假期｜ issue 核發｜ loss 損失

17. (D)

翻譯 我們正計劃創建一個新網站。

解析 動詞 plan 要用 to 不定詞當受詞，答案是選項（D）。

單字 plan 計劃｜ create 創建

18. (A)

翻譯 她已修好洗衣機。

解析 動詞 finish 要用動名詞當受詞，答案是選項（A）。

19. (B)

翻譯 每個人都對那項決定感到很失望。

解析 動詞 disappoint 是「使失望」的意思，從句意上來看是讓每個人失望，所以是被動語態，空格要放過去分詞，答案是選項（B）。

單字 disappoint 失望｜ decision 決定

20. (C)

翻譯 由於執行長的背書，這個提案獲得很多正面回應。

解析 空格位在分詞構句中。省略前面的 Being，只留下過去分詞，就能清楚掌握句子結構。答案是選項（C）。

單字 proposal 提案｜ positive 正面的｜ response 回應

21. (B)

翻譯 許多教師仍然相信書本對學生來說是很好的工具。

解析 空格位在不定冠詞和名詞之間，所以空格要放修飾名詞的形容詞。從句意來看，「有用的」工具，是最適合的，答案是選項（B）。

單字 tool 工具｜ careless 粗心的

22. (D)

翻譯 你可以從成功的人那裡學到很多東西。

解析 要放能修飾名詞 people 的字，答案是選項（D）。

23. (A)

翻譯 俱樂部的規則如有更改，恕不另行通知。

解析 「be subject to」，是主詞「受到……的影響」之意。答案是選項（A）。

24. (D)

翻譯 她很有創意，可以發明很多東西。

解析 本題考片語「so . . . that . . . 」。如果選成選項（A），creative 和 that 中間就必須要有一個名詞。答案是選項（D）。

單字 invent 發明

25. (D)

翻譯 專家說讚美比處罰對小孩更有效果。

解析 看到空格後出現的 than，就可以知道這題在考比較級。答案是選項（D）。

單字 expert 專家｜praise 讚美｜effective 有效的｜punishment 處罰

26. (B)

翻譯 我們出席在首爾舉辦的大會。

解析 看到空格後出現 hold 的過去分詞 held，可以知道空格接受過去分詞 held 的修飾。因為 hold 是舉辦的意思，所以最適合被舉辦的名詞只有選項（B）。

單字 attend 出席｜conference 大會｜effect 效果

27. (B)

翻譯 對多數人來說，泡菜不但有益健康，也很美味。

解析 看到空格後出現動名詞，可以判斷空格要放以動名詞為目的，並有「為了」之意的字，答案是選項（B）。

單字 in addition to 除了……尚有｜tasty 美味的

28. (D)

翻譯 約翰和他哥哥都不能參加比賽。

解析 相關連接詞 neither A nor B，動詞型態要取決於最靠近動詞的名詞。在本句中，動詞型態要符合 B，也就是 his brother，答案是選項（D）。

單字 race 比賽

29. (C)

翻譯 儘管不擅長歌唱，他們還是為了公司參加比賽。

解析 空格要放連接子句的連接詞，從句意來看，需要放表讓步的連接詞，答案是選項（C）。

單字 contest 比賽｜be good at 擅長

30. (A)

翻譯 官員造訪公司這件事非常不尋常。

解析 空格要放連接子句的連接詞，同時又是該子句的主詞。能將前面的子句整個當作先行詞的連接詞，最合適的是選項（A）which。

單字 official 官員

31–34.

翻譯 收件者：robert@digilog.com
寄件者：xenon@email.com
日期：六月 12 日
主旨：感謝函

親愛的羅伯特：
我很高興聽到你的消息。我知道你最近一直努力工作，因此我一直很擔心你。沒錯，工作很重要，但你得要好好照顧自己。

解析

31. (B)

用 to 不定詞的副詞用法，來表達感情。答案是選項（B）。

32. (C)

因為 that 後接子句，所以空格要放符合第二人稱主詞的動詞，所以答案是選項（C）。

33. (B)

前一句提到努力工作，後一句提到要照顧自己，空格句子要放在這兩句中間。推測脈絡是，雖然很努力工作，但太過度會有礙健康，所以很替他擔心。答案是選項（B）。

34. (C)

因為是自己照顧自己，所以空格要放反身代名詞 yourself。

35–38.

翻譯 **韓國歷史劇**

近來很多人對韓國歷史有興趣。如果你是其中之一，我們衷心推薦你觀賞韓國戲劇。韓劇不僅很有意思，而且有助於學習韓國歷史。

解析

35. (C)

這題考片語「be interested in」，答案是選項（C）。

36. (A)

空格前的句意是，很多人對韓國歷史有興趣，空格後出現了代名詞 they，空格中要放 they 所指稱的複數事物或人物。選項（A）提到了和歷史有關的戲劇，所以答案是選項（A）。

37. (C)

在片語「not only A but also B」中，A 和 B 的格一定要一樣，因為在 B 位置上的是形容詞 helpful，所以可以考慮能當形容詞的選項（C）和（D）。不過因為 they 所指稱的是韓國歷史劇要用現在分詞，答案是選項（C）。

38. (A)

空格要放介系詞的受詞，所以要放是動名詞的選項（A）。

單字 **benefit** 好處 | **relationship** 關係

39–42.

翻譯 **來參觀我們的網站吧！**

你想認識新朋友嗎？你享受品嚐美食嗎？來我們的網站吧！我們的網站可以讓你和有趣的人交朋友。另外，我們推薦好餐廳，你和你的新朋友可以在那裡一起享用美食。

39. (B)

動詞 want 要用 to 不定詞當受詞，答案是選項（B）。

40. (D)

enjoy 要用動名詞當受詞的動詞，答案是選項（D）。

41. (C)

空格後的意思是「此外，我們還推薦能和新朋友一起享用美食的餐廳」，所以邏輯上，空格應該是在談有關交新朋友的事，答案是選項（C）。

42. (B)

前面 so 和 that 中間沒有加入形容詞或副詞，兩個字連在一起時，是「以便」的意思。所以空格放「能」的意思是最適合的。答案是選項（B）。

43–46.

翻譯 投資新創公司會有風險。然而藉由這個網站的幫助，我賺了很多錢。這個網站可以讓我尋找值得投資的優秀新創公司。當初如果沒有使用這個網站，我就不會賺那麼多錢。

解析

43. (D)

從空格後出現的 but，可以知道前後句的句意相反。後一句是「這個網站幫我賺大錢」，所以空格應該是相反的意思，投資一家新公司是「很冒險的」，所以答案是選項（D）。

44. (D)

考片語「be able + to 不定詞」這。答案是選項（D）。

45. (B)

allow 接受詞補語，要用 to 不定詞，答案是選項（B）。

46. (C)

不是要找因果關係的句子，而是要找符合文章脈絡的句子。
選項（A）突然冒出花錢在娛樂上，和文脈不符。
選項（B）提到不能理解為什麼有人要創立新公司，和文章所談的投資新公司無關。
選項（D）提到創立新公司要再三思考，也和前面所講的投資新公司無關。

選項（C）用假設法提到，過去要是沒使用這網站，就不能賺這麼多錢了，符合前面的脈絡，所以選項（C）是答案。

單字 invest 投資｜risky 有風險的｜
earn 賺錢｜useless 無用處的

Parts 7
單篇閱讀文章/多篇文章

❶ 各類型試題說明

類型 **01 綜合資訊**

D 應用練習　　P. 357

1. (B)

翻譯 您計劃造訪英語系國家嗎？您想用英語和別人溝通嗎？那麼即刻下載我們的「簡單口譯通」APP 吧！只要用您的母語對這個 APP 說話。然後，簡單口譯通就會把您說的話翻譯成英語，並替您發聲。您還在等什麼？現在就下載這個令人驚豔的 APP 吧！

⋯⋯⋯⋯⋯⋯⋯⋯⋯⋯⋯⋯⋯⋯⋯⋯⋯⋯⋯⋯

廣告的主要內容是什麼？
(A) 學習外語有效率的方法
(B) 將使用者母語翻譯成英語的 APP

解析 單從第一句話無法知道這是什麼廣告，但是透過提到下載 app 的第三句話和最後一句話，就可以知道這是 app 的廣告。其他部分是在說明 app 的功能和用法，答案是選項（B）。

單字 make . . . p.p. 使⋯⋯｜
interpretation 翻譯｜
native language 母語｜
translate A into B 將 A 翻譯成 B

---

2. (B)

翻譯 收件者：全體員工
寄件者：艾麗絲・潭南執行長
日期：3 月 25 日
主旨：本公司的家庭友善政策

我們是個對家庭友善的公司。因此，我們實行對家庭友善的政策。然而並沒有很多員工從這些政策中受惠，這是因為他們不知道政策的內容。所以，我們決定出版小冊子解釋我們所有的家庭友善政策。

備忘錄撰寫的動機是什麼？
(A) 說明公司是家族企業
(B) 解釋為何公司會出版小冊子

解析 文章主題通常會出現在第一句或最後一句。第一句提到的 family-friendly 是「家庭友善」的意思，和選項（A）的 family-run（家族經營）意思不同。最後一句提到，為了介紹家族友善政策，要印小冊子，從這裡可以知道文章主要的目的是什麼，答案是選項（B）。

單字 staff 員工 | subject 主旨 |
family-friendly 家庭友善的 |
policy 政策 | pursue 實行 |
benefit from 從……受惠 |
decide to 決定 | publish 出版 |
explain 解釋

類型 02 細節資訊

Ⓓ 應用練習　　P. 363

1. (A)

翻譯 **保羅・史密斯 下午 2:00**
克萊拉，你可以到機場接茉莉亞・勞倫斯嗎？

克萊拉・迦納 下午 2:05
你好，保羅。你說的是那家新服飾公司的執行長嗎？

保羅・史密斯 下午 2:10
沒錯。雖然她的公司才成立不久，但經營得非常成功。

誰是勞倫斯小姐？
(A) 一家成功公司的經營者
(B) 想要新創服飾公司的人

解析 在克萊拉的對話中提到茉莉亞・勞倫斯是新服飾公司的執行長（CEO of the new clothing company）。保羅・史密斯提到，該公司相當成功。所以可以知道茉莉亞・勞倫斯是位經營成功的服裝公司的執行長。

單字 pick up 接送 |
CEO (chief executive officer) 執行長 |
clothing company 服飾公司 |
executive 經營者

---

2. (B)

翻譯 **珍・亞當斯 上午 9:30**
嗨，我們可以在下午見面討論季度報告嗎？

凱文・強森 上午 9:31
嗨，我在下午會和一位新客戶見面。她想在電視上廣告宣傳自己的商品。

珍・亞當斯 上午 9:30
好吧。你可以建議她做網路廣告嗎？或許我們明天可以見面。

亞當斯小姐希望強森先生做什麼？
(A) 在電視上廣告一些商品
(B) 要求客戶改變她的想法

解析 強森先生說，下午要和想在電視上做產品廣告的客戶開會，亞當斯小姐對強森先生說，可不可以建議她在網路上做廣告，改變客戶的心意，所以選項（B）是對的。

單字 quarterly report 季度報告 |
advertise 廣告 | product 商品 |
advise 建議 |
change one's mind 改變某人的心意

D 應用練習　P. 369

1. (A)

翻譯 親愛的保羅：

我剛閱讀了你的文章，是有關吃肉的危害，-[1]- 吃太多肉可能對你的健康有不良影響。然而專家說我們都需要吃一些肉。如果我們完全不吃肉，就無法保持健康。-[2]- 所以，我認為你應該重寫你的文章。

----

[1] 和 [2] 哪個位置最適合插入以下句子？
「吃太多肉可能對你的健康有不良影響。」
(A) [1]
(B) [2]

解析 〔1〕後面用 but 連接了專家的意見，專家說肉類是必要的。所以 but 前面的內容，要和它相反，因此放入提示句是很適合的。相反的，〔2〕前面是在說吃肉類的好處，若放入提示句會很奇怪。

單字 article 文章｜danger 危害｜meat 肉類｜expert 專家｜stay healthy 保持健康｜rewrite 重寫｜be good for 適合

2. (A)

翻譯 我們是一家非常在乎顧客的公司。-[1]- 因此，我們很想知道顧客對我們的商品有什麼看法。他們對商品感到滿意嗎？還是對它們感到失望？我們邀請顧客瀏覽我們的特別網站 www.yourvoicematters.com，並告訴我們他們的意見。-[2]-

----

[1] 和 [2] 哪個位置最適合插入以下句子？
「因此，我們很想知道顧客對我們的商品有什麼看法。」
(A) [1]
(B) [2]

解析 要插入的句子包含「顧客對產品的想法（what they think about our products）」，〔1〕後面是「他們滿意嗎？（Are they satisfied?）」、「他們失望嗎？」（Are they disappointed?），因此在〔1〕插入提示句是最合適的。

單字 care about 在乎｜customer 顧客｜be satisfied with 對……感到滿意｜be disappointed with 對……感到失望｜product 商品

類型 **04** 掌握目的

D 應用練習　P. 375

1. (B)

翻譯 **梅蘭妮・麥克林 下午 3:15**
詹姆斯，你看過艾美那本書的封面了嗎？

詹姆斯・史密斯 下午 3:25
我看過了。我認為那會吸引兒童。

梅蘭妮・麥克林 下午 3:27
我很高興聽你那麼說。她的書要訴求的讀者就是兒童。

在下午 3:27 時，麥克林小姐說「我很高興聽你那麼說」是什麼意思？
(A) 她很高興聽到史密斯先生已經讀過艾美的書
(B) 她很高興知道艾美那本書的封面會吸引兒童

解析 麥克林小姐高興的原因可以從前一句話得知，前面史密斯先生說「書的封面會吸引兒童（I think it will appeal to children）」，所以答案是選項（B）。

單字 take a look at 看｜cover 封面｜appeal to 吸引｜be aimed at 訴求目標｜attract 吸引

2. (A)

翻譯 **珍蘇珊 · 萊斯** （下午 4:30）
史考特，你對執行長的提案有什麼看法？

史考特 · 博爾 （下午 4:31）
跟你說實話，我不認為員工會支持提案。

蘇珊 · 萊斯 （下午 4:32）
你為何那麼想？我預期很多員工會喜歡這個提案。

在下午 4:32 時，萊斯小姐說「你為何那麼想」是什麼意思？
(A) 她不同意博爾先生的看法
(B) 她想要和執行長討論這個提案

解析 從「What makes you think so？」這句話前後兩句兩人的想法，就會知道答案。博爾先生認為員工不會支持，相反的，萊斯小姐說會有很多員工支持，從這裡可以看出兩人意見不同。所以答案是選項（A）。

單字 **proposal** 提案 |
employee 員工 | **support** 支持 |
what make you 是什麼讓你…… |
expect 預期 | **agree with** 同意

類型 **05** 推測題

Ⓓ 應用練習 P. 381

1. (B)

翻譯 收件者：erica@yaho.com
寄件者：robert@solute.com
主旨：執行長會議
日期：六月二日

親愛的艾瑞卡：

我寫信來回應您的問題。我想在週五和貴公司執行長見面。如您所知，我會在週三對一些大學生進行演講。執行長可能對我演講的主題有興趣。內容是關於如何在全球化世界保持更大的競爭力。

以下關於執行長的暗示何者為真？
(A) 她自從她成立公司後就一直與艾瑞卡共事
(B) 她可能對提升競爭力有興趣

解析 透過最後兩句話可以知道，收件者公司的執行長會對寄件者的演講感興趣，該演講的內容是有關在全球化的世界中強化競爭力，所以可以推測公司執行長會對提升競爭力有興趣，選項（B）的內容是正確的。

單字 **in response to** 回應 |
give a speech to 演講 |
topic 主題 | **competitive** 有競爭力的 |
globalized 全球化的 | **found** 創立 |
improve 提升 |
competitiveness 競爭力

2. (B)

翻譯 **阿曼達 · 庫柏** （下午 3:15）
傑克，你可以到我的辦公室修理我的電腦嗎？

傑克 · 帕瑪 （下午 3:16）
現在不行。我正在處理一件急事。

阿曼達 · 庫柏 （下午 3:17）
了解。那麼，告訴我你何時可以到我的辦公室。

以下關於帕瑪先生的推測何者為真？
(A) 他是庫柏小姐的主管
(B) 他可以維修電腦問題

解析 單從對話無法得知兩人的關係，不過看到庫柏小姐的電腦壞了，並拜託帕瑪先生來修理，可以知道帕瑪是會維修電腦的人，所以答案是選項（B）。

單字 **repair** 維修 | **deal with** 處理 |
urgent 緊急的 | **matter** 事情 |
supervisor 主管 | **fix** 修理

D 應用練習　　　P. 387

1. (B)

翻譯 收件者：Jennifer@sunwto.com
發信者：robert@sunwto.com
主旨：關於調職
日期：五月三日

親愛的珍妮佛：

我們聽說你會轉調至我們的倫敦分公司。遺憾地是，那個分公司有某些人不太友善，我們希望你對那樣的同事有所提防。當然，那裡也有和善又體貼的員工，你會分辨得出哪些同事是和善的。和他們好好相處，然後你在倫敦分公司就會工作得更順利。

第六行中的「分辨」最接近什麼意思？
(A) 不喜歡
(B) 知道

解析 句子如果是「不喜歡（dislike）」親切的員工是不符合句意的，所以應該是「知道、分辨得出」親切的員工。答案是選項（B）。

單字 transfer 轉調 | branch 分公司 |
employee 員工 |
prepare oneself 自我準備 |
thoughtful 體貼的 | tell 分辨 |
get along with 相處融洽

2. (B)

翻譯 我們很高興宣布我們將為新成立的公立圖書館舉辦命名競賽。如同一市公民所知，這間新圖書館可以收藏數百萬本書籍和雜誌。除此之外，它還可以讓使用者經由網路取得其他的公立圖書館的資源。您希望我們用什麼名字稱呼這間超棒的圖書館呢？請將您的建議用電子郵件寄到 chean@lakecity.library.org。

第四行中的「取得」最接近什麼意思？
(A) 阻斷
(B) 使用

解析 透過網路能取得（access）許多圖書館的各種資訊，所以換個詞「使用（use）」其他圖書館也可以。

單字 announce 宣布 | hold 舉辦 |
name 命名 | contest 競賽 |
allow . . . to . . . 讓……得以…… |
user 使用者 | access 取用權 |
suggestion 建議

Quick Test　　　P. 388

1. (B)　2. (A)　3. (A)

4. (A)　5. (B)　6. (B)

1. (B)

翻譯 **跨國搬家**

搬到另一個國家是項重大決定。那也表示你有很多事情需要處理。但別擔心！「愉快國際搬運公司」會逐步協助您處理每件事項。事實上，我們對客戶友善的服務會讓您覺得跨國搬家輕鬆無比。因此，您還在等什麼？請上我們的網站 www.funmovinginternational 瀏覽更多資訊。

廣告的主要內容是什麼？
(A) 讓旅客出國玩得很愉快的公司
(B) 幫客戶搬家到國外的公司

解析 從廣告的標題可以知道這不是關於旅行（traveling）而是關於搬家（move）的廣告。所以選項（B）說這是幫忙客戶搬家到國外的廣告，是最合適的。

單字 decision 決策 | take care of 處理 |
customer-friendly 對客戶友善的

2. (A)

翻譯 **梅蘭妮・強森** （上午 **10:20**）
保羅，你的預算報告重寫好了嗎？

保羅・亞當斯 （上午 **10:21**）
還沒寫完。我的時間不多，我有太多事情要做。

梅蘭妮・強森 （上午 **10:22**）
了解。我會試著找方法減輕你的負擔。

為什麼亞當斯先生還沒完成他的工作？
(A) 他沒有足夠時間完成他的工作
(B) 他沒有任何同事幫他

解析 兩個人的對話中完全沒提到同事（coworker），透過亞當斯先生對話中的 I don't have much time，可以知道他時間有限，答案是選項（A）。

單字 **finish** 完成｜**rewrite** 重寫｜**budget** 預算｜**try to** 嘗試｜**ease** 減輕｜**burden** 負擔｜**coworker** 同事

3. (A)

翻譯 收件者：lawrence@empul.com
寄件者：evans@schospital.org
主旨：志工準則
日期：12 月 11 日

親愛的勞倫斯小姐：

感謝您聯絡我們關於想擔任我們一間醫院的志工。您似乎非常關心孩童，因此，我們認為您可能可以擔任陽光兒童醫院的志工。請寄信到莎拉・布雷克的電子郵件信箱 sarah_black@schospital.org，她會給您更多有關在醫院照顧兒童病患的資訊。

[1] 和 [2] 哪一個位置最適合插入以下句子？
「因此，我們認為您可能可以擔任陽光兒童醫院的志工。」
(A) [1]
(B) [2]

解析 提示句 so 之後的內容，必須是前一句話的結果。因為前面出現了原因，想到醫院當志工，而且也喜歡照顧兒童，所以在〔1〕這裡接提示句是最適合的

單字 **volunteer** 志工｜**guide** 準則｜**thank you for** 為……致謝｜**contact** 聯絡｜**care about** 關心

4. (A)

翻譯 **珍・庫伯** 上午 **10:15**
艾瑞克，你對芳達小姐有什麼看法？

艾瑞克・史密斯 上午 **10:25**
她具備了這個職位的必備的技能。

珍・庫伯 上午 **10:27**
我也有同感。我會立刻打電話給她。

在上午 10:27，庫伯小姐說「我也有同感」是什麼意思？
(A) 她相信芳達小姐可以擔任他們討論的職位
(B) 她相信芳達小姐需要再找另一家公司

解析 「我也有同感」是認同對方時所說的話。看到前面艾瑞克對芳達的評論就知道答案。艾瑞克說芳達具有該職位必備的技能，庫伯也同意這想法，答案是選項（A）。

單字 **necessary** 必備的｜**skill** 技能｜**position** 職位｜**right away** 立刻｜**fill** 擔任｜**discuss** 討論

5. (B)

翻譯 瑪莉・帕克擔任獵人頭顧問已超過十年。帕克說很多公司不知道他們想僱用什麼樣的員工。她相信要成為優秀的獵人頭顧問，你要耐心地與不同的公司互動。根據她的說法，這是因為了解公司的目標要花很多時間。

以下關於獵人頭顧問的推測何者為真？
(A) 他們應該到很多不同的國家旅遊
(B) 他們應該嘗試深入了解公司

解析 選項（A）重複出現了報導內提到的 different，這是用來誤導的陷阱選項。recruitment agent 做的工作是提供有關求才的資訊，所以不用考慮選項（A）。另外，透過最後一句話，它提到「要了解公司的目標」，所以答案是選項（B）。

單字 recruitment 徵才｜ agent 仲介｜ employ 僱用｜ interact with 互動｜ patiently 耐心地｜ take time 花時間｜ be supposed to 應該要｜ travel 旅遊

6. (B)

翻譯 **回收的重要性**
市政府知道環境對每個人來說都很重要。因此市政府建議每位市民都回收並重複使用物品。當你回收物品，它會轉變成另外的東西。當你重複使用物品，它就不會被浪費。不管你回收或重複使用物品，你都為環保盡了一份心力。

第五行中的「保護」最接近什麼意思？
(A) 讓某樣東西失去用處
(B) 讓某樣東西保持安全

解析 想到回收利用或重複使用對環境的影響，這題就很容易了，因為再回收利用或重複使用能減少對環境的不良影響。選項（A）和內文意思完全相反，所以不用考慮。protect 是「保護」的意思，和選項（B）keep something safe 的意思相同，所以選項（B）是答案。

單字 government 政府｜ recycle 回收｜ environment 環境｜ that is why 因此｜ advise 建議｜ citizen 市民｜ reuse 重複使用｜ item 物品｜ waste 浪費｜ protect 保護｜ useless 無用的｜ safe 安全

❷ 各類型文章說明

類型 01 信件和電子郵件

D 應用練習　　P. 397

1. (B)

翻譯 四月三日
親愛的霍夫曼先生：
我是你咖啡店的常客。我喜歡這裡的氣氛。我也很喜歡在這裡工作的每個人，除了一位員工。我不想告訴你他或她是哪一位，但你一定聽過其他客人的類似投訴。我想要你鼓勵那位員工對客人更友善些，畢竟那是員工的職責。

第六行中的「投訴」最接近什麼意思？
(A) 你稱讚某人行為的言論
(B) 你對某事表達不悅的言論

解析 出現 complaints 的句子裡表示「一定已經聽到其他顧客有相同的抱怨」，所以從寄件者在這句話之前所講的內容，可以判斷是令人不高興的事情，所以和選項（B）相符，答案是選項（B）。

單字 regular customer 常客｜ atmosphere 氣氛｜ employee 員工｜ similar 類似的｜ complaint 投訴｜ encourage 鼓勵｜ praise 讚美

2. (A)

翻譯 收件者：employees@alrado.net
寄件者：representative@alrado.net
主旨：退休派對
日期：7 月 13 日

親愛的全體員工：

如同你們有些人所知，艾麗絲・林區小姐將在下個月退休。她與我們共事近 20 年，她引進革新的方法改善員工生產力。多虧她的方法，我們公司獲得極大的成功。我們想要感謝她，並且將為她舉辦退休派對。我希望所有員工參加派對，並感謝她的貢獻。

為林區小姐舉辦派對的原因是什麼？
(A) 因為她的公司想感謝她的貢獻
(B) 因為她的公司想要解僱她

解析 透過電子郵件最後一句話「I would like all . . . for her hard work」，可以知道公司是要感謝林區小姐的辛勞。即使不知道電子郵件詳細的內容，選項（B）出現的「解僱（lay off）」，和試題中提到的「舉辦宴會」是不符的。

單字 retirement party 退休派對 |
innovative method 革新方式 |
improve 改善 | productivity 生產力 |
hold 舉辦 | lay off 解僱

類型 02 廣告

D 應用練習　　P. 403

1. (A)

翻譯 **智慧數位照相機**

許多人認為數位照相機不再有用處，他們說智慧手機可以取代照相機。請試用我們最新款的數位照相機，然後你會發現它比一般智慧手機更好用。你也會發現為不同事物拍照會讓你很有成就感。請上我們的網站 www.smartdigitalcam.com 瀏覽更多訊息。

第二行中的「取代」最接近什麼意思？
(A) 代替
(B) 利用

解析 首先要知道 replace 後接的 them 是指數位相機（digital cameras）。因為智慧型手機不會利用（make use of）數位相機，所以選項（B）是錯的。所以具「取代」之意的選項（A）是答案。

單字 replace 取代 | ordinary 一般的 |
rewarding 有成就感的 |
take place of 取代 |
make use of 利用

2. (B)

翻譯
莎莉廚房
不是普通的餐廳
739-9932

莎莉廚房不是一家普通的餐廳。當然，我們供應美味的餐點。同時，我們也將協助您烹飪您最喜歡的菜餚。只要在您來之前告訴我們您想做什麼菜。然後，我們會為這道菜準備所有食材。我們親切的廚師會協助您料理您選擇的菜。如果您想要有這種美妙的經驗，今天就打 739-9932 和我們聯繫！

第二行的「普通的」最接近什麼意思？
(A) 出色的
(B) 平常的

解析 一般來說，廣告的目的就是要讓人們知道廣告產品的特色，所以第一句話應該要提到莎莉廚房的特色，但因為前面有 not，所以 ordinary 若是選項（A），第一句話就變成「不特別」，不符合廣告的目的。

選項（B）的 usual 是「一般的」的意思，加上 not 就變成「與一般不同」的意思，選項（B）是答案。

單字 serve 供應 | dish 菜餚 |
ingredient 食材 | exceptional 出色的

1. (B)

翻譯　傑克‧史密斯　　　　下午 2:45
威羅，你和格林先生談過了嗎？

威羅‧博爾　　　　下午 2:48
還沒有。我有急事要處理。

傑克‧史密斯　　　　下午 2:55
那麼，我想我可以和他談他的訂單。把他的電話號碼給我吧。

關於史密斯先生的推測何者為真？
(A) 他之前和格林先生見過。
(B) 他想處理格林先生的訂單。

解析　傑克‧史密斯的最後一條訊息表達可以直接處理訂單，因此答案是選項（B）。

單字　urgent 緊急的 ｜ matter 事件

2. (A)

翻譯　艾美‧格蘭特 （上午 11:20）
我很高興我們提前完成了這個專案。

艾瑞克‧強森 （上午 11:21）
大家都很努力。我認為我們的團隊很棒。

艾美‧格蘭特 （上午 11:22）
我也有同感。只要我們團結合作，無事不成。

在上午 11：22 時，格蘭特小姐說「我也有同感」是什麼意思？
(A) 她相信她的團隊很有效率。
(B) 她相信她的團隊需要更努力。

解析　格蘭特小姐說「我也這麼認為」，表示她同意前面強森先生所說的話。所以選項（A）說「她的團隊很有效率（her team is efficient）」是答案。

單字　complete 完成 ｜ ahead of 提前
schedule 時程表 ｜ efficient 有效率的

1. (B)

翻譯　**重大聲明**

近來有些報導說本公司解僱了史提夫‧李，據說因為我們決定解僱他，讓他感到很生氣，那完全背離事實。李先生在過去是位很盡職的員工，因為他的太太生了重病，他告訴我們他想要多花點時間陪她。因此，他必須離開我們的公司，但我們和他仍舊保持良好關係。

撰寫這份備忘錄的動機是什麼？
(A) 鼓勵員工和李先生維持更好的關係
(B) 解釋李先生為什麼離開公司

解析　掌握文章脈絡就能解題。內容表示事實和某些報導的內容完全不同。李先生離開公司的原因是出自於私人原因，並且是自願離職，這是本備忘錄的重點。單從本文最後一句話，就可以知道選項（A）是錯的。

單字　fire 解僱 ｜ decision 決定 ｜
let go 解僱 ｜ nothing could be
further from the truth 完全背離事實 ｜
dedicated 盡心盡力的 ｜
relationship 關係 ｜ encourage 鼓勵

2. (A)

翻譯　**重要通知**

本公司的經營哲學是為有需要的顧客服務。作為新進員工，你可能會想知道為有需求的顧客服務和服飾公司有什麼關係。我們的經驗讓我們學會只有為有需求的顧客服務，服飾公司才會成功。為了幫助你學到那一課，我們要你尋找有需求的人。請聯繫人力資源部門獲取進一步的細節。

第一行的「經營哲學」最接近什麼意思？

(A) 定義機構行為的概念

(B) 難以理解的概念

解析 公告的內容是要告訴新進員工「公司的經營哲學」。即使不知道 philosophy 的意思，後面仍一直提到要幫助有需求的人，並提到這是公司成功的方式，所以選項（A）是答案。

單字 notice 公告｜ philosophy 哲學｜ in need 有需要的｜ wonder 納悶｜ have something to do with 與……相關｜ in an effort to 為了致力｜ for further details 進一步的細節｜ define 定義｜ organization 機構｜ behavior 行為

類型 05 報導和介紹

D 應用練習　　P. 421

1. (B)

翻譯 卡迪夫博物館宣布將舉辦南韓藝術家特展。南韓並非一般美國人熟悉的國家。博物館希望這項展覽可以幫助美國人更了解韓國藝術。展覽開放給一般大眾參觀，時間是三月二日至四月一日，上午十點到晚上六點。卡迪夫居民可以免費入場。

關於卡迪夫博物館何者為真？

(A) 它的創建人是南韓移民

(B) 它想要讓美國人熟悉韓國藝術

解析 文中並沒有提到卡迪夫博物館是誰創建的。透過報導的第三句話，「博物館希望這項展覽可以幫助美國人更了解韓國藝術」，可以知道選項（B）是答案。

單字 announce 宣布 hold 舉辦｜ exhibition 展覽｜ general public 民眾｜ admission 入場費｜ resident 居民｜ found 創建｜ immigrant 移民｜ familiarize 使熟悉

2. (B)

翻譯 感謝您選擇查理漢堡。如果您吃我們的漢堡，就是幫助別人維持健康。-[1]- 因為我們要求食用雞供應商不使用藥物飼養雞隻。如果使用藥物飼養雞隻，可能會造成大眾健康的問題。-[2]- 因為我們的供應商不使用藥物飼養雞隻，我們就可以避免那樣的問題。請點擊以下連結和朋友分享這個很棒的故事。

[1] 和 [2] 哪一個位置最適合插入以下句子？

「因為我們的供應商不使用藥物飼養雞隻，我們就可以避免那樣的問題。」

(A) [1]

(B) [2]

解析 作答時要先了解欲插入句中的「such problems」是什麼。在提示句之前的句子中有提到問題是用藥物飼養雞隻所造成的健康問題，所以將句子放在〔2〕最合適。

單字 stay healthy 維持健康｜ supplier 供應商｜ raise 飼養｜ drug 藥物｜ public health problem 大眾健康問題｜ share 分享｜ prevent 避免

D 應用練習　　　P. 427

1. (B)

翻譯　如果你想將你的商品賣給其他希納顧客，只要填寫以下表格。

商品類型：＿＿＿＿＿＿＿＿＿＿＿＿
商品購買地點在 ＿＿＿＿＿＿＿＿＿
商品狀況：＿＿＿＿＿＿＿＿＿＿＿＿
賣價：＿＿＿＿＿＿＿＿＿＿＿＿＿＿
國際運送：有 ＿＿＿　無 ＿＿＿

……………………………………………

這個網頁的推測何者為真？
(A) 顧客不能將他們的書籍賣給其他希納顧客
(B) 外籍人士也可以成為希納顧客。

解析　希納網頁的第一句話提到要販售商品給其他顧客就要填表格，所以可以知道選項（A）是錯的。
表格中有一項「國際運送（International Shipping）」，由此可以推測，外國人可以利用這個網站購物，答案是選項（B）。

單字　**item** 商品｜ **fill out a form** 填寫表格｜ **condition** 狀況｜ **asking price** 賣價｜ **international shipping** 國際運送

2. (B)

翻譯　**進行客訴**
如果您需要立即協助，可以隨時打 080-7552-8282 和我們聯繫。或者您可以填寫以下線上表格進行投訴。我們會盡快與您聯繫以解決您的問題。

您的全名：＿＿＿＿＿＿＿＿＿＿＿
您的電話號碼：＿＿＿＿＿＿＿＿＿
您要我們解決的問題？
＿＿＿＿＿＿＿＿＿＿＿＿＿＿＿＿＿
投訴細節：
＿＿＿＿＿＿＿＿＿＿＿＿＿＿＿＿＿
＿＿＿＿＿＿＿＿＿＿＿＿＿＿＿＿＿

關於電話號碼 080-7552-8282 何者為真？
(A) 只有享特權的顧客可以打這支電話號碼
(B) 每天 24 小時都可以打這支電話

解析　網頁的第一句話提到「需要立即協助的人，可以打電話來」，這句話中的「隨時（anytime）」，跟選項（B）中所說的 24 hours a day, 7 days a week 是一樣的意思，所以選項（B）是答案。

單字　**make a complaint** 進行客訴｜ **assistance** 協助｜ **resolve** 解決｜ **issue** 問題｜ **full name** 全名｜ **privileged** 享特權的｜ **accessible** 可取得的

D 應用練習　　　P. 433

1. (B)

翻譯　親愛的莎莉：

我在倫敦玩得很愉快，這裡有許多迷人的景點可看。我也在這裡遇到一些很棒的人：丹尼、艾薇和李奧。丹尼是英國人，我在迷路時遇到他。他很友善，為我指引到飯店的路，多虧他的幫助我才能安全回去。艾薇和李奧是一起旅行的華裔美國人。

……………………………………………

艾瑞卡第一次遊覽倫敦時，她只想要盡情玩樂。然而她迷路了，而且不知所措。幸運地是，丹尼遇見了她，並告訴她如何回她的飯店。多虧丹尼的好心，艾瑞卡愛上了倫敦。她宣布她和丹尼將在今夏結婚。

……………………………………………

關於莎莉的推測何者為真？
(A) 她在美國認識了艾薇和李奧
(B) 她是艾瑞卡的一位朋友

解析 這封信和報導的地點是在倫敦，第一封信闡明艾薇和李奧在倫敦相遇，所以選項（A）是錯的。

文中並未明確指出莎莉和艾瑞卡是什麼關係，不過從艾瑞卡去倫敦旅行還寄信給莎莉，可以推測她們應該是朋友。答案是選項（B）。

單字 fascinating 迷人的 ｜ get lost 迷路 ｜ show the way to 指引到……的路 ｜ get back 回來 ｜ thanks to 多虧 ｜ come across 遇見 ｜ kindness 好心 ｜ announce 宣布 ｜ get married 結婚

類型 **08** 三篇文章

Ⓓ 應用練習　　　P. 439

1. (B)

翻譯 克里斯是位非常喜歡冒險的男孩。他總是喜歡嘗試新事物，毫不害怕可能要面對的風險。尤其是，他喜歡極限運動，像是跳傘和高空彈跳。他的父母總是擔心他們的獨子可能會受傷。

收件者：艾美・強森
　　　　　<johnson@campred.com>
寄件者：珍・史密斯
　　　　　<smith@edwardmail.net>
主旨：我熱愛冒險的兒子
日期：4 月 10 日

親愛的強森醫生：

你可能讀過關於我兒子的短訊。他太喜歡極限運動了。我的丈夫和我不知道該怎麼辦。

收件者：珍・史密斯
　　　　　<smith@edwardmail.net>
寄件者：艾美・強森
　　　　　<johnson@campred.com>
主旨：回覆：我熱愛冒險的兒子
日期：4 月 11 日

親愛的珍・史密斯小姐：
您的兒子真的很熱愛冒險。然而有些極限運動特別危險。我建議您的兒子不要從空中的飛機跳下來。

強森醫生要克里斯不要做什麼？
(A) 開車
(B) 跳傘

解析 若要知道克里斯熱愛的極限運動有什麼，可以從第一篇文章的第三句話 skydiving 和 bungee jumping 而得知。第三篇文章的最後一句話提到了「從空中的飛機跳下來」，所以選項（B）skydiving 是答案。

單字 adventurous 有冒險精神的 ｜ risk 風險 ｜ face 面對 ｜ in particular 尤其 ｜ extreme sports 極限運動 ｜ advise 建議

Quick Test　　　　P. 440

1. (A)　2. (B)　3. (B)　4. (B)　5. (A)

1. (A)

翻譯 **艾瑞卡・史密斯**　　（上午 10:20）
你認為我們應該投資庭柏公司嗎？

保羅・迦納　　（上午 10:22）
我不這麼認為。這家公司目前遭遇很多困難。

上午 10:22 時，迦納先生說「我不這麼認為」是什麼意思？
(A) 他不想投資這家公司
(B) 他認為為窮人募資不是好點子

解析 「I don't think so」是回應史密斯小姐的疑問,她不知道該不該投資庭柏公司。「I don't think so」表示「不認為應該投資」,所以答案是選項(A)。

單字 **invest** 投資 | **difficulties** 困難 | **raise money** 募資 | **the poor** 窮人

2. (B)

翻譯 親愛的蘇珊・布雷克小姐:
明天我要跟您提過的執行長會面,我要向她提出我的企劃。如果她喜歡,她就會資助這個企劃。我的企劃案會幫助孩童藉由參觀博物館了解過去。我認為了解過去對每位孩童都很重要。

關於作者的推測何者為真?
(A) 她已經參觀過在家鄉的每間博物館
(B) 她相信歷史對孩童的生活有幫助

解析 最後一句話說「我認為了解過去對每位孩童都很重要」,選項(B)利用相似字換了一種說法,所以答案是選項(B),將 learning about the past 換成了 history;將 important to every child 換成了 helpful in children's lives。

單字 **present** 提出 | **support** 支持 | **financially** 經濟上地 | **museum** 博物館 | **past** 過去

3. (B)

翻譯 葛林公司的執行長勞勃・李昨天辭職了。李是一位成功的企業家,在石油業中廣受敬重。這家公司並沒有解釋他下台的原因。因此,很多人對這家公司的經營狀況感到疑惑。

第一行的「辭職」最接近的意思是什麼?
(A) 開始他的工作
(B) 離開他的工作

解析 透過第一句話可以知道勞勃・李是葛林公司的執行長,接著說他昨天辭職(resigned)了,這和「開始工作(started his job)」的意思完全相反。resign 和第三句話的 step down 意思相同,就是從原來的位置「下台、卸任」的意思,答案是選項(B)。

單字 **resign** 辭職 | **widely** 廣泛地 | **respect** 敬重 | **oil industry** 石油業 | **explain** 解釋 | **step down** 下台

4. (B)

翻譯 收件者:white@emvimt.net
寄件者:robert@savechildren.org
主旨:馬來西亞的志工計劃
日期:2 月 11 日

親愛的懷特先生:
感謝您的來信,我真的很感激,我們一直協助數千名志工出國幫助有需求的人。您似乎有興趣幫助馬來西亞貧困的孩童,而我們在該國家也有數項志工計劃。您可以到我的辦公室和我討論那些計劃嗎?我相信您會讓馬來西亞的貧困孩童生命從此不同。

撰寫這封電子郵件的動機是什麼?
(A) 鼓勵懷特先生幫助歐洲的貧困孩童
(B) 邀請懷特先生討論志工計劃

解析 文中提到的貧困孩童,不在歐洲(in Europe)是在馬來西亞(in Malaysia)。寫這封電子郵件的目的有在最後面提到,想請懷特先生到辦公室討論計劃,答案是選項(B)。

單字 **volunteering project** 志工計劃 | **appreciate** 感激 | **volunteer** 志工 | **go abroad** 出國 | **in need** 有需求的 | **make a difference** 改變現況

5. (A)

翻譯 瑪莉旅行社

導覽是探索外國城市的絕佳方式。問題是，要找合格的導遊很難。然而，如果您選擇瑪莉旅行社，就完全不用擔心。我們所有的導遊都非常關心您，他們會盡其所能地讓您擁有愉悅歡暢的旅行經驗。現在就打 373-7883 和我們聯繫，然後享受一場難忘的旅行體驗。

收件者：瑪莉・布朗
寄件者：蘇珊・李
主旨：無
日期：三月三日

親愛的布朗小姐：

我最近到南韓首爾旅行。我原本很擔心，因為我不曾去過那個城市。然而你們的導遊蘇米非常和善又有效率。多虧她誠摯的服務，我真的很享受我的首爾之旅。所以，我已將你的旅行社推薦給瑪麗・史密斯，她是我的一位好友，她不久就會和你的旅行社聯繫。

史密斯小姐在不久後會做什麼？
(A) 打 373-7883 這支電話
(B) 和一位朋友到首爾旅行

解析 瑪麗・史密斯是寫這封電子郵件的蘇珊・李的朋友。透過郵件的最後一句話，蘇珊・李將收件者瑪莉・布朗的旅行社推薦給瑪麗・史密斯，並說她很快就會打電話給旅行社，廣告中有旅行社的電話號碼 373-7883，答案是選項（A）。

單字 travel agency 旅行社｜
guided tour 導覽｜explore 探索｜
qualified 合格的｜choose 選擇｜
efficient 有效率的｜sincere 誠摯的｜
dial 撥打（電話）

Practice Test　　　　P. 444

1. (C)　2. (D)　3. (B)　4. (D)　5. (A)
6. (D)　7. (C)　8. (B)　9. (B)　10. (D)

1. (C)

翻譯 瑪莉・亞當斯　　下午 3:20
唐納德，你知道我們的行銷活動的花費嗎？

唐納德・強森　　下午 3:21
300 萬元。我認為那筆錢花得很值得。

瑪莉・亞當斯　　下午 3:22
我同意，我們的業績在行銷活動後就已大幅改善。

在下午 3:22 時，亞當斯小姐說「我同意」是什麼意思？
(A) 她認為公司應該花超過 300 萬元在行銷上
(B) 她不了解為何公司浪費那麼多錢
(C) 她認為在行銷活動上投資 300 萬元的決策很明智
(D) 她不認為強森先生有說實話

解析 因為亞當斯說「我同意（I agree）」，表示她同意對方所說的話。對方唐納德說「300 萬花得很值得」，表示行銷活動是好事，答案是選項(C)。

單字 marketing campaign 行銷活動｜
significantly 明顯地｜waste 浪費｜
decision 決策｜invest 投資

2. (D)

翻譯 我們所有在極光飯店的員工都非常在乎您，我們堅信顧客的滿意程度是我們飯店的存在的原因。所以，在您離開之前，請務必完成我們的顧客滿意度問卷，我們會立即處理您在我們飯店的任何問題。同時，您的回覆也可以幫助我們改善服務。

關於極光飯店何者為真？
(A) 它不太重視顧客
(B) 它不要顧客投訴它的服務
(C) 它營業已經超過五年
(D) 它想要改善它的服務

解析 首先，這篇公告並沒有提到飯店經營了多久，所以選項(C)是錯的。

選項(A)說飯店不重視顧客，和第一句話「非常在乎顧客」意思相反，所以選項(A)也不對。

選項(B)說「不希望顧客客訴」和第四句話「有任何問題會立刻處理」也完全不同。

這份公告的目的是要顧客填寫問卷表，以便改善服務，選項(D)是答案。

單字 firmly 堅決地｜customer satisfaction 顧客滿意程度｜exist 存在｜questionnaire 問卷｜issue 問題｜response 回覆｜improve 改善｜think highly of 重視｜complain 投訴

3. (B)

翻譯 我們格林汽車公司相信安全是汽車工業最重要的層面。因此，我們很遺憾要通知顧客，我們將召回一些休旅車。我們要召回的是新型 2009 休旅車、新型 3010 休旅車以及新型 5012 休旅車。遺憾地是，這些休旅車對我們的顧客來說可能不安全。請打 555-7882 和我們洽詢進一步細節。

為何新型 5012 休旅車要被召回？
(A) 因為格林汽車公司將不再生產休旅車
(B) 因為休旅車可能會將駕駛置於危險之中
(C) 因為休旅車不受年輕人的歡迎
(D) 因為休旅車沒有產生利潤

解析 第三句話提到了要召回的車種，接著第四句話闡明了召回車子的原因是由於「無法保障駕駛的安全」，所以選項(B)換個說法說「會陷駕駛於危險中」是一樣的意思，選項(B)是答案。

單字 aspect 層面｜automobile industry 汽車工業｜regret to 遺憾地要｜inform 通知｜recall 召回｜SUV (=sports utility vehicle) 休旅車｜produce 生產｜put . . . in danger 置……於危險之中｜generate 產生｜profit 利潤

4. (D)

翻譯 **我們線上服務的註冊表**

請提供以下資訊，我們才能為您提供線上服務。我們不會和任何人分享您的資訊。
全名：＿＿＿＿＿＿＿＿＿＿＿＿＿＿
出生日期：＿＿＿＿＿＿＿＿＿＿＿＿
SES 帳戶號碼：＿＿＿＿＿＿＿＿＿＿
地址：＿＿＿＿＿＿＿＿＿＿＿＿＿＿
電話號碼：＿＿＿＿＿＿＿＿＿＿＿＿

線上註冊不需要什麼資訊？
(A) 您的姓氏
(B) 您的聯絡資訊
(C) 您的帳戶號碼
(D) 您的出身地

解析 看一下網頁上的項目，並將各項目對照選項就能解題。沒有出現在網頁上的是選項(D)出生地（your place of birth）。

單字 registration 註冊｜form 表格｜provide A with B 把 A 提供給 B｜share 分享｜full name 全名｜account number 帳戶號碼｜last name 姓氏｜place of birth 出身地

5. (A)

翻譯 **地球一小時**

地球一小時是由「世界自然基金會」舉辦的全球活動，活動時間在每年三月的最後一個星期六。在這一天，我們鼓勵家庭和企業把非必要的燈光關閉一小時，目的是提高人們的節能意識。這個活動在 2007 年首度於澳洲雪梨舉辦，當時有 220 萬參與活動的人為了節省電力而關燈。

關於地球一小時何者為否？
(A) 通常延續 12 小時
(B) 每年都會舉辦
(C) 是為了倡導人們節能
(D) 首度在澳洲舉辦

解析 看一下第三句話，提到了地球一小時的活動，就是讓家庭及公司關閉不必要的燈一小時。所以活動持續的時間不是 12 小時，是一小時，所以選項(A)錯了。

單字 **organized by** 由……舉辦 | **be held** 被舉辦 | **household** 家庭 | **nonessential** 非必要的 | **be meant to** 目的在於 | **raise** 提高 | **awareness** 意識 | **concerning** 與……有關 | **take place** 舉辦 | **participate** 參與 | **electricity** 電力 | **last for** 延續 | **on a yearly basis** 一年一度 | **aim to** 目的是

6. (D)

翻譯 **紅番椒食譜**

紅番椒是一種容易準備的菜餚。首先，將兩顆大洋蔥切碎，然後用少量油煎炒。接著，加上一些大蒜和切成丁的辣椒。洋蔥變軟後，加上兩磅的絞牛肉。攪拌直到牛肉變成棕色表示已完全熟透，再撒上一些紅辣椒粉。

第一行的「準備」最接近的意思是什麼？
(A) 籌備一場活動
(B) 訓練人員
(C) 擬定執行計劃
(D) 烹調菜餚

解析 最上面的標題是「紅番椒食譜」，所以選項中和料理(dish)無關的「籌辦活動(organize an event)」、「訓練人員(train people)」、「擬定計劃(make plans to do something)」等，都可以立刻刪除。答案是選項(D)。

單字 **recipe** 食譜 | **cut up** 切碎 | **fry** 煎炒 | **add** 加上 | **garlic** 大蒜 | **diced** 切丁 | **pepper** 辣椒 | **ground** 磨碎的 | **stir** 攪拌 | **sprinkle** 撒上 | **powder** 粉

7. (C)

翻譯 當你到習俗和傳統不一樣的新目的地旅行，很容易就會經歷文化衝擊。儘管文化衝擊並不是會威脅生命的疾病，它可能會導致一些像是睡眠剝奪和沮喪的嚴重問題。然而，藉由簡單的預防措施，你就可以避免這些問題，並能完全享受你的旅途。

關於文化衝擊何者為否？
(A) 它可能會讓你難以入眠
(B) 它可能會讓你不愉快
(C) 它通常對你的全身健康有好處
(D) 有辦法可以克服它

解析 選項(A)的「難以入眠」，和選項(B)的「會讓你不愉快」，都相當於文章中提到的 sleep deprivation 和 depression。文章最後一句話提到「只要採取簡單的預防措施，就能解決問題」，和選項(D)的意思一樣。所以答案是選項(C)。

單字 destination 目的地 | custom 習俗 |
culture shock 文化衝擊 |
life-threatening 威脅生命的 |
disease 疾病 | lead to 導致 |
sleep deprivation 睡眠剝奪 |
depression 沮喪 |
take a precaution 預防 | avoid 避免 |
physical health 身體健康 |
overcome 克服

8. (B)

翻譯 「我們去喝咖啡吧！」你的美國朋友這
麼說。-[1]- 在整個北美區，人們喜歡在
咖啡店見面。-[2]- 咖啡店有一種讓人願
意聊天的非正式氛圍。人們在那邊坐下
來討論當天的業務、新聞和運動、個人
擔憂的事，或只是聊八卦。-[3]- 人們到
咖啡店不只是和親友社交，也可以洽談
公事或請他們的員工吃點心。-[4]- 有些
人則到那邊則是閱讀報紙或他們最喜歡
的雜誌。

[1]、[2]、[3] 和 [4] 哪一個位置最適合插
入以下句子？
「咖啡店有一種讓人願意聊天的非正式
氛圍。」
(A) [1]
(B) [2]
(C) [3]
(D) [4]

解析 因為插入句中提到「咖啡店的氣氛鼓勵
人們聊天」，所以這句話之後提到「人們
在咖啡店聊天說地」是最合適的，選項
（B）是答案。

單字 personal concern 私人擔憂事項 |
gossip 八卦 | socialize 社交 |
treat 請客 |

9. (B)

翻譯 英國以運動聞名於世，許多運動像是足
球、英式橄欖球和板球都源自於英國。
這個國家也以文學知名，並且培育出像
威廉‧莎士比亞和 C. S. 路易斯等的偉
大作家。英國的名氣也來自於它是 2012
年倫敦奧運的主辦國。由於它獨特的文
化，英國有來自全世界的遊客。

收件者：艾瑞克‧史密斯
寄件者：艾瑞卡‧強森
主旨：關於英國的文章
日期：七月三日

親愛的史密斯先生：

我閱讀了您這篇有關英國的文章後深感
興趣。我經營一家製造運動用品的小公
司，我想知道哪一種運動在英國最受歡
迎。我對您在文章提到的三種運動特
別有興趣。請寄信到 erica_johnson@
sportstop.com 與我聯繫。

這封電子郵件的作者對下列哪種運動並
不特別有興趣？
(A) 足球
(B) 馬球
(C) 板球
(D) 橄欖球

解析 在電子郵件的第三句話中提到，對史密
斯先生文中提到的三種運動很感興趣，
所以只要找到文中沒提到的項目就能解
題。第一篇文章提到了足球（soccer）、
板球（cricket）、英式橄欖球（rugby），
沒有提到 polo，所以選項（B）是答案。

單字 Great Britain 英國 |
be originated 源自於 | literature 文學 |
be known as 以……知名 |
host 主辦國 | run 經營 |
manufacture 製造 |
sporting goods 運動用品 |
mention 提到

10. (D)

翻譯 剛出生的小熊貓是一隻無助的小動物。牠的身體出奇地小，前三週眼睛都閉著。小熊貓高度依賴媽媽，唯一的食物來源就是母奶。母熊貓對小熊貓的關心和愛護廣為人知。牠們在移動時會輕輕用嘴巴叼著小熊貓。

收件者：kevin@danomen.net
寄件者：johnson@mconerce.com
主旨：剛出生的小熊貓
日期：5 月 14 日

親愛的史諾先生：

歡迎加入我們！蒙哥馬利動物園是很適合工作的地方。由於你負責照顧小熊貓，你必須要了解這些小動物的特性。

收件者：johnson@mconerce.com
寄件者：kevin@danomen.net
主旨：回覆：剛出生的小熊貓
日期：5 月 14 日

親愛的強森小姐：

謝謝你。幸運地，我剛讀了一篇有關小熊貓的有趣文章。或許我們可以邀請這位記者到我們的動物園。

為何史諾先生要邀請記者到動物園？
(A) 因為記者養了小熊貓當寵物
(B) 因為史諾先生每天閱讀報紙
(C) 因為他將寫一本有關小熊貓的書
(D) 因為記者可以協助他讓工作有效率

解析 在史諾先生電子郵件中提到他讀到一篇有關小熊貓的有趣報導，接著提到「可以邀請記者來動物園」。由於在前一篇強森小姐寫給史諾先生的電郵中提到，要照顧小熊貓的話，要先了解牠們（you need to learn about these little creatures），所以可以推測那篇報導，對史諾先生照顧小熊貓是有幫助的。答案是選項(D)。

單字 newborn 新生的 | helpless 無助的 | creature 生物 | remain 維持 | be dependent on 依賴 | be known for 以……聞名 | protective 有保護欲的 | carry 攜帶 | gently 輕柔地 | be on the move 行動 | welcome aboard 歡迎加入

國家圖書館出版品預行編目 (CIP) 資料

Start 新制多益：給新手的聽力閱讀解題攻略
（寂天雲隨身聽 APP 版）/ Mu Ryong Kim,
The Mozilge Language Research Institute
作；江奇忠，彭尊聖譯 . -- 初版 . -- 臺北市：
寂天文化 , 2021.04 印刷
　面；　公分
ISBN 978-626-300-003-2（16K 平裝）
1. 多益測驗

805.1895　　　　　　　　　110004694

START 新制多益：給新手的聽力閱讀解題攻略

作　　者	Mu Ryong Kim, The Mozilge Language Research Institute
翻　　譯	江奇忠（英）／彭尊聖（韓）
審　　訂	Helen Yeh
編　　輯	Gina Wang
校　　對	許嘉華
內文排版	劉秋筑
封面設計	林書玉
製程管理	洪巧玲
出 版 者	寂天文化事業股份有限公司
發 行 人	黃朝萍
電　　話	+886-(0)2-2365-9739
傳　　真	+886-(0)2-2365-9835
網　　址	www.icosmos.com.tw
讀者服務	onlineservice@icosmos.com.tw
出版日期	2022 年 08 月 初版再刷（寂天雲隨身聽 APP 版）（0102）